HER
Cold
HEART

BOOKS BY PAMELA FAGAN HUTCHINS

Detective Delaney Pace series

Her Silent Bones

Her Hidden Grave

Her Last Cry

Her Forgotten Shadow

Her Burning Lies

Patrick Flint series

Switchback

Snake Oil

Sawbones

Scapegoat

Snaggle Tooth

Stag Party

Sitting Duck

Skin and Bones

Jenn Herrington series

Big Horn

Walker Prairie

Maggie Killian series

Live Wire

Sick Puppy

Dead Pile

HER Cold HEART

PAMELA FAGAN HUTCHINS

bookouture

Published by Bookouture in 2025

An imprint of Storyfire Ltd.
Carmelite House
50 Victoria Embankment
London EC4Y 0DZ

www.bookouture.com

The authorised representative in the EEA is Hachette Ireland
8 Castlecourt Centre
Dublin 15 D15 XTP3
Ireland
(email: info@hbgi.ie)

ISBN: 978-1-80550-118-3
eBook ISBN: 978-1-80550-117-6

To the one who sees the warmth in my heart.

PROLOGUE
BEFORE

The truck lost traction on the downhill curve and began a slow, silent slide toward the guard rail. The driver tapped the brakes and white knuckled the steering wheel. Tabby Teller closed her eyes and gripped the passenger assist handle, or, as she'd heard it called when she was growing up, the holy moly handle. Her hands were slick with sweat, so she gripped it so hard her hand hurt.

"Whoever treated these roads needs to be fired," the driver said, his breath coming out in sharp pants.

How could he be thinking about that when they were about to go over the drop-off? Right now, all she wanted was to feel the tires grip the road. She'd trade her left breast for it—hell, she'd trade both of them. She'd lost so much of her life just because she'd let the wrong guy buy her a drink and crawl into her bed. Her job. Her friends. Her future, if she had one after tonight.

And the crazy thing was she'd wanted to go on this ride.

The driver had asked for help. Claimed he was too recognizable, like he'd been in the news or something. She guessed he was memorable. Not because he was good looking. The opposite, with a big, flat nose, pale skin, a chin that stuck out, and graying dark hair. He smelled like a billy goat. Plus, he was big. Tall and thick.

She'd been volunteered. At first she'd been appalled. This driver was a creep fest. But then she'd remembered what freedom had felt like without a hand gripping her arm, eyes searching her out everywhere she went, questions hammering her if another guy so much as looked at her. Like she didn't know what would happen to her if she talked to one of them. Not that some hadn't tried to get close to her on the rare times she was alone. On her. Inside her. If one of them would have rescued her from her boyfriend, she would have let him do anything he wanted to her.

None of them would have. Hitting on a leader's squeeze away from prying eyes was one thing. Straight up defying him and stealing his woman was the road to an unmarked grave, after he made a lesson out of him.

Tabby peeked out a slitted lid only to get an eyeful of a white abyss. She whimpered and shut it tight just as the back end of the truck crashed into something. The impact wrenched her shoulder, and the truck made a terrible screeching noise. Her teeth ground into her lips.

"Hold on," the driver said.

"I am!" she shouted, tasting blood.

The scraping sound grew louder, the front end swung toward the middle of the road, and the truck skated sideways. Then, with a jolt, it regained traction, but only in the back. The front end slid in a semi-circle back out toward the edge again.

Tabby screamed. She ducked her head and threw her free arm over it, bracing her feet on the floorboard and her hand on the grip. Anticipating the sensation of floating. Of falling. In her mind, she pictured herself leaping off the rocks in Bastards

Cove at Summersville Lake. Accepting the dare. Fighting her fear. The sun on her face, the wind in her hair, the tug of gravity as she plummeted feet first down to the water. The shock of water up her nose, ripping off her bathing suit top and shoving her bottoms into a wedgie. Surfacing, surviving.

Then the front wheels gripped pavement. The truck stopped rotating toward the cliff. The road leveled out onto a flatter stretch.

The driver whooped and smacked the dashboard with his palm. "That was a close one!"

She laughed, limp with relief, savoring the moment with her head on her knees. Then something slammed into the back of the truck. Her head smashed into the dash, cushioned by her fingers. The truck started sliding again, but faster this time, too fast for her to gather her wits. When the plummet off the road came, it bounced her body upright. She saw white ground out her window. *We went off on the uphill side.* No cliff. Instead, they careened toward snow-covered trees.

"Damnation!" the driver yelled, as he stomped at the brake pedal and fought the steering wheel, which was jerking back and forth.

Ahead of them, snow flew in the air and onto the wind-shield as the truck pushed through. Obstacles would appear suddenly in their headlights then flash by in Tabby's peripheral vision, like she was stuck in a real-life video game. There were too many, and the truck wasn't maneuverable in the snow. Each one they missed seemed like a miracle. Missing them all seemed impossible.

She braced one hand against the dash, still holding the grip, ready for the inevitable impact. She forced herself to close her eyes again.

Help me, help me, help me. Or would death be better? An escape... A sense of peace settled over her. *Just don't let it hurt.*

After what felt like an eternity, the truck bogged down, and they were still. Her ears were ringing like a legion of cicadas buzzing. The heater was still blasting, and the interior felt humid and smelled like sweat. She was safe, and she wasn't sure how she felt about it.

"Are you okay?" The driver cut his eyes to her. He looked unharmed.

She put a hand to her head. Her fingers came back sticky. "I'm bleeding."

"It doesn't look too bad."

She rolled her neck. Everything hurt, but he was right. It could have been far worse.

"I gotta go see how we're getting the truck out of here."

"Will it run?" She imagined a mangled undercarriage, leaking fuel tanks. Popped tires.

"Still is." He patted the dash. "We just got tapped from behind and slid off the road on the good side. Somehow we didn't hit anything. A little snow won't hurt us."

She felt the rumble of the engine now. The whining noise in her ears had drowned it out.

He opened the door. Wind blasted the interior, swirling snow in with it. Sharp crystals pelted her face. She wrapped her arms around herself. She was already dressed in all her outerwear for the elements, including the snow boots her boyfriend had given her for Christmas. They were warm and functional but a little edgy, with black fur. Suitable for the moll of a militia group leader, she supposed.

"Oh, my God, are you okay in there?" a man's voice said through the open door. He sounded panicked. It had to be someone from the vehicle that had slammed into them.

The driver's back flattened against the seat, and he put a hand toward her, patting down the air. *Be cool,* he was saying. "Yes, sir, we're just fine."

The man's head appeared in Tabby's line of vision. A wool

Carhartt cap. Ruddy skin. Concerned dark eyes. "We... Oh, shit, you have a woman in here with you. Ma'am, I'm so sorry. The conditions got the better of me." Then he winced. "You're hurt."

"It's not as bad as it looks."

"I can call an ambulance. Or take her to the hospital in Billings myself."

Tabby hadn't seen this coming. Freedom wasn't just getting out of the compound for a few days. Or the death that she'd faced a few minutes before. Freedom could be disappearing in a city and *never going back*. Never facing the things he had been doing to her more and more lately. Things that hurt. Things that were wrong. Things she suspected he had done to other girls before her. There were whispers. People looked the other way when her eyes were blackened. One way or another, she had become sure he would never let her leave.

Maybe this was a chance for real freedom.

The driver said, "She doesn't—"

She groaned and put a hand to her head. "I think I'm going to be sick."

The man said, "I'll come around and help you out."

The driver raised his voice, his tone hard. "The good Lord and me got her. We don't need you." She watched his hand move to his waist where she knew he kept a handgun holstered.

The man bit his lip. He gave Tabby one last glance, then deliberately looked away from her. "I, um. I apologize. I can see you've got it. Would you, um, could I, uh—how about I give you a pull so you can be on your way?"

The driver shot Tabby a glare. Then he said, "Well, you have put us in a bind. You got a winch?"

Tabby pressed her knuckles against her lips, fighting back tears. Now it was like her pain and predicament were invisible to the stranger. How easily he'd been dissuaded from helping her, even though it was clear that she'd needed it. She couldn't blame him for not playing the hero. They were miles from town in terrible conditions, and the driver was menacing. But it was still bitter medicine.

The man said, "A winch and a tow package. Are you loaded?"

"Empty. That's why we made such a great skateboard."

The man forced a laugh. "Yeah, okay. Well, let's get you out of here then."

"Right behind you."

The stranger tromped out of Tabby's sight.

The driver wheeled on her. "You want to get us both killed? And him, too?"

She pouted as prettily as she could. "Of course not. I just don't feel good."

"Or maybe you were trying to run away." He'd seen through her act. There would be repercussions, she knew.

She eyed her canvas holdall in the floorboard. A determination came over her. Escape had been so close. She had to try. If she was going to face consequences anyway, what did she have to lose?

She snorted, almost choking as she forced out the words, trying to make them sound convincing. "I would never. Look at how good I have it. I'm with an important man who loves me."

The suspicion in his eyes faded. "I'll doctor your cut. Just don't involve strangers."

"Okay."

"Stay put. I have to go get us hooked up."

She nodded.

He got out, shutting the door behind him. Tabby didn't have much time. Five minutes, maybe, before he came back? Another five before his truck would be free of the snow drift? There wasn't enough time. She knew there wasn't, barring a miracle. But she had to try. She'd have ten minutes to run as far as she could away from the truck and the nice stranger. She knew a thing or two about wilderness survival after the last year. She'd be fine once she got on the road, unless the driver caught her. *Don't think about that.* But her path would be trackable in this snow. Worse, if she succeeded, her boyfriend could find her by her phone. She put it on the floorboard. She'd have to leave it.

Okay, then. She didn't have time for second-guessing or being scared. *Get moving.*

She took a deep breath and released it. Hefting her bag, she opened the door and jumped out, landing in a heap and sliding away from the truck, which was parked on slanted ground. It knocked the breath out of her. She clambered back to her feet like a bear on roller skates. *No way am I wasting time closing the truck door.* She leaned low and started fighting her way through the snow, then stopped by the front tire.

She had an idea about how to buy herself precious seconds.

She knelt beside the front tire and dug through her holdall until she found her journal. Her boyfriend hated that she kept it. She had to let him read it when he wanted to, which meant that she censored herself, but she loved to write about the beauty of Montana. She pulled an ink pen from inside its pages. Then she located the valve stem on the tire, uncapped it, and jammed the blunt end of the pen in, trying to connect with the metal pin. A satisfying hiss told her it was working. The process was slow, and she had to readjust her pen when it lost contact a few times, but after a minute or so the truck sagged down on its rim.

She salvaged her pen, zipped it in her bag, and took off again, first heading away from the vehicles, parallel to the road. She needed to get out of the range of their headlights. Within fifteen seconds, her breaths were searing her lungs. If it hadn't been for all the high-altitude training she'd done with her boyfriend and the guys, she wasn't sure whether she could have done this. At first she'd argued and pleaded to get out of it. Hadn't seen the reason for it. But he hadn't given her a choice.

They'd drilled in all conditions. Practiced being the hunter and the hunted. Now, she was seasoned at maneuvering in deep snow. At pushing past pain and what she'd believed were her limits. She had been weak before. Easy prey. She was stronger now, but she wasn't going to thank him for it. For being in this situation.

Sweat dripped down her back. By her estimation, she'd been running for three minutes. The illumination from the vehicle lights was less intense now. It was time to cut across to the road. The pitch of the ground back to the pavement was steep and slippery. Her footing, precarious. She fell on her face. *Fine.* She crawled on her hands and knees, like an animal, and it improved her footing. *God made them with four-wheel drive.* It was better to keep a lower profile, anyway. A boot came off, costing her priceless time between retrieving it, dumping out snow, shoving it back on, and tying it tighter.

But she made it up the embankment to the pavement where she struggled to her feet.

Behind her, she heard the driver's shouts. He'd discovered she was missing, which meant that he'd probably gone back to the truck to steer it out. She was down to just a few minutes head start. She needed more distance between them. Like miles and miles and miles of distance. He wouldn't be able to come after her in the truck until it was towed out, and then he'd have to change the tire, but after that he would make up ground fast. She had no idea how far it was to a town or a lodge or anything with people.

She began running. Her feet didn't have any better traction than the truck had when it had slid off the road, and within ten feet, she'd crashed to the ground. She was breathing so hard that she couldn't hear the driver yelling anymore, if he still was. She tried to get up and fell again, her legs weak from crawling through the snow.

For a moment, she dropped her head and let tears form in

her eyes while she caught her breath. How was she going to run in these boots? How was she going to get anywhere in these conditions?

And that's when she found herself in the headlights of an oncoming vehicle.

ONE

TEN MONTHS LATER

Deputy Delaney Pace faceplanted at the base of the bunny hill, just before reaching her daughters and their friends, and right after promising herself she wouldn't let her ski tips cross again. Now she had neither ski on, neither pole in her hands, and was without her hat. Her goggles were around her nose. At least with the wind calm for once and the temperature nearly twenty degrees, it was practically balmy out. She groaned and raised both her hands in the air in mock surrender, then spit snow out of her mouth.

An argument caught her attention in the midst of her humiliation. A man in head-to-toe green camo was shouting in the face of a woman holding skis. She was small and not much older than Carrie. Delaney made a quick mental note in case things escalated. Jeans, Ian Munsick concert sweatshirt, big black cap, pretty, no hair showing. The guy's white-blond hair wasn't covered. He had a rather small head and face for his size.

The woman shoved him in the chest. "I said leave me alone. Get away from me. I am not interested. We are not dating. Don't make me report you."

Her shove didn't move him, but after a moment, he took a step back. "You'll change your mind."

"I never will."

She walked up the hill toward the lodge. He watched her for a moment, then headed in the opposite direction, toward the equipment shop.

"Nice, Melaney," Carrie said, poling toward her and using the name she and her younger sister Kateena had coined as a blend of Mom and Delaney. Delaney redirected her attention to her daughter. The high school senior was dressed as a rainbow, in a yellow cap, pink coat, purple pants, and orange gloves. She high-fived her friend Victoria, who stood a foot taller than Carrie and was top rebounder on their state champion high school basketball team. Victoria had opted for a more subdued look in black mittens, ranch overalls, and jacket—navy blue— sans hat.

Thirteen-year-old Kat was adjusting the headband holding back her black curls and giggling at something her boyfriend Freddy was whispering in her ear. She didn't seem to notice the yard sale of ski wear and equipment at their feet. She socked Freddy's arm. "You won't be saying that someday when I win barrel racing at the National Finals Rodeo." She glanced up and at Delaney. "Clara says it will all start happening for me *when I get my own horse.*"

Delaney made a mental note to have a talk with Clara Eckhardt, the sheriff's department's chief admin and personal rodeo coach to Kat. The girl had only been riding for six months. Was Kat far enough along for Delaney to make that kind of commitment? She managed every penny of her finances, stretching them to the point of breaking. That went double for her bank of time. And if Kat lost interest in the sport, Delaney was the one who would end up with a high-strung horse to take care of.

Victoria elbowed Carrie. "Tell her. You promised you were going to."

Delaney lifted her head. "Tell me what?"

A schussing sound too close to her ear claimed Delaney's attention. "You're supposed to wear the skis."

She rolled over to see the handsome face of Sheriff Leo Palmer. Amused blue eyes, chiseled cheeks above a well-shaped winter-length beard. He filled out a pair of ski pants pretty nicely, too. "What if I was injured?"

He bent and took her hand. "Are you?" He pulled her up, and she flew to her feet and then some, landing lip to lip with him.

"Only my pride."

He smiled against her mouth. "Good to hear. Because tonight is date night. I want to see what color you've painted your toenails."

She pressed her lips into his. They were shockingly cold, and hard little icicles in his beard pushed into her chin. She liked it. She'd been experimenting with colors from Carrie's endless supply of nail polish. Today was a deep purple. She'd let him discover it for himself. "I thought this was our date."

Between two teens at home and the demands of her work as a detective, alone time with Leo was scarce for Delaney. The situation had been compounded until recently since Freddy and his mom Adriana had lived with Leo. Adriana had saved up for months to move out by working at the Loafing Shed—the family bar and restaurant operated by Delaney in trust for Kat, who had inherited it from her believed-to-be-dead father, Liam. At least Delaney prayed her brother was dead. He was one of the most dangerous criminals in the state of Wyoming.

She lived in constant fear that he'd show up again in their lives, leaving another trail of dead bodies in his wake. Her last memory of him kept her up at night. A snowy cliff high in the mountains. The two siblings alone, facing off. Her gun pointed at him.

He'd said, "If you kill me now, you'll never get a touching reunion with our mother."

Her finger had begun to shake on the trigger. "Our mother?! Is she alive?"

His smile was toothy and evil. "Very much so."

But she had shot him, intending to wound him and take him in to face the justice system. Instead, the impact of the shot had sent him tumbling backwards and over the cliff face. His body had never been found.

Freddy said, "Yo, Uncle Leo, we're like heading up the lift, um-kay?"

His words brought Delaney back to the present. She looked over at Freddy and Kat. He was a good-looking kid. Or young man, rather. Wavy dark hair like his mom and uncle, tall, with sleepy eyes and long lashes. Sprouting whiskers that he stroked unconsciously. Not too long ago, the boy had thrown a pot party at his uncle's house, thinking Leo and Adriana were safely away at work for hours. Leo had dropped by home to grab a heavier jacket and found a dozen stoned teenagers. He'd had no choice but to turn his nephew in. Freddy had gotten a slap on the wrist. Leo had been hauled in front of the county commissioners over the scandal.

Delaney was more worried about Freddy's suddenly deeper voice and the new facial hair than the pot. All those hormones were up close and personal with Kat on a daily basis.

Leo backed away from Delaney. "Okay. We'll catch up with you guys at noon. Leave your phones on."

"No signal up here."

"Duh. Okay—see you inside at lunch."

The three girls and Freddy skied toward the lift.

Delaney brushed snow off her pants. "If this is a date, I can't wait to see what tonight will bring, since it's starting with you trying to kill me."

Leo gathered Delaney's equipment. "You're doing great. No way I could let a Wyomingite native to these mountains pass the prime of her life without learning to ski."

She took a step toward him and wobbled, so she stood with her hands on her hips. Walking in hard plastic boots on slick snow was no easy task. "So, you're saving me from some kind of ignominy?"

He looked up and grinned. "No. I'm ensuring that we have years of skiing together ahead of us, if you learn now." Leo had told her he'd loved the sport since childhood trips to Lake Tahoe with his family.

A warm tingling spread through her cheeks and ears at his words. She savored the sound of years together. "My body is telling me thirty-six is already past my prime."

"Au contraire. It's the beginning of your best years." He dropped her skis beside her then handed over her hat and poles. "It does blow my mind how you could grow up here without skiing, though."

She pulled her hat over her ears, glad she'd worn her long hair in a French braid. "No money. Or what money we had when I was young my dad spent on racing things with motors. And then, foster care."

"Makes sense."

She stepped into one ski. It slid outward, putting her in a splits stance. "Why is this so damn hard?"

Leo wedged his ski against hers to keep her steady. "I've got you."

She pressed her boot toe first into the binding of the other ski without falling. "Is it noon yet?"

He moved his ski away, leaving Delaney unsupported. She managed not to fall. "Nope. We've got time to ride the big lift up before lunch."

The lift had been Delaney's nemesis so far. She hadn't made it through loading or unloading yet without falling. It was normal on the lower lift, which accessed all the beginner slopes. The Summit Chair was a different story. The more experienced skiers used it.

"Are there green slopes up there?" It was only her second day on the mountain and her first without a ski instructor. She hadn't studied the maps for trails down from the Summit Chair. And even though she'd picnicked and hiked the Elk Ridge trails in the summer years ago, it had changed since those days. The ski resort had closed when she was a kid, then reopened as a community-funded recreation area only a few years before. New runs were being added as funding became available.

"I wouldn't call them green, but there's definitely a way down you'll be fine on with me. Yes?" Leo held up a fist for her to touch.

Delaney felt a flicker of unease. She'd faced down the ice roads of Canada in her semi, Gabrielle, she'd adopted two teenage girls, and she'd bested perps bigger and stronger than her. What was making her so nervous about this? She couldn't embarrass herself in front of Leo and the kids any more than she already had.

A lesson drilled into students over and over at commercial driving school came back to her. One they'd hear when they'd balk at some of the scarier physical challenges the instructors put them through. *You only learn it if you do it.* It had been true. She hadn't wanted to jack up a twenty-thousand-pound tractor and crawl under it to change a flat tire alone the first time she'd done it. She'd seen videos and listened to instructions. But she'd learned more from doing it than she had from the lessons. And damn if she hadn't had to use that skill alone in minus fifty Fahrenheit on a frozen lake in the dark, too, with no cell signal to look up a YouTube video.

While skiing wasn't required for her job, it was important to

Leo. She'd be careful, cautious, mindful. In half an hour, she and Leo would be cheerfully overspending to feed four teenagers. Then, later, they'd ditch the skis, and the real fun would start. They'd brought their snowmobiles on a trailer behind Leo's truck. He'd promised her two hours on the sleds in the afternoon.

Everything will be fine.

She forced the carbon dioxide out of her lungs and bumped his fist with hers. "Okay. Let's do it."

"You go first. That way I can stop and help you if you need it. Which you won't."

"Oh, you know I will."

Delaney started toward the lift. The ground sloped upwards, so she widened the tips of her skis, doing a sort of reverse pizza walk. The incline flattened and she poled over to the mostly empty lift lines. Elk Ridge was popular with locals but not easy for travelers to visit. The equipment and staff were more than sufficient to keep skiers on the mountain instead of standing around waiting. A wave of dizziness ran through her. She paused at the entrance to the roped chutes to regain her equilibrium and motioned a few groups ahead of her.

Leo stopped behind her. "You okay?"

"Yes. Just catching my breath."

A woman skied up beside Delaney. "I think I'll take a rest, too."

Delaney glanced at her, which made the mountain-scape tip for a moment. The woman was young—maybe mid-twenties —and dressed in jeans and a sweatshirt. Pretty, too, even behind giant goggles and with wisps of red hair escaping from a big black cap. She'd seen her before. The woman who'd been arguing with the man in the camo gear. She was alone now. Apparently, she'd gotten her point across. She almost asked her if she was okay, but she clearly was, and Delaney didn't want to pry.

"Are you new to skiing?" the woman said.

Delaney leaned on her poles. "Yes. Brand new."

"I just started, too. It's fun, but tiring."

"Very."

"Do you live in Sheridan?"

"Kearny." Delaney drew in a steadying breath. Her dizziness was receding. Maybe she was dehydrated. She'd always had a tendency to drink too little and underestimate the liquids and electrolytes she was losing in winter months. She tried to remember if she'd drank water that day.

"I'm in Sheridan. Better jobs."

Delaney nodded, her thoughts now on fixing her dehydration issue.

Leo scooted forward into the tight space on the other side of her. He whispered in her ear. "You don't have to do this. I know you're a bad ass. We can find lots of other things to do together besides ski."

The young woman started backing up. "Oh! I didn't realize you were skiing with a partner. I'll get out of your way."

"You're fine," Delaney said.

But the girl had already scooted behind her and Leo.

"Thank you." To Leo, Delaney said, "I *am* nervous, but it's okay. I'm feeling dehydrated. Do you still have that water bottle in your waist bag?"

"I do." He reached for the bottom hem of his coat and lifted it, revealing his bag.

She held up a hand. "I'll drink on the lift." She turned back to the young woman. "Have a good day."

The young woman gave her a toothy smile. "You, too."

Then Delaney propelled herself down to the lift. Leo moved easily beside her until they were in place and next up. A chair passed them. Leo gave her a nod and glided into position. She pushed with her poles, overshooting the spot where she was supposed to stand.

Leo caught her upper arm to stop her forward momentum, then tugged her back a few inches. "Got you. Are you ready?"

Caught in her head, she couldn't answer him. She moved her poles to her inside hand and looked over her outside shoulder. She felt overheated and sweaty. She saw the young woman in jeans behind them in line. The girl waved and gave a thumbs-up. Delaney knew she should wave or nod or smile or something, but she saw the chair coming fast, and all of her attention focused on it. She reached to her right, waited for the seat to bump her legs, and sat down with a death grip on the outside arm of the chair.

"Our Father who art in Heaven, hallowed be they name," she muttered.

The chair sagged, then lurched forward and lifted from the ground. Her stomach stayed on terra firma.

Leo squeezed her knee. "You did it! Do you want the footrest down?"

The chair rocked front to back, front to back.

Her tension increased. This lift was higher than the one for the baby slopes. "Just don't knock my skis off."

"I'll be very careful." He brought the footrest down. "Okay, lift your feet and slide them on."

"My poles." Her throat was tight. Her words clipped.

"Take it slow and maneuver them however you want. I can even hold them for you."

She carefully put her skis on the support, then slid her poles into her lap. It felt like a monumental achievement. "I'm good."

Leo gestured around them. "It looks so different from up here. Even more beautiful."

"Uh huh." He was right. They had a snow globe view from the chair. A white wonderland spread below them, with tiny skiers clad in colorful clothes careening down sculpted hills, through glades of toy-sized trees. She loved it, even if she didn't love being this high, dangling from a wire in an open chair.

"You're even more beautiful, too."

She shook her head. "I probably have frozen snot running down my face."

"Beautiful frozen snot."

"You're crazy. And I've never wished more for someone to call us in for an incident."

He laughed. "Don't jinx us." He took off his gloves, tucking them under his thigh. Then he retrieved a metal water bottle from his zippered waist bag and handed it to her. "Now, tough guy, hydrate."

Delaney took several long chugs from the bottle and offered it to him. He shook his head, so she put the top back on, and he secured it in his pouch and gloved back up.

"Better?"

"Better."

She snuggled her head into his shoulder and tried to relax. To make the most of this weekend off, which was rare, and to enjoy it together, which was unheard of. Leo had recently been elected sheriff of Kearny County. This, despite his best efforts to divert his supporters to write-in nominating votes for former Wyoming State Police officer Clint Rock-Below, which he'd done because of his new relationship with Delaney. Also on the ballot had been Deputy Joe Tarver, but he'd made a dismal showing, thanks in part to shooting Leo a week before the primaries. Joe had been suspended without pay for a few weeks for reckless discharge of a firearm post investigation into the incident.

After Leo had won the nomination and later the election, the county commissioners had marched Delaney and Leo in to talk about their relationship—*that had been fun*—and decided to grandfather it in before implementation of a new non-fraternization policy that prohibited dating within chain of command in all county roles. Then the city of Kearny tapped Clint as the new chief of police. They'd asked Delaney first, something she would never disclose to Clint, who was a friend. But she'd stayed true to her commitment to focus her excess time and energy on her newly adopted daughters. The police chief job, like the sheriff's job, required more than she was willing to give.

Before the county commissioners' decision, she'd almost resigned herself to calling Clark Applewood—a douchey federal agent with the Bureau of Alcohol, Tobacco, and Firearms—or, as she preferred to think of ATF, the Bureau of Addled Twats and Fleabags— about the job he'd offered her. She was glad it hadn't come to that. The whole premise of ATF was anti-Wyoming, where people lived the second amendment and stayed baked most of the long, harsh winter, just to make it through. Besides, Delaney loved working with Leo.

Leo broke her reverie. "Time to lift the footrest."

She was shocked. She'd managed to relax and forget she was dangling thirty feet in the air. "We're already there?"

"It's only an eight-minute ride."

Panic clawed at Delaney's chest. Her relaxation had been short-lived. She slipped her feet off the support and clutched her poles. "I'm going to fall."

Leo lifted the footrest and let it swing back in place above them. "You won't."

The lift operator hut was in view, and it felt like they were being towed straight up now. "What if I do?"

"Then I'll help you get back up."

She nodded too many times. "Okay."

"Want me to hold on to you?"

"No. I don't want to pull you down, too." The landing zone was ten feet away, slightly above them.

"Here we go."

The ground was rushing at Delaney's skis. They were even with it.

"Now." Leo stood and let the chair give him a little push.

Delaney stood, too, but she'd waited too long. The chair not only pushed her, it shoved her ass over tea kettle. She fell in slow motion, arms out, legs splayed. As she fell, she realized that behind her was another chair. Inevitably. And behind that yet another. Every chair loaded with skiers.

She heard skis hit the snow. Delaney tried to make herself small, fully expecting to be run over and cursed out. But what she didn't expect was to hear the crack of a rifle. Screams. And then to feel a body tumbling on top of her, twitching as blood gushed crimson over Delaney and the snow.

TWO

Sheriff Leo Palmer felt like a nuclear bomb had just exploded in his chest. One minute he was getting ready to help Delaney out of the way of oncoming skiers unloading from the lift. The next, reverberations from a gunshot shook the snow off the trees overhead. By the time he'd reversed course, Delaney was down in a pool of blood, her honey-colored hair spilled out in the snow.

His only thought was to cover her. *Too late, too late.*

He launched himself through space, noticing as he landed that a second body had fallen with her. Was it the shooter? Had Delaney just taken a pointblank bullet? But, no—he'd definitely heard the crack of a rifle. And there was no rifle on the ground or in the pile of humanity under him. A rifle was a firearm shot from a distance, not close range.

A rifle. There's a shooter out there. The kids! All of these people!

"Delaney, Delaney! Can you hear me?" He felt breathless and close to panic. Delaney was his person. But he had to dial it back. The safety of everyone on the mountain was at stake.

Delaney answered, her voice muffled but strong. "I'm okay. I wasn't the one hit."

"Thank God." He squeezed her body up and into him. His relief was short-lived, though. It wasn't her blood, but it was someone's. This other person tangled up with Delaney.

When he loosened his grip on her, she locked her stunning green eyes on him, stopping his heart for a second. *I cannot lose her.* "Who is it?"

He rolled away to allow Delaney to wriggle free and got his first look at the other person. Small. Young but adult. Female. She lay in a contorted position with her back and neck bent unnaturally. Clad in jeans and a sweatshirt. On the snow lay what was left of a cap that used to be black, because this had been a headshot. Blood. So much blood. Obscuring her face. On her, in the snow, on Delaney. He touched the young woman's shoulder and closed his eyes for a split second. *I'm so sorry this happened to you.* Seeing the effects of violence up close didn't ever get easier.

"Oh, no! I know her. She's the one I was talking to in the lift line." Delaney grabbed the woman's wrist, searching for a pulse. "She was arguing with a tall blond guy in camo down at the base, too."

Leo knew Delaney wouldn't find a sign of life. "There's a shooter out there somewhere." He looked around them. Skiers were lying on the ground or huddled in the trees. The lift had been turned off, and the operator was nowhere to be seen. The chairs were swaying. The line was bouncing. The people riding the lift were moaning, crying, and screaming. Riders clung to each other. As he watched, one skier jumped from a chair. Then another. *Shit!* He envisioned broken legs. Necks. Backs. Things were getting worse.

Delaney was shaking her head. "No pulse." She gently turned the woman's bloody chin, exposing her ruined forehead. "The bullet entered the temple from the right. Someone is a damn good shot."

"We can't move her body before we get crime scene up

here. Can you get the lift operator to send people in the chairs back around to the base, then close off the scene? I'll call for help and see what we can do about getting people off the mountain."

"We need to go after him." Delaney was scanning the trees in the direction the shot came from.

"Agreed. But public safety first. Then we can try to find him."

"God, I hope the kids are okay." She pulled her phone from her pocket. "No signal. How do we even reach them?"

"I'll find someone who can radio the base. We'll get them a message."

Delaney's forehead was creased with worry. "Should we have Carrie drive them home or Skeeter come get them?"

Skeeter was a sometimes bodyguard, often babysitter, part-time private investigator, and always someone Leo and Delaney could count on. Lately, he'd been hard at work trying to locate the mother Delaney hadn't seen since she was eleven years old. Like Delaney, Leo had a hard time believing Fabiola Pace was still alive. If she was, surely she wouldn't have left Delaney to suffer through a succession of foster homes in her teens after her father died? If Skeeter did find Fabi, Leo wasn't sure Delaney would ever forgive her.

"We'll have to see how this plays out," he said.

Delaney gave the dead woman a last look, nodded, then got up, removed her skis, and trotted toward the lift operator's booth. Leo guessed it had been sixty seconds since the rifle shot. He noted the time on his smart watch, then skied away from the lift to the nearest group of people. One of the skiers was dressed in ski patrol gear. Another looked to be an instructor with a group of students. He held up a finger to ask for a minute and spoke into the lapel radio that he had come so close to leaving in his truck that day. His sense of responsibility as sheriff wasn't something he could turn off. He'd imagined scenarios where it would be useful and brought it. None like this one, though.

"This is Kearny County Sheriff Leo Palmer. I'm at the summit of Elk Ridge. There's been a shooting. We need an ambulance and additional personnel to work the scene, contain it, and take statements."

"This is Clara at base, Sheriff. I'm on it."

Leo and Clara spoke briefly as he gave her additional instructions. Technically, Elk Ridge was in Big Horn County, outside his jurisdiction, although Wyoming law enforcement seamlessly provided mutual aid to each other throughout the state, based on custom and state law. Clara would coordinate with Big Horn County directly and get the closest possible officers to respond, but she would send Kearny's dedicated crime scene unit. They'd been fortunate because of county rare mineral funds to be able to set up their own crime scene unit and share it with their part of the state, while other counties had to rely on support from Cheyenne.

He added, "Be on the lookout for a person of interest. Caucasian male, tall, blond, wearing camo." He knew it wasn't much, but better to be over-inclusive for now.

When the conversation ended, he moved over to the ski patrol, a lanky fellow in red and black whose head grazed the branches above him. The guy had to be six-five plus. A lot over that with his helmet. "I'm Sheriff Leo Palmer with Kearny County. Can I get your help?"

"Yes, sir. What happened? We heard a gunshot."

"We need everyone off the mountain. The lifts shut down. The runs closed." Leo had to figure out how to contain people within the resort, while at the same time not exposing anyone to risk. "Additional law enforcement is on the way. Please spread the word that people will have to give statements to law enforcement before leaving. This is critical, and we'll move as quickly as possible."

The tall fellow was nodding.

"You can make sure the lifts are shut down and trails are closed?"

"Yes, sir. I'll see to it."

"What's your name?"

"Sammy. Sammy Ryan."

"Sammy, do you have a radio that you can let me use to communicate with all the ski patrol?"

"Uh, yeah."

"Why don't you introduce me, then I'll take over."

Sammy nodded, got out his radio, and said, "Calling all ski patrol and resort personnel. Emergency at the summit. I have the Kearny County Sheriff up here with me. He's gonna take over now." He handed the radio to Leo.

Leo repeated his instructions. "Thank you, everyone." He returned the radio.

"So, it was a shooting?" Sammy said.

"Yes. And now I have to find who did it. Did you see anything weird? Anyone carrying something that might have been a rifle?"

Sammy shook his head.

"Okay. By the time you're done, there should be law enforcement arriving on scene. They'll handle the parking lot and taking people's statements. They may have additional requests for you guys."

"Yes, sir."

"Oh, and one last thing. My partner's daughters Kat and Carrie should be down there with my nephew Freddy and another friend. Carrie is seventeen and dressed like, um, all the colors of sherbert. Orange, pink, yellow. She should be easy to spot. They need to know why we can't come down. Can you ask someone to tell them to wait to hear from us?"

"No problem." Sammy skied to the student group.

By the time Leo returned to the lift, he could hear Sammy

urging people down the mountain in a loud, firm voice. The chair lift had been switched back on. Delaney was standing in front of it, reassuring frantic riders—most of whom were asking about friends and family on the mountain—and instructing them to unload at the base.

When she saw Leo, she turned to him but kept waving people to ride the lift through its descent. "I think we've almost reached critical mass. People can see the others riding down and understand. The lift operator is pretty panicked, though. That shot came toward him, too. He is supposed to be gathering some net we can use to close off the scene."

Leo checked the time. Five minutes since the shooting. The door to the booth opened. His radio squawked. Delaney caught his eye and nodded that she had things covered.

"Sheriff Palmer," he said into his mic.

The lift operator approached with an armload of netting, which he dropped at Delaney's feet. The guy was swiping at his eyes.

A voice boomed from the radio. "This is Sheriff Shannon Wilcox with Big Horn County. I'm en route and have my entire force on their way. What's going on out there?"

Leo knew the sheriff from the western side of the Bighorn Mountains, of course. Shannon had been in office for decades, but still did his job with the energy of someone newly elected. "I'm here with Deputy Delaney Pace. We have one person shot coming off the summit lift and confirmed dead. No sign of the shooter. We're securing the body and scene and have marshalled ski patrol to help us get everyone off the mountain and to close the lifts and trails. They're spreading word that people will need to give statements before they leave." He told them about the man Delaney had seen arguing with the woman. "Sorry we don't have more specifics."

Wilcox said they'd try to find him. "Could it have been a hunting accident?"

"I can't imagine a hunter would mistakenly think they're aiming at an animal. The maps clearly show the resort, plus it's noisy. Filled with movement and color. But anything's possible."

"It's just a thought. Sometimes hunters wear ear plugs and get singularly focused when they're in pursuit of big game."

"Well, I haven't seen any big game. But we'll look for hunters."

"Okay. Containment and statements will be job one for my deputies first on scene. Then we'll—"

Whatever else Sheriff Wilcox said, Leo didn't hear it. His words were interrupted by a loud shout nearby.

"He's getting away! He's getting away!"

Leo spoke into his mic without hesitation—the essentials had already been passed. "We have a lead on a suspect, Shannon. I've gotta go." He stowed his mic, then shouted, "Delaney!"

But she was already slip-sliding her way toward the person who'd seen the shooter.

THREE

TEN MONTHS EARLIER

I stood in front of the leadership, holding myself to my full height, which was half a head taller than the younger man who was speaking, the person I reported to onsite. We were inside an outfitter's tent, the one that was serving as a sort of winter head-quarters for the camp. The camp moved around. The accommo-dations rotated between a few locations. This winter they were in Montana, in the Custer National Forest, right outside the Crow Reservation. It was stark territory, but I liked it. Liked seeing the occasional big horn sheep and the wild horses on my way in and out. The locations were always hard to access, espe-cially when the snow flew. I didn't mind the drive. I didn't live and train with the rest of the guys. I was integrated into the outside world for my work with them, which was part armored transport, part bag man, and part delivery driver.

My boss in here could kill me if he felt like it. My boss in the outside world would put me away for life if I messed up. Neither was good. But I lost everything I had to live for a few months before. My bride. My sister. My home. Death didn't scare me anymore.

I'd delivered my report to the leadership, and I would face

their judgment. I knew it would be bad. My boss was volatile, especially when it came to women. With him, there was always a woman, too.

He glared at me through beady, dark eyes. "I must not have understood you right the first time. Was that some kind of joke? Tell me again. Where is she?"

I pulled my shoulders back and raised my chin, conscious I was shivering slightly. A fire crackled in the wood burning stove, but it wasn't doing much good. "There was ice up on the pass. We slid around but God saw us through. Then some fool lost control and ran us off the road. We got stuck out there for a bit."

His hand was up, his finger pointing in my face. "You're wasting my time. The only part that matters is where she is."

I hated his high-pitched voice. "The other vehicle stopped. A fellow came to help. We were hooking my truck up for him to give us a tow out. I was only gone from the cab for a few minutes. She, uh, she ran off through the woods."

He crossed his arms, shaking his head. "She's a woman. Tell me a big guy like you didn't let a woman get away from him?"

I pictured Tabby as she'd tried to wheedle help from the other guy. Hair that looked unnaturally blonde. Big blue eyes. A curvy figure. She was pretty, but I wouldn't have been interested in her even if she wasn't off limits to me. She was unclean. God gave me my women before they were sullied. I would not have helped her escape, nor would it have mattered to me if I'd been forced to hurt her to keep her from getting away. I knew now that I should have tied her up in the truck. She'd tricked me into believing she would stay, which upset me very much. If I had caught her, I would have taught her a lesson she never would have forgotten. "She made it to the road before I was towed out. Someone stopped and picked her up. By the time I got there, she was gone."

He snorted, a disgusted sound. "Like I said."

"She left her phone." I held it up. My stomach growled, long and loud. The tent smelled like the sirloin steaks the leadership had been eating before I came.

He refused to take the phone. "That does us no good."

A second man set his fork and knife down and pushed his plate away. A new guy, but he must be important if he was here for this. "It might."

"We can only locate her if it's with her," my boss snarled.

"Maybe so, right now. But eventually, if you want to find her, she's going to do something we'll catch her on. Use an old email address. Her iMessages. Log in to a social media account on there. Call a number we find on it and can monitor. Accidentally have a one-time password sent to this number. It will be useful. I mean, I haven't met her, but I think these things will be useful."

"We don't know her code. We can't get in."

"Leave that to me." He winked, flashing green eyes like a cat. A big scary mountain lion of a cat.

"How long will that take?"

"Hopefully not too long. We'll get to work on it." The new guy turned and held out his hand to the driver for the phone. "Did you get a make and model on the car that picked her up? A license plate?"

I handed the phone to the new guy. "It was a big SUV. Dark. But I didn't see any more than that."

"Which direction did it take her?"

"North. Toward Billings."

"Okay, then. We'll focus our initial efforts there." He shifted back to the driver's boss. "Does she have money? A home to go back to? A job skill?"

He was pacing. "No money. She ran away from home after high school. She worked in a roadhouse in Bozeman. Bartending and waiting tables. She used to dance, but she quit and said she never wanted to go back. She dated a guy who pushed her around. The guy before that did, too."

"So, she has a type." The new guy was rubbing wiry chin whiskers. "Then we have plenty of leads."

He pounded his fist in his hand. "She must be found." He turned on the driver. "You. You'll pay for letting this happen."

I clenched my fists then opened them. I was outnumbered. I couldn't fight. I was ready to accept pain and injury. Part of me hoped for death. It would solve so many problems.

The third man finally spoke from the other side of the table from the new guy. The leader of the whole group. The same height as my boss but double his body weight, all of the extra in muscle, with hair so blond it was almost white, plus his most striking features—his scars. They ran down the side of his cheek, red and angry, through his hairline, and into his hair. The story was a grizzly had got him a few years before, and an older brother had saved him. A brother who was now in federal prison down in Colorado. "Quit sniveling like a baby. It was your idea to let her go. You have to learn to deal with your problems if you can't keep from creating them. Like me. You have one month to bring her back. After that, it's my call."

"One month isn't enough."

"I'll tell you what is enough and what isn't. And I'll tell you what the consequences are. From now on, you're stripped of your leadership responsibilities. I'm promoting him in your place." He thumbed at the new guy. "You'll report to him, in fact."

"You can't do that!"

"I just did. And if you want, I can make a phone call to DC and get a second opinion."

"No. I, uh. Just, no."

"As for him," he looked over at me, "you should be apologizing that he was in that position. Now, all of you, get out of here and get some work done. Little brother, I think they can use your help with latrine duty."

I said, "Thank you, sir." I was surprised but found I didn't care one way or the other. I walked toward the door.

My boss caught up with me outside. He spat on the ground at my feet. "You think this is over? It won't ever be over between you and me. Not ever."

FOUR

Delaney caught herself on the shoulder of a man she'd never met, which kept her from crashing to the ground and sliding halfway to the lodge down the steep slope.

Breathless, she said, "Sorry. Deputy Pace." Leo skied up beside them. "This is Sheriff Palmer. Tell us what you saw."

The man—or kid, as he looked late teens at most—was wide-eyed under an orange cap made for hunters. "It's over this way. A rifle. And tracks heading out the back."

"What do you mean 'out the back'?" Leo asked.

The kid waved his hand. "The front of this hill is the ski area. The back is outside the boundary. At the bottom are the snowmobile trails."

"Did you see him?"

"No, man. I was about to go backcountry skiing. Off trail. I heard the shot and people screaming. I skied back and there was the gun and the tracks. I could have been caught in the crossfire, you know?"

Delaney said, "What kind of tracks?"

The kid frowned, looking uncertain, and thought for a second. "Not skis. Snowshoes."

"Could you have skied where the tracks went?"

He shook his head with more confidence. "Not right there. Too gnarly with rocks and trees. Maybe somebody better than me could have."

Leo turned to Delaney. "Do you know the area?"

She brushed hair from her eyes. "The snowmobile trail, yes. The back of the ski mountain down to it, no. If we hurry, I can get us around to that trail on our snow machines. Maybe we'd catch up to him since he's on snowshoes." She had downloaded trail maps to her phone when she'd moved back to Kearny. Hiking trails. Snowmobile trails. Off-road vehicle trails. Maps of back roads. Maps of areas with no roads at all. In their rugged and vast area to enforce the law, they were nothing without maps. Maybe with them she could guesstimate where the snowshoer—the shooter—would come out. "I can't imagine anyone would snowshoe away from a crime scene. That's thousands of acres of rough terrain back there. He's got to have a snowmobile waiting on him."

Leo was nodding. "Let me radio instructions. You get your skis on."

She gave a violent head shake. "That's not happening. I'm riding the lift down."

Leo was speaking into his lapel radio, but he shot her a thumbs-up. "A backcountry skier found the weapon. I'll have him wait for someone at the summit and take them there. Delaney and I have a lead on the shooter. We're coming down the lift and going after him." When he'd finished he spoke to the kid again. "Can you wait here for the next officer? And not tell anyone else where the gun is?"

Delaney was making the slippery walk back to the lift, jamming the toes of her ski boots into the snow for traction and trying to look slightly uphill, away from the sensation pulling her toward the incline from her peripheral vision.

Behind her, the young man said, "Yes, sir."

Then Leo skied up beside her. "I'll get the lift operator to let us on."

Thirty minutes later, Delaney was flying across the groomed snowmobile trail that started at Adelaide Pass and continued toward Mockingbird Creek and beyond. Adelaide Pass was one of the most popular places for sledders to park their vehicles and trailers for day rides, but she and Leo had ridden to an intersecting point of the trail from the ski area and turned west on it there.

They'd encountered about a dozen people so far. She'd watched the other sleds for snowshoes to no avail yet.

Every minute or so, she'd look to make sure Leo was still there, far enough back to avoid snow and debris thrown up by her machine, but close enough to be within sight. His snow sledding skills had improved since he'd first moved to the area, but she was pushing their speed to the limit of his abilities. She couldn't help but remember a year before when he'd gotten stuck during a wellness check they'd made in the mountains that had turned into one of the biggest murder cases of her career. Speed wasn't her only worry for him now, though, since 'groomed' was a relative term. The grooming didn't happen every day. The powder from the night before could catch a ski and bog a sledder down or pull them off trail.

Because of the uncertainty of where they were headed and the likelihood of it being remote, she'd taken a minute in the Elk Ridge parking lot to prep and stow gear bags and add to her clothing layers. Neither had their duty belts, but they'd made do with items in their trucks. Both of them had unlocked their weapons from their vehicular gun safes and brought them. She'd also managed to connect with her daughters face to face. Carrie would be driving the teens home in Delaney's truck. The kids had sworn they'd leave after they gave their statements, but their dilated pupils and fast talking told Delaney the drama of the moment had them in its grip. It would be tempting for them to stay and gossip a while longer.

Now, out on the snowmobile trail, the backside of Elk Ridge loomed to her right, per the map she'd been checking. She pointed with two fingers, holding the pose to give Leo time to see it.

She slowed her speed and scanned the snow between the trail and the hill, looking for tracks. It was highly unlikely that the murderer would have left a snowmobile on the trail itself. That might have triggered attempts to assist by passing Good Samaritans. But the snow immediately off the groomed portion of the trail was very deep. It would take a skilled rider to drive across it without getting stuck and would leave very obvious marks in the snow. She would see them if that had been what happened.

She saw nothing. Could the murderer have left a sled elsewhere and be taking a longer walk through the woods to get to it?

She stopped and turned off her machine then flipped up her face shield. Leo pulled up beside her and did the same.

He said, "What do you think?"

"No sign of him yet." She waved her hand at the expanse of unmarked snow on the hill. "No snowshoe tracks, no sled tracks."

"Could he still be up there?"

"Maybe. If he's waiting on someone or hurt. Otherwise, he'd be out of there. Going down that hill wouldn't take this long."

"So, where the heck is he?"

She took it as a rhetorical question. "I've been trying to put myself into the mind of someone fleeing the scene of a shooting on a ski mountain. If it were me, I'd prioritize moving deliberately and carefully. The worst thing that could happen would be getting injured or trapped. That would slow our guy down or derail him completely. But a close second would be to draw attention to himself. To make himself memorable. If I were him, I'd be acting like a recreational sledder. Driving quickly but not racing away in a panic."

"I'm with you."

"A recreational sledder wouldn't be traveling solo. But two people means a murder conspiracy. If our guy is acting alone, there will be only one sled."

"There might only be one sled if someone came and picked him up double, too."

"True. I'm beginning to think that's likely, based on the lack of tracks. But I still don't see snowshoe tracks anywhere."

"Me, either. And I haven't seen anyone I thought could be our guy. Although what do I know? He might have ditched his snowshoes just like he ditched his gun. Maybe we should have stopped other riders and asked about him."

She shook her head. "We still should see tracks. That's virgin snow on that hill."

"True."

"So, I think we keep going. I'm hoping this means he was walking down the mountain at an angle. It might also mean we have a little more time to catch him if he had a longer walk."

"What's in that direction?"

"Mockingbird Creek. It has a campground with a handful of cabins for overnighters and parking for day riders. Also, access to Highway 14 down to Greybull or back across to Sheridan."

"Let's get going, then. I'm right behind you."

She nodded, flipped her shield back down, started her sled's engine, and took off at half throttle, torn between the desperate urge to chase after their killer at full speed and the need for good visibility of any disturbances in the white landscape. Eyeing the shape of the hill, she saw what looked like a ridgeline along the southern edge. It was a likely route to descend. Not as steep as coming straight down off the back. Optimism surged through her, buoyed her. She gave her sled a little more gas, aiming for the base of the ridgeline.

When she judged she was nearing it, she backed off the throttle and stood to get a better view. Twenty yards ahead, the forest came close to the trail. Her heart rate accelerated. The perfect spot. She edged to the left on the trail, hoping to keep from inadvertently destroying any tracks.

And then she saw them. Snowshoe marks. Lots of them. From the tree line and around the edge of the trail. She pulled to a stop. The tracks were even on the trail. Someone had walked out of that forest and gotten on a snowmobile in this very spot.

She pumped her fist and whooped, her voice loud inside her helmet and the exhalation of breath fogging her shield. She held up her hand to signal Leo to stop, then took off her entire helmet and shut off her sled. Which way had the snowmobile gone?

She stayed on her runners, standing on her tiptoes. She imagined the scene as if a snowmobile were here. The tracks would be going around the back end of the snowmobile for the snowshoer to mount. It was easier than going around the unwieldy skis in front. It's what she would have done. Based on that, she was certain the sled had headed toward Mockingbird Creek. She pulled out her phone and took pictures as best she could of the tracks, zooming in to get good shots.

"What do you see?" Leo shouted.

"He came out here. Lots of snowshoe tracks, even on the trail. They're headed toward Mockingbird Creek. But the snowmobile didn't turn around."

"He was heading in the opposite direction from where he came?"

"Or someone dropped him off, went and turned around at Adelaide Pass, and came back and picked him up."

"Or he did the turnaround at Adelaide Pass himself and left it parked here."

Leo was right, even if she didn't think it was likely the killer would have left his getaway vehicle unattended and in plain sight on the trail. "All we know is which way he was going. Not how many people there are, gender, age, how many sleds, what he's wearing. Nothing."

"An order to 'stop that snowmobile' won't do much."

Just then, a line of snowmobiles zipped around them, each rider holding up a hand in greeting. The first rider held up five fingers, the second one four, the third three, the fourth two, the fifth one, and the last rider a closed fist. It was the safety sign language to let other trail users know how many vehicles to expect.

Leo groaned. "And we now know there are six additional riders on this section of trail. I'll see about getting it closed off."

"There are a lot of side trails for people to come on and off from. I don't think closing is feasible."

Leo spoke into his radio. "Sheriff Palmer for Sheriff Wilcox. Come in Sheriff Wilcox."

Delaney pulled up the map on her phone. It was only a couple of miles—less than five—from where they were parked to Mockingbird Creek.

"This is Sheriff Wilcox. What's up, Leo?"

"We think we've found where the suspect exited the back of the ski area on snowshoes and got on a snowmobile headed toward Mockingbird Creek. Unfortunately, that's all we know, and there are sledders out here unrelated to the incident. I was thinking you might want to start interviewing people that come through the trail at the campground?"

"Damn. Manpower is an issue. I've called for help. I'll work it out, but if your suspect is already en route, we won't catch him. We're too far away."

Delaney was putting her helmet back on. She gave a twirling "let's go" signal to Leo.

Leo said, "We'll keep you posted. We're going after him." He put his mic away and was getting ready before Wilcox had confirmed the transmission.

Delaney started her engine and waited for Leo to signal her that he was ready, then she gave her snowmobile all the throttle it had.

FIVE

Leo's thumb ached from holding his snowmobile at full throttle. Driving all out, he and Delaney had overtaken the group of six that had passed them by earlier, then several other small groups. What they hadn't found was anyone with snowshoes—and they were now positive that the killer hadn't left them on the mountain or the trail.

A few times on their ride the bite of the wind had been so cold that he'd had to huddle down into his clothing. When they'd left the ski resort, the wind had been mild. Now it was whipping up little snow tornados in front of him. A glance up over the trees and the top of the next mountain beyond had been sobering. To the north, the sky was dark and heavy. The falling temperatures and wind were the prologue to the real story. A storm was moving in. He tried to calculate how far they'd ridden. His watch told him they'd left Elk Ridge less than an hour ago. Maybe ten miles? With the stops and conversations and twists and turns it was hard to be sure.

Delaney stopped at a fork in the trail. Leo immediately turned off his machine and lifted his shield.

She pointed to the right. "About three miles to Highway 14

and Mockingbird Creek Campground. Rustling Creek Snowmobile parking beyond that." She swung her arm to point ahead of them. "About twenty-one miles to the Flint Rock Lodge, which is after the Flint Rock Lakes. Then it's ungroomed trails along the western edge of the Bighorns." She waved to her left. "All up in there is Cloud Peak Wilderness. Not a place you want to be this time of year."

"Don't you think our guy would be headed to a vehicle and a getaway?"

"That seems the most likely bet. I can't imagine he'd be marooning himself out at the lodge or a campsite out here. If there's safety in numbers, there's risk in the opposite, right?"

Just then two snowmobiles approached from the Mockingbird Creek connector. Leo waved them to a stop and held up his badge.

The first person to reach them was a man possibly in his forties if the lines around his eyes were telling an accurate story, which he saw when the man lifted his shield. He was wearing navy Carhartt from head to toe.

"Sheriff Leo Palmer, Kearny County," Leo said.

"Are you lost? This is Big Horn." The man's eyes sparkled with good humor.

Leo smiled at him. "Have you seen a snowmobile headed toward Mockingbird Creek in the last few minutes carrying snowshoes?"

"Snowshoes?"

Behind him, a man had taken off his helmet. He looked young enough to be the man's son and was dressed almost identically except in black. "I didn't see anyone with snowshoes. I used to carry them all the time when I snowmobiled off trail, so I notice."

The six snowmobilers overtook them again, shooting curious looks. The third person in line gave them a questioning thumbs-up. Leo returned it to assure them no one needed help.

A buzz of engines approached from ahead of Leo and Delaney.

"Thanks, guys," he said to the two men.

"What's this about?" the older guy asked.

The murder at Elk Ridge was no secret. "We're looking for a person who might have information about an incident at the ski area. As always when you're out in the national forest, let us know if you see something that doesn't seem right."

"If you see something, say something," the younger man said. "Will do."

The two of them were on their way east toward Adelaide Pass before the group coming from the direction of Flint Rock Lakes had reached them. Again, Leo held up his badge and waved them over. Four snowmobiles pulled to a stop in a semi-circle around him and Delaney, blocking the entire trail. The sleds were new. The outfits were colorful. Four helmets came off, revealing tanned faces with mussed hair. Two men, two women.

Leo introduced himself then Delaney. She raised a hand in greeting. "We're looking for a snowmobiler who's carrying a set of snowshoes."

One of the women frowned. "That's not much of a description to go by."

"Sorry. It's all we've got. If you haven't noticed anyone with snowshoes, you can be on your way."

Her voice turned edgy. Almost snotty. "Is it a crime to carry snowshoes out there?"

The other woman laughed.

One of the men said, "Come to think of it, that's not a bad idea. If you got stuck, walking out would be near impossible."

Leo licked his lips. The odor of whiskey was wafting through the air. He didn't mind a hot toddy on a cold day, but driving while intoxicated was no more legal on a snowmobile than in a wheeled vehicle. And possibly much more dangerous.

Sixty-five percent of fatal crashes of off-road vehicles including snowmobiles involved drugs or alcohol. It also made witnesses more challenging to communicate with. "We sure would appreciate your help. So, is it a yes or a no—did any of you notice a sled with snowshoes?"

Finally, the second man spoke up. His eyebrows were furrowed in a deep V. "I did. Not too long ago. Maybe ten minutes?"

The first woman laughed as snow began to float toward the ground. "Listen to you, Mr. Back the Blue, standing on the right side of the thin blue line."

Leo saw a murderous look cross Delaney's face, but she remained silent, only turning to look at him and nod toward the cooperative guy.

"Thank you, sir. That's extremely helpful. Was it more than one sled?"

"Two, I think," the man said. "One was yellow and black, the one with the snowshoes. It looked pretty old. The other was bigger. It had blue on it. Mostly blue. Maybe some black. They went by pretty fast."

The first woman sounded even snottier now. "You mean you didn't already know this? You're just chasing after snowshoes?"

Leo felt snowflakes hitting his face and melting. "Sir, could you tell if the drivers were male or female?"

"No, I couldn't."

"Or maybe you have an impression of what they were wearing—was it flashy and colorful? Black? White?"

"White. They were both in white."

"All right, then. Thank you—"

"Seriously—not impressive, officers." The sarcastic woman leaned toward the other woman. "And I thought the cops back home were morons."

Leo held out a hand, but Delaney ignored it.

"Ma'am, unless you'd like us to have you hauled into town for drug and alcohol testing, your best course of action is to head straight to the nearest place you can sit out your intoxication—I recommend Mockingbird Creek Campgrounds—and to not say another word to us while you're doing it. There's been a murder at the ski resort up the road and we're in pursuit of a person of interest who fled the scene on snowshoes and appears to have left on a snowmobile. Congratulations. You're officially the only ones to have seen him. Another reason to go take shelter in a hurry. He's likely to be displeased you saw him. Meanwhile, we're going to take our moronic selves off into the wilderness to try to catch a killer, if you'll excuse us. Unless you want that ride into town for testing?"

The woman started to speak, but the helpful man cut her off with a raised hand and curt voice. "Not one more word out of any of you. Thank you, Sherriff. Deputy."

Delaney smiled at him. She brushed snow off her shoulders and face shield.

Leo pointed toward Mockingbird Creek. The four riders roared away in that direction. He radioed the information to Sheriff Wilcox. Then he turned to his partner.

"We have suspects," he said to her. "This is progress."

"They have a significant head start."

"Ah, yes, but they have no idea we're on to them." He was about to mention the weather and suggest they go to Mockingbird Creek for backup and more gear. But he was too late.

Delaney had already accelerated ahead of him.

"Dammit, Delaney." He floored it but soon was having trouble keeping up with her.

The weather beat at his back. His gloved hands—protected by the windshield—were accumulating snow. Visibility was getting worse by the second. He switched on his headlight and gritted his teeth against the cold.

He loved Delaney's passion for her job. Her determination.

Her toughness on the outside and softness on the inside. He loved just about everything about her. But right that second he loved her rugged individuality a little less than usual. Working as partners for a year before getting together, he knew her well. So far, their fledgling relationship hadn't interfered with their jobs. If anything, they tried harder than ever to keep things professional and respect each other's roles and wishes. But then again, there hadn't been a high-stakes case lately. The kind that sucked the deputy in and spit her back out as a lone wolf vigilante with a badge. The kind that elevated public scrutiny of him and his sense of personal responsibility for delivering justice within the bounds of the law.

It had put them at odds before. And now... she was zooming ahead of him in strange terrain and deadly conditions. He knew time was of the essence, but not at the expense of her safety. Or his.

A group of riders passed him going the other direction. He watched them instead of the trail, only for second. His skids caught powder, and he fought the steering. For a long, torturous moment, he was sure he was going to flip over. When he'd stabilized, it took a few moments to slow his breathing. Could Delaney even be sure he was back here? Before that line of thought could overstress him, he realized that she could. She had a rearview mirror. He was using his headlight. He couldn't see her, though, and he wasn't feeling confident about staying in the center of the trail, which was growing less groomed by the second.

Suddenly, headlights were coming back in his direction. As they drew nearer, he felt a wave of warm relief. It was Delaney.

They huddled to talk.

Leo said, "My machine isn't as fast as yours. I'm having trouble keeping up. And this weather is going to the dogs." Delaney drove her personal snowmobile. Leo hadn't made that kind of investment and was riding one that belonged to the department. She'd given him a hard time about it earlier. "Inappropriate use of department equipment, Sheriff?" To which he'd replied that he'd be scouting territory to prepare for future cases. It had been funny at the time. Now, it seemed prophetic.

Delaney's green eyes were glowing with fire. "I have an idea. I try to catch them, and I fake a problem to get them to help me. Then you'll show up, and we'll take them in."

"No. Let's stay together."

"Leo, it's a groomed trail. Neither of us gets off of it. I either catch up to them and this works or it doesn't, and I turn around and we go back together. It's not like I'm going to miss you in that bright red helmet of yours." She dusted her hands against each other, like she was describing the easiest thing in the world.

Leo had refused the department-issue helmet and bought his own. The thought of helmet sharing had not been appealing to him. He'd caught a lot of grief for his color choice. "I could have trouble and not reach you."

"I'll turn around in an hour, no matter what. Agreed?"

"You could have trouble and not be able to come back."

She threw an arm out, pointing back the way they'd come. "We passed a safety shelter a few miles back. If you have trouble, hitch a ride there and wait for me. Or if you don't like that, go all the way to Mockingbird Creek Campground. They have cabins. It's not like we're alone out here. This is a popular trail with people in nice, warm buildings at both ends. I'll do the same. We just have to agree to stay on the trail."

"That's easier said than done if this turns into a blizzard."

"One hour, Leo. I studied the forecast today, and this isn't expected to be more than just a little snow. So, watch for the reflectors on the trees that mark the edge of the trail. Turn back if it gets bad." She nodded and stomped back to her machine.

"If I give you a direct order to turn around, are you going to ignore it?"

"Yes."

"If I threaten to fire you?"

"Makes no difference."

"If I tell you that I'm just a scared computer nerd from California?"

"You wouldn't put that in my head."

"I have a radio, and you don't."

"So, don't go off trail. Radio for help if you have trouble. Radio for help if you think I have. I'm a child of the mountains, Leo. I'll be fine." She pushed the button to turn on her engine and sped away like a rocket into the night.

Leo gritted his teeth and shook his head. He couldn't have stopped her even if he'd pulled a gun on her, and how ridiculous would that have been? Her plan was awful but in character. All he needed to do was drive the trail at a reasonable speed.

He took off after his star deputy—the best friend who always led him astray, and the confounding, irritating, remarkable love of his life—with a bad feeling in the pit of his stomach.

SIX

Carrie Hoff pulled to a stop outside the back door to the Loafing Shed. She was dropping Freddy there, where his mom Adriana was working. A handful of employee cars were parked beside Carrie's, and wonderful smells were leaking out of every gap in the old boards. Saturday night meant barbecue ribs. Her stomach rumbled. She wondered if they had anything good in the refrigerator at home. Maybe leftover pizza? She'd have to get to them before Kat ate her share and Carrie's too. The opening of Billie Eilish's "What Was I Made For?" came on Spotify, and Carrie cranked up the volume. She shared a smile with Victoria. They loved the song. Lately Carrie could really relate to the lyrics.

Freddy opened the back door. Kat did the same. Carrie turned, scowling.

"Y'all don't get too loaded at the Loading Shed," Victoria said, laughing at her own joke.

To Melaney's chagrin, everyone in town insisted on calling the bar and restaurant the Loading Shed, like a place to get loaded, instead of the Loafing Shed, which was its real name and meant to suggest a safe shelter to loaf around in. It had been named after the loafing sheds for livestock all over Wyoming ranches. Carrie used to call it the Loading Shed, too, but lately she'd been secondhand irritated on Melaney's behalf every time someone said it.

"No way, *Kateena* Pace. We're heading home," Carrie said.

"Who died and made you Queen of America?" Kat already had one foot out the door.

"Melaney left me in charge. I'm responsible for you, and I'm not coming back to get you later."

"Freddy's mom can give me a ride home."

Freddy was standing by the truck. It wasn't snowing as hard here as it had been on the mountain but flakes still wafted in. The drive home had been long and given Carrie a headache, probably from clenching her teeth and shoulders. She was a good driver. She should be. She'd been driving her twin brother's truck since he died. As in *was murdered.* Most of the time she pretended she was back to normal since that and a lot of other horrible stuff that she tried not to think about had happened, but what was normal really? Everything inside her felt like it had changed.

God, where was I? Down a mental rabbit hole. Again. Anyway, she was a pretty decent driver. But the mountain roads in a storm was a lot. She'd been scared, and everyone else in the car had just chattered on and fought over what music was playing without a clue about her stress.

Carrie felt manipulated and taken for granted and her head hurt, on top of having a teenage existential crisis. Maybe she shouldn't have quit therapy. "You didn't even *ask.*"

"I'm asking now."

Oh, that tone! Kat had a way of making Carrie feel sorry for Melaney. "Do you have homework?"

"It's Saturday, Care Bear. As if." Kat rolled her eyes.

Victoria said, "If you were my sister I'd let you stay."

Kat pumped a fist. "Yes! I knew Vic was my favorite person in the world. Did you hear, that, Carrie? Now you have to let me."

Carrie sighed. It was more like a deep chest growl. "Fine. But if I get in trouble for this, I'm ratting you out for last weekend." She had the ammunition. Kat had been at Freddy's infamous pot party. Carrie had whisked her away only minutes before the group had been busted, information Melaney was not privy to. Carrie intended to hold it over Kat's head the rest of her life, or until it became critically necessary to use it.

"You can't do that!"

"Try me."

Kat huffed. "Fine."

"Fine."

Kat slammed the door and flounced away, one hand in Freddy's, already chattering.

Victoria snorted. "How much longer until she gives up horses because of him?"

Carrie frowned as she pulled around the side of the building. The parking area was packed with trucks and SUVs. She was the only one allowed to bash her little sister, with the sometimes-possible exception of Melaney. "She won't. When Kat gets something in her head, she is dogged." She liked using the vocabulary words she'd learned studying for college entrance exams. Not that they were going to matter.

"Seems like lately all that's there is Freddy."

At the exit from the parking lot, there was no traffic in either direction. Carrie turned onto the roadway, right toward town. Why was Victoria acting like she knew Kat better than Carrie did? She didn't. Carrie didn't respond.

A few minutes later, Victoria touched Carrie's hand. "I didn't mean to upset you."

Carrie put her hand on the steering wheel. "It's fine."

"You want to spend the night at my place?"

"No. Who knows when Freddy's mom will bring Kat home. I need to be there. Besides, Dudley has been home alone all day." Dudley was Kat's little Frenchie. The dog snored even with his eyes open, bounced like he had springs in his feet, and tried to fight the vacuum cleaner. He was your basic adorable nightmare.

"I can stay with you, then, so you won't be alone. If you want."

"I won't be alone. Duds is there. Kat will be back. And probably Melaney. Then I have to work in the morning." She had a longer-than-usual Sunday shift at the Loafing Shed because she'd taken today off to ski. Mary counted on her. Carrie had less time for hobbies like gaming because of the job, but she loved having her own money. Victoria worked there as backup sometimes, too.

"Are you trying to ditch me?"

"No, of course not." Carrie smiled at her. But she could feel that it was a little off. She was lying. Something was getting to her about Victoria, but she couldn't explain it. She didn't even know what it was herself.

Victoria crossed her arms over her chest. "You didn't tell your mom today."

"There wasn't a chance."

"You promised you would."

"A woman was murdered. What was I supposed to do?" She braked too hard in front of Victoria's house, rocking both of them forward in their seatbelts. It was an accident at the wrong time.

"Sorry. I'm just trying to help, like you said you wanted." A tear welled in Victoria's eye.

Carrie sucked a deep breath through her nose. "I'll do it. I promise."

Victoria nodded. "'Kay then." She fumbled at her seat belt.

The tear rolled down her cheek. "Bye." She leapt out of the truck.

Carrie felt a stab of guilt in the center of her chest. "Victoria, wait. I'm—"

But Victoria slammed the door shut and ran inside without looking back.

SEVEN

Delaney guesstimated she was close to Flint Rock Lake and the end of the groomed trail based on the length of time she'd been driving and her speed. There was no way she'd catch a glimpse of the lake, though—it was too far off trail to see in the storm. She had her headlight on but couldn't see as far as the light's reach. It was like being in a white cave, hemmed in by the trees on each side and the snow all around her. The visibility was so bad that she'd almost given up five minutes before, but it was at that moment that she'd caught sight of bouncing lights in front of her. Smelled acrid exhaust.

Was this her suspect and his co-conspirator? There was no way to know until she caught them. Her speed was already maxed out. It was now a race against time. Could she make up the last of the ground between her and them before they reached the ungroomed trails? If not, her only hope was that they stopped at Flint Rock Lodge. She would not, could not pursue past there. Not with Leo expecting to find her. Not alone. Not in these conditions. Even if she wanted to, which she very badly did.

A snowmobile whizzed by in the opposite direction. She

turned to check for snowshoes. There were none. How she wished she was with them, suspects in custody. An hour away from hot coffee before a roaring fire at Mockingbird Creek. Less than that from rejoining Leo and finishing this together. She hadn't seen his headlight in a while now. Despite her bravado earlier, being separated from him worried her. It was the only way, though, since his machine had all the get up and go of a land tortoise. It was the job. He understood, even if he didn't like it.

Ahead of her, the snowmobile taillight suddenly seemed much closer. It had stopped, she realized, easing off her throttle just a little. She strained to see though the snow—fighting the fading light now, too—and could identify only one rider. She squinted, hoping for a glimpse of a second snowmobile, but didn't find one. Her disappointment was bitter. These weren't her suspects. She'd come all this way and was facing failure.

The deputy in her couldn't pass a snowmobile in a storm without checking on the wellness of its rider. She neared a big black and yellow machine and her interest level increased. When she was nearly upon it, the rider turned. She frowned. His upper body seemed incredibly long and his head small and pointed. It wasn't until she was upon him that she realized two snowshoes were strapped to his back. Her breath caught. Snowshoes. But only one machine and one rider. It was then she took stock of his clothing. His clothes were such a bright white, he almost glowed in the dark. *White. We were told they're wearing white.* Her heart took off at a full gallop. This was him. This was it.

But then she replayed the image of the rider who'd driven past in the other direction a minute before. Tried to pull from it what the rider had been wearing. What the snowmobile looked like. She had clocked no snowshoes. She hadn't been paying close enough attention to the other details, distracted by the weather and her growing weariness. A clear picture formed.

The snowmobile had been dark, in contrast with the rider, who was light. A black machine and a rider in a white suit?!

The other suspect. They'd split up. She was in the presence of one of them.

But the other was heading back toward Leo.

EIGHT

Leo hurtled through the white kaleidoscope of snow, keeping his eyes low and in constant movement. His sense of balance and distance was shot. If he hadn't believed in gravity, he wouldn't have been able to tell up from down. He slowed down a little more. Delaney was ahead, out there somewhere, chasing after a murderer and his accomplice, but he'd do her no good if he got lost or hurt. Unfortunately, his visibility didn't improve much with the decrease in speed. He wrestled with whether to drive all-out again. Part of him wanted to, but he just couldn't make himself squeeze the throttle any tighter. Twenty-five miles per hour in this weather was going to have to do it. He slowed more. No, twenty. He had to be able to make the turns that were coming upon him at the last second now.

Darkness loomed on either side of him, which he took as a good sign that he was still on the trail. Dark meant trees. Or rocks. *Keep yourself in the white part.*

The darkness on his right seemed to move closer. He eased into a turn, relying on the feel of the trail—its smoothness, its levelness—to guide him. The turn grew sharper. He slowed more and leaned into it.

And then a moving darkness was in front of him. *What in God's name?* Directly in front of him. He gripped the brakes but too late. His snowmobile was going under something tall—a moose and it smelled like a wet, skunky dog!—that at the last second smashed his windshield and knocked him flying from the seat. He heard the whine of his engine as his body hit the ground and began to roll down an incline. *A hill? A cliff?*

His helmet hit something as hard as a rock. Maybe an actual rock. He heard a crack. *Not good.* Then he stopped rolling. He'd reached flat ground. A very cold flat ground, much harder than the trail or the hill had been. He lay dazed and motionless for long seconds, letting awareness creep back over him, flexing his hands and feet and turning his head from side to side.

He wasn't injured. At least not badly. He heard a groan and another crack. He felt this one, deep into his bones.

His eyes flew open. He suddenly knew exactly where he was. Or at least what he was on.

Ice. He'd landed off trail on ice. He was on a frozen lake.

NINE

Delaney eased to a stop beside the stranger with the snowshoes. His tinted face shield was down, but his machine's engine was off.

She lifted her own shield. She forced a fragility and desperation into her voice. "Oh, my God! I'm so glad to see you!"

The helmet tilted, just enough that she took it as an invitation to continue with the story she'd planned, one as close to the truth as possible.

"I'm Laney. I was out here with my boyfriend, but we got separated, and now I'm lost." She paused, waiting for him to show concern. Sympathy. Interest. But he displayed zero emotion, zero reaction. She squeezed her eyes, thinking about the time her daughters had been kidnapped by her horrible brother Liam, to form tears. "Can you, c-c-c-can you help me?"

The man leaned forward on his handlebars. The silence seemed interminable. He lifted his face shield, releasing the smell of cigarettes. She only had a second to pray she didn't know him. That he didn't know her and what her job was. That he wouldn't be saying, "Really, *Deputy*? Somehow I don't believe that."

His face was covered by a balaclava, but his intense dark eyes held her gaze. Could this be the camo-clad guy from the ski slopes? The one with white-blond hair and the small face and head who had tormented the woman who was killed? She couldn't tell. His body didn't seem large, but it was hard to know how tall someone was with their legs folded and torso leaning forward on a snowmachine. "You look okay to me. Your sled's in good shape. You got gas?"

"Um, I don't know. This is my first time driving a snowmobile. My boyfriend is the expert." She wiped at the meager tears she'd produced. "What's your name?"

"You can call me Slim."

"Slim. Thank you, Slim. I feel better just talking to you." She considered attempting to arrest him herself. What were her chances of success out here? She had a gun and flexicuffs. But this guy had a partner who could be back any moment. *You have two daughters who count on you and a man who loves you. Multiple people who want you to come back alive.* "Is this the gas gauge?" She pointed at her dash.

With her other hand, she removed her gloves, stuck them under her leg, and took out her phone, pointing it at her face to open it. Her fingers were aching and stiff within seconds from the cold. But she forced them to work anyway, angling her phone to capture him and taking a burst of photos with the flash off, careful to keep it out of his sight.

He didn't move to check out her gauges, just looked back down the trail over her shoulder. "It'll light up if you get low."

Stall, she told herself. *Give Leo time to get here.* "Can you maybe help me find my way back?"

"Back to where?"

"We were staying at a lodge."

"Mockingbird Creek?"

"No. You have to drive to get to it."

"Where'd you park?"

"It was high up in the mountains and really snowy. He told me the name, but I don't remember. Oh, my gosh, what if something has happened to him?"

"How long ago did you seem him?"

"A long time. Maybe an hour. Two hours. Are you riding by yourself?"

"Lady, you need to turn around and head back the way you came. There's only one trail out and you're on it."

"In this storm? Honestly, I'm sc-sc-sc-scared."

He didn't respond, other than to make a sound. A slightly disgusted sound.

"Where are you going? Maybe I can go there with you?"

"You don't want to go with me, lady. I can promise you that."

She scaled her voice to pre-wail. "It will be past dark soon, and I have no idea where I'm going. Maybe if I were somewhere with phone service. Or Wi-Fi. Or a radio. Do they have those where you're going?"

"You'd better get on your way. I'm heading in the opposite direction, and I don't have time for this."

She let her jaw drop and tremble. "But you were just sitting out here. Alone."

"Not that it's any of your damn business, but my buddy dropped something and went back for it. Which just puts us further behind. Take this trail to Mockingbird Creek Campground. It'll be twenty miles. There'll be a sign for it. Turn left at the sign, and then you're almost there. They'll have phones and know what to do with you. You'll be there in two hours. Maybe half that if you hustle. Go. Your daylight is wasting."

It was now or never. Delaney couldn't make up her mind about whether to try to arrest him or not. As soon as she did, she had to be prepared for him to bolt. She'd have to lunge for him. Holding a gun on him would do no good. He'd just drive away, and she'd be firing in bad visibility at a moving target without adequate justification to risk killing him. She should prepare to knock him out and tie him on behind her. How big was he? Was she going to be able to handle his weight in this snow depth? And what if his buddy came back while she was doing it? Or saw her carrying him out and came after her? Were they armed? The shooter had dropped the rifle, but she guessed they probably were.

She was still waffling when a radio squawked. A staticky male voice spoke, but what he said was just numbers. "Thirteen, twenty-two, zero."

She repeated it to herself a few times, committing it to memory. "I thought you didn't have communications equipment. Can I use that to call for help?"

"It's a walkie-talkie, lady. You can't call anyone on it but my buddy. And now I gotta go."

Before she could draw her weapon, much less place him under arrest and leap onto him, he turned on his machine, reversed course in a laborious K-turn as changing directions mid trail was no simple business, and sped away, back toward Mockingbird Creek. She took a picture of his machine then sat for a moment, thinking. She had a picture of Slim's machine and his body type. She knew he was with a buddy. She got the impression they were heading somewhere out here around Flint Rock. Maybe further.

It wasn't much, but it was all she was going to get. Because she had made a commitment to Leo, and she was going to keep it, as much as she wanted to take off after the suspects and trust Leo to read her mind. Yes, she would try to talk him into continuing after the suspects when she found him, but first she had to find him.

She looked for his location on her phone, hoping for the miracle of signal. But the last ping had been several hours ago. She looked at the time. It was far later than she'd thought. And that was when she really started to worry. If he was still riding, he should have caught up with her by now. That made finding him her highest priority. Because this was a big wilderness, and the storm was getting worse by the minute, proving the forecast a bunch of hogwash. Maybe he was on the trail somewhere, waiting for her. Maybe in the emergency warming hut.

Or maybe not.

People died out here in these conditions. She couldn't let Leo or herself be one of them.

TEN

Leo's heart was a bass drum in his ears, but he could still hear his panting breath. Ice. He was on ice. How thick was it? Had it been cold enough long enough for a solid freeze? If so, why was he hearing the noises and feeling the cracking?

He tried to remember what—if anything—he knew about ice. He'd grown up in Southern California. What little he'd learned was in Coast Guard, but even there, he was land based. Law enforcement special ops. He had one and a half years of Wyoming marked off on his personal calendar, and none of that to date had included frozen bodies of water.

So, basically, almost nothing.

Stop it. His thoughts were coming off the flywheel. *This is no time for panic.*

He evaluated his options. Definitely he should not stand up. That would put all his body weight in one spot. Best to keep his weight spread as wide as possible, to lighten the load on any individual patch of ice. He could slither on his belly as fast as he could to shore, or he could stay still. *Think. Think before doing.* Which way to the shore? His vision was obscured. Something was on the inside of his shield, and he noticed a coppery scent.

Blood. It had to be his nose. He carefully lifted his face shield, which got stuck, and he realized it had been smashed, but he was able to see below it.

He'd survive a bloody nose. Back to what was important. He turned his head and looked one way. *Nope, too flat. That's ice.* Then the other. Still ice. It was either in front of him or behind him and he was betting behind. He lifted his head. More ice. *Behind me. Okay.*

His original panic was ebbing enough that his brain was functioning, and his breathing was easier without the shield over his mouth and nose. But he still should take his helmet off. If he went under, it would trap water around his head. He pried it off and held the chin strap in one hand.

A snowmobile engine in the distance caught his attention. *Delaney!* She was coming back for him.

He started a slow, careful rotation of his body, trying to gently spin instead of digging in with his hands or feet. The helmet bumped and slid with his progress. The ice was shockingly cold on his cheek. The skin on his face felt wet. His balaclava had slipped off, he realized, probably with his helmet. He hoped it wasn't laying on the ice behind him now, because he would not be going back for it. How quickly would frostbite set in out in this cold, with snow falling and melting on his skin and his face pressed against ice?

Leave it. Better to have frostbite than to do something foolish in a hurry and end up underwater.

He kept rotating, guessing he was halfway turned by now. The snowmobile engine noise slowed and idled. It sounded close. Then it revved again and came nearer. It switched off. *Yes!!*

"Delaney," he shouted. "I'm over here." He imagined her warm face against his as he told her about hitting the moose, which they could laugh about later. How great it would be to curl up with a movie beside her on his couch after they handed the case over to Sheriff Wilcox and his crew.

There was no answer.

"Delaney, is that you?" Why wasn't she answering? Maybe she couldn't hear him over the wind.

Now he could hear footsteps in the snow. *The shore—it's not far!* He finished his rotation and began a salamander crawl toward the sound. He lifted his gaze and saw a path through the snow cover where his body had landed, and slid out over the frozen water. He inched closer. At least now if he broke through it would be shallow. He might freeze to death, but his chance of drowning was slim. *Which was a worse way to die?*

He saw booted feet and the bottom of someone's legs at the edge of the ice. Big feet in big boots. *That's not Delaney.* Then the color of the pants registered. White. *One of our suspects?* But white wasn't an unusual color. It could be anyone.

He touched the shore and kept crawling until his upper body was on solid ground, inches from the boots. "Man, am I ever glad to see you. I hit a moose and went flying." He levered himself up and walked on his knees, slipping once, then landing fully on terra firma. Smiling and holding out his hand, he looked up at the white-suited person and forced a guileless smile. All he saw was a big body, white balaclava, and helmet. "My name's Leo, Leo—"

The person's arm swung down. Leo saw the movement, saw the long black object in his hand. Had time to duck but not get away. Felt the impact on his head.

Then he didn't see or feel anything else as blackness descended on him.

ELEVEN

Delaney drove like the hounds of hell were on her tail all the way back toward Mockingbird Creek. And she felt like she was *in* hell. A cold, dark, snowy version of it. The wind was howling and blowing up snow at the same time as it was falling in a curtain around her. The wind chill made the temperature feel even colder. What light had been coming through the clouds was gone.

Her search for Leo wasn't going well. She was swiveling her head, looking for him on the trail, to the point of dizziness. She couldn't imagine him going off trail. At worst, he'd be at the edge. But she hadn't seen him or his snowmobile, and she'd covered half the twenty miles back to the turnoff. She was certain she'd still had his headlight in her sideview mirror at this point in the trail when she was heading out. If he'd been waiting on her, she'd have seen him by now.

Flickers of fear were rising inside her, but she beat them back. She'd told him to turn around if he had trouble. So that was it. That was what he'd done. She'd check the warming hut and if he wasn't there in front of a fire he'd made with provisions stocked for winter visitors, he'd be at Mockingbird Creek

Campground, just like they'd agreed—only he'd be worried out of his mind about her and probably a little bit pissed. She'd been gone a long time. Out in the wilderness alone in bad weather. He had a right to be upset.

But she had some news for him. Descriptions. A possible name. Again, she second-guessed herself. Could she have brought Slim in? Had she just missed her only opportunity to take a killer out of the community? She had a feeling she was going to question herself about it for a long time.

Thinking about their suspect, something hit her. It wasn't just Leo she hadn't seen on the trail. She hadn't seen either of the white-suited men. That was weird. They'd been headed across the mountain, Slim had said. At least up to Flint Rock Lodge. Slim said the only reason his partner had turned back was to pick up something he'd dropped.

Either he'd dropped it way back up the trail or they'd changed their minds. Or he'd lied. She mulled it over, still scanning for Leo. She needed a windshield wiper for her face shield. The weather was absolute crap. The suspects had probably decided it was too dangerous and headed in, too.

Then she shook her head. *No.* These guys were fleeing the scene of a crime. They weren't going to backtrack toward where law enforcement would be looking for suspects. They were out here somewhere. Maybe they'd been doubling back to see if they were being followed. The dropped item could have been a ruse. She thought about the radio call in numbers. That had been weird. "Thirteen, twenty-two, zero." Obviously, it had been a code. Had it been a location? A backup plan? An order to *change* plans? It had come in *after* Slim told her he and his buddy were headed out beyond the lodge.

Her neck tingled. Were they out there somewhere watching and waiting for her to go by? Or would she open the door to the shelter and find not Leo but the two of them?

The snow was coming down so hard now that she had to

drop her speed or risk missing the turnoff to the hut. And she hadn't been clocking time versus the speed, so she wasn't sure how far she had left to go.

Rookie move, Delaney. Get your head on straight. She had to ignore everything else spinning through her brain—her fears and doubts and second-guessing—and just execute the plan. So, her best estimation was that she had gone nearly the entire twenty miles. The shelter would be on her left. It was before the junction that led to Mockingbird Creek, on the left and off trail at a fairly significant curve. That much she knew. Unfortunately, she'd never stopped there. Worry gnawed at her. If she was having this much trouble figuring out where it was, Leo would have, too.

Maybe she should just go on to Mockingbird Creek. She could double back to the hut if he wasn't at the campground.

But then she saw a line too straight to be made in nature. An angle that had to be a roof line. She whooped and turned toward it. But she immediately stopped. The drifts on the little road leading toward it were monstrous. There was no way she'd make it through them. She stood on her machine's seat and lifted her face shield, squinting to keep snowflakes out of her eyes. Unless someone had parked around back, there were no snowmobiles at the shelter, but there was no sign of recent tracks through the drifts. There was no smoke coming out of the chimney.

He's not there. And neither were her suspects. Her stomach felt hollow. Her heart felt empty and echoey. She pushed the feelings aside. He'd be at the campground, with the people Wilcox had sent there after Leo had contacted him earlier.

Then she remembered—Leo had a radio! If he'd had any trouble, he would have used it. He'd probably already radioed in an update, summoning more officers to search this area in the morning.

It made her feel better for about two seconds.

She redirected her machine to the trail and the few remaining miles before the campground, driving too fast for the conditions. Driving reckless and nearly blind. Fighting panic. Fighting tears.

Ten harried minutes later, she stopped inches from a Big Horn County Sheriff's Department truck. The door to a small log cabin opened, letting out the scent of a wood fire. She recognized the man framed in the doorway. She flipped up her face shield and ran toward him through the deep snow, stumbling in her heavy boots.

"Leo," she cried.

"Haven't seen him," Sheriff Wilcox told her.

And she fell to her knees and clutched her helmet.

TWELVE

The bright lights and loud music inside the Loafing Shed were giving Kat Pace a headache. She swung her legs under the high-top table and looked through the open door to the kitchen. Freddy's mom was still running around telling people what to do. Mary was doing the same thing at the bar in the center of the big room. The place might *never* close. She hated to admit it, but she was sleepy. She and Freddy had been here for hours, and it had already been a long day. Getting up early, skiing, the woman murdered. It had been crazy. Maybe that was why she was so tired.

But she'd tried to rally. They'd eaten twice. Cheeseburgers and fries once and then chicken strips and gravy. Her clothes smelled like the fry vat in the kitchen—not a good thing. She'd downed four Shirley Temples, which Freddy made fun of her for drinking, but good was good. They'd played for hours on the old-school arcade game that had been delivered a few weeks before. Kat wasn't gonna lie—she loved *Centipede* and was way better at it than Freddy. She'd also spent her entire week's allowance loading up songs on the super cool TouchTunes. It had been fun to make the old fogies groan when all she played was Beyoncé and Olivia Rodrigo and Taylor Swift, but even that wasn't enough to keep her going.

She was close to calling Carrie and asking for a ride home.

Freddy bumped her knee with his under the table. "Yo, Kat. You with me?"

She bumped him back. "Right in front of you. Or beside you." She giggled.

"Wanna go out back and," he winked at her, "watch the snow fall?"

"Do I want to freeze my butt off? Uh, no."

"I can keep you warm."

Freddy had a lot of interest in trying to keep her warm, if that's what you wanted to call it. More than she did. She'd been super into kissing at first. It was so exciting. Freddy finally liked her back! And it was fun, too.

But that wasn't the only thing he wanted to do. The more she and Freddy made out, the more uncomfortable she was getting. He was starting to try to touch her. He usually stopped when she asked him to. Last weekend, though, when he'd been smoking pot—and she hadn't, by the way—he had just laughed at her and kept trying. She'd been so upset she'd called Carrie for a ride home from Leo's house, and left in tears. She was only thirteen. Freddy was nearly fifteen, and Melaney and Carrie both said that was a big age difference when it came to stuff like that.

Then Leo came home early and busted the party. Freddy got in sooo much trouble. He was grounded now. In fact, the only reason he'd gotten to go skiing today was because his uncle was with him. His mom still seemed pissed and had been shooting eye daggers at him all night.

Kat wanted to talk to him about what had happened between them at the party, but she didn't know how. He didn't even seem to remember that she'd run out of the house crying. It was a little upsetting, to be honest. Should she just let it go? She did feel sorry for him about being grounded.

But she didn't want to go out to "watch the snow fall" with him. She kept her voice light and jokey. "Gonna have to pass."

"My mom's car would be nice and warm." His hand was on her knee.

"I have to be at Clara's early tomorrow morning. I'm making up for missing today."

His eyebrows shot up. "You pick shoveling horse shit over me?"

The first and last thing Clara had her do every visit to the ranch was take care of the animals, and that included mucking out. "I didn't say that. But I'm tie-urd. So tired."

He looked away, then frowned. "You're not that into me anymore, are you?"

"What? How can you say that?" She reached for his hand, but he pulled it away.

"I don't want to come in second to a bunch of nags."

Suddenly, she was wide awake again. She hadn't meant to make him feel bad. She liked him a lot. She really did. She had for, like, *forever*. "Freddy, no." She leaned over and put her head on his shoulder. She had to fix this. "You're not second to anything. And you know what? I like watching snow fall with you."

He stuck his lower lip out in a big pout. "You say that now."

She felt weak with relief. "I say that always."

He stood up and held out his hand. "Mom keeps her keys in her purse. It's in the office."

Kat gave him a big smile. She let him lead her down the hallway, feeling only a little nervous. She'd just tell him no hand stuff as soon as they got outside. He'd understand, especially since they'd be in a parking lot where anyone who walked by could see in the car.

Wouldn't he?

THIRTEEN

All Delaney heard for long moments was a loud buzzing noise, like she was a mosquito frying in a bug light. Where was Leo? How could she have missed him?

A voice broke through to her. "Delaney? Deputy Pace, are you okay?" A hand descended on her shoulder. Shook it.

She looked up into the probing eyes of Sheriff Shannon Wilcox. "I, um, Leo was supposed to meet me at the warming hut. He wasn't there. Our fallback was here."

"You weren't together?"

"We were. But we were on the suspect's tail. He and another guy were getting away. We decided—" but Delaney had a stricken moment wondering if it was really *we* or just *her*. Her voice broke. "I was supposed to catch up to them. Stall them. Play like I was lost. Which I did. At least with one of them. They split up, too. Leo was going to stay on the trail and just follow. But he never caught me. So, I came back to our meeting points. And he's not anywhere he was supposed to be."

Shannon helped her to her feet. He was strong and lifted her a few inches higher than necessary. "All right. Let's take a deep breath and think this through."

Delaney pulled back from him, suddenly electrified. "He probably missed the turn. He could be back to Adelaide Pass by now."

"Good thinking. We've got officers up there. I'll radio them."

"And he has his radio. You can contact him."

"Now we're getting somewhere."

She was heading for her snowmobile. "But I need to drive the trail up to Adelaide."

Shannon held up a hand in the "stop" gesture. "Let's get you warm and dry first. Feed you and hydrate you while I handle these radio calls."

"I don't need anything."

"Humor me, deputy. The calls will only take a minute. Bathroom. Gatorade."

The last thing Delaney wanted while Leo was alone, maybe lost, and freezing in a mountain storm was to comfortably warm herself by a toasty fire with a beverage. It was obscene. But she followed Shannon inside. *Just while he radios.*

She'd never been in one of the Mockingbird Creek cabins before. It was functional and inviting. The curtains were gingham, the table and chairs pine. The kitchenette floors were a discolored linoleum that was probably white once upon a time. The countertop was almond-colored Formica. Two inches of coffee remained in a glass carafe. It smelled burned. This unit had several bedrooms off a small sitting area. And, of course, the fireplace, which was made of stone, radiated heat from the center of the room. In front of it were two other cops. One, Kearny Police Chief Clint Rock-Below, the other Caitlin Porter, a Kearny officer. Clint was a member of the Crow Tribe and had dimples as deep as Big Horn Canyon. Auburn haired and milky pale, Caitlin stood as tall as her boss.

Clint met Delaney in two strides, his eyes locked on hers.

He held out his arms. Delaney accepted a hug but extricated herself quickly.

Shannon pulled off his cap, revealing a shaved head with a port wine birthmark shaped, he claimed, like the state of Wyoming. Delaney didn't see it. "We're looking for Leo Palmer. He was last seen on his snowmobile out toward Flint Rock. Caitlin, can you radio up to Adelaide Pass and see if he's there? Clint, you try Elk Ridge. I'm going to see if I can raise him directly. Delaney is going to ride out to both places after some self-care."

Delaney took a few steps toward the kitchenette, but she froze and listened as the three officers worked their radios all at once, their voices overlapping. The room started to sway. Light-headedness had come on fast with the sudden heat in the small space. Maybe she really was dehydrated. She opened the small refrigerator and found bottles of red Gatorade. She unscrewed a top and drank one down in a series of gulps, wiped her mouth with the back of her hand, and threw the bottle in the trash.

Shannon nodded at her, clicked his mic and repeated his message. "This is Sheriff Shannon Wilcox for Sheriff Leo Palmer. Come in, Leo. Or anyone who has seen him. Over."

Caitlin was first off her radio. "They haven't seen him at Adelaide Pass."

Delaney took a shaky breath. "Okay."

Clint said, "They're looking around at Elk Ridge. I don't have a no, yet."

She nodded. It had been what she was afraid of. She needed to get back out there looking for him.

Shannon was still speaking into his radio every few seconds, repeating a version of his original message. Then he said, "If he's riding, he might not hear me. I'll try again in a minute."

A voice came through over Clint's radio. "No one has seen Leo here, Clint."

He responded with a quick, "Thank you. Radio Sheriff Wilcox if Leo shows up."

"Will do."

Delaney clenched and unclenched her fists. The heat seemed to be coming as much from inside her as from the temperature in the cabin. She was sweating, could even smell herself, the odor of her stress and anguish. She had to get control of her emotions. She'd had her moment. It was time for rationality and focus. For action uncompromised by her feelings. To treat this like she would if it was any other co-worker or community member. She counted ten breaths, feeling a modicum of calmness settle over her. It had to be enough. "He could be injured and freeze to death out there. Time for me to go."

Clint said, "I'm coming with you." He grabbed his coat from a hook by the door and started putting it on.

Delaney nodded, teeth gritted. *No emotions.* So why did she feel like crying again? Searching for a lost snowmobiler in these conditions wasn't going to be without risk. And this lost snowmobiler was Leo, who still held some jealousy that Delaney and Clint had dated and wasn't always nice to him. But Clint hadn't hesitated. "Thank you. Very, very much."

Caitlin was stuffing nutrition bars and drinks into a backpack. "The Gatorade will freeze if you don't drink it soon. Hydrate or die out there."

"Thanks."

"Do you need any more gear? Dry gloves? A fresh balaclava or hat?"

"No. I'm fine."

Caitlin handed her the backpack. "Take my radio and duty belt, too."

"I can't do that." Like Clint, Caitlin was putting her personal issues aside. She'd never liked Delaney and had made a big play for Leo the year before. But in this moment, she couldn't have been more kind and helpful.

"You can. I'll be with Sheriff Wilcox. You and Clint need them more than we do."

"That's huge. Thanks again." Delaney set the backpack on the floor and took a moment to get the radio attached properly, then buckled on the duty belt.

Clint snatched up the backpack. "I'll meet you outside. I'm going to warm up my machine."

Shannon said, "I need you to take a minute and tell me everything you know about those suspects. Like, did either of them match the description of our person of interest?"

Delaney felt impatience rise up like a dragon inside her, but she fought it down. Shannon was right. She had important information. "I can't be sure. There were two guys. Last seen wearing white snowmobile suits."

"Both of them?" Clint said.

"That's what I was told."

"Like they were in a club or on a team?"

"I don't know."

"Hmm. It sounds like James Bond. One of the winter movies. You know, those paramilitary groups."

Delaney hadn't seen the suspects together, but she could agree that it was odd for two men to be dressed identically for no reason. "Something to think about. One may go by the name Slim. Caucasian, thin, didn't see him standing up, and he was wearing a face covering. Beady eyes, dark. I didn't see his hair or face. He was driving an old black and yellow Skidoo. Like maybe fifteen years old or so. The other guy was on a newer machine. Black and blue. I didn't see it. They seemed to be headed to the Flint Rock Lodge area or further at first. I caught up with Slim near there. But his partner had turned back. Slim said he'd dropped something and had gone looking for it. Then some guy radioed Slim. They had walkie-talkies. All he said was, 'Thirteen, twenty-two, zero.' Slim took off after him, back toward Mockingbird Creek. But when I drove back a few minutes later, they were nowhere to be seen." While she was talking, she'd pulled her phone out of her pocket, unlocked it with facial recognition and pulled up the photo.

"Airdrop me that," Shannon said.

She did as he asked.

"Did they know you were a cop?"

"I don't think so. I called myself Laney and played damsel in distress, but Slim just told me to turn around and follow the trail back to Mockingbird Creek. He didn't know Leo was with me. I don't think the other guy did either."

"How did you know it was our guy?"

"I didn't. I don't. But he had snowshoes strapped to his back, and the guy we think is our suspect is believed to have snowshoed off the back of Elk Ridge. We found snowshoe prints coming out of the woods at the base of a ridge right onto the trail, where it appears he got on a snowmobile. When we reached Mockingbird Creek, some snowmobilers coming back from Flint Rock Lakes said they'd seen a guy with snowshoes and described him and another guy with him and their machines. The guys I saw matched the descriptions and were in the right place in the right time frame. And no one else was."

"Got it. It's helpful unless our shooter strapped on skis and went down the face of the mountain to the lodge, of course. Good work."

"All except the part where I lost my partner." *My lover. My friend. Freddy's uncle. Adriana's brother. Our sheriff.* He was so much to so many people and everything to her. She bit the inside of her lip.

"I'll call Flint Rock Lodge when you leave and ask about Leo. Just in case."

"Good idea. Did you get any identifying information from the rifle?"

"No. Your crime scene team couldn't get any prints off it or the ammunition, and Sugar said the serial number had been filed off."

"Of course."

"I'll update you on Jackie Spurrier when you're back with Leo." At Delaney's blank look he said, "The woman who was killed at the ski resort." Delaney nodded. "In the meantime, we'll contact you when we hear from him," the sheriff said. "Can you check in with us every fifteen minutes?"

"Every half hour."

"That will work. Be careful out there."

Delaney hated the delay, but something about reciting the investigation findings had settled her. The only thing that would have been better was Leo typing it all in on his tablet into one of his investigation templates. She nodded brusquely and then left the warmth of the cabin, heading back into the storm.

Three hours later, Delaney and Clint had covered the trail from Mockingbird Creek to Adelaide Pass, then they'd retraced the original path Leo and Delaney had taken out of Elk Ridge. They'd doubled back and ridden past Mockingbird Creek to the warming hut and then on to where she'd talked to Slim. The sheriff reported on one of their check-ins that he had talked to the manager of Flint Rock Lodge. Leo hadn't been there.

"I want to keep going," she said to Clint, as she stared ahead into the dark toward Flint Rock Lodge and the ungroomed mountainside trails beyond it.

"Delaney, do you realize how unlikely it is that you missed Leo on the trail, and that he missed you and yet still kept going further?" Clint's voice was kind, but his words still stung. "If we were talking about you, maybe. But we are talking about *Leo*."

"But it's not impossible." Clint was right, but admitting it meant they were out of options. "I hear you, though. Let's just check the Flint Rock safety shelter. It's close."

Clint nodded. "But then we turn back."

"Then we turn back."

So, they'd continued to the safety shelter. It was cold and empty, like Delaney felt. *Where are you, Leo? Please send me a sign. Anything.* She hoped he knew she was trying to find him. Knew in the marrow of his bones that she would not give up until he was home safe.

Without further protest, Delaney rode ahead of Clint back toward Mockingbird Creek, blinded by tears for the first five minutes. When they stopped, she realized it wasn't snowing anymore and the clouds were less dense. As she neared Lower Flint Rock Lake, the moon broke through and shone brilliantly onto the icy surface. She looked over the flat expanse. With this much snow on the lake, it was like a white meadow.

As her eyes cut back to the trail, something out of place caught her eye. Something red in the moonlight.

She held up her fist and hit the brakes. When Clint had pulled up beside her, she pointed back to where she'd seen whatever it was, then put her machine in reverse. Feeling her emotions well up again, she eased off the gas. *Careful. Don't do something stupid now.* She backed up until she felt like she was even with the red object, but she couldn't see it from that angle. She switched off her engine and waded through the snow down to the shoreline, her breath like a stormtrooper inside her helmet.

She reached the edge of the ice and looked back to her left. Then she screamed, not caring that she was trapped inside with the penetrating shrillness of her own voice.

It was a red snowmobile helmet. Like Leo's.

FOURTEEN

Leo's eyes fluttered open. Tiny ice crystals cut into his face. Wind bit into the skin of his exposed neck and made its frigid way under his clothes. He was face down, bouncing. Bouncing. Bouncing. He was moving, flying across the snow, away from where he was supposed to meet Delaney. He tried to get up but couldn't. He tried to move his arms, but they seemed stuck. What was holding him down? The attempt to move hurt his head. Nausea overtook him and he vomited.

A man shouted curse words.

The bouncing slowed. A loud noise grew softer. Then something hard crashed down on his head. His last thoughts as he slipped away were that Delaney would be worried, and a worried Delaney did crazy, dangerous things.

FIFTEEN

Delaney picked up the helmet. On the back in small letters was Leo's handwriting. PALMER, in black sharpie. She shouted back at Clint. "It's Leo's helmet!"

Clint was slip-sliding in sidesteps down the embankment. "Are you sure?"

She held it up for him to see. With horror she jerked down the cracked face shield. "Blood."

"Let's stay calm. That's only a smear. The shield probably cut his face or busted his nose when it broke. It's not enough for a major wound."

She did not feel calm. She turned back to the ice. Only a few feet from the shore was a darker patch where there was no snow. "Oh, God. Look." She pointed. "Is the ice broken?"

Clint peered over the lake, then stepped back. "I think it is."

Delaney lunged toward the lake, but Clint grabbed her arm and hauled her back.

"You don't do him any good if you go under."

Her face felt frozen from her tears. Had Clint ever been in love, did he understand the torment she was going through?

The pain and fear was more excruciating than anything she'd ever experienced. "If he's there... if he's under there..."

Clint held up the helmet. "His helmet's dry. The chin strap is unbuckled and intact. He took this off. I don't think he went in the water."

Delaney tried to latch onto his words, to wrap herself up in the hope of them. "But what if he did?" She looked around, frantic, and saw track marks leading to the lake's edge. "A snowmobile went in, Clint. You can see it, too. I know you can."

"We're going to find out what's in there, together. After we radio for help."

She snatched Caitlin's mic and held the button. "Deputy Pace for Sheriff Wilcox. Come in." Her breaths were ragged and raw in her chest. She was feeling lightheaded. *Hyperventilation.* Clint was right. She had to calm down. Concentrating on long, deep breaths, she called again. "Delaney for Sheriff Wilcox. Please come in, Shannon."

The radio crackled. "This is Sheriff Wilcox. What do you have, Delaney?"

"We're at Lower Flint Rock Lake. I found Leo's helmet on the bank. There's a large hole in the ice. Clint and I have to check it out. We need help." Her voice broke on the last word.

After a brief pause, the sheriff answered. "Copy that. Deputy, do not go into that water until we arrive with survival gear. We will be on our way as quickly as we can."

"Thank you. Delaney out." Delaney returned the mic to its holster. There was no use lying to the man, and there was no pretending that if Leo was in that water that she wouldn't go after him. She would jump in without a second thought if it meant bringing Leo out alive.

Clint was sliding down the incline with bags of gear in both arms, retrieved from their machines. *Did he hear the sheriff order them to stay dry?* "I'll shimmy out on the ice with a rope around my waist. I already tied the other end off to my machine. It won't be deep there. I've got a flashlight and a ski pole."

She didn't bother asking him why he had a pole, just moved on to the salient point. "You're heavier than me. I'm going out. I think at an angle from the left. Away from the path the snowmobile took." She held out her hand for the light and the pole.

He looked like he wanted to argue. Instead, he sighed and handed her the equipment. "Be careful, Delaney. I have extra socks and gloves, but I don't have a full set of clothes. And we both know we should be waiting on help. But this is about Leo. I get it."

Fresh tears sprang to her eyes. Clint was a good friend. A good person.

He tied the rope snugly around her waist. He placed a second coiled rope over her shoulder. "In case you need to pull something out."

She nodded, lips pressed tightly together.

Then she knelt in the snow and scooted herself onto the ice like she was pushing off from the side of a pool. But unlike in a pool where she got a face full of nice, warm water, here she got a load of cold snow up her nose and down her collar. She felt like she'd been shocked, but she welcomed it. She needed to be alert, sharp, ready. And to overcome her fear—she was separated from frigid water by a layer of ice with no idea how thick it was. She'd never been into ice skating growing up. Had only been ice fishing once, and that was just to drink beer in a hut when she was underage. She'd lasted fifteen minutes before she'd headed back to a truck on terra firma.

She didn't trust ice. From her years driving an eighteen-wheeler on it, she had learned its dangers. Had seen trucks break through. Had watched heavily laden trailers sink. She had always studied the ice thickness and weather patterns before she risked her life on it. She stuck to the path where the thickness could be verified, knowing it could vary greatly across one body of water.

She didn't have the luxury of study and knowledge here. Couldn't say what the temperatures had been in the last few months and what the condition of the ice was. Not only that, there were thermals throughout the mountains where warm water bubbled up and could erode the ice layer even in weather cold enough to otherwise create great ice.

And a snowmobile had broken through. While a snowmobile was heavier than a person, how much lighter did she have to be not to crack the ice?

Right now, though, none of that mattered, because Leo could be in that water.

As she crept her way forward, Clint put his hands on the back of her ankles. It didn't restrict her movement, but it made her nervous.

She moved a few more inches across the ice. "You should keep your weight off the ice, Clint. I'm tied off."

"I'm on land," he said. "All good."

Her feet were no longer touching the shore. A gruesome image formed in her mind. Leo. Floating. Trapped under the ice below her, his body tap, tap, tapping for her. She made a sound that was half cry, half moan.

"Are you okay?" Clint said.

"Yes. No. Yes."

"You're almost there. I'm coming out on the ice a little way with you. Don't worry. I'm on my belly, too."

She imagined the combination of his weight and hers, even though she knew that the impact of both their bodies was lessened by their horizontal disbursement. She visualized the ice cracking open and the cold water claiming them both. But she kept wriggling forward.

The opening was within reach now, the surface of the ice wet on her gloves. Was it thinning here or had it been cleanly broken? Her throat felt thick. She didn't know if it would make it better or worse if she knew the answer to her question. "I'm here. How close should I get?"

"Does it feel solid?"

"So far. I don't hear anything. Don't feel anything moving or cracking."

"You want to be close enough to shine that light in. You might be best off perpendicular to the hole. So that your head is close without having to hang your body over."

"I'll move a little further out beside it. Are you still touching shore?"

"No. But I'm not too far. We're okay."

"You can let go of my legs."

"I'd rather not. I don't want to have to explain to Leo how I let you freeze to death in this water."

She closed her eyes. His optimism about Leo helped, a little. Wriggling her head closer, she held up her flashlight and shined it into the dark, cold water.

SIXTEEN

Kearny Police Chief Clint Rock-Below had only ever loved one woman in his life, and it had taken a fair amount of stoicism to hide that from her and the rest of the world when she hadn't felt the same way back. He had a lifetime of practice, given his rough childhood on the Crow reservation. He'd perfected a disarming smile to cover all types of emotions.

But he wasn't smiling now. He checked the rope between the snowmobile and the woman, using only one hand and keeping the other on her ankle. Her. Delaney. *Leo's woman.* The rope was loose. He took it up. He didn't want any slack in case she went in.

He swallowed down a lump. He had a healthy respect for situations like these. In grade school, one of his best friends had driven an off-road vehicle onto the reservoir and through the ice. Clint and his big brother had been standing beside the rescue team when they hauled his body out. It had made Clint careful, more careful than he would have been otherwise. Playing hockey on ponds. Ice fishing on Lake Desmet. He'd never forgotten that the water was a cruel beast with an unpredictable appetite.

He squeezed Delaney's leg, just to reassure himself she was still there.

She gasped.

At first, he thought he'd hurt her. "What is it?" he said.

"Handlebars. They're barely even under the surface. The back end sunk."

"Is it Leo's machine?"

Her voice was muffled. *She's crying.* It felt like a pitchfork to his heart. He would do anything to stop her from hurting. Even wish for her boyfriend to be alive, well, and warm. Leo was a decent guy. He wanted good things for Leo. He just didn't want Delaney for him. "Yes."

"Is there anyone in the water?" *Please, no.*

"I don't see anyone. Or anything else. Except... Oh, my God, Clint. The throttle. The handlebar with the throttle."

"What, Delaney? What do you see?"

"There's something holding it at full throttle. Like an extra wide rubber band or something. This machine has been tampered with."

He closed his eyes, picturing it. "Someone sent it out on the water without a rider."

She turned to look over her shoulder. "Like they tried to hide it. But why? And where is Leo?"

SEVENTEEN

Delaney stood on the seat of her snowmobile, peering into the woods beside the trail. The area north of Lower Flint Rock Lake was lit up with temporary light kits and filled with vehicles—all snow machines. But they'd arrived well after she and Clint had finished their search of the lake—probing under the ice and down to the shallow lake bottom with the pole, then breaking away the ice into a wider opening. When they felt sure there was no one in the water, they'd moved their investigation to the shore where they'd spent the last half hour trying to recreate what had happened.

She had theories but no facts except that Leo had been here and now wasn't. *Leo is missing.* The thought echoed in her hollow insides. She wrapped her arms around her middle.

Caitlin climbed onto the snowmobile next to Delaney's. "Do you want me to shine a light in there for you?"

"No. I think I have better depth perception without the glare off the snow."

Caitlin nodded. "What do you think happened?"

Delaney pointed back at the ice. "What I know is Leo's snowmobile was sunk deliberately."

"Any thoughts on why?"

Delaney flexed her toes inside her boots to keep them warm. "No idea yet. It makes no sense unless someone wanted to hide it. Or slow down law enforcement."

"Yeah. We're all going to be working this for a while."

"Clint and I found activity over here in the woods—a lot of disturbed snow and some snowmobile tracks in the trees."

"Like people parked in there? More than one snowmobile?"

"In my opinion, yes. And as I was walking around up there, I couldn't help but kick up some snow. I uncovered moose droppings and pieces of plastic. The face shield on Leo's helmet was broken."

Caitlin's eyes widened. "He hit a moose."

"Probably. Which could mean he had a wreck. Maybe other people stopped to help."

"That makes sense."

"Yeah. Except for the part where his snowmobile was sunk. And he's not here but his helmet is."

Caitlin tilted her head in her giant snowmobile helmet. "Maybe he had a concussion and got disoriented. Walked off in the wrong direction. Forgot his helmet. Then some kids came along drunk or high and sunk the snowmobile for a lark."

Delaney shrugged. "Hard to imagine, but it's not impossible. We didn't find him down the trail, though. And we haven't found any tracks that suggest he walked off into the trees."

"Maybe he drove off with someone?" Her face fell. "Oh, man. What I should be saying is, I'm sorry. I know you two, um, that you're together. I don't mean to upset you."

Delaney waved a hand. "Thank you. It's okay. And you're not saying anything I haven't already been thinking. Keep brainstorming."

Caitlin bit her lip. "There's no blood. Moose or person."

"There was a little in the face shield of his helmet. But not enough to be worried about."

"Closed head injury?"

"A possibility. One theory Clint and I have is that he landed on the ice. There were little spots of blood and patterns on the ice that suggested someone had been out there before us and slithered back."

"Or was dragged."

Delaney felt a coldness seep over her. "I hadn't thought of that."

Caitlin held up her hands. "Again, no blood. I'm not thinking predators."

Not an animal *predator.* Delaney pictured Slim. Unfriendly. Likely a murderer. And his buddy, a conspirator who in the eyes of the law was a murderer, too. But Slim and Leo hadn't been here when she'd driven by. No one had. *Not that I saw.* She looked at the disturbed snow in the trees where snowmobiles had been parked. If they'd been back there, she might not have noticed them. And another thing—she'd had plenty of time to run her memory of the lake back through her mind. There had been no hole in the ice when she passed here on the way to Mockingbird Creek. Leo's sled was sunk *after.* She was positive.

Caitlin continued. "He didn't necessarily take that helmet off himself, if he was unconscious."

"That's what I'm afraid of."

"Maybe it isn't a bad thing. They might have taken him to safety. He might be in a hospital in Sheridan as we speak."

This was the first positive thought Delaney had had in hours, and she banished the sunken snowmobile from her mind for a moment. "Has anyone checked hospitals?"

Caitlin pursed her lips. "I don't think so."

Delaney picked up her mic. "This is Deputy Delaney Pace. I need someone with law enforcement who has cell service. This is an emergency."

Within seconds, a male voice answered, chopped and staticky.

"If you can hear me, I can't understand you. But I need someone to check area hospitals and see if anyone matching Sheriff Leo Palmer's description has been brought in tonight. Click twice to confirm."

The radio clicked twice.

"Thank you. Please contact me as soon as you know something."

The radio clicked twice again.

Delaney nodded at Caitlin. "Thank you. That was smart."

For a second she regretted that she hadn't asked them to get in touch with Carrie and Kat to let them know she'd be late. Maybe to call Skeeter to see if he could stay over with them. But she had hours before those things were problems. She'd get hold of them next time, when there was better reception.

Shannon stalked over on snowshoes. Delaney wished she'd brought a pair for herself. They were shaping up to be the must-have accessory of the day, for the bad guys and law enforcement both. He was pointing at her. "I've already blistered Clint for that stunt the two of you pulled. You could have gotten yourself killed, and maybe endangered more of the team in the process."

Delaney summoned inner peace. She'd known this was coming. Even agreed it was necessary. Nothing would have changed her decision, though. "Yes, sir."

"I've heard you're a cowgirl, but no rodeo shit in my county, understood?"

She nodded. "I hear you."

"You and Leo shouldn't have split up in the first place. This is Big Horn County. This murder is my case. Finding Leo is my case. You are mine when you're here and you will act like it."

She bit down hard, grinding enamel. Red seeped into her vision. "With all due respect, I didn't break any laws, Sheriff. And I don't work for you, even when I'm here."

"Then get your ass out of this crime scene."

She crossed her arms. "I have as much right to be on this trail as anyone. I don't see tape. In fact, I don't know, nor do you, whether a crime even occurred here. But my boss is missing, and I—"

"Your boss? You're out here because he's your boss? I don't think so." His tone, which had been aggressive before, turned snide.

Delaney hadn't seen this side of Shannon before. He'd been so kind earlier. But she'd heard rumors of his chameleon personality. She raised a finger and pointed it at him. "Yes, he's my boss. And I would be out here for anyone in our community who was in trouble. Like I was out here tonight for a woman I didn't know who was murdered, something I care about very much. Leo is also important to me as an individual—"

The sheriff snorted. "Now the truth is coming out."

Suddenly, Clint was beside her. He stepped between Delaney and Shannon. "I didn't hear any lies told or truth withheld. But let me just say it was my decision to help Delaney check that ice. I have a lot of experience. We did it safely and together. We're grown-ups, Sheriff. Skilled at what we do and trying to protect and serve. Let's all back this up and focus on what's important here. Finding Leo. Bringing in a murderer or two. Getting everyone safely off this mountain tonight without freezing to death."

Clint squeezed Delaney's shoulder then let his hand drop.

The sheriff was mumbling to himself, but he walked away and started shouting orders at his deputies.

"I had it, but thanks for the support," Delaney said.

Clint nodded at her and motioned for Caitlin to move closer. When he had the two women near enough for a discreet conversation, he said, "The sheriff is very interested in pursuing the suspect Delaney identified for him. Just between us, he's throwing his hat in the ring for governor next term, and he doesn't stumble upon many chances for the spotlight. I'd bet he sees these cases as his big opportunity. Anyway, I'd like to volunteer Kearny PD and Kearny County to bring in a tracking dog and spearhead the search for Leo. It means we'd all need to be a little sweeter to Shannon. Do I have your support and cooperation?"

"I'm in," Caitlin said.

Delaney's radio squawked. "Deputy Drew Knowles for Deputy Investigator Delaney Pace, come in Delaney." She nodded at Clint. "Yes, yes." Then she hit her mic button. "You've got me, Drew. Tell me something good."

"I wish I could."

Delaney's knees felt weak. *Please, God, don't let him tell me Leo's dead.*

EIGHTEEN

Deputy Drew Knowles drummed his fingers on the desk in his sheriff's department cubicle as he tried to radio Delaney again. Their first connection had been horrible. He had a vague idea of where she was, from looking up Lower Flint Rock Lake on a map. As much as he'd longed to ride as a kid, his parents had never had the money for snowmobiling. He was learning as an adult, but he hadn't taken to snowmachines naturally, even though he was a Wyoming native. His exploration so far consisted of the easy trail, which was nothing more than a snow-covered dirt road at a lower elevation. Leo had told him that his own skills weren't much better not long ago.

And yet the sheriff had found himself in a rugged and remote area snowmobiling in the Bighorns today, in a blizzard. Drew loved the excitement of his job as a deputy, but maybe he didn't want to learn. Then he'd have a reason not to sign up for that duty roster.

His Monster was empty. He threw it in the trash and tried Delaney again. "Deputy Knowles for Deputy Pace. Come in, Delaney. Can you hear me? This is Drew."

This was going to be a hard conversation, with anyone and

everyone in law enforcement able to listen in over the radio. Damn, Leo was his boss. Leo was Delaney's boyfriend and partner—technically her boss but it was hard to call him that, not the way the two of them worked together.

Static on his radio made him sit up straight. Delaney's voice came in clear as a bell. "Drew, can you hear me? Is this better?"

"Delaney, you've got me!"

"I rode up to a higher section of the trail with some open terrain around me. Just tell me what you have to tell me. I'm ready."

Drew closed his eyes. He couldn't help hesitating. He respected Delaney more than almost anyone he knew, and Leo was one of his favorite people. Drew, as a black man, had learned that race did not matter to Leo, except to the extent that he acknowledged gaps in understanding and experiences. Hell, he dated Leo's sister. Lived with her. He wanted to tell Delaney that Leo was beside him and doing great. Had wanted to tell Adriana that.

But he couldn't.

"I'm sorry. I couldn't find him, Delaney. I called every hospital on both sides of the mountains. I talked to them about him. Gave his description. Asked them about John Does. Nobody has seen him. Adriana and Freddy haven't heard from him, either. Everyone knows to call me if he shows up."

There was silence on the other end. He was afraid they'd lost connection again.

Then her voice crackled through. "Okay. It was worth a try. Thank you."

"What else can I be doing for you?"

"Personally, I need someone to call my daughters and tell them I won't be home tonight. And to ask Skeeter Rawlins if he can stay over with them." Drew typed the two requests into a list.

"No problem."

"As for work, in Leo's absence, I'm at the helm. Sheriff Wilcox of Big Horn County has agreed that Kearny PD and County will lead the search for Leo while Big Horn focuses on the murder. So, the next thing I need is a search dog and handler. Can you get us one, ASAP?"

He typed SEARCH DOG and HANDLER in all caps. "Absolutely. The second we hang up, I'm on it. Do you want me up in the mountains with you?"

"Where's Joe?"

"Still in Cabo San Lucas on vacation. Due back Monday morning."

"Eloise?"

Eloise Shaw was their newest deputy. So new that she wasn't official yet. "Another week of training in Douglas."

"Sounds like our best plan is to keep you where you can work the phones, radio, and computer, and respond to anything locally. We're going to need to lean on you."

Drew looked around the empty office. With everyone on the police side deployed and it being the night shift, the quiet was eerie, but that was okay. Adriana would understand if he had to sleep here. He'd cancel his personal training clients and skip his own workouts tomorrow, even though every missed session hurt him in his preparation for his upcoming body-building competition.

"A few more things. Find a way to get in touch with every lodge, ranch, outfitter, and anything else with a telephone on the west side of the mountain, please. Ask them to look around their properties for Leo. Oh—and the local snowmobile club. See if they can send people up to scour the area. All the little offshoot trails that only the hardcore take, in case Leo got disoriented in the snowfall and ended up on one of them."

Drew's fingers could hardly keep up with her now. "Good idea." Some of these things didn't require special expertise. If he hadn't gotten a handle on them by morning, he could call Clara and ask her to come help. She'd do anything for Leo, even if it would be Sunday.

Delaney was still talking fast. "Get Adriana to do an interview with the press, asking for information leading to the safe return of the sheriff. A public plea. Share it all over social media. Share a post about it in the meantime, until you can get her on camera. Oh, and add that we are seeking the identity of a person of interest. A tall, extremely blond man who was at Elk Ridge earlier today. He was wearing green camo, and he was seen talking to Jackie Spurrier."

Adriana would want to do her video immediately. "Could I just have Adriana send me a video for the social?"

"That will work."

"People will ask about a reward."

"Not the ones who will actually look for him."

"But it gets attention. Makes people talk about it."

"I don't have time to work on that now, nor will you, but put it on your list as something to look into later. Let's keep moving on my needs while we have a good connection. I have a picture of the snowmobile one of the murder suspects was driving. See what you can find on it and maybe him. White male, thirties, dark, beady eyes, on the thin side. He gave his name as Slim, but I think he was lying. Leo was up on the trail at the same time as this guy and his buddy. I don't want to get sideways with Sheriff Wilcox—more sideways than I already am, which is a story for another time—but there's a chance our cases are related. A very good chance. I want to find these guys as much as Wilcox does."

"On it."

"And for that reason, we need to try to trace them to the woman they murdered as well. I don't know much about her except that she lived in Sheridan."

Drew stood up and walked over to a whiteboard by the cubicles. He'd written down everything he knew about the murdered woman on one side. He'd saved the other but hoped he wouldn't have to use it for Leo's case. "Jackie Spurrier. I probably have a lot more to go on than you, there."

He couldn't help feeling queasy trepidation. Everyone on their team had unique skills. Delaney was great with witnesses and quick deductions. Leo was able to put people at ease because of his position and had a knack for dredging up information. Joe was methodical and relentless. Drew was fearless and enthusiastic, but at less than six months on the job he was green, and he knew it. He'd lucked out being tapped to even help on past investigations. Most deputies of his experience were driving around the county on patrol. He had to show the confidence in him was merited, even though he had a terrible case of imposter syndrome right now. He was going to have to step up. Leo needed him. Delaney was counting on him.

"Great. Thank you, Drew."

"I'll get on all of this, as soon as I get your daughters squared away."

"I hate to scare them about Leo."

No one in Drew's personal life had kids until Adriana. Living with teenage Freddy had proved Drew wasn't exactly an expert at child relations, which is why he was going to let Adriana handle talking to Delaney's girls. "The whole town already knows. Freddy told Adriana before I got to her. But I hear you."

Delaney's voice turned to static again, then faded to nothing.

"Delaney? Delaney?"

There was no reply.

Drew steadied himself with a deep breath. He was on his own. He could *not* screw this thing up.

NINETEEN

Leo's first thought upon waking was that something in his head was about to explode. His next was how much worse it would hurt if he gave in to the nausea that accompanied the pain. The stench contributed to that problem. It only took a few seconds for him to realize that he was the source, and that he had emptied his stomach while unconscious. He rolled away from the damp, knowing that it came with him. The repositioning almost pushed him over the edge. He clamped his teeth and held as still as possible. Even the breaths shifting his head made the upset worse, and the pulse in his temples vibrated his tender brain—a mallet to a gong.

Opening his eyes might help. He did it and discovered inky dark shot through with sparklers. He shut them quickly. *Too much.*

He tried to lift a hand. His wrists were bound in front of him. That was better than... when? Before, at least. He reached his hands up and carefully touched the most tender places on his head, checking for what, he wasn't sure. Shrapnel? Bone fragments? Missing hunks of skull? Not likely, or he wouldn't be awake. Even alive. Despite his caution, the probing set off more fireworks, this time behind closed eyes. The pain was redlined or close to it. It was all relative, and any increase was hard to quantify.

His fingers came away dry. *Closed head injury.* That wasn't necessarily good news, as it gave the swelling no way to resolve itself. And swelling was his enemy. He needed his head elevated. Something cold for it. Anti-inflammatories. And while he was wishing for horses, he would hope to ride off to a hospital for brain injury care.

None of those things were going to happen, and he knew it.

"Is anyone out there?" he said in a whispery croak. Little more than a rattle, yet still each syllable was excruciating. He licked his lips, summoning saliva, then tried again. "Anyone?"

A cacophony of silence met his words. No one was here.

But where was here? His senses were so short-circuited he wasn't sure if he was inside or out. In hard-packed snow or on a feather bed. He exhaled slowly through closed lips, willing himself to awareness. How did his *skin* feel? It was definitely cold—hypothermia cold—though not below freezing. There wasn't a breath of wind. His face and body seemed dry, except for where he'd been in his own... ugh, he couldn't think about it. From the dryness, he concluded he wasn't on snow, but the surface was very hard. He ran his joined hands across it. Not wood, linoleum, or carpet. Frozen ground or concrete. Polished concrete, not rough.

He focused on listening. No outside noises. He had to be inside solid walls.

Inside. Okay, what does that mean? He still had no idea where he was or how he'd gotten here. No recollection of what had happened to him. Who or what had done this to him. His circumstances should have terrified him, but his brain was over-taxed. He found himself shutting down.

Waves of sleepiness lapped over him. Blessed waves that he wanted to drown in. A rational part of him softly suggested he stay awake. Sit up. Look around. Assess dangers. Try to find help. Get the hell out of here and find home. *Home. Delaney.* His primal survival instincts shot up a weak flare. *Danger. Danger. You are in danger.* But his brain had already disengaged from conscious thought, and he slipped once more into unconsciousness.

TWENTY

Kat sucked in a rapturous breath as she leaned against the stall door at the Eckhardt ranch, taking in the sight of Leopard, an appaloosa mare with beautiful red spots across her haunches in her otherwise blue roan coat. She even smelled good—sweet and sunshiny—but then all horses did to her.

She had nearly turned off her alarm and lazed in bed that morning. She was sooo tired. She'd stayed up worrying about Melaney and Leo half the night. Because Leo was missing. It was awful. The only thing worse would have been for it to be Melaney.

When Freddy's friend had texted him the night before that Leo was lost in the mountains, Kat and Freddy had been arguing in his mom's car because Kat told him she wasn't ready for hand stuff. Freddy had accused her *again* of not being into him. She was afraid they were about to break up. Then he'd gotten that text, and they'd run inside to tell his mom. Freddy had been super upset, even though earlier he'd still been kinda pissed about Leo turning him in over the pot party incident. His mom seemed scared but like she was trying to be brave. She said everything was going to be all right.

Kat knew saying that didn't make it true. Bad things happened. They had happened to her. She hoped they hadn't happened to Leo. But Melaney hadn't come home from the mountains with him yet, and that wasn't good.

Anyway, she was glad she'd come to the ranch. Skeeter had stayed over with her and Carrie, so he'd heard her alarm and shouted for her to get ready, then he'd given her a ride. She probably wouldn't have made it without him. But honestly, she'd made the effort because she'd known Leopard would be here. Clara helped people train their horses all the time. Leopard was going to be for sale soon, and her owner wanted Clara to tune her up, so she'd have the best possible chance of selling well—as in, for a lot of money.

"She's beautiful," Kat said.

Clara Eckhardt put a hand on Kat's shoulder. She wasn't much bigger than Kat, but she could handle the strongest, most willful horses on the ranch. She told Kat she did it with the power of her mind. "She really is. Would you like to help me work with her?"

"Yes! Is she fast?"

"Very."

"Has she run barrels?"

"Has she ever!" Clara tried to tuck her white hair behind her ears, but it was too short. She'd cut it super short after a crazy lady who'd murdered a bunch of girls had chopped Clara's hair off. It turned out Clara was the crazy lady's mother. And the mother of that lady's sister Shirleen, who wasn't crazy and had been spending a lot of time at the ranch with Clara learning to ride, sometimes when Kat was there. Kat liked her a lot.

The haircut *had* been ugly. The new one was cute.

"In rodeos?"

"For five years."

"What division?" Barrel racing divisions were based on

time and performance with the best scoring teams of horse and rider competing in 1D and moving on down through 4D and in some rodeos even 5D and 6D. Whatever her division, Leopard would start over building scores with a new rider.

"She was winning in 3D and had just moved up to 2D."

"How old is she?"

"She's ten now."

Kat had been learning a lot in the months she'd worked with Clara. This meant Leopard probably had ten years of racing left, if she stayed fit and healthy. What a wonderful horse she'd be for someone. For her, maybe? She'd been too scared to ask Melaney for a horse yet. She'd hinted. She'd left HORSE FOR SALE flyers around and online horse ads on her laptop screen with the sleep and screensaver functions turned off, hoping Melaney would see them. But she knew money was tight because they were saving up for Carrie to go to college. Leopard would probably be really expensive. Even if Melaney said yes to a horse, Kat knew she shouldn't get her hopes up about a horse like Leopard. But how could she help it?

Clara's phone rang. She frowned at the screen. "I need to get this, Kat."

"'Kay." Kat stroked Leopard's nose but watched Clara. This could be about Leo or Melaney.

"Hello, Clara Eckhardt speaking." Clara listened, her lips rolled inward. "I've actually got her younger daughter with me now." Silence. "What about asking Skeeter to help us?" Silence. "Yes, absolutely. I'll be on my way shortly." She put the phone back in her pocket and gestured for Kat to precede her toward the barn doors.

A text came in on Kat's phone, which was conveniently in her hand. She was expecting Freddy since they texted twenty-four seven, but it was a number she didn't recognize.

Is this Kateena?

Who called her Kateena anymore? She frowned, scrunching her nose and shaking her head. She answered with *Who dis?* That's when she realized that the phone number wasn't a Wyoming 307 area code. Where was 253?

Walking behind her, Clara said, "Kat, that was the sheriff's department."

Kat looked up from her phone. "Do you need to go?"

"Sorry, but I do. I'll drop you on my way."

Kat was kinda bummed. She'd been hoping to ride Leopard. Plus, she loved talking to Clara after her rides. She treated Kat like a grown-up. She wanted to ask what to do about Freddy. She'd tried to talk to Carrie the night before, but she'd been snappy and mean.

But the expression on Clara's face made Kat feel breathless. Clara looked worried.

She stopped beside her outside the barn. "Is it about my aunt?"

"No, sweetie. It's about helping Drew. He's short-handed."

"Helping him find Leo?"

Clara sucked in a big breath, held it, then let it out slowly. "Yes."

"But if Delaney was in trouble, you'd tell me, right?"

"Mm-hmm," Clara said, avoiding Kat's eyes as she latched the barn doors.

Kat got a very bad feeling in her stomach. She'd always trusted Clara, but she was pretty sure that Clara had just lied to her. So, was Melaney really okay? And who could she trust to tell her the truth if she wasn't?

TWENTY-ONE

Drew sat at the head of the sheriff's department conference room feeling like a kid pretending to be a detective. He'd done it enough in grade school. Twirling imaginary six-shooters and blowing smoke off their barrels, grilling suspects, and arresting criminals. This was nothing like that. It was much harder. He didn't have the authority to deputize anyone, but he felt certain that Delaney would approve of Skeeter volunteering and Clara stepping up.

He cleared his throat, then began filling Clara and Skeeter in on his progress to date in the search for Leo and the work ahead of them. They listened attentively with good questions. *I can do this.* Gradually, his nerves receded.

He said, "The search dog and handler should be there by now. I hope to hear from Delaney soon, wanting an update."

Skeeter took a gargantuan bite out of a breakfast burrito. Some of its contents spurted onto the shelf of his pot belly, but he didn't seem to notice. The big man had brought a bag full of them, piping hot, straight from the Loafing Shed. Drew had found a note in the bag. ADRI LOVES DK. But he would have recognized her signature steak and poutine burrito even without it. Smelled like heaven and tasted like sin. Currently, he was trying to cut things like French fries, red meat, and gravy out of his diet to shed excess body fat. His goal was to dip below five percent. The prospect of flexing onstage in a Speedo while greased up like a turkey going into the oven—a black turkey, the one standing out amongst all the other white turkeys—had given him willpower. Only not today.

Clara said, "You want me to start with the social media and PR?"

"Yes, please. I'll be calling all the local lodge and landowners." Adriana had recorded video to use, but he hadn't had time to deal with it yet. As it was, he'd worked until four a.m. before catching a few hours of sleep. He'd found a dog and handler and got them deployed, and he'd messaged the snowmobile club. They'd agreed to be at Mockingbird Creek that morning with volunteers at first light to help search. He'd also started developing a list of properties, and he'd looked for an old snowmobile titled to someone named Slim, with no luck. And that morning, he'd fielded an emotional inquisition from Adriana.

She'd asked him an odd question. "Do you think it could be the cartel?" Then she'd told him about Leo working undercover and that being part of why they'd all moved to Wyoming, to get away from them. He'd assured her that all the evidence pointed elsewhere, but she made him promise to ask Delaney. And he would, soon.

Clara leaned forward like she was about to stand up. "Any reason I should stick around and not get going on this?"

Weight lifted off Drew. He smiled at her. "No, feel free to run with it. There's more work where that came from when you're ready."

She nodded and moved briskly out of the room.

"Skeeter, could you try to find out everything there is to know about Jackie Spurrier?"

Skeeter talked through his half-full mouth, waving his

burrito and scattering gravy and fries on the tabletop. "Already started when I heard the news yesterday. Got a durn good head start."

"That's great."

Drew's radio came to life with Delaney's voice at ear-splitting volume. He dialed the volume down as she spoke.

"Deputy Pace for Deputy Knowles. Come in." She sounded tired. A little frayed. Drew wondered if she had slept at all.

He pressed his mic button. "Good morning. Deputy Knowles here with Skeeter. He's in helping us with background on Jackie Spurrier. I'm working the other side of the equation. Clara is doing social media and PR."

"Hi, Skeeter. Did you stay with the girls?"

There was a pause as Skeeter swallowed a bite sooner than was probably optimal. "Yes, ma'am. Carrie is at work, which is good. She was shell-shocked about Leo and worried about you. She's a good girl. Kat got home late with Adriana and Freddy. I took her to Clara's this morning, and Clara took her to pick up Dudley and dropped her at the Loading Shed on her way here."

"Loafing."

Drew smiled. Delaney had some gas left in the tank for today if she bothered to rise to Skeeter's bait.

Skeeter's eyes twinkled. "My bad."

"Thank you so much, Skeeter."

"No problem."

"Clara's helping, too?"

Drew said, "Yes. The gang's all here. Although she's not in the room. Do you have any news?"

Delaney said, "Well, we haven't found Leo. But we're working hard and ready for a big day. Thanks for the snowmobile club—they've been searching for hours already. And the dog and handler. We're almost set to send them out on the mountain."

"Glad they made it."

"I thought of a few things you need to know. First, Sugar's team didn't find any prints on the rifle used to shoot Jackie. The serial number was filed off. So that's a dead end. But do keep an eye out for the guy I told you about yesterday, the big, blond one who was harassing Jackie at the ski resort. Also, be sure you don't step on Sheriff Wilcox's toes. If you find out something he needs, please share. I may not be reachable to coordinate.

"Sounds good. You have time for an update?"

"Five minutes."

"I'll be fast. The snowmobile is registered to a single-member limited liability company out of Big Horn County. That LLC is owned by a trust. Far West Ventures LLC. Far West Ventures Trust."

"Jesus, Joseph, and Mary. Any humans?"

"I have a copy of the trust certificate. The trustees are all out of the Washington, DC, area. I don't know anything about them yet."

"This is a nightmare."

"I did run a search on the trust name through property tax records."

"Yeah?"

"I found other LLCs."

"Of course."

"One name rang a bell. Snow Hare Ranch. I looked and found it on the map near where you guys are."

Her voice perked up. "You're brilliant. I know where that is. Any phone numbers, email, human names, web addresses?"

"I found a phone number, but I can't tell if it's really for the lodge or not. There's no voicemail or answering service. The site I found it on wasn't like a website for the lodge. In fact, I couldn't find an ad or web address for visitors. So, I don't think it's a public lodge, like it's not open for guests. I think the number came off some kind of web crawler that spits back information or something. I was going to call it soon. In fact, I have a list of properties I was going to start calling in the area, but I just hadn't gotten to it yet. The dog and handler took a lot of time. And after those things I thought I'd try to run down the trustees of Far West."

"Thank you. Snow Hare makes me think of snowsuits and an idea Clint had. Can you see if any clubs or teams or groups in the area have all-white snowmobile outfits? Failing that, look for other groups that would wear them. Military or para-military."

Drew felt a quickening. "Because both the suspects were seen wearing all white."

"Yes."

"Okay. Um, also, Adriana wants to know if you think there's any chance this is cartel related."

Dead silence for three-two-one... then, "I hadn't thought of that. I don't see it. But I'll watch for it. Tell her thanks. Listen, I'd better—"

"Skeeter has information on the woman who was shot. I haven't even heard it yet."

"You've gotta make it fast, Skeeter. Clint Rock-Below has the dog and handler ready."

Skeeter's words came out rapid fire. "Jackie Spurrier. Twenty-two years old. Been tending bar in the Best Western sports pub in Sheridan. She was living and working as Janet Strom. Her legal name came out when she died because of her ID. When I tried to trace Janet Strom, I couldn't find her before Sheridan, which only goes back six months. For Jackie Spurrier, I got the opposite problem. She posted hundreds—maybe thousands—of selfies to her socials in South Carolina then in Bozeman. That stopped eighteen months ago. She disappeared for a year, then popped back up as Janet Strom in Sheridan."

"Hmm. Sounds like she was running from something."

"That's what I think, boss-lady."

"We need to know who or what. Why she went off the radar."

"Working on it. We're all rooting for you. And I know you. You're going to find him and bring him home safe and sound."

Drew added, "Be careful out there."

Delaney clicked her mic twice then said, "Thank you all, more than I can say."

Then she was gone. Drew was at a loss for words. Skeeter looked down at his second—or was it third?—half-eaten burrito. He pushed it back a few inches then wrapped it up and stuffed it back in the bag.

In the silence, Clara poked her head around the door. "I've got a camera crew headed to the Loafing Shed to interview Adriana for radio and TV. But I took that personal video she posted and shared it. There's already action on social media. Something you need to see."

Drew raised his brows. "Already?"

She handed him her phone with a grim expression. Drew's mouth dropped open as he read the screen.

TWENTY-TWO

TWELVE HOURS BEFORE

The rider dragged his quarry up the incline from Lower Flint Rock Lake.

When he'd seen the wrecked snowmobile, he'd started to drive past it. He thought he knew where he'd dropped his rucksack. It had been when he ignored the sensation of something brushing his coat, assuming it was snow or a pinecone or the wind. *Stupid, stupid, stupid.* It wasn't that much further back along the trail.

He hated wasting time to retrieve it, but there were items in it that traced back to his identity, and there were fingerprints to confirm it. A woman had just been murdered a few miles from here. He hadn't pulled the trigger, but he'd been the lookout. His prints were in the system. There was no way he was taking a chance this would be pinned on him. Not after keeping himself off law enforcement radar for this long. Not when things were finally—finally!—gathering momentum for him. To have it all end in a massive manhunt was not going to happen.

So, yeah, he'd nearly left the wrecked rider wherever he or she was. But something in his gut made him brake. A quick impression from his glimpse of the machine. When he stopped and turned back, he saw it.

He'd whispered an expletive.

It was a Kearny County sled. The license plate was exempt, without a registration sticker. Given the circumstances of the woman shot at the ski area, he felt certain it was a Kearny County law enforcement sled, because the odds of any other type of county employee randomly being out here seemed minuscule.

They were hunting for him. Him and his partner.

He looked around for a body, which wasn't easy with the snow coming down like a bride's panties on her wedding night. Movement out on the ice caught his eyes. *There you are.* The figure was face down and stretched out. *Just let the pig break through and drown.* But no—it was working its way toward shore. The rider couldn't take a chance. He lifted his seat and pulled a collapsible club from its well-stocked depths. He extended it to its full length then drove his sled as close to the lake as he could get it. He cut the engine and walked the shoreline, feeling confident that with his face covering and helmet he was unrecognizable.

The cop shouted, "Delaney! I'm over here!" A man's voice.

The rider smiled. Delaney? As in Deputy Delaney Pace? He didn't reply, because he wasn't Delaney, which the cop would know soon enough.

Then his smile reversed itself. He should have known the guy wouldn't be alone. Deputy Delaney Pace was out here, too. The cops were separated but together. Where was she? He scanned in every direction as far as he could see but there was no sign of another sled.

In front of him, the cop was slithering on his belly, almost to terra firma, undrowned and dragging his helmet. The night would have gone so much more pleasantly if he didn't have to do this. But in seconds, the cop was going to be asking his name and thanking him for stopping to help. And minutes after that he'd be searching for someone who shot a woman with a rifle from the summit of Elk Ridge. The real question was whether to kill him and stash his body or leave him out here to die.

"Delaney, is that you?"

He'll know I'm not her by now. He hefted his club, ready.

The cop was on the shore now, lifting his head. "Man, am I ever glad to see you. I hit a moose and went flying. My name's Leo, Leo—"

The rider brought the club down on his head. Aloud, he said, "Tell me something I don't know." He'd recognized Sheriff Leo Palmer. And he'd decided alive was better than dead.

He radioed using the numeric code that was as familiar to him as words after the last year. "Thirteen, twenty-two, zero." It meant *trouble, cops, come to me.* He knew there would be no reply. They kept off the walkie-talkies unless it was a real emergency. His partner would be here soon. Less than ten minutes. But Delaney was out there somewhere, and she'd be looking for her pretty boy partner soon if she wasn't already.

This changed everything. The plan had been to take the long way back to the others. A horrible backcountry route through rough territory, but one that wouldn't lead any pursuers to their veritable doorstep. Breakdown in the plan. Move on to a new one.

He had known he had to move fast.

So, that's why he'd been dragging Leo Palmer up a slippery, steep slope in powder halfway up his shins. His breathing was ragged, but whatever. He pushed himself harder. *Climb faster. Don't wuss out.* He looked back at Leo. He'd been dragging him through snow deeper than the guy's head. He stopped and brushed the snow away, listening for breath sounds.

Yeah, he was still sucking in air. At least he'd been face up.

Turning Leo, he switched to arm dragging. He reached the tree line and went past it, out of sight of the trail in this weather, and propped him against a tree. With rope from under his seat, he tied him upright. His hand brushed something hard under Leo's coat. Weapons? He unzipped the coat. A nice handgun and two extra clips in a belly holster. He took them and put them under his seat. He powered down and pocketed a phone and smashed a smart watch. Buried the watch pieces deep under the snow. But his real find was a radio.

A police radio would be *extremely* useful.

He removed the unit and stowed it under the seat, too, along with a pocketknife and a multi-tool. Then he ran back to the wrecked sled. It wasn't running and was on its side, probably flooded. No matter what, the first thing to do was get it upright. He stood on the upper side of the track holding on to the handlebars and bounced his weight until it tipped back over. He tried starting it, but that was a no-go. He kicked it. He didn't have time for it to recover from the flooding, if that was what was wrong with it. He dragged it toward the trees, and it took everything he had in him. In seconds, he was cursing his leaden thighs and the shooting pains in his back, cursing Leo Palmer and the moose, cursing the snowmachine. But none of it mattered. All that mattered was Delaney Pace not seeing her partner and his sled. That they be hidden long enough for a getaway.

It had to be. Because if it wasn't, he was going to have to add murdering two cops to his list of crimes.

When he had the snowmobile where he wanted it, he drove his own sled in beside Palmer, far enough off trail to be hidden, too. Now, how to get his buddy's attention? He felt a little silly adopting the rules of using no names—going so far as to train themselves not even to think the names—during operations, to ensure they didn't betray themselves. It was effective, though. So, his *partner.* There was no guarantee the next person coming down this trail wasn't going to be Delaney Pace.

He didn't have the first clue how to do it.

But in the end, he got lucky because his buddy was driving with his headlight off. For whatever reason, the rider had no idea. It's not like the whole county couldn't smell that old snowmobile coming. The rider could see just well enough to recognize the distinctive black and yellow paint job and body style. Besides, there was no way a cop would be flying through the dark with no headlight, especially not if she was searching for bad guys and her partner.

He leapt into the trail waving his arms, then, when the snowmobile slowed down, motioning for him to pull off far into the trees. The snowmobile veered toward the tree line, slowed, then wallowed its way into the dark of the forest.

The rider lumbered to him and started speaking as soon as the engine cut out. He pointed at Leo. "Meet the sheriff of Kearny County."

His partner looked like he'd been punched in the solar plexus. His voice turned grim. "I know who he is."

"I know you do. And not in a good way."

"No. Not in a good way. What happened?"

"The dumbass hit a moose. He ended up thrown out on the ice. I met him just as he made it back to shore."

"Why did you stop?"

"Are you kidding me? If I hadn't, we'd be bumbling around out here with two cops."

"Two?"

"His colleague. He was calling for her. Delaney Pace."

"*Delaney? Deputy* Delaney Pace? I just was talking to some chick named Laney. She was lost and scared and I pointed her back to Mockingbird Creek. That was Delaney Pace?"

"You're lucky you're not wearing zip ties on your hands and feet."

He snorted. "I'm not scared of a woman."

"Then you're an idiot."

The sound of a snowmobile engine pushing max RPMs came screaming out of the south.

"Hush," the rider said.

When the sound had grown as it passed and then faded into the distance, the rider's breath came out in a rush.

"Was that her?" he said.

"Yeah. Woman alone on a snowmobile. That was her."

"Great. Then let's get the hell out of here." He clapped his partner on the back and walked toward Palmer, who was still unconscious. He stopped for a moment, thinking. They needed distractions. They needed ways to slow the cops down. An idea formed. He grinned. "Hey, can you go sink his snowmobile?"

"Why me?"

The rider laughed. "Come on, just stand on the edge of the lake beside it, rev it up good and tie the throttle at full with the brake on, then release the brake. It'll fall through the ice. Sounds fun, right?"

"A little." His partner grinned. "Okay, it sounds good."

The rider dug under his seat and handed the other an extra-wide rubber band. "Use this."

"Okay. I'll be right back."

The rider busied himself getting his snowmobile back on the trail and loading Palmer onto the front of its seat. He would carry him across the saddle like a field-dressed elk, wedged between his own body and the front end. His only problem would be when the sheriff woke up, but he'd just give him another knock on the head with his metal club if that happened. With the change in plans he was about to announce, they'd be back with the others before too long anyway.

He heard the racing engine of Palmer's snowmobile, then a crack. The engine noise struggled and then stopped.

Two minutes later, his partner was hauling his own sled out of the trees.

"How did it go?" the rider asked.

"Piece of cake." His partner stopped, frowning. "Wait—did you get your rucksack?"

The rider closed his eyes and squeezed them tight. "Dammit. I didn't get it."

"Should one of us go look for it?"

The rider thought about the clues to his identity and his prints. The falling snow. The looming, almost-sure arrival of a second cop. The uncertainty of his partner even finding the rucksack—because there was no way the rider could personally go after it and risk another run-in with Delaney Pace. "No. This is turning out to be a big snow. It will be buried until spring. It's the lesser risk. That deputy could still turn around. We need to get out of here and back to the others."

"Are we going to bury him under snow here or back at camp?"

The rider laughed. "He's alive."

"Do I get the honors or do you?" He was already reaching for his gun.

"We're not killing him."

"You-know-who's not going to like that."

"Ah, but you and I don't care about him. Is he out here with you? No. I am. Me. I'm more of a brother to you than he'll ever be. And I've been telling you, he's just in your way."

"I don't get it. Why do we want to keep him alive?"

The rider waved his hand at Leo. "You're looking at the answer to our prayers."

TWENTY-THREE

Standing once again beside Lower Flint Rock Lake on the snowmobile trail—which was now packed down from foot and snowmobile traffic—Delaney's stomach burned from too much bad coffee and too little food. The caffeine hadn't done much to make her alert, but the pain was keeping her awake. She yawned anyway. Clint offered her his thermos.

"I can't take any more."

"Good call. It tastes like battery acid smells." Clint stretched his arms up and out like he was just getting out of bed, tilting his face to the brilliant sun and bright blue, cloudless sky. The weather in Wyoming suffered from multiple personality disorder; in Delaney's opinion, anyway.

Leslie Underwood, the dog handler from Cheyenne, was fitting snow booties to the paws of a brindle Belgian Malinois named Ace. Dressed in a fleece jacket, Ace looked like a greyhound with fur. His eyes were bright and pointed ears alert. Only a few other snowmobiles and officers were present, since Leslie had asked for them to clear the scene for the sake of the dog's clarity.

Leslie rose. "I'm ready for the clothing item with Leo's scent."

In anticipation of this request, Delaney had sent a volunteer from Mockingbird Creek to fetch Leo's street clothes from his truck, which was still parked at Elk Ridge. They'd been retrieved in a gallon Ziplock bag. Delaney opened it and offered it to Leslie. "He had all of these on yesterday morning."

The handler peered in, lips pursed, nodding. "How about the T-shirt, please. That would have been in close contact with the widest area of his body in the parts most likely to produce his scent signature."

Delaney pulled the Kearny County Sheriff's Department summer picnic T-shirt from the bag and handed it over. She found scent dogs fascinating. The last time she'd worked with one had been after spring thaw when they'd tried to track Liam from where she'd last seen him. The dog had failed because the scent had disappeared with the snow. Some had theorized a predator had removed Liam's body during the winter. Delaney didn't believe it. Liam had always been like a mutating virus, reinventing himself out there somewhere until he was ready to attack again. "Do you think this is enough?"

"It will be if we can get physically close enough to Leo's trail. Ace is top notch. Dogs like him detect scent differences between people that even DNA can't differentiate. Like between identical twins. It's amazing really. He's also cross-trained for grid search work. The two things—scent and search—are really integral skills, and we'll use them both today." She presented Leo's T-shirt to Ace. The dog huffed it with enthusiasm, then started spinning around and sniffing the snow. He returned to the shirt. "Good boy." Leslie unsnapped his leash. "Find it. Find it."

Delaney had expected Ace to go crazy when he was released based on his excitement level after smelling the shirt. But instead, the dog, while energized and moving fast, seemed strangely settled. He started in a circle. Almost immediately, he found Leo's scent. Leslie rewarded him and urged him to continue. He ran out onto the ice, seemed to identify where Leo had been, then turned and raced back up the bank and across the trail, tail up and head down.

It was electrifying to watch, even if Delaney knew this was only the beginning. They'd already known Leo had been here. It was where he went after that they needed Ace for.

The dog bounded around in the disturbed area of snow under the trees where Delaney and Clint had found evidence of snowmobiles off trail.

"Ace is telling us he was up there in the trees." Leslie went after Ace and rewarded him. She directed him out to search.

He started circling, first returning to where he'd started. Leslie sent him out again, and he circled under the trees. After a few minutes, the dog appeared to disengage. He whined and returned to Leslie.

She spoke in soft tones to the dog, then said, "He's not finding a clear trail away from here. Is it possible Leo was transported?"

Clint closed his eyes.

Delaney said, "Yes, unfortunately."

"Okay. It would be a serious waste of Ace's energy and enthusiasm to ask him to run searches all along the trail. The snow is deep, and it's very cold. What I propose is I give him a break until you develop other leads. We'll remain at your service. I can redeploy him any time you think there's a chance of crossing a scent trail."

Delaney wanted to scream with frustration. It was what she had feared, but not what she'd hoped. But then she remembered her conversation with Drew and Skeeter.

"I have an idea," she said.

TWENTY-FOUR

Taking a seat in Starbuck's, Skeeter sucked down a sip of his Mocha Cookie Crumble Frappuccino as a chaser to a bite of Sausage Cheddar and Egg Sandwich. Starbuck's made a tasty drink, although he still preferred a Frosty from Wendy's. The pleasing scent of coffee in here was better than the Wendy's smell though. Wendy's sometimes smelled like the teenage kid who mopped the floors didn't ever change the mop water. Skeeter should know. He'd had that job in high school.

He pulled up the list of witnesses he'd chased down online and picked up his phone. He'd just made his fastest drive ever from Kearny to Sheridan. He couldn't remember wanting anything worse than he wanted to be the one to break this case and bring Leo home alive. Ever since last year when he'd helped rescue Ashley Klinkosh, a teenage Crow girl who'd been kidnapped, he'd felt rejuvenated. He could do stuff that mattered. He could still prove the people who hadn't hired him for law enforcement jobs had been wrong.

In Ashley's case, all of his secrets had spilled out to the people he cared about. His financial mistakes. Bad past relation-ships. Drinking. Some drugs. The worst secret was that he had made some really bad decisions when investigating the disappearance of a teenage girl five years before. She'd ended up dead after years of being held prisoner by a man who took young girls as his so-called brides. The same man who took Ashley. You name it—Delaney, Leo, and Mary had heard about him doing it. But they'd had his back. With their help, he was putting the past in the past.

Now, they were giving him a future. Leo kept sending him county work. There was a little more supervision, but that was okay. He'd been dead certain Delaney would never trust him again with her daughters. But she'd called him family. She'd hired him to help her find her mother. She'd warned him to never, ever make that kind of mistake again—and he wouldn't, not on his life, nor on Kat's or Carrie's, nor Mary's son Juan Julio's—and told him that she knew her girls were safe with him. Mary didn't pull Juan Julio away from his care. She also made sure he kept his drinking social. In the old days, he would have tied one on so he wouldn't have to think about how hard things were.

He wasn't ashamed to admit he'd cried like a little girl more than once about the whole thing. He didn't deserve friends like he had. He owed them the world. That meant he had to produce real leads that led to Leo's return.

So, he was nodding, and the set of his mouth was determined—albeit chewing—as he dialed the number for Jackie's roommate in Sheridan. The young woman was also her fellow bartender at the Best Western. If anyone knew anything about Jackie's life, it was most likely to be her.

"Hello?" It was a female voice. The woman sounded like she'd been crying.

"Alisha Patterson?" he asked.

"Who's this?"

"I'm... Rawlins. I'm working with the Kearny County Sheriff's Department." He felt a thrill at the words he'd wanted to say for so long. It wasn't as good as being a deputy. That would never happen. But it was still like jumping in Lake Michigan on a hot August day. "I hate to bother you, ma'am, as I'm sure this is a sad time for you, but we need information about your roommate to help us find her killer."

"Are you the one who left me the message earlier? I'm sorry I didn't call back yet. It's just been so—so—so—"

"Nope. I'm glad I caught you. I'm at the Starbuck's. Any chance we can talk face to face."

"That's weird."

"Why?"

"I'm in the drive-up line."

"Sounds like good luck to me."

"Give me a minute and I'll come inside."

Skeeter fought back a wave of nerves. He'd interviewed people plenty of times as a private investigator, but never on a case for the county. His work from Leo was usually about skip traces and background information. What Skeeter thought of as busy work. No one saw *him*. He put his sandwich in its bag and stuffed that in his briefcase. He brushed crumbs off the table. He slurped down the last of his Frappuccino and threw the empty cup in the trash.

He'd just arranged a pen and paper on the table when a young woman with a tear-streaked, puffy face pushed through the door, one hand holding a tall coffee cup. He waved at her. She took a seat across the table from him and pulled off her wool cap, revealing a completely bald head.

"Thanks for coming in," he said, trying not to stare at her head. Or her forehead, where there were no eyebrows.

"Chemotherapy. I'm twenty-four, and I have ovarian cancer." She wiped her face with a napkin.

"I'm sorry. That's tough stuff."

"I thought it was bad before this happened. This is just awful. The worst. Janet—I mean I guess it's Jackie, but I knew her as Janet. She was just so nice and positive and supportive. She was the one who'd take me to and from chemo. When my hair started falling out, she shaved my head."

"How did you meet her?"

"In the bathroom at Walmart, actually. She was putting a color rinse on her hair in the sink. Kind of purple-ish. I told her I'd done my hair that color once and gave her some tips on how to keep it fresh. Ironic, huh? She was like, kind of shy, but she was really grateful because she'd never done a rinse before."

Skeeter didn't even know what a rinse was, but Carrie put some weird colors in her hair, so he assumed it was the same thing. He smiled at her. "That sounds... cool." The word felt weird in his mouth, but it seemed to work with Alisha.

"Yeah. It was. She asked me if I lived in Sheridan. We talked about my apartment and where I worked. She'd just moved to town and didn't have a place or a job yet. We'd really hit it off, so I told her to apply at the hotel where I worked. They're always looking for good people, you know? They hired her on the spot. She had a lot of experience and stuff."

"I'll bet she appreciated that."

"Oh, yeah, she did. We went to get a bite to eat, and she crashed at my place. Then she just never left." Alisha laughed, which brought more tears. "Until now, of course. Oh, my gosh, I can't stop crying. It's just, it's just, I mean, why her?"

"That's what we want to find out. Did she have a boyfriend?"

"No. She was super pretty but she didn't date at all. Not that lots of guys didn't ask. I tried setting her up with friends—nice guys—but she wouldn't. Said her last boyfriend had been so bad that she was going to see if she could be a lesbian." Alisha nodded. "That was a joke. She didn't apply or anything." When Skeeter looked confused she added, "That was also a joke. There's no application. Sorry, I think I'm making bad jokes because I'm nervous, and sad, and a little scared. All those things mixed up in me at once."

"That's okay. Did she tell you his name? The ex-boyfriend?"

"She refused to say it. She said it might summon him like a demon. She just called him The Asshole."

"Was she scared of him?"

"I think so. She stayed off social media and stuff and wouldn't let me post pictures with her in them. She said he was super controlling, like she was basically his prisoner, and he wouldn't even let her talk to other guys."

Skeeter felt sweat roll into the crease across his belly and under his chest. A young woman who was a prisoner to a controlling man? Why did his first case for the sheriff's department have to be so similar to the case that had haunted him as a PI? He couldn't screw this up. He wouldn't. "Did she have pictures of him? Or ever get messages, like texts or email?"

Alisha shook her head.

"Did anyone ever ask about her in town? Show up at work or your place? Scare her?"

"There was this one guy that followed her around like a puppy dog. I never saw him, but she told me it was getting old."

"Description?"

"She said he was weird looking. Tall with a pin head. Dark eyes and platinum hair. The funny thing was that he never showed up here or at work, so I sometimes wondered about it."

"In what way?"

"I mean, where was he following her to? She took me to and from chemo, we'd shop together, stuff like that. I never saw him. But she wasn't, like, a liar. It was just... strange."

Skeeter made a note. The guy matched the person-of-interest information he'd been given, but this wasn't much to go on. "What about friends and family? Did she talk to anyone or have visitors?"

Alisha looked thoughtful, sipped her coffee, then frowned. "You know what? I never heard her talking to family. She talked about them. Said they were awful and that she was out of there without looking back as soon as she graduated high school. Dumped her high school boyfriend and ran off with a cowboy headed to Montana. But her parents never called, and she literally was, like, never on her phone. I don't know if they even had her number. I mean, I need to take a break from my phone sometimes. I should do that more, really. But she was on, like, a permanent break."

Skeeter couldn't think of any other questions. He wished he had a Kearny County business card to give Alisha, like Delaney did after her interviews. There was no way he was handing her his private investigator card. "If you think of anything else, give me a call. I'm out of cards." He recited his number.

Alisha typed it into her phone. Then she stood but didn't leave. "I've never known anyone who was murdered before. It's really awful." She bit her lip. "But now I'm wondering if we were really as close as I thought if she never told me the truth about her name. Maybe she never told me the truth about anything at all. Maybe there was no ex-boyfriend. Maybe she'd never even bartended before."

Skeeter nodded, wondering something different. He wondered why people had to suffer so much. Alisha, with cancer. Jackie and all she went through only to end up murdered. The girls in the case, the one he didn't want to remember. His dad used to say that no one ever said life was fair. His dad had been wrong about a lot of things, like that Skeeter was brain damaged and would never amount to anything. But he was damn straight about that one.

He stood and put out his hand. She took it but instead of shaking it, she leveraged it into a hug. A strange wave of emotion flooded him. "You got a ride to and from those chemo appointments now?"

She released him. "Yeah. It won't be the same, but I do. I don't care if she wasn't who I thought she was. I loved her. Please find out who did this to her and make sure they pay for it."

All Skeeter could do was nod. The lump in his throat was too big to get the words past. But inside a fire was burning. He would do this for Leo. And he would do it for Jackie or Janet or whatever she called herself. And Alisha. And Ashley. And all the people who got taken or murdered. All of them.

TWENTY-FIVE

Delaney and Clint left the handler and her dog at the warming hut where Leslie would feed Ace and provide him with a physical and mental break. The two officers went outside.

She raised Drew on her radio, shutting her eyes against the sun. "Any progress connecting with someone about Snow Hare Ranch?"

Clint brushed snow off the bench of a picnic table and took a seat, listening in.

Drew sounded frustrated. "I haven't been able to get an answer on the number I think is theirs. Every other lodge or ranch or cabin in the area has been contacted, and they've been helpful and cooperative. No one has seen Leo—some aren't up in the mountains, since it's winter—but they've all given permission for law enforcement to enter their properties and search. Many have asked us to contact them if we want help, and most have said they'll be conducting searches to the extent they can themselves."

"That's good about the others, but Clint and I are going to pay them a little visit at Snow Hare. We need your eyes."

"How can I help?"

"Go to my cubicle. You're going to look at a map for me." She described its location.

Delaney was a devotee of cartography. The way some people passed the time with games on their phone, reading, or needlepoint, she entertained herself with maps. On her cubicle walls, maps were plastered edge to edge. She'd started with maps of the municipality of Kearny and then added the county and the state. Month by month she hung more, many with increasing detail. She believed with her entire being that it was her responsibility as a deputy to know the land intimately and that it was key to serving her community. In her mind, Wyoming—with the lowest population density per square mile in the forty-eight contiguous states—faced a larger impact from terrain and weather on public safety than elsewhere. Throw in that the terrain was rugged and weather extreme, and the risks to human life increased exponentially. Just traversing the sheer number of square miles in Kearny County to aid a citizen in jeopardy was time-consuming and at times, sadly, impossible. She needed to know and understand the topography, the property owners, the roads, and the structures. Intimately.

Right now, she was kicking herself for inadequate study of the Big Horn County maps, especially given that it was adjacent to Kearny County. However, she could picture the map she needed, and it was in her cubicle. A few months before, she'd printed a beautiful, detailed close-up aerial of the territory along the north–south stretch of the snowmobile trail they were on. It was fairly new, too, with the boundaries of Snow Hare Ranch and other properties superimposed and helpful notations added. What she couldn't remember about the ranch were its access points, any seasonal roads leading into it, and whether there were structures on it.

"Heading there now. Give me a sec. Okay, I'm in your chair. I see it."

"Great. It actually folds out. You'll want to do that."

"Ah. Cool. Yeah, this is much easier to read."

"Good. Are there any buildings on Snow Hare?"

"Uhhhh... I think so. It says Snow Hare Lodge and there appears to be a group of buildings beside the words. Like a house, some large outbuildings, some smaller ones. Hard to say for sure."

"That's helpful. How do you think we get there from Mockingbird Creek campground?"

"Gosh. Okay. Well, there's one road in. It splits into two... one direction connects with the snowmobile trail, the other goes west and... I can't see that it connects to anything. It kind of just ends."

"All right. Where's the entrance off the trail?"

"I'd say just two miles or so from the turn-off between Adelaide and the snowmobile trail. It's not that far. Then it's only a few hundred yards to the structures."

"Thanks, Drew."

His voice took on a hopeful note. "Did the dog find Leo's trail leading there?"

"No. The handler's conclusion is that Leo was transported away from the lake. My guess is that Snow Hare is a good place to continue the search. Any news on your end?"

"Clara and I are starting research on the trustees of Far West now. Skeeter has been talking to people Janet—aka Jackie—worked with and getting nowhere. He's going to start tracking down contacts from social media from Jackie's prior life. But we have one piece of news. It has to do with the social media posts."

"What's up?"

"Someone claims to have found a rucksack on the snowmobile trail near Lower Flint Rock Lake last night. Was Leo carrying one?"

"No. All our gear was under our seats."

"I mean, it could be anyone's, but..."

"A long shot is better than no shot. See if they'll bring it in. We're too short-staffed to send someone for it."

"That's the thing. They live over in Worland."

"Then have them drop it off at the sheriff's department in Big Horn County. I'll give Shannon a heads-up that its germane to us finding Leo and claim sharesies."

"Got it. Thanks."

"I'll check back later." Delaney signed off.

Clint was smiling. "I take it our visit to Snow Hare will be a surprise, then."

"You take it right."

Delaney nearly flew right past the main entrance to Snow Hare Ranch on their approach. She gripped the brakes after sensing cleared trees. Backing up, she peered into the distance, recognizing the width of a mountain road. But its intersection with the snowmobile trail was nothing but snow piled high from the winter trail grooming. At both edges, a chain rose from the snow and attached to D-rings on trees with locks, ostensibly blocking vehicular traffic. A PRIVATE PROPERTY NO TRESPASSING sign nailed on the right-side tree warned trail users away. No one had accessed this road with wheeled or tracked vehicles for a long time. If Delaney and Clint wanted to use it, they'd have to cut the chain.

Twenty feet later, however, she spotted a much narrower trail with clear evidence of recent usage by tracked vehicles, angled so that it was hard to see from the direction of their approach. Tree branches further obscured it, but when she drew near, she could tell many of the branches were damaged from the impact of vehicles.

She swung wide to make a nearly one-hundred-and-eighty-degree turn to catch the trail. Behind her, the sound of Clint's engine reassured her he was doing the same thing. The new path took all of her attention, as it immediately swung back to the left and then zigzagged through the forest on a crazy series of rollercoaster-like hills. Branches whipped her across the torso and head. Fortunately, the snow was packed down from regular usage and possibly grooming. Within a hundred yards, the trail straightened, widened, and the branches were trimmed back.

A sense of foreboding stole over her. Someone had taken great pains to camouflage winter access to this property. This went beyond not monitoring or answering a phone. If those people were here, they were likely to be extremely displeased about unannounced visitors. By her reckoning, their trail could empty out by the front door of the house or lodge any second. The sound of their snowmachines might have already alerted any occupants, as sound carried crazily well in the mountains. Those used to the sound of snowmobiles accessing their trail would be able to recognize when someone was approaching on it, as opposed to using the public trails.

She came to a halt and cut her engine.

Clint pulled up beside her and did the same. "I was hoping you'd stop. Damn, this place is spooky already."

"Signs suggest we need to prepare for a poor reception. Especially if they've got Leo here and are harboring a murderer."

Clint was already checking his weapon for ammunition. She pulled hers out, too. "The trail is well used. Even since the snow last night."

Delaney put her own gun back in its holster, her inspection of it complete. "I don't want to be sneaky about this. I want to park out front where we can be seen and knock on the front door, unless you talk me out of it. We don't have the information or manpower for a power play."

"Ninety-nine percent agreement. All of that, but one of us hangs back in case of trouble. Covers, gets ready to summon help."

She nodded. Suddenly, she was fighting a lump in her throat. Clint was a good cop and a more than capable outdoorsman. But she missed Leo and their banter, their spark, their near-mind-reading level of communication, and even their head butting. It should be Leo here right now. Instead, it was Leo they were looking for.

"Hey," Clint said. "Are you all right?"

"Yeah. I'm just... I'm worried and trying not to let it bog me down. And it won't. It just got to me for a second."

He leaned over and put a hand on the wrist of her heavy coat. "Understandable. Anytime you need a pause, tell me, and we'll take a deep breath while it passes over you."

Delaney nodded. "I'm ready now."

"Wait. Who's covering and who's knocking?"

"I'll knock. A woman may be less threatening, especially since I'm not in uniform."

"Works for me."

She lowered her face shield and accelerated ahead of Clint, taking deep breaths to get herself fully back to equilibrium.

Sure enough, fifty yards later, the forest opened onto an expanse of white backed by a snowy ranch compound. At its edge was an imposing log structure with a sign above the door. SNOW HARE LODGE.

Go time.

She revved her engine several times to announce her presence as she drove the last few yards, parking at a rock barrier in an area that had been cleared. If she hadn't been sure from the trail usage that the house was occupied, the obvious plowing around the lodge as well as the plume of smoke rising from a chimney was a dead giveaway. She no longer heard Clint behind her and assumed he'd found a good place to hide and cover.

Snow crunched under her boots as she walked to the door. She felt nervy and exposed. The door opened when she was ten feet away to reveal a man in winter white camo gear holding a shotgun leveled at her chest. From the neck up, he looked like he could have been a cast member of *Jersey Shore*.

She raised her hands and stopped. "Good day to you. No need for weapons."

The gun barrel wagged at the trees. "Tell that to your buddy." His voice matched his look. If not Jersey, then somewhere close to it. What the heck was he doing up here? She remembered the trustees were from DC, which was not exactly next door to Wyoming either.

She lowered her hands. "Fair point. We'd been trying to call the phone number listed for this place and couldn't get an answer, so we were being cautious. I'll wave him off." She turned toward where she thought Clint should be and waved, then took off her glove and gave him an okay sign. Clint had binoculars, and she hoped he was using them. If so, he could see for himself things were not really okay and that he should remain on high alert, no matter what signal she acted out for the benefit of the guy in the doorway.

"What do you want?" She was pretty sure the odor emanating from his person was Jack Daniels. But the one coming from the house was Mary Jane, as in cannabis.

"Let's start over. My name is Delaney Pace. You don't sound like you're from around here. Where are you from? What's your name?"

"What do you want, Delaney Pace?"

"I'm looking for my boyfriend. We were snowmobiling last night and got separated. I can't find him. His name is Leo."

"Haven't seen him."

"I haven't even described him yet."

His upper lip curled in a sneer. "Same answer."

This place and this person were setting off her alarm bells. She gave his description. "When I'm not snowmobiling, my job is deputy with Kearny County. Leo is our sheriff, Leo Palmer."

"Still the same answer."

"We're also looking for a couple of guys in white snowma-chine outfits. Probably a lot like yours. One of them may be a big guy with platinum blond hair. Would you mind if Kearny Police Chief Clint Rock-Below—that's him out there waiting for me—and I ride around your property and look around for Leo and them?"

"I mind."

"I can come back with a warrant, or you can help us locate a missing person now, before he freezes to death?"

He crossed his arms. "Warrant."

"Does that mean you have something to hide?"

"Warrant."

"Can you start searching your place in the meantime? A man's life is at stake."

"Lady—"

"Deputy."

He pointed a finger in her face. "Lady deputy, get off this property. You're trespassing. If we find your boyfriend on our place, we're more likely to pepper him with lead than give him a cup of hot cocoa and read him a bedtime story."

It was the first time he'd used the word *we*. But of course, there would be more than one person. Very few people would solo in these mountains in the winter. The question was who, how many, and what in the heck this place was about. *Might as well be direct. May not get another chance to chat.*

"Who is we?"

He glared at her.

"Who do you work for?"

His eyes were flat. "Trust me—you don't want to find out. You need to leave. For your sake. This is the last time I'm saying it nicely."

Delaney raised her hands again as she backed away. "See you soon then."

"Not if we see you first."

"Not if we see you first."

TWENTY-SIX

"Wake up." A man's authoritative voice penetrated Leo's eardrums and ricocheted into his tender brain. His eyes reacted by popping open, then retracting to slits. Bright light hit them like a head-on collision with a semi. He groaned, unseeing.

"He's coming around," another man said, then blew out a stream of cigarette smoke. His voice was higher in pitch. Almost whiny.

The voices didn't sound friendly.

Leo batted his eyelids against the light, trying to work them apart again. His headache was intense, but not as bad as the last time he'd woken up. He'd been alone then. Unable to think. Unable to function. Now, memories blitzed him with the speed of an aerial assault. Chasing suspects behind the ski resort. Delaney riding ahead. Hitting the moose. Slithering off ice. Meeting a silent man in white. An incredibly hard blow to his head. Vomiting. Pain. His skull taking hit after hit. Realizing he'd let Delaney down.

None of it was good. Maybe oblivion had been a blessing. Concussion, drugs, or both? he wondered. The effects were wearing off now, whatever it had been.

He held up his joined hands to block the worst of the direct light. It helped. He looked up to see several backlit figures standing faceless in front of him. He counted heads. They swum before him. Maybe three?

He said, "I'm awake." His voice was raw and thready.

A new voice spoke. Overly confident. It was coming from the middle figure. The first guy had sounded authoritative, but Leo decided this was the man who thought he was in charge. "Don't forget we've instituted 1100. No names. Don't even think them."

"Yes, sir. Amnesia protocol," the whiny one said.

The boss guy cleared his throat. "Welcome, Sheriff."

For a split second, Leo considered playing dumb. But he'd had his wallet and badge on him. He'd been riding a county snowmobile. Carrying a police radio. "You know who I am. Who are you?" He sat up, holding his weight on his wrists. The room swayed dangerously.

"I told you it was him." The higher, whiny voice. The one standing to the right. He leaned over and ground his cigarette out on the concrete floor then left the butt there.

Boss man said, "I don't listen to you. You've been demoted. You're lucky I don't kill you for raining hell down on us over that girl."

Whiny guy killed the girl at the ski resort?

"You told me she had to—"

"In a public place? Like that? You don't have the brains of a hamster on life support whose family is about to turn off the machines." Then he added, "Excuse me, Sheriff. Where are my manners? Nice to meet you. I'm your host."

And Boss ordered her dead? Was Boss the guy who knocked me out at Flint Rock Lake?

Leo spoke, his voice a little stronger, matching Boss's pretense of social niceties. "You'll forgive me if I don't compliment you on your hospitality. I'll be rating you a one star for uncomfortable accommodation, a lack of food and water so I can't speak to their quality, and no turn-down service. Some medical attention would have salvaged my review, but..." He raised his hands and dropped them.

Boss dropped the pretense. His voice was cold and matter-of fact. "You may think you're special, but to me, all you are is trouble."

"And you stink," Whiner said.

Leo knew he was right. The room was rank with his own human odors. It was a humiliation he didn't have the luxury of dwelling on.

Boss said, "You're here against my vote. For now, you're alive and out of the elements, which is considerate under the circumstances."

"Which are what? Last I remember I ran into a moose and went ice skating," Leo said.

The first speaker finally rejoined the conversation. The voice came from the tallest of the three men. The one who sounded like a possible challenger to the boss's status. "We don't like cops chasing us around."

Something pinged in Leo's brain. Did he recognize that voice? *Maybe this was the one from Lower Flint Rock.* "Was I chasing you?"

Whiner spoke. "Weren't you? Your partner fed me some cock-and-bull story about getting separated from her boyfriend." He threw his voice to mock Delaney. "'I'm scared, please help me.' Bullshit. She was trying to trap me."

Leo's pulse accelerated. Whiner had met Delaney. He was one of the white-suited snowmobilers.

Boss must have had a similar thought. "Remind everyone to dress civilian today on the way out. That lady cop saw you in our winter white suits. There can't be anything to link them to each other or us." When Whiner didn't move, Boss said, "I mean, now."

Whiner took a walkie-talkie from a holster. "Uh, sixteen for uh, sixty. I mean, six hundred." He reholstered the walkie-talkie.

Leo said, "Where is Delaney now?"

The challenger laughed. He held up a dark object. Leo heard a click, like a knob turned until power engaged for something electrical. Then Delaney's voice filled the room, staticky but clear. His radio. They had his radio. *"We're coming back to get a probable cause warrant. The caretaker at Snow Hare Ranch wouldn't let us search for Leo."*

She's looking for me. According to Whiner, she'd seen him. Talked to him. Leo felt sure she'd recognized him as the suspect. She'd be able to give a description. He didn't want her stumbling into this hornets' nest. The thought of what these men had done to him and might do to her was terrifying. *I have to get out of here myself before that can happen.*

"I'll get it started for you. See you soon." Sheriff Wilcox's voice.

All three men laughed.

Challenger said, "That was interesting. Thanks for the radio, Sheriff. It's kept us entertained. And up to date."

Boss said, "Too close for comfort. Time to wrap this up."

Leo rocked into a cross-legged position with his arms in front of him, taking pressure off his wrists. "I don't understand why I'm here in the first place. Is this about the woman at the ski resort?"

Boss's tone turned ugly. "My brother is the gift that keeps on giving. I still don't understand, either. Why is the sheriff of Kearny County here?"

Whiner and Boss are brothers.

The room felt charged, like air before a lightning strike. Leo held his breath, feeling exposed to a deadly crossfire.

Challenger answered before Whiner could speak. "There's no risk Delaney Pace won't take for Leo Palmer."

Leo felt a cold tingling in the nerve endings all through his body. *Not Delaney. Anything, anyone but Delaney.*

"Why does that matter to me? More to the point, why would it matter to my sister?" Boss said.

"Think of her as your genie in a bottle. What wish would you guys like her to grant?"

Leo closed his eyes. *I should have told her no. I should have insisted we stay together or wait for daylight. She's compromised, because of me. All because of me.*

Boss was quiet for a moment. "She's not stupid."

"No, but she's in love."

Whiner guffawed.

Leo had to try. He had to redirect. He injected all the nonchalance he could into his tone. Like the topic meant very little to him, when it meant everything. "She's a trained law enforcement officer who follows procedures working within a system designed to prevent *granting special wishes.*" He emphasized the last words.

Boss snorted. "For your sake, I hope you're wrong. Now, get up. We've got to get out of here without getting caught or killed, thanks to my dumbass brother and you."

TWENTY-SEVEN

Their expedited probable cause warrant to search Snow Hare Ranch came through via email an hour later, which was how long it took for Delaney to ride with a Big Horn deputy to reach Greybull, where he received and printed the warrant. With it came a message from the judge that they were "pushing the limits of probable cause." He would go no further than this. She didn't care. It was all she needed. Leo was there. Her gut told her so. This piece of paper was enough for her to prove it, if their earlier visit hadn't sent his captors scurrying away with him. It couldn't be helped. Time had not been on their side, and they'd had nothing to support a warrant before. Nor had they the manpower or the evidence to muster a raid.

The drive back would be interminable, especially since it would be with the Greybull mayor, a nice enough woman, but a complete stranger and Delaney's only option for a lift at short notice for her and the deputy. At least she had cell phone signal at lower elevations. With apologies to the mayor, she made a quick call to Carrie. No answer. She was probably working, and Mary had a no cell phone rule. Then she tried Kat, who she knew was also at the Loafing Shed or had been a few hours before.

Her younger daughter picked up. "Did you find him?"

"Not yet."

"I'm sorry, Melaney."

"Me, too. But we're going to find him. Are you okay?"

"Oh, you know. Freaking out about Leo. And I have stuff I need to talk to you about when you get home."

"What kind of stuff?"

"Freddy."

"As soon as I get there, I promise."

"That's weird."

"What did I say?"

"Not what you said. I just got another text from someone at a 253 area code. Where is that?"

Delaney googled it on her phone. Northern Washington. She got an uneasy feeling in her stomach. "Is it someone you know?"

"No, but they know my name. Or at least my old name. *Kuh-teen-uh,*" Kat said, dramatically.

Delaney's uneasy feeling turned into queasiness. Granted, her emotional bandwidth was nearly depleted from Leo's situation and her lack of sleep, but, still, she found it disturbing that an unknown out-of-state person was texting her naïve thirteen-year-old daughter and calling her by name. "Kat, don't answer those texts!"

"I'm just going to ask who it is."

"No! Kat, don't answer them. Wait for me to get home!"

"Huh? You're breaking up."

The call went dead.

Delaney pressed her knuckles to her mouth. Was she wrong to be upset? Maybe it was just a friend who'd moved. Or a person who had lost their phone and was using someone else's. *God, my nerves are shot.* She spent the rest of the drive in thought that must have morphed into a nap at some point, because the truck bumped to a stop. *Leo,* she thought. Then remembered the call before she fell asleep. *Kat.*

The mayor was parked at Mockingbird Creek Campground. Clint was standing beside his snowmobile, a fuel can in his hand, watching them.

"Thanks for the lift," she said as she got out.

The mayor shrugged off her thanks and went to distribute donated drinks and snacks to law enforcement and volunteers.

Delaney squared her shoulders. Kat's texter wasn't an emergency. Right now, she had a warrant to serve. With any luck, she'd be bringing back a murderer and a sheriff who just happened to be her boyfriend.

TWENTY-EIGHT
ONE HOUR EARLIER

At leadership's emergency request, I met a helicopter at the base of the mountain, in the middle of a badlands ranch where the group sometimes camped in the spring. I couldn't have been happier about it. I'd been due to stock winter camp, but this was easier. Every monthly winter camp visit was a grueling ordeal. I'd spend a week offloading into a pickup truck and meeting a Snowcat at the end of the forest road, over and over.

It was early for it, but I had assumed the campsite was changing. I was waiting for word that I'd drop the entirety of my load there. The winter this year was harsh. I wouldn't have blamed them for bailing out.

Three people leapt out of the helicopter, its blade whipping snow into a whiteout around them. Two of them turned back to grab what I expected would be baggage.

It was not.

It was a man. One carried him by the shoulders, the other by the feet. The man's head was up, and he was looking around, although his neck was loose. He seemed loopy. Was he sick? Injured? As they all got closer, I saw the binding around the man's wrists and ankles.

He's a prisoner. Great. That means they'll be using 1100. The Amnesia protocol. It meant I should not give my name nor use anyone else's.

The first person to reach his truck was the one I least wanted to see. He was holding the prisoner's shoulders and panting with effort. "Hey, asshole. Don't think I've forgotten what you cost me. Or what it's going to cost you. But for now, make room for us. We need a ride."

"I'm not unloading here?" I said.

"Did I stutter?"

Apparently, I'd assumed wrong about moving winter camp. It was disappointing. "I don't have room."

"Make room and make it fast. We need to get out of here."

"I don't know..."

"Listen. Dump the shit on the ground. You can fetch it later if the coyotes don't get it. But right now, make room and get us the hell out of here."

"Where is everybody going?"

He didn't answer.

The group leader suddenly appeared in my window. I jumped.

He said, "I swear to God, I'm going to shoot you if you don't get moving."

I turned to look at the leader's younger brother one last time before jumping out to move his duffel bag and his cooler of snacks and drinks to the back of the truck. It would be a tight squeeze for five men in a space that sat three.

As I walked to the back of the truck, I saw the face of their prisoner.

Suddenly, the big hurry they were in made a lot more sense.

TWENTY-NINE

As Delaney walked toward Clint, she heard a steady buzz of snowmobiles in the distance. Not like one or two. Like twenty. Or more. The cacophony was disconcerting in the quiet of the mountains.

Clint began pouring fuel into his snowmobile. "You got the warrant?"

"Yes. What's going on out there?" She threw a hand toward the racket.

Out of nowhere, Shannon barged between the two of them and held up his hands, like a cross guard telling traffic in both directions to stop. "We need to talk."

Clint pulled a "who does he think he is" face behind Shannon's back.

Delaney wasn't feeling warm and fuzzy toward Shannon either. She crossed her arms. "We do. I'd like a quick update."

"As would I."

"Fine. I'll go first. One of your deputies got us a probable cause warrant to search Snow Hare Ranch where we think Leo is being held. As soon as you're finished with us, Clint and I want to take the search dog and our team back out there to serve it. They're the only property that hasn't cooperated with us on this side of the mountains."

"I'll need to swear the two of you in as special deputies for Big Horn County, then."

"No time like the present."

She and Clint raised their right hands and Shannon swore them in.

Delaney said, "Thanks. Now, your turn."

"We haven't come up with an identity yet on your snowmobiler suspect. We're in contact with the family of the murder victim and are reaching out to her friends and co-workers. You know her name is Jackie Spurrier, but she was working under a different name for the last few months in Sheridan. She didn't have any actions pending in Wyoming like charges against exes, complaints about stalking, or restraining orders."

Delaney nodded. No need to tell him her team had all of the same information already. "Have you run across the guy I saw on the slopes? The blond giant?"

"Not as of yet."

She hoped Skeeter was having more luck.

The sheriff continued. "We're having a lot of activity on the trail."

Delaney said, "I hear it."

"In the last hour and a half, there's been a steady stream of snowmobilers coming south to north heading for Elk Ridge and Adelaide Pass and on toward Burgess Junction. My staff have been stopping everyone since yesterday afternoon with instructions to alert me about anything odd. They're looking for men and machines matching the descriptions you gave us, as well as for Leo, of course. No one has passed that has raised their suspicions, but the sheer volume has us concerned."

"What's going on?"

"They claim to have been on a men's winter camping retreat."

"With what organization?"

"No organization. Just friends."

"How many?"

"Forty so far."

Delaney didn't think she'd had forty friends in her entire life. "That's a lot of friends. Do they have gear?"

"Quite a bit of it."

"Are you getting names and contact information?"

"We are."

But there was no way to check veracity without detaining all of them. Not since they had no phone connection from the mountains. "It's giving me a bad feeling."

"That's not all." The sheriff looked like he had eaten a bag of bolts.

Delaney's stomach tightened.

"The game warden has been getting calls about a helicopter on the west side of the mountains."

"From where to where?"

"Heading off the mountains."

"From. Where. To. Where," she repeated, with emphasis.

"Not really any idea. It's not in the air anymore that we can tell."

She started shaking her head and gnashing her teeth.

"I'm upset, too, but hear me out. The reason people were calling it in to the game warden is because they thought someone was herding wildlife." Herding wildlife by aircraft or any means was illegal. That didn't stop outfitters and property owners from trying, though. Out-of-state hunters paid big bucks for a chance at a trophy elk or big horn sheep.

"Did no one up here see or hear it?" She turned to her temporary partner. "Clint?"

Clint gave an eyebrow-up wide-eyed shrug. "All I've heard is the snowmobile regatta. I didn't see a thing."

"Convenient timing."

"The thought occurred to me as well," the sheriff said.

"If I were a suspicious person, I'd think this was precipitated by our first visit to Snow Hare, Delaney," Clint said.

All Delaney said was "Dammit, dammit, dammit," as she ran for her snowmobile.

THIRTY

Clint and Buck, one of the Big Horn County deputies, served the warrant on the surly and sole occupant of the lodge at Snow Hare Ranch. Or at least he claimed to be alone. Since the guy—who had now provided ID in the name of Mark Scarpetta—had earlier told Delaney there was a "we" at the lodge, Clint wasn't sure whether to believe him or not.

"I don't have the authority to say yes to this," Mark said.

Buck—tall, thin, and stooped—snorted. "You don't have the authority to say no to it. We have the right to do it with or without anyone's permission or presence. In fact, if you do anything to obstruct Big Horn County from fully enforcing the warrant, we'll arrest you. And if you don't put that gun away, I'll arrest you anyway."

"The hell you will." Mark tightened his grip on the stock of the gun, but his eyes were darting around nervously, looking for help that apparently wasn't coming.

"I have too much to do to keep arguing with you."

Mark lowered the gun.

"Here's your copy." Buck handed him the warrant.

Mark took the warrant and pretended to read it, which was difficult with a shotgun still hanging from the crook of his arm.

"Clint, you got this?"

"I do," Clint said. "Thanks, Buck."

"I'm going to check on things outside." Buck walked out the front door.

"Take all the time you want. I'll just be getting started in here," Clint said, sidling past Mark and his gun, then pausing.

The gun came up and swung around toward Clint. "Stop. You can't do that."

Clint's hand shot out, grabbed the gun just above the stock, and twisted it out of Mark's hands. "Mark Scarpetta, put your hands on your head and stand with your feet hip width apart. Are you carrying any other weapons?"

Mark's hands came up in a fighting stance for a moment, then they fell. Slowly, he raised them. "What the hell?" He moved his feet into position.

"Are you carrying any other weapons?"

"No."

Clint patted him down. He removed a holstered handgun. "Don't lie to a cop, Marky Mark. Now, you're under arrest for aggravated assault and battery for drawing and threatening to use that firearm on me, Mr. Scarpetta."

"This is bullshit."

"Put your wrists together in front of you."

"The hell I will."

"Great. Behind you then. You've got until the count of right now to do it before I charge you with resisting arrest."

Mark began spewing a litany of unpleasant slurs against Clint's race, chosen profession, and person in general while complying with his instruction. Clint put flexicuffs around his wrists and made sure he wasn't gentle.

"I'm going to read you your rights. You need to shut up and

listen." He recited them to Mark then said, "Do you understand these rights as I have told them to you?"

"Whatever."

"My bodycam will confirm that they were read to you. Now, if you'll have a seat here..." He took Mark to the kitchen by his elbow. The room reeked of rotten garbage and unwashed dishes. Clint guided Mark into a chair where he used another flexicuff to secure him in place.

He needed to get outside, but he couldn't leave Mark alone. Delaney had been a jackrabbit's whisker from coming undone ever since she'd learned about the helicopter and the mass exodus of snowmobilers. He should be out there with her, whether he was the one she wanted by her side or not. But Delaney and Leslie weren't set up for Ace to work yet, and the rest of the team of deputies and city cops they'd gathered to search the buildings on foot and the property on snowmobile and snowshoe were also still in prep mode. He also suspected Mark held a caretaker role and was the custodian of the keys to all the places on the property they'd want to search.

Outside, Clint heard the sounds of a very agitated dog.

He pointed at Mark. "You're coming with me and we're going to find another cop to go with you to unlock every door in this compound. Every single one. And don't make me come back for another conversation about adding more charges against you."

He cut Mark free from the chair and frogmarched him outside to see what Ace was so upset about.

THIRTY-ONE

THE NIGHT BEFORE

Tabby hooked her knee then tucked her stiletto-clad foot around the pole. She held on with one hand and leaned over, arching her back, letting her long hair fall. She wasn't thinking about the pole, even though the routine was strenuous and difficult to pull off while almost naked. She was wondering if she was going to get lung cancer from the secondhand smoke she was breathing. The e-cigarette trend had helped, but manly men in the west still lit up. The heat was suffocating, too. The manager of XstaC overcompensated for the constant influx of cold Montana air with the comings and goings of patrons.

She couldn't believe she was back to this life. Lap dances for low rollers in a blue-collar town. Singles, fives, tens, and the occasional twenty tucked in her thong. Once a guy had actually retrieved his twenty and lurched out in a drunken huff when she had informed him club rules prevented him from touching her.

Her time in purgatory over, she climbed offstage with her head high, picturing herself as a model on a catwalk a world away in Milan. Then a roughneck or railroad guy or something like that motioned her over as his friends whooped and pounded a table. He waved his stack of ones and fives like she was going to swoon over them. *Fat chance.*

The bubble of Milan burst in her mind. *Still in Helena.* Tabby imagined she was an actress playing a dancer in a movie, instead of herself working as one in real life. She sauntered to the table. *I am Jennifer Lopez.*

"Give us a lap dance, sweetheart," the man said. He leaned back with his legs spread and arms behind his head.

So, she began, disassociating, performing a memorized dance she'd perfected to convince each recipient he was special and that it wasn't being done by rote. Her mind floated away as small bills accumulated on her hips. *And the Academy Award goes to...*

Even as she acted her heart out, a little voice inside her told her this wasn't good. But it was still better than what her life had turned into with *him*. The violence. The humiliation. The control. The fear. Every night since she'd escaped, she'd been having nightmares, not just about what he did to her, but about women like her. The dreams were so vivid, she had started to believe the women had been real. And in her dreams, they were running away from him, like her, only they got caught. Always. Most nights, she woke sweating and terrified right before he killed them. The worst version was when she dreamed about a girl who was hiding in the barn. He'd found her there. She'd fought him with an old metal rake. The tines dug into his cheek and dragged bloody gaping wounds into his flesh. She didn't wake up in time and he killed the girl with the rake she'd used on him.

That nightmare was a screamer. Just thinking about it made her miss a step, but the horny guys didn't seem to notice.

So, yeah, she had to dance, because she had to make money as fast as she could. Some things had gone right for her. The kind older woman who had picked her up on the side of that mountain road in her SUV had offered her a place to stay in her guest house until Tabby could get on her feet. Tabby had said yes and thank you please. Now she was saving up for a bus ticket home, to West Virginia, which sounded like heaven to her. Why had she ever left in the first place?

And she was getting close. So close. If she had a good week, she'd leave next Monday.

Her routine ended to leers and catcalls. Dirty one-dollar bills jutted at obscene angles from the strings on her hips. She smiled with her mouth, like a wooden puppet, and firmly pushed grabby hands away from her butt.

That bus ticket could not come soon enough.

THIRTY-TWO

"What kind of alert is this one?" Delaney asked.

Ace was barking and pawing the ground at the end of his leash. Delaney wanted to bark and paw with the canine. But Leslie had told them earlier that Ace alerted in different ways for different finds, since he also was trained for cadavers. She really prayed this was for a live find.

Leslie issued a few firm commands to Ace, then released him. The dog circled, almost pretzeling his body as he wound up like a spring then bounded across the snow, past the house, and toward an old log barn with a new red metal roof.

Leslie lumbered after him in big, heavy boots. She shouted back, "He's on the scent we gave him."

Delaney started running, too. She was glad the place had been plowed so there were only a few inches of snow cover on most of the ground, although the wind had blown up a few taller drifts. The altitude didn't help. As it was, her heart was pounding out of her chest and she could barely breathe, but most of that was emotion. Because she knew what Ace was excited about. *Leo. Ace is on to Leo.*

Leslie reached the barn first, where Ace was trying to scratch a hole in the door. There was a padlock holding it closed. "Who's got the keys?"

Clint came running up behind them. "The caretaker, Mark Scarpetta. I had to put him under arrest. Long story. He's with one of my officers getting his keys. We shouldn't wait on them." He whistled to get the attention of one of his officers. "Come cut this for us," he shouted, waving him over.

Devon Peele—a blond, short, and stocky Kearny officer Delaney had worked with in the past—unstrapped long-handled metal cutters from a snowmobile and trotted over. He made quick work of the U bolts the lock was attached to. The lock fell to the ground.

"Thank you," Delaney said.

Clint and Devon pulled the doors open. Ace sprinted inside. Leslie gave him room to work but stayed close behind him. Delaney paced her.

"Hey, don't be cutting our locks," the caretaker shouted. *Mark?* He and a Greybull cop had entered the barn.

"Exigent circumstances," Clint said. "Five-dollar piece of hardware on a five-million-dollar property. It's going to be all right, Mark."

Ace wasn't showing indecision or hesitation. He made his way to a storeroom door and repeated his pawing maneuver. Every fiber of Delaney's being was feeling that dog. She wanted to lower herself to her knees and scratch through with her fingernails beside him.

"Leo!" she shouted. "Leo, are you in there?"

But Leo did not answer.

Leslie said, "You're overdoing it a bit, buddy." To Delaney she said, "He's the most enthusiastic dog I've ever worked with." She tried the door handle. "This one is locked, too."

"Leo!" Delaney called. "If you're in there, we're here. We'll have you out soon."

Still, there was no reply.

"Keys, please," Leslie called.

Clint marched Mark to the door.

"I can't do anything with my hands behind my back," Mark said.

Clint used a pocketknife to cut the flexicuffs. "You're still under arrest."

Mark tried multiple keys, but none worked.

"I don't get it. They must have changed the locks. We didn't have a deadbolt on here before."

"Who's they?" Delaney said.

Mark's eyes shifted down and to the right. "I don't know, man. We get lots of people through. Groups of hunters mostly."

Lie. Delaney tabled it. For now.

Clint rushed the door, putting his weight into it. It didn't give at all. Clint winced and rubbed his shoulder. "It's solid."

"Is there another way in?" Delaney said.

Mark shook his head. "No. No other doors, no windows. No cellar."

"Leo!" she screamed.

There was no answer.

Delaney's panic ratcheted higher. She looked at the door. "We'll take off the hinges, then."

Clint immediately went to a work bench and started rummaging through tools on top of it. "Flat head or Phillips?"

Delaney squinted in the low light. "Phillips."

In seconds, he was back with two of them, one larger than the other. He handed the smaller one to Delaney and kept the other. The two set to work. Delaney's slipped every few turns, a little too small, but workable. Clint's fit and he made a faster job of it.

Ace continued his frenzied efforts to get inside.

"As I'm sure you can tell, there's a very strong scent signature in this room," Leslie said. She issued a command for Ace to settle. He did, a little, but his whine was piteous.

Clint finished his hinge and took over Delaney's. She made a lap of the barn's interior, looking for something to open the door. She heard the second hinge clatter to the concrete floor as she spotted a pry bar. *Perfect.* She grabbed it, ran back to the door, jammed the wedge end into the opening, and pried with her full weight. The door inched outwards. Clint slipped his hands in below the pry bar and began to pull the door.

The lock groaned but held tight at the other edge. However, the door was now open wide enough that the frantic off-task Malinois and the humans were able to shimmy through.

Inside, Ace ran in circles, nose to the ground. Finally, he stopped and sat. He gave one look back at Leslie.

"Good boy." She got out a rubber toy and began playing tug of war with him. "This is how I reward him."

Delaney turned to Leslie. "Would he tell us if Leo was dead? If it had been a dead body here?"

"I think so. He'd be giving me mixed signals at least."

Delaney circled like Ace. The room was completely empty. There was no furniture, no supplies, no equipment, and no Leo. Not even a piece of trash or a discarded glove. But on the ground, the dirt floor was pressed in a shape that suggested a body had lain there.

"He was here. He was here when we were here earlier." Murder in her eyes, she advanced on Mark. Lunged at him, screaming, "You piece of—"

Clint intercepted her, catching her just before she tackled Mark, intent on pummeling him. "Whoa, whoa, whoa. Let's put that energy toward finding him."

"She's crazy. She was attacking me! You all saw her," Mark said.

No one paid attention to him.

Delaney struggled against Clint. "Leo should be with us right now. If it wasn't for him—"

"I didn't do nothing. If he was in here, I didn't know shit." Mark backed up against the wall.

"Where are the people who were here?" Delaney shouted, still pushing against Clint's arms but with less violence.

"They left."

"When?"

"An hour or two ago."

"Why?"

"They said it was time for them to go. They'd already packed up, so they just got the hell out."

"How? How did they get out?"

"Snowmobiles. Snow cats."

Clint said, "I don't think we had any snow cats come by on the trail." He released Delaney, but she could feel his eyes on her.

"Which direction did they go?" Delaney said, flexing and closing her fists.

Mark had his hands up and his voice was a lot less tough. "Every direction. It was a big group."

"And the snow cat?"

"I think it went on the road out to Big Bear Park. Away from the trails and Mockingbird Creek."

"How far to the park?"

"A few miles."

She lowered her voice to a lethal whisper. "Who are they, Mark?"

"I swear, I don't know. I stay away from the people onsite. I just take orders over phone and email. They don't tell me nothing."

Delaney closed her eyes. Then she pushed past the door and out of the storeroom. For the first time, she clocked the mess of the main barn. All the items she hadn't seen in the storeroom she found there, especially trash. Trash for the officers to search. People had been here. People had left in a hurry.

The others had gathered behind her.

She turned to face them. "The helicopter Shannon told us about. The snow cat to Big Bear Park. My money is on Leo being taken out of here on that helicopter, down the mountains to the west. But why? With who? And where is he now?"

Back at Mockingbird Creek nearly two hours later, Delaney paced, fumed, and cursed as she waited outside for Sheriff Wilcox to arrive, her head still filled with the horrifying vision of the two long, narrow helicopter skids she'd seen in the snow of Big Bear Park. They'd been next to an abandoned snow cat. She felt certain that Leo had left the mountain on a helicopter with persons unknown for reasons unknown to parts unknown. But if he had, Ace had not been able to confirm it. Leslie called it inconclusive. She said that sometimes happened if the scent exposure had been indirect and brief.

Mark Scarpetta had been taken down to the Big Horn County Sheriff's Department for questioning and processing into their jail. They could hold him for forty-eight business hours pending a decision whether to press charges. The clock was ticking to get information from him. So far, he was refusing to speak without a lawyer present. He'd been given his one phone call. Now they waited for his attorney to arrive.

Meanwhile, officers were still searching Snow Hare Ranch and would be for many hours. Leslie and Ace had stayed as well. She said it was a great place to do a few training exercises, if they didn't mind. They did not.

Delaney and Clint had radioed for assistance and had officers contact every airport within range of where the helicopter could have flown from and to that day, no matter the size. None of them had any helpful information. If it had fueled up, taken off, or landed, it wasn't at an airport they had been able to identify.

Drew's voice came over Caitlin's radio.

"Yes?" Delaney said, her voice like an ax.

"I've got a federal agent in the lobby here demanding to meet with you," Drew said.

She didn't need the feds slowing them down. "Send them to Sheriff Wilcox."

"I don't think that will work. He's Special Agent Clark Applewood. He's with—"

"He's with the ATF."

"Alcohol, Tobacco, Firearms, and Explosives. Yes. He said you know him?"

"Oh, I know him. Take your radio out to him. It's the only way he's going to get to talk to me."

"Okay. He's kind of a superior jerk, by the way."

"You just described every federal agent I've ever met."

"My ex isn't so bad."

Delaney remembered his former girlfriend was FBI out of Casper. She'd even helped them once. "The exception that proves the rule."

"Okay, here's Special Agent Applewood."

"This is Deputy Investigator Pace," Delaney said.

"—is a private conversation, Deputy Knowles." It was Clark's voice.

"I'm not leaving my radio." The cut-off in Clark's words seemed to indicate that Drew was holding the mic button down himself.

Delaney sighed. "Clark, I don't have time for this. If you want to talk to me, it's under our terms. I'm not within an hour of phone signal, and my radio signal is in and out. Make up your mind and make it fast."

She saw Clint take notice of the conversation and begin walking toward her.

After a few clicks, Clark spoke in an annoyed voice. "Your co-worker isn't read in for this. Neither are you, but I was going to make an exception."

Clint was now standing beside her, and his eyebrows were halfway up his forehead.

She rolled her eyes at him and shook her head. She didn't let Clark know that yet another person who was not "read in" was now party to their conversation. "I'm interrupting the search for my partner to speak to you. You've got five seconds to convince me not to turn my radio off."

"Fine. We have a confidential informant who saw Leo Palmer today."

She froze. "What did you say?"

"You heard me."

She was losing her patience fast with him. "Where?"

"Somewhere he is not anymore."

"Where is he now?" she yelled.

Clint moved back a step.

"Our CI doesn't know. The CI saw him several hours ago. The CI gave him and a few other people a ride."

"Did it involve a helicopter?"

"I don't know."

"Clark, who has Leo?"

"That information is classified as it has national security implications. I wanted to let you know we'll handle it from here."

"Handle what?"

"The kidnapping of your sheriff. Anyone outside the team authorized by the ATF needs to back off."

"The hell I'll back off." She gritted her teeth. "The next time I see you, you'll understand how many fucks I give about your national security implications, in a very personal way. Where the hell is Leo? Who has him? No more shit. If you didn't want me to know, you wouldn't have contacted me."

"We've talked about the lack of wisdom in threatening a federal agent before. I thought we might discuss a way for you to get that clearance, so I could tell you more."

"You're using *this* to manipulate me? You are a morally bankrupt son of a bitch." She was screaming now. Her voice cracked. "Tell me. Tell me or I swear, I'll—"

Clint grabbed the mic from her hands. Her colorful threat never reached Clark's ears.

She balled her fists and glared at Clint.

He pressed the button to talk. "Kearny Police Chief Clint Rock-Below here. This sounds like obstruction of justice. From what I am hearing, your confidential informant has confirmed our fear that the sheriff of our county has been abducted. A fellow law enforcement officer. The best course of action seems to be to work together to make sure he comes home safe."

"Not if it compromises our investigation. If he were here, I'm sure he'd tell you that."

"Well, he's not, so we can't be sure of anything. Except that you seemed willing to overlook that if Delaney would do something for you."

"Honestly, I didn't realize she had me on blast for everyone in Wyoming to hear."

"They're called radios. They're all we have up here. And I'm willing to testify to what I just heard. I'd imagine Deputy Knowles is as well. In the meantime, we'll need a helluva lot more than a radio call from someone claiming to be a federal agent to halt our search."

The door to the cabin flew open. Caitlin burst out, head moving back and forth. It stopped when she saw Delaney, and she ran toward her. She was speaking rapidly into her mic, eyes locked on Delaney's the whole way. The look in them was sheer panic.

Delaney forgot all about Clark Applewood.

"What is it?" she said to Caitlin. "What?"

Not Leo. Please, not Leo. She braced herself, terrified of what she was about to hear.

Caitlin stopped just short of Delaney. She was speaking into a mic and carrying the unit in her arms, since Delaney was actually wearing Caitlin's radio. "I have Delaney right here." Then, to Delaney she said, "It's your daughter. Clara helped her radio up to us."

Delaney felt her mouth drop. It wasn't what she'd expected. She threw her shoulders back, a conscious effort to recenter herself. She wasn't going to let Kat or Carrie experience this version of her. The one reeling from her conversation with Clark Applewood in disbelief, anger, and desperation. The one who was shaken to her core and scared to her marrow that Leo was gone, gone, GONE. They needed her to be the strong one. But how much longer could she pretend she was that person when the man she loved had been taken from her? She'd been through loss before. With her mom. Then her dad. She'd held so tightly to her heart in fear of a moment exactly like this one. *But right now isn't about you.* She took a few deep breaths, counting up four, down four, up four, down four, then said, "Carrie? Or Kat?"

Caitlin adjusted the channels on Delaney's radio. "Here you go. It's Clara with Kateena."

Thank you, Delaney mouthed at her.

Caitlin returned to the cabin.

"Melaney? Are you there?" Kat's melodic, high-pitched voice filled the air.

The sound made her feel strangely weak. Leo was not the only person she loved and who loved her. She had this beautiful girl, and she had Carrie. *You are not alone. You cannot forget that you are not alone.* "Hey, sweetie. It's me. How are you?"

"We got cut off."

"Yes. I lost signal in the mountains. Are you okay?"

"Well, kind of not really. You know that strange number that was texting me?"

"Yes. The one I told you not to text back."

"You did? Well, I didn't hear that part. I asked who it was. She said she was my grandmother."

That was... weird. "Your mother's mother?" Delaney didn't know anything about Lila Pace's family, other than she'd been told Lila had cut off contact with all of them in her early twenties when she'd married Liam, who they hadn't liked, for good reason it turned out. He'd killed their daughter and held his own daughter and Carrie hostage. Delaney had reached out to the family when Lila passed and learned her father's death had preceded hers. Her mother had declined to come to the funeral or meet Kateena. Delaney had written her off. She'd been down a similar road before. She'd do everything she could to protect Kat from the pain of that rejection.

"I don't think so. She said that Liam was her son. So, that's *Dad's* mother. Your mother. You and Skeeter were looking for her, right? So, like, maybe he found her?"

The man grimaced and moved the phone an inch further from his ear. He was trapped in a vehicle racing west along the Interstate with a woman shouting at him from all the way across the country. Could the others hear her shoveling shit on him and see that he was having to eat it? Rage flowed through him like an advancing lava flow. He barely registered as they crossed the Yellowstone River, which he normally liked to check for ice and water level. He didn't stop at a dispensary, even though pain from breaking his femur in a training exercise a few years back was making him want to chew off his own fingers.

Her diatribe was continuing. "I have a career and another life. I will not let you take me down with your mess."

"My brother's mess. Again," the man said through gritted teeth. Losing his temper with her did no good. Arguing with her was a losing proposition. The only thing that worked was not talking to her at all.

"Under your watch. Again. And oh, by the way, that phone number no one is supposed to know about has twenty missed calls." She paused to reload.

He wanted to scream at her that she was ungrateful, had a

short memory, and owed him for the cush life she had in her fancy townhouse with a maid and car service. It was him who footed the bills for her degrees at private schools. "It's been a series of unfortunate events."

"You were camped out at Snow Hare Lodge for the last two months. I let you stay there. And now it's crawling with cops who are looking for *you*."

"Slight correction. They're looking for one of us. But it isn't me." What he didn't tell her, couldn't tell her, was what they were likely to find. She could disclaim knowledge. Hell, she'd never set foot on the place as far as he knew. But shit was about to go down. He'd deal with it when it did. One crisis at a time.

Her voice changed to a hiss. "Seriously, what the *hell* is going on now?"

"You need plausible deniability."

"That's just great. Well, you promised me he wouldn't be a problem anymore. If you can't handle it, I'll find someone who can. Someone less costly."

Less costly? That was rich, coming from half a married couple whose combined household income was mid seven figures annually. But it was that money and their reputation that provided the shield for all of them and was the reason he was ready to grovel now. "You have my word of honor. My days of complacency with him are over. He's not just a problem. He's a danger." He didn't mind if everyone in the vehicle overheard this. He wanted his brother to feel his wrath, his disdain. He wanted him to feel like the worm he was. If he hadn't seen their mother pregnant with him, he'd never have believed they shared any DNA. He was half convinced a genetic test would show they had different fathers. "But, in the meantime, we need a place to hole up."

"You and the whole group?"

"No. We instituted the Covey protocol." They had many protocols, meticulously planned out in case of a variety of foreseeable problems, most having to do with anticipated government raids after their group had been involved in different kinds of public *disturbances*—their operations. In this case, they'd scattered like a covey of quail in all directions. They would each fall back to the safety of their home bases and rally when he called them back, later.

"Who, then?"

"Just four of us."

"I asked you *who* will be staying at my property if I make it available to you."

Wealth had turned her into a real bitch. He smiled to keep from responding in the way he wanted to. "Little brother, unfortunately, plus my number two and his guest." His number two—who was driving the truck they'd picked up out of storage—nodded in acknowledgement. The sheriff was gagged and bound on the floorboard of the backseat.

"The same number two I sent you last year?"

She never misses a chance to take credit for anything. "Yes, your former client. And I appreciate it."

She huffed. "I'm hearing about some cop who went missing. That wasn't you, was it?"

Her phrasing sucked for her and allowed him to answer truthfully. "No, it was not." *It was my dumbass brother.* He also decided not to tell her how much pleasure he was going to get out of killing the cop and his girlfriend, when their roles were over. Something slow and painful.

The dumbass brother in question was sitting sideways in the backseat, feet up, picking his teeth with a half-bitten fingernail, a bitter look in his glazed eyes because he'd been told he couldn't smoke in the truck. Now the whole interior smelled like rotten eggs, and it was an easy bet he was polluting it on purpose.

"This is the last time."

"Thank you. I won't forget it."

"Seriously. I will not bail you out for him again. Not in this lifetime or any other."

"Don't worry. I won't ask you to."

"In fact, this is the last time you're staying anywhere my name is associated with. The murder of young women isn't in the mission statement."

Public murder. "Wait a damn second. That eliminates basically all our sites."

"Not my problem."

He seethed, grinding his teeth. "Is this you speaking or that white glove featherweight you married?"

A voice that was lower but not by much said, "This call has ended. We'll send you the information, encoded."

"I wasn't aware I was on speaker."

Her voice again. "You were recorded, too."

"You're my attorney and my fixer. Don't do this."

The line went dead.

He screamed so loud and hard that his lips stretched taut, and his jaw trembled. Then he calmed and let his face go slack. They had a safe place to stay, or soon would. That was all that mattered. For now.

THIRTY-FIVE

Delaney dropped to her butt in the snow, like her legs had liquified. Fabiola Pace. *No.* It couldn't be her. The delicate gold anklet with the dangling cross burned against her skin under her wool socks, a gift from her mother. She wore it on days when she leaned toward a belief that her mother was dead and hadn't left her. Now she was barely able to find the words to answer Kat. "We were looking but Skeeter couldn't find her. People can trick you on text and online. Unless you're face to face, you don't really know who you're talking to."

"But she knew me. It wasn't like some random stranger. It could be her, right?"

Delaney tore off her glove, stuck her hand in the snow, then put the coldness on her face. "I don't know." She felt like all the warmth in her body had seeped away except in her face, leaving her as nothing but a cold empty shell with a head on fire. Her mother. After all this time. On Kat's phone.

Clint sat down beside her. He held out his hand. She shook her head. He was too touchy-feely lately. She didn't want sympathy. She didn't want to be touched. She got up and moved away from him.

"She said she has to talk to you. She asked me for your phone number."

I don't have time for a mommy-daughter reunion now. "Kat..."

"She said it was a matter of life or death."

The manipulation after all this time should have made her mad, but instead it made her feel tired. She needed to find her fire, end this conversation, and get back to the search for Leo. But all she managed to say was, "She had twenty-five years to try to find me. Her emergency is not mine right now."

"OK. I'll tell her."

Delaney leaned down, scooped up snow, and applied it directly to her forehead. "No. Don't tell her anything. Don't talk to her anymore. If it even is her." *If it's not her, how would this person know to impersonate Fabi? Whether it's her or not, how did they get Kat's number?* Kat. Carrie. Her daughters. If someone was contacting Kat, were they watching her, too? She had to call Skeeter. Ask him to trace the number, find the caller. She had to get protection in place for the girls. Move them to a safer place. Block the caller's number. *Oh, God. How can I do everything all at once?*

"Oops. Sorry, I type too fast. I already did."

"Kat! You have to stop."

"Wait. She's typing a reply."

"Stop engaging with her, Kat. Now, I'm sorry, but I have to go. Things are really tense here. I'm going to send Skeeter over to help you, if I can."

"Melaney?" Kat's voice sounded funny. Less her breezy self. Like she'd had the wind punched out of her.

"What's wrong?"

"She said I should read something to you."

"Fine. But then that's it. I really have to go."

"Okay. Um. But I feel weird reading this."

"Just do it. You'll be okay."

Kat cleared her throat. In a voice that wavered, she said, "*Delaney, it's about Leo. Call me if you ever want to see him alive again.*"

Delaney dropped the mic, horror-stricken. Her mother. Her mother was involved in Leo's kidnapping. *No.* It made no sense. It could *not be.*

But before she even had time to process it, Clint was in her face. "Not now, Clint," she snapped. She fumbled for the dangling mic and tried to walk away again.

He blocked her, and she wanted to punch him.

"This had better be critical information to interrupt me with my child."

He looked straight into her eyes, unwavering, unblinking. "The Snow Hare Lodge team just radioed in. Ace and Leslie just found two buried bodies. Fresh, unmarked graves. And they said to tell you it looks like there may be more."

Delaney shook her head, trying to catch up. Unmarked graves. New ones. At the ranch where the murderer of a young woman had fled to. Where Leo had been only a short time ago.

Leo... *Dear God, don't let it be Leo!!* Kat's texter had suggested he was alive. Who knew who she really was, though, and what was true?

And then two words popped into her head unbidden.

Serial killer.

THIRTY-SIX
THREE HOURS EARLIER

Drew hung up the phone from his latest futile call, which he'd squeezed in amongst the other activities and requests that were bombarding him. With the acting sheriff and the police chief out of cell phone range yet leading the effort to find Leo, he was de facto coordinator for non-radio communications. It was his job to protect them, too. He had to solve the problems and stop people from insisting on speaking only with them.

He sighed, ticking items on his whiteboard. His personal to-do list wasn't daunting on the face of it. Find out about these trustees and track down any ties to the white snow suits. He'd delegated social media and public relations to Clara. Skeeter was investigating Jackie's past to find possible murder–kidnappers lurking there. What didn't appear on the board was managing them and the coordinator role, plus communications with the team on the mountain. It made it really hard to get to his list. His stress was high, and this situation wasn't even twenty-four hours old. He needed a punishing workout and a serious sweat, but he wasn't going to get it. Short of that, forget-the-world sex would help. That was also not going to be on the table. Adri was shattered about Leo's disappearance. Not being there for her now when she needed him was adding to his stress.

Back to the calls.

He'd given up on the number he'd found for the lodge on Snow Hare Ranch originally, which he'd discovered when he crosschecked it matched the one in the state filings for Far West LLC and Far West Trust. He'd called it nearly twenty times. There was no voicemail on it, and, if it was capturing his incoming number, no one had bothered to call him back. Maybe it was unmonitored or out of date. The name of the registered agent was a no-go, too. When he googled the name—Leticia Letourneau—there was no such person in Wyoming. Or, by that spelling, anywhere, much less at the Cheyenne address given.

Thus, he was trying to reach the only humans he could find associated with Snow Hare Ranch. Those were the trustees of Far West Trust, which owned Far West LLC, which owned the ranch itself. It was so confusing that he'd drawn a picture of the relationship on the flipside of the whiteboard.

There were three trustees. He'd found some info about them online, at least about their professions. Elan Mitchell was a billionaire who made his money in gun manufacturing. Inherited it, rather, as a great-grandfather on his mother's side was one of the most famous names in the history of firearms. Greg Sones owned a political consulting company. Tanya Sones was an attorney. He hadn't dug far enough to uncover a familial relationship between Greg and Tanya, but he expected to since they shared a last name. The trustees shared a common trait— they didn't exist online beyond sterile professional bios without reference to where they lived, their marital status, or whether they had children, pets, hobbies, or—more helpful—criminal records. No social media presence, no lifestyle interviews, no glowing testimonials about them.

He'd switched to trying to contact the trustees directly. He had numbers for what he thought were their offices, which tossed him into automated systems and left him unable to leave messages or talk to humans. He'd filled out online contact forms asking to be put in touch with them. He'd tried to find home numbers but gotten nowhere on that.

It didn't help that it was a Sunday. Even normal people would be hard to reach on their downtime. Was he going to have to show up on their doorsteps? If he could even find their homes. He lowered his head to his desk with a thunk. Then he lifted it. *No. I call the local cops and ask for their help if it comes to that.*

Feeling buoyed by eliminating this avenue of doom, he flipped over to his browser. He'd found what might be a home address for Elan. It was, in a word, palatial. A mansion overlooking Potomac Bay. But was it his home? And if so, how likely was it that he'd be there as opposed to one of the many other homes a billionaire probably had? He would have to find them all. It was shaping up to be a time-consuming process with a low probability of success. Even as he contemplated the crushing load, he fielded a string of seven phone calls.

Clara. The property research was a job for her. The properties the trustees owned individually, the properties owned by the trust and the LLC. He drafted an email asking for her help then walked to her desk.

When he reached her, she looked up and said, "On it already."

He wiggled his fingers at her. "Look at you. Any questions?"

"Nope."

"That was easy."

She nodded. "Shoo. I'm working."

He glanced at the time on the phone above her desk. Eleven a.m. Whatever he was going to do, he had to get some food and a nap. His low battery warning was down to one percent. His brain had gone into power-saving mode hours ago. He patted his pockets. He had his phone, keys, and wallet. "Hey, I'm going to run home for a shower and a half-hour nap."

She didn't take her eyes from her keyboard. "You look like you need it."

He didn't think he would feel like laughing about anything today, but her words broke through, and he did. "See you in a bit."

After yesterday's darkness during the storm and twenty-four hours spent in the station, walking outside to brilliant sunshine was disconcerting. He'd left his sunglasses in his truck and had to squint away the rays. His boots crunched the packed snow in the parking lot and then on the sidewalk as he made the five-minute walk to his house. He wished he'd driven in, because the cold air was waking him up.

As he reached the front walkway to his house, though, tiredness hit again. He'd pass on food for now and just hit the rack.

The front door flew open. Adriana stood in the doorway wearing tight jeans and a faded red T-shirt that hugged her curves. She put her fists on her hips. "I've been calling and texting."

The morning had been so intense that he'd ignored all personal calls and messages. "I'm sorry. I've been focused only on your brother." He wiped his feet on the door mat.

"Did you find him?"

"Not yet."

"Tell me the truth. Did this happen because of her?"

"Her?"

"Delaney."

"It appears that he hit a moose and that someone... gave him a ride... somewhere."

"Are you being obtuse on purpose?"

"There's a lot we don't know yet. Give us time, Adri. Everyone is working hard to find him."

She waved her hand like she was clearing away smoke. "I

know her, Leo. I need you to tell me the truth. Is he missing because of her?"

He thought about what he'd been told. That Delaney had ridden ahead of Leo in that middle-of-the-night blizzard. She was a rule breaker. A risk taker. He would never have gotten away with pulling a stunt like that, but Delaney got results.

And she's Leo's girlfriend.

His thinking pause was just a little too long.

"I knew it! I knew it was her fault!" Adriana was shaking her head and pointing at the street. "You're the only one I can count on, Drew. You have to go back. Go back and don't come back until you find him." Then she swayed like an aspen tree in the wind for a moment before crumpling into his arms and sobbing.

And Drew knew that he would skip sleep and food and anything else this woman asked him to for as long as she needed, if it would keep her from crying like this.

THIRTY-SEVEN

Delaney white knuckled Leo's truck out of the mountains from Elk Ridge toward Kearny. After the radio conversation with Kat and hearing about the unmarked graves from Clint, she'd been torn. Part of her had wanted to return to Snow Hare Ranch and dig the graves up with her bare hands, but the possibility that Leo was alive spurred her to instead race her snowmobile back to the ski resort, load it in Leo's truck, and use her spare set of keys to drive home, ten miles over the speed limit the whole way —a feat in the winter with snow still on the steep, winding roads. Clint and Caitlin were tailing her and having trouble keeping up. A platoon of officers remained at Snow Hare Ranch processing the avalanche of evidence from the people who had recently vacated the property and around the graves.

While it was circumstantial, Delaney believed it was possible there was a serial killer at work here. Not just the murderer of one young woman, but the murderer of multiple other people. *Just as long as it's not Leo.* People buried their grandma in the back forty sometimes. Maybe they didn't get a death certificate to avoid probate or taxation or out of ignorance. Alarm bells were ringing across northern Wyoming. Across the state. Sheriff Wilcox's eyes had been bugging out of his face when she'd left. He may have been secretly thrilled to handle a single murder case, but a potential serial killer in his county? He was wading in quicksand without anyone around to pull him out.

She held the steering wheel firm as the tires squealed around a curve. So, who knew? Maybe the sheriff would luck out and there would be innocent reasons behind the back-country burials. In the end, it would not be her case. But her heart didn't seem to be getting that message, and she just couldn't wrap her head around Kat's texter. The one who hinted Leo was alive. Her mother. If it really *was* Fabiola Pace. Which would be surreal. Insane.

Delaney pumped the brakes to slow down quickly for a hairpin curve. Luckily, the pavement was dry. She smelled burning rubber. As soon as she came out the turn, though, her mind took off again. Why hadn't this person contacted her directly? Did they not have access to her number? All she had—outside of work—was a mobile number. Same for Kat. It's not like mobile numbers were part of a public directory. Someone who knew Kat's number must be behind this. Either directly or indirectly through passing it along. It could have been as innocent as a group chat or responding to a request from a trusted person. Or it could have been something more sinister. Could be *someone* more sinister. A bully. A predator. Or both.

Delaney had to face an ugly possibility. It could be Liam Pace.

The trees were thinning, and her ears were popping. She checked her phone for signal, desperate to initiate the call to the number Kat had given her. No bars yet.

She'd never once thought about Liam having Kat's phone number. In guilt and horror, she realized Kat probably had the same number now as before she lost her parents.

Big miss. Big, big miss.

If Liam was alive... if this *was* Liam... or if Liam was behind this... Delaney didn't know what to think. What to do.

She negotiated a sharp left curve against a north wind that caught her broadwise and buffeted the truck. Caitlin and Clint weren't visible in her rearview mirror anymore. Ahead of her was a straightaway into the little town of Dayton. She checked for phone signal. Two bars. Finally.

First things first. "Siri, text Skeeter." She dictated a text asking him to trace the number.

Then on to the harder thing, and Siri couldn't help with that. Taking a deep breath, she typed in the number with one hand, glancing back and forth at the road, caring about safety a little only because of Leo and her girls. If she hit an elk or a mule deer that decided to cross the road while she was driving seventy-five miles an hour downhill, who would make this call? Who would find Leo?

Certainly not that asswipe Clark Applewood.

The number began to ring through the speakers. The ringing ended when the call was picked up on the other end. There was a tinny quality to the sound. No one spoke.

"Who is this?" Delaney said.

After a slight delay, a distorted voice. "Is this Delaney Pace?" *Voice changing app.*

"I asked first."

"This is your mother."

The words packed an emotional wallop, even in the unrecognizable, robotic voice. "I highly doubt that."

"It is."

"What do you want?"

"I want to talk to you about Leo."

"Then be honest with me about who you are."

"I am."

It took every bit of Delaney's self-control to fight back the urge to scream, to lash out, to tell this machine or person or animal how much Fabiola Pace had hurt her. She needed information from this conversation, not to make herself feel better. "Prove it."

"How?"

"Tell me something only the two of us know."

"It was so long ago."

Delaney's voice dripped sarcasm like ice cream down a cone in August. "You're telling me."

"My memory is not what it once was. I'm an old woman now."

"Middle-aged, not old. You're fine."

The sigh was a gust of wind in Delaney's ear. "Okay. You had a stuffed dragon that watched you while you slept to protect you from the monsters under your bed."

How could her words wring every feeling at once from Delaney? Sadness. Hope. Love. Anger. Fear. Because the only people who could have known about the dragon were family. The dragon she'd buried behind the barn six months after her mother had disappeared. No matter who this was, they were connected to someone from her past who should have loved her and cared for her but did not. "Lots of people knew that. They could have told you. It wasn't only you and me."

"To prove to you that your dragon was a good dragon, I sewed a silver heart inside and told you that the dragon had my heart. It was the pendant your father gave me when you were born, and you'd always loved it. We made a pact never to tell anyone because I was afraid it would hurt his feelings."

Sweat beaded on Delaney's forehead. Her hands suddenly felt slick on the wheel. She slowed the truck and pulled over on the side of the road, afraid she was going to throw up.

The woman on the other end of the phone really was her mother.

THIRTY-EIGHT
THREE HOURS EARLIER

Skeeter licked the last of the glaze from a bear claw off his hands, inhaling the cinnamon scent. He'd brought a dozen assorted doughnuts into the station on his way back from Sheridan, but Drew didn't let gluten or processed food pass his lips, and Clara said the sugar would make her crash. He'd had no choice but to eat them himself. He was working in Delaney's colorful cubicle surrounded by her maps—it wasn't somewhere you'd want to be with a hangover, but it was nice—so he brushed his crumbs into the trash. She wouldn't appreciate him leaving her a mess.

Then he drew a breath for courage. He couldn't put it off any longer—he had to call the parents of the girl who had died. There was nothing worse than that kind of sadness.

He dialed the number he'd found for them. It was still Sunday morning church service time in Wyoming, but two hours later in South Carolina.

The phone rang four times before a shaky female voice answered. "Hello?"

"Skeeter Rawlins for Mrs. Spurrier, please." If it had been a man, he would have asked for Mr. Spurrier. He wanted whoever answered to stay on the line.

"This is she. I apologize, but now isn't a very good time. Please call b—"

Skeeter rushed to speak before she could hang up. "I'm with the sheriff's department in Kearny County, Wyoming, ma'am. I'm so sorry for your loss. I need to speak to you about your daughter Jackie."

"We already got a call. We were told she's d-d-d-dead."

"Yes, ma'am, and this is a follow-up."

"You don't sound like you're from Wyoming. Your accent. It's more..."

"Wisconsin."

"I was going to say Minnesota."

Skeeter eyed the doughnut box, then pushed it out of reach. "They're very similar. Ma'am, I need to ask you some questions that will help us find who did this to your daughter."

"What do you mean? We know who did this."

"I'm sorry?" Skeeter put a hand to his forehead. His fingers were sticky. Had he missed an announcement, an arrest?

"Her father and I are quite sure it's that man she went to Montana with."

"Where'd she meet him?"

"Here. In Huntington. He was in town with a load of horses he delivered. She was in high school. She hadn't even graduated yet, and he was a grown man. He preyed on her."

"What was his name?"

"I thought my husband told you this already."

"We ask the same questions. It's a way of making sure none of us miss nothing important."

"Okay. Well, his name is Herb Tilton."

Skeeter scribbled notes. The pen felt awkward in his sticky fingers. "Did you know Mr. Tilton?"

"We met him once. That's when we forbade her to see him.

Two weeks later, she was gone. We never saw her again." She broke into sobs. Loud, wracking, painful sobs.

"Tammy, what the hell's the matter with you?" a man's voice said.

"I'm talking to the police. About Jackie."

"Give me the phone."

Skeeter winced. Lyle's tone with his wife was not nice.

A man's voice spoke sharply. "This is Lyle Spurrier. You've upset my wife. Don't call her again."

"We're just trying to find a killer, Mr. Spurrier. But she said you both think it's Herb Tilton."

"Of course we do."

"Anything in particular to make you believe it was him? Did he make threats? Or did he ever physically hurt her?"

"He forced her to run away from home. She was never the same again. Ended her relationship with her mother, which was very hurtful. Plus, you yourself said she was living in another town under a new name. Do the math."

Skeeter didn't bother explaining that he wasn't the one they'd talked to before who'd said that. Or that the math wasn't clear to him yet, but then again, he'd never passed algebra in high school. All that *solve for* X stuff made his head spin. And he still felt like X was a mystery in this problem. "When was the last time you talked to Jackie?"

"Is that a trick question?"

"No, sir. It's straight up."

"Saturday. She called us Saturday. First time in two years." His voice trembled slightly.

Skeeter stood, surprised. The mother had said... wait, she'd said they hadn't ever seen her again. Not that they'd never talked to her. "Did she talk about Herb?"

"No."

"Or mention having problems with or being worried about anyone or anything?"

"No. She invited her mother and I out to visit her in Wyoming."

Skeeter had thought the mother's tears would be the worst part of this conversation, but he was wrong. The noise Lyle Spurrier made sounded like the death throes of a wolf. Raspy. Loud. Breathless. Skeeter wanted to howl with him.

"I'm sorry," he said, his own voice soft.

And then he ended the call and drew two big stars by the name Herb Tilton.

THIRTY-NINE

"Delaney? Did you hear my answer? Have I passed your test?" Fabi Pace said.

Three mule deer leapt out of a gully beside the highway and bounded across the road, their enormous ears alert for danger.

Delaney put her forehead on her steering wheel. Even with the distorted, robotic voice, she now believed it was her mother. "I'm... I'm here. You've, uh, you've confirmed your identity."

"Is that all you have to say after twenty-plus years?"

"I'm not the one with any explaining to do. But now is not the time for that anyway. Sheriff Leo Palmer. Where is he?"

"You'll get him back if you follow the instructions."

Delaney breathed in bullish snorts through her nose. *Wasting time. She's wasting time. But does this mean he's really alive and not buried at Snow Hare Ranch?* "Where are you, mother?"

"I'm at my home."

"And where is that?"

"If you're trying to ask if Leo is with me, he's not. I've never laid eyes on the man."

Delaney saw flashing blue and white lights in her rearview mirror. Clint and Caitlin had pulled up behind her. "Let's back up. Is this your phone number?"

"Temporarily."

"Whose idea was it to distort your voice?"

"It was set up on the phone this way. I don't know how to change it. I'm not into computers and technology."

"How did you get Kat's number?"

"Kat?"

"Your granddaughter. Kateena. She goes by Kat."

A knock at the window made Delaney turn. Clint was standing outside, his brows knit into deep furrows. She gave him a thumbs-up that she knew didn't match the look on her face, then closed her eyes to concentrate on Fabi, who had said something Delaney didn't catch. "Can you repeat that?"

"It was given to me by someone."

"Okay. Let's just assume that's my *dead* brother for a moment. Why did you contact her?"

"I was asked to. Someone thought it would be the best way to get your attention."

For a split second, Delaney allowed herself to acknowledge her grief and disappointment in this version of her mother. It wasn't just that Fabi had left her to rot in foster care. This woman was an ally of her truly evil son. "You have my attention now. Don't ever text or call her again. I am your sole point of contact with my daughter. Understood?"

"Your daughter? She's Liam's daughter."

"Not according to the State of Wyoming."

"I was hoping to get to know her."

"We will talk about that only when Leo is safely back home. So, let's talk about Leo's return. How do we get him home?"

"I have instructions to read to you."

Delaney shoved her hand into the crown of her hair.

Fabi cleared her throat. "You are to bring a load of items from Calgary across the border."

Delaney gripped her hair. *What in God's name is Liam up to?* "A load of what?"

"Something special."

Code for highly illegal. Code for Liam setting me up for arrest at the border as payback for shooting him? "I don't know what kind of vehicle to drive unless you tell me."

"Um..." Delaney heard rustling paper. "Bring Gabrielle. And a flatbed trailer."

"Great. Now, where am I delivering to?"

The voice sounded like it was reading. "Check back when you're in Canada, and I'll give you pick-up instructions. When you're ready to return, I'll give you partial delivery instructions. When you near the destination, you'll get final instructions. But you have to come alone, and you can't tell anyone. You will be monitored for compliance."

"I'm a deputy. Our sheriff is missing. I'm the acting sheriff. I can't just disappear."

"You'll think of something."

"And if I do everything I'm told?"

"You'll get Leo back."

"Alive? He's not already dead?"

"Yes. Alive."

"Because Liam has him?"

"I didn't say that."

She didn't have to. Liam either had him or had control or influence over whoever did. *Or he's manipulating you, and Leo is buried up at Snow Hare Ranch.* People Delaney had reason to believe had committed not just one but multiple murders. "And if I don't do everything I'm told? Liam is willing to kill a law enforcement officer in cold blood?"

"Delaney, you have the wrong idea about your brother. He

was always a good boy. He took care of me when no one else would for years. He—"

"Spare me the Sermon on the Mount speech. He's not Saint Liam. And the one who had no one to care for them for years was me. Your daughter. Your child."

"You don't understand what they did to me. I was—"

"You were a mother. I was a child. Enough." Her voice rose and she choked it back. Stayed silent and swallowed until she regained control of her emotions. "Back to what matters. I do nothing without proof of life."

"Proof of what?"

"I need proof that Leo is alive, this very second, and at every second during my journey."

"I'll see what I can do."

"Tell Liam this is absolutely non-negotiable."

"I can't—"

Delaney hung up the phone and finally allowed herself a long, primal scream.

FORTY

Standing halfway out in the road, Clint knocked on the driver's side window to get Delaney's attention. The face she turned to him was agitated. But she gave him a thumbs-up. He paused at the back bumper of the truck, now feeling agitated himself. Delaney had been coming out of her skin when they'd left Elk Ridge. He'd offered to drive, but she'd shot him down. He'd acquiesced because he knew she needed space, emotional and physical. Then her driving had been reckless. He hadn't been able to keep up. He'd been convinced they were going to round a bend and see smoke rising from a wrecked truck hundreds of feet below them at the foot of a cliff, with her inside it.

He should have insisted she give him the keys.

He walked back to his own truck, opened his door, and leaned in. "Can you drive down? I'm going to ride with Delaney."

Caitlin's eyes were bright. "Yes, sir."

"Thanks."

Caitlin was one of the best officers he had. Hardworking, smart, confident, calm, and good with the public. When Clint had taken the police chief role, she had confessed that her past relationship with Delaney had not been great, mostly because of issues related to former chief Mara Yellowtail. Caitlin had expressed a desire to mend fences. Since then, he'd been pleased with how well the two women worked together, when necessary. Yet he had also noticed that Caitlin had puppy dog eyes for Leo. He suspected that had impacted on past difficulties.

"Do you want me to wait?"

"Yes. Let's stick together."

"Will do." Caitlin was already moving herself awkwardly over the console and into the driver's seat. Personally, he would have walked around. In different circumstances, he would have laughed.

Clint stationed himself outside Delaney's door, ready to throw himself into the backseat if she tore out of there. He watched and listened. He needn't have worried. Her full-throated scream was a pretty good indication she was off the call.

He pulled the door open. "I'm driving. We're talking."

"Zero chance I give up the wheel. But get in if you want to."

He should have expected her reaction. Delaney needed to be in control, never more than when driving. And she was an exceptional driver. Just surviving her drive down the mountain was proof of that. But working for the state, he'd spent too many years pulling people with big emotions out of car wrecks. He wasn't going to wrestle her over the steering wheel, though. He'd help her stay focused and calm. Or at least under a semblance of control.

He dashed around the front of the truck and jumped in. The interior smelled like wet boots and had the tang of stress and sweat. She was accelerating onto the road before he had his seatbelt fastened.

"Well?" he said, when she didn't say anything. "Was it your mother?"

Her voice was flat. "I think so."

"I heard what was said when I walked up back on the mountain."

"What do you mean?"

"That you were to call her if you ever wanted to see Leo again."

Delaney's jaw flexed. "Which would be better than him occupying one of those graves up at Snow Hare."

He'd been afraid she'd made that connection. It was a strong possibility, although he hated to admit it. "Is she involved? With Leo, I mean?"

Her face was stone. "Somehow."

"And what are you to do if you want Leo back?"

"I've been sworn to secrecy."

"That won't work."

"I know. But until I know whether or not they have a way of monitoring me, this is a solo mission."

"What is a solo mission?"

"Something I have to do to get Leo back."

"Do you have proof of life?"

"Hoping to soon."

"Delaney, this is a kidnapping conspiracy. Murder, too, most likely. And now we're talking obstruction of justice. You, you're the one obstructing justice. Other people could have heard that radio call besides me."

"I know that," she snapped. "I'll tell them it amounted to nothing but the ramblings of a crazy woman if I'm asked. Because, Clint, she is that. If nothing else, she is that."

"That doesn't fix it. You can't withhold what you're doing or keep anyone's identity or whereabouts a secret."

Delaney slowed as they entered Dayton. "I can't reveal what I don't know. She used a voice changing app. She wouldn't tell me where she is. I don't know where Leo is. I don't know anything yet. About what I'm doing or who I'm talking to. I'll find out when I get where I'm going."

"How did she get Kat's number? What is her contact point in this whole mess?"

She navigated a dog ear to the right, then to the left, ending up on the straightaway through the tiny, picturesque downtown. "I don't know. She could be delusional."

Clint had been thinking about this on the drive down. Who would contact Kat. Who would use her and Fabiola Pace to get to Delaney. Who would use Leo to get to Delaney. "It's your brother, isn't it? It's Li—"

"Don't say that name to me. I know nothing."

"You're just going to throw your career out the window to protect a brother who would just as soon see you dead?"

She whirled and the truck veered off the road just before the bridge over the Tongue River. Without even looking at the road, she set it back on course, eyes locked on him. "I would never. I'm going to protect *Leo*."

Clint refused to reach out to brace himself. They passed over the bridge. He leaned toward her, matching her glare and intensity. "And I'm going to protect you."

She recoiled, then she seemed to get bigger, to glow, to thrum. "If you endanger Leo, I will do crazy things."

He retreated, shook his head, looked at the road ahead of them. "I won't, okay? That's not what I meant. You need someone helping you."

She mashed the accelerator, gaining speed quickly. "I need someone helping us find out who has Leo and where they are. Someone working around Clark Applewood and his federal cronies. Coordinating with Wilcox. Covering for me while I'm out in the field following leads—because that's what I'll be doing and what we're going to tell everyone."

"That's fine. But don't shut me out. I need to know where you are and when to call for help."

Her jaw clenched and jutted. Long seconds passed. "It's my fault, Clint. If I hadn't ridden ahead. I was just so upset about that young woman who got shot. So many young women. I couldn't stand it. I just... I just... I got carried away. And Leo paid the price."

"We don't know that. We don't know what happened."

Her face sagged. All her toughness gone, *poof*, in a blink. "Yes, we do. If I'd been with him, no one would have come after him. We would have been equally matched. I left him without backup. For all we know, the guy I talked to realized I was a cop and went straight back for Leo."

Clint hurt for her. But he knew she had to go through some of these feelings. He didn't agree it was her fault, but he did think those big feelings could fuel her, drive her, sustain her. "Did Leo order you to stay with him?"

"It doesn't matter." A tear slid down her cheek. She turned her green eyes on him. Her damp, electric green eyes. "Promise me you won't tell anyone that it really was my mother until I'm ready. Or speculate that it is my brother. Not until we know."

"Delaney..."

"Help me figure it out if you want, but don't put him at risk. It was made very clear to me not to involve anyone else. They said I'll be monitored. I gave the number to Skeeter. I asked him to trace it back. I'm not ignoring any part of it. I just care about finding Leo more than anything else."

"I—"

Her phone rang. She drew in a sharp breath. "It's... the caller. Her."

"Ready?" Clint said.

She nodded.

He pressed to accept the call through the stereo.

Delaney swallowed. "Hello."

"You asked for proof that Leo is alive."

Clint frowned at the weird voice. It didn't sound like a woman in her late fifties.

"Yes."

"I've texted you a video."

Clint grabbed Delaney's phone from its dash holster and opened her texts. In the text string with the caller, there was a video message. He pressed play.

The car filled with Leo's voice. He sounded sleepy or drugged. Slurring. *"This is Sheriff Leo Palmer with the proof of life. Tell Delaney I love her and not to do anything stupid. I hit a moose. Knocked me out on the lake."* There was a scuffle and a grunt. In the background, you could hear Leo say, *"Hey. Gimme that back."*

The video ended.

"You got it?" the voice said.

Delaney answered in a strong voice completely different from the anguished one she'd spoken in a minute before when expressing the guilt she was feeling. "Yes."

"I can tell someone you're on your way?"

Delaney straightened her arms on the steering wheel, squeezing it tightly with both hands. She shot Clint a look. "You can tell that son of a bitch who shares my DNA that I'm on my way."

And it was at that moment that Clint figured out what he needed to do.

FORTY-ONE

As Leo walked from the truck, he had the impression of mountains rising in every direction on the edges of a snowy, prairie-like expanse. The air was so cold his nostril hairs froze in seconds, but he was glad to have a break from wearing a bag over his head. He wasn't sure why the men had removed it, but he still hadn't seen their faces. They were walking behind him. He thought about wheeling around but staying alive until he could escape was more important than their identities. They were armed. Hopefully he'd get a chance later.

A hand pushed Leo into a stumble that ended with him on the ground, unable to break his fall because his hands were bound behind his back. His shackled feet hadn't helped much either. Small rocks dug into his face. His wind was knocked out of him in a rush, but he didn't make a sound.

The men behind him laughed.

Leo gritted his teeth and inchwormed his knees under himself then pushed off his chin and chest. He was glad for the cross training and yoga he did with Delaney, even though he usually tried to get out of going.

Delaney. He hated that he was putting her through his absence. His kidnapping. What an idiot he'd been. The moose and the wreck hadn't been his fault, most likely. But he should have had his guard up. He'd been alone, chasing murder suspects. He'd just let a stranger walk up to him without exercising appropriate situational awareness and caution. It went further than that. He should have insisted Delaney and him stay together. Or that they brought more officers with them. He could have suspended the search until conditions improved. All of those were things within his control. Any one of them would have prevented this fiasco. Now, what she would do to try to find him and bring him home was as worrisome as his own predicament.

He'd been really groggy earlier—they were definitely spiking his water with something strong—when during the drive one of the guys had ripped the bag off his head, stuck a phone in his face, and ordered him to identify himself and offer it as proof of life. It took a second or two for his brain to respond, and when he spoke it was like he was watching himself from a distance. "This is Sheriff Leo Palmer with the proof of life. Tell Delaney I love her and not to do anything stupid. I hit a moose. Knocked me out on the lake."

That had earned him a punch in the gut for some reason. They'd snatched up the phone and put his hood back on.

It had been pathetic, really. He'd had the chance to send a message in code. But what would he have said? He didn't know who he was with or where he was. If the worst came, at least he'd told Delaney he loved her one last time. The thought was a twist in his gut.

He climbed from his knees to his feet then shuffled forward.

"Through the door, Sheriff." It was Boss. "It's been unlocked for us."

Leo looked around for a house, but all he saw was an

earthen berm rising from the snow. But it did have a door in it. A short door. An arm reached ahead of him and opened it. There was no light inside. He hesitated.

"Take four steps and get on your knees."

Leo hated the orders. He hated taking them. But he did as he was told. The darkness was thick. Unable to put his hands in front of him, he moved cautiously. After he counted four steps, he knelt, hyperaware of the sound of his own breathing in the quiet. It smelled musty and of something else. Mothballs, maybe? An old scent memory from his grandmother's closet. The air wasn't much warmer than outside in here, either. Under his knees the floor was hard, but not like tile. Sod hard.

The lights flicked on. He just had time to take in a downward slanting floor in a low-ceilinged room with a kitchen on one side, table and chairs in the center, and a sitting area on the other before the hood was jerked down over his head again. Final impressions registered. No windows. Underground. That meant sound and temperature insulation.

"Put the truck in the garage," Boss said.

"You do it," Whiner said. *My God, they bicker like brothers.*

"I can." The voice of Challenger. Helping, but driving a wedge at the same time. He was sly, clever, subversive.

Boss said, "I want you to put our pet sheriff away."

Are they avoiding using names so I don't hear them? Smart.

"You're an asshole," Whiner said.

"And you're an idiot."

Leo needed to slow things down. "I have to go to the bathroom." He was also hungry and extremely thirsty, but he would abstain from food and water for as long as possible. He wanted to put off the possibility of ingesting more drugs.

Boss said, "Lucky for you, your accommodation comes with one of those what-do-you-call-em bathrooms."

"En suite," Challenger said.

"Those. Take him away."

A hand grabbed his elbow and jerked Leo to his feet so roughly that for a moment he thought his shoulder was going to come out of its socket. He bit down on the inside of his lip.

"Let's go." Challenger didn't release his arm, just pushed him forward.

Leo shuffled forward.

"Turn left."

Leo adjusted what he hoped was ninety degrees to the left.

"Forward again. Five steps."

After five steps, Leo stopped.

"Sit."

"On the ground?"

"Yes. I'll be back."

"The bathroom?"

"Just a second."

While he waited, Leo counted. One one thousand. Two one thousand. He'd made it to thirty when Challenger returned. He heard what sounded like a plastic bucket with a metal handle hit the floor. Then something softer. A bag? And, finally, the *thwump* of plastic with liquid in it. Water bottle. *Funny how recognizable sounds are when you can't see.*

Challenger's steps moved away from him. A door creaked.

"The bathroom?" Leo said.

"You've got everything you need."

"My hands are behind my back."

"Put his hands in front of him," Boss shouted. "I don't want to listen to him bitching."

The footsteps returned. "Lucky son of a bitch. Don't forget I'm holding a knife and have a gun on my hip." Something pulled at the plastic around his wrists, then it broke apart.

Leo wanted to jump the man, but even if there'd been no knife, his own arms were limp and leaden. And there were armed men outside the door. Close outside.

"Put your hands in front, the inside of your wrists against each other."

He held them out.

What felt like flexicuffs were cinched around them. "Don't give me reason to remember you're in here."

The footsteps walked away. The door closed, then Leo heard a deadbolt turn.

Leo yanked the hood off. He was rewarded with easier breathing, but inky blackness broken only by a thin line of light from under the door made it impossible to see anything. *Maybe my eyes will adjust.* He rotated on his butt using his feet. They didn't hit anything. He scooted to where he'd heard the bucket. When his feet tapped it, he stopped beside it. Put his hands in. It was empty.

En suite bathroom, he realized.

He patted the bag. Reached inside. Found what felt like food bars. Oranges. Apples. Kicked the plastic bottle and heard sloshing. The food was probably safe, but the water he assumed was loaded with tranquilizers.

He sat in the dark, listening. Low voices were talking, close enough that he could make out their words, just barely.

"What are we going to do with him?" Whiner said.

Boss spoke. "We sent the video. But I think the risk of keeping him alive is too high."

"But it's the only way to ensure continued cooperation," Challenger countered, his voice calm and measured. "She said she's going to want ongoing videos to keep cooperating."

"Fine. But not one minute longer than we have to. Besides, we'll have enough on our hands just dealing with her when she gets here."

Her? She?

"Are you sure she isn't going to bring half the cops in Wyoming with her?" Whiner said.

"I'm telling you, she'd do anything for this guy." Challenger sounded smug.

"Why?" Boss asked.

"Because she's not just his co-worker. She's his lover. And I want her watching when I kill him."

Leo lowered his head to his knees. *No!* Delaney was walking into a trap, and it was all because of him.

FORTY-TWO

Skeeter read the message from Delaney.

Track down a name and address for this phone number. Just between you and me.

He felt a lift in his shoulders. She trusted only him with this job. He didn't have a login at the sheriff's department, but he had buddies he could call on for favors. This sounded like something to get on to right away. He ran searches through all the databases he had access to and came up empty, making sure no one was watching over his shoulder. When he struck out, he fired off a volley of emails.

That should do it.

He smiled. He'd get that information for Delaney. She could count on him.

FORTY-THREE

SEVENTEEN HOURS LATER

Driving through endless white prairie into Lethbridge, Alberta, Delaney was fighting fatigue. She pulled Gabrielle over at a Petro-Canada truck stop. When was the last time she'd slept, other than a two-hour nap before she left? Friday night with Jackie Spurrier's murder near midday on Saturday, Leo taken on Saturday night, and now it was Monday morning after ten hours of driving.

She'd taken the quickest route—Interstate 15 through Great Falls, Montana, despite wind advisories. Gabrielle had a high profile, but the flatbed trailer didn't. It had been nearly two years since she'd driven Gabrielle on a long haul, and she wasn't conditioned for it. Physically or mentally.

She was having difficulty keeping her mind on the road. Her brain pingponged back and forth in a crazy volley. Leo really was alive. So, who were the people in the other graves? Where was Leo now? How had the people in the graves died? Had they hurt Leo? Who had killed the victims? Did Leo know she was coming for him?

Finally, she'd forced herself into future-focused thought patterns. When Leo made it home, what would they do first?

What would she say to him? He'd been trying to coax her into taking a trip with him. A real vacation, just the two of them. She would definitely do it. Immediately. She couldn't even remember why she'd said no before. She'd switched things up and visualized Liam and the other faceless perpetrators as they were tried and found guilty and locked up for life in prison. The loved ones who would receive closure because of Leslie and Ace's find. It was more positive, but still wearing her down more than the wind.

The night was otherwise uneventful.

She'd planned her crossing at the Coutts–Sweetgrass border station in the wee hours, when the lines were short and the cold bitter. She'd kept the interior of Gabrielle hovering ten degrees above freezing to minimize the difference she'd face outside if she had trouble and to keep herself awake. It had worked so far for the latter. Luckily, she'd had no problems. There had been very few vehicles on the road, other than a white SUV she'd seen behind her off and on all night. The monitoring Fabi had mentioned?

She'd prayed and bartered with God as a Canadian agent examined her papers. She'd received them via a spurious email address before she got on the road and checked them thoroughly, like her life depended on it. More thoroughly than that, because Leo's did. But she couldn't control whether the buyer or seller would cause her to be flagged at the border. Nor whether the agent would get overzealous and search Gabrielle. If he checked the sleeper cab he might find the arsenal she'd stashed quite illegally under the false bottom of her bunk.

She must have offered something the Big Guy liked, because she'd been waved through with a cursory check, her weapons safe and secure.

Now, at the truck stop, she shivered and turned up her collar. The temperature gauge in the cab read ten Fahrenheit. She filled Gabrielle's fuel tanks and other fluids, washed her windshields, and did a walk around the tractor and trailer, checking connections and looking for problems that might get her pulled over or cause difficulties on the road. Because it reassured her, she verified nothing had happened to her chains, flares, or emergency kit since her last stop. Then she restocked on energy drinks. She knew they were horrible for her. Normally, she didn't touch them. Prohibited the girls from drinking them, at least in her presence—they were popular with teens. But this drive was about survival. She needed sharp wits, and the energy drinks were unmatched for that—if she stayed with legal solutions anyway. Which she would do. She'd never gone in for the uppers lifestyle that jacked some truckers through the long days and nights.

Loading herself and her bags of supplies back into the truck, she drove away from the pumps and reparked. She saw a white SUV. Was it the same one from the night before? She couldn't be sure, but she didn't like it. A Nissan Rogue with North Dakota plates. She would be sure not to miss it if it turned up again. The driver was turned away from her, digging in the backseat. It was probably just headed to Calgary like her. North central Montana and southern Alberta were barren. There were no other routes.

She texted Fabi. Her mother. It had been too early when she crossed, especially if Fabi really was in Washington like the area code of her number suggested, where it was an hour earlier.

I'm in Lethbridge. Send instructions.

While she waited, she read her messages.

From Kat: *When will you be back?*

From Carrie: *Kat's acting weird.*

Her interaction with her daughters had been hurried before her surprise departure. Kat had been quiet. Almost sullen. They would have to talk when she got back. Carrie had argued vehemently that she should be allowed to go with Delaney as her backup driver because she loved Leo, too. That had been a flat no—she would never put one of her girls knowingly in this kind of danger. Mary and Juan Julio were staying with them. The girls planned to accompany her to the Loafing Shed and not stay home alone. Normally Skeeter would have been the one to bunk over, but Delaney needed him on the case. He would still drop by a couple of times a day, though.

School was still out for winter break, so her girls wouldn't be up yet. She sent a group text to them.

I love you guys. Call me anytime.

Fabi still hadn't replied, so Delaney segued to work. She'd left Sunday evening and let the team know she was following leads in the field and was certain to need their help Monday, probably late into the night. As the acting sheriff in Leo's absence, she'd ordered them to get a good night's sleep. *Acting sheriff.* The title did not feel good. It was Leo's, and she wanted him back in it.

Only Clint knew the slightest thing about what Delaney was really up to, and he'd agreed to cover for her if she lost contact. There would come a point where she read the others in, but for Leo's protection, she would not yet.

She texted Skeeter.

Any progress on that phone number?

A message came in from Fabi. It was an address in Calgary. Delaney shot back an immediate reply.

What am I picking up?

It's on your paperwork.

On the paperwork, it just said vehicle parts. If it were only that, they wouldn't have needed her. There wasn't a lot she could do about it now, no matter what it was. She typed, *Is it paid for? Who do I ask for? What time do they expect me?* and hit send.

Three dots appeared. Disappeared. Reappeared.

Jordan Iles at noon. You'll pick up the trailer at one. Head south into Montana.

She shook her head.

After I eat and sleep. I'll get on the road at dusk.

No. You leave immediately.

Delaney growled. No one wanted her there faster than she did, no matter what was waiting for her when she arrived. *As long as Leo is there.* But did they want her to have a wreck with their important cargo?

She texted, *This is not negotiable. Leaving at dusk. Where do I map to?*

The dots danced again. Delaney's eyes swam. She cracked open a Monster.

Map to Helena.

That's not very specific.

Text me after you cross the border for details.

Proof of life.

When you get to Calgary.

Delaney gulped her Monster, then shifted Gabrielle and eased her forward, watching for the white Nissan Rogue in her sideview mirrors. If they wouldn't tell her what she was picking up, she was going to have to figure it out herself.

In Calgary.

FORTY-FOUR

Skeeter was in tube socks and a giant robe eating cereal in his apartment when his mobile rang. It was not quite seven in the ding-dang morning. Maybe it was one of his contacts about the phone number for Delaney. But what he saw on his screen was the number for Jackie's friend Louanne in Bozeman. He answered it. "Skeeter Rawlins."

The voice on the other end wasn't a woman. "This is Dickie. Who's this?"

Maybe Louanne had changed her number. "I'm, uh, with the Kearny County Sheriff's Department in Wyoming. I'm calling for Louanne. Is this her phone?"

"What do you want her for?"

"It's about an old friend of hers. Jackie Spurrier."

"Yeah. Well, Louanne is scared as crap on account of how Jackie was murdered. She don't want no part of that."

Skeeter stood up, cradling the phone between his neck and shoulder as he retied his robe. His apartment was freezing. "So, she's talked to you about Jackie?"

"Of course."

"You're her boyfriend or husband or what?"

"Boyfriend."

"Why's she scared, Dickie?"

"Because she knew people, you know? And if the people she knew are the ones who killed Jackie and she says something, maybe she's next."

Skeeter had to think for a second to unwind the words from Dickie's mouth. "If she knows something, they may do that anyway. I'd say it's safer to help us catch them."

Silence on the other end of the line.

"You still there?" Skeeter walked to the thermostat. He turned the heat up three degrees. He could afford it with all the extra hours he was working to help find Leo.

"Yeah. Man, I tend to agree with you. The thing is, Jackie had this old high school boyfriend. He was a steroid head crazy asshole. He followed her out here."

"Was she still dating him?" Skeeter moved to the couch where he had a pen and paper on his coffee table.

"No. She dated a guy here. Herb something. She dumped Herb because he was too nice. Then she met another guy. The high school ex didn't show up until he found out she was head over heels about her newest boyfriend. Then she took off with new guy to get away from the ex. Louanne hasn't seen her since. I don't think she'd even heard from her."

Jackie got new boyfriends about as often as I get new drawers. "Is Herb's last name Tilton?"

"Sounds right." Skeeter started taking notes.

"Do you know the high school boyfriend's name?"

"I do, actually. Louanne and I were already hanging out, and I called the police on him once. He was trying to bust down their door. I'll never forget him. Muscly with a shaved head and veins popping out."

"His name?"

"Robby Sanders."

"What did he do when she took off?"

"Kept harassing everyone who knew her until the cops escorted him to the city limits. I don't know where he went after that."

Skeeter was writing as fast as he could. This ex sounded unstable. Like a good lead. "What about the new boyfriend? Do you have a name or address?"

"No address. I met him once. He worked out of town. He was all right. His name was—oh, shit. It was on the tip of my tongue."

"Take your time."

"Yeah. Randall something. Randall. I may not have ever known his last name."

"All right. Anything else you can think of that might help us—problems Jackie had with co-workers or customers?"

"Not that I heard about."

Skeeter gave Dickie his phone number. "It would be good if Louanne could call me back. Really helpful to us."

"Yeah. Another cop left a number, too. I'll tell her what you said. About how Sanders knows she knows. Try to get her to call you." Dickie frowned. "But, dude, be careful. Sanders is dangerous. Jackie told us he used to kill things when he was a teenager. He killed her dog when she broke up with him. That dog was like family to her. What kind of person does that?"

Skeeter knew exactly what kind. A damn good suspect. And then he had a thought. Jackie had been hiding from someone, and she'd been killed just one week after she called her parents.

What was the chance those two things *weren't* related?

If they were, he hoped her parents never found out.

FORTY-FIVE

Leo awoke sputtering with a sharp pain in his ribs. He gasped and fought to catch his breath.

"Wake up, Sheriff," Whiner said. "Or I'll kick you again."

Leo batted his eyes open to blackness. He reached to rub them, and his hands met fabric. The hood was back on. When had that happened? He must have fallen asleep. More than that. He had to have been drugged again. But he hadn't drank the water. In fact, he was thirsty. Tongue stuck to the roof of his mouth thirsty. *The fruit. Maybe they injected it?* It was hot and humid inside the hood. They must have dropped it on the table next to the food, because it smelled like lasagna. The thought made his stomach cramp.

"The hood..." he said.

"Is staying on. I'm videoing you. I need you to state your name and the date."

"I don't know the date."

"Yesterday was..."

"I don't know."

Whiner sighed, sounding exasperated. "What day were you on the snowmobile trail?"

"Saturday night."

"And the next morning?"

"Sunday. I was in a—I was somewhere. Inside a building."

"Good. Where next?"

"A car. Then here. By nighttime, I think."

"Right. Sunday night."

"How long has it been since then?"

"It's the next morning."

"Monday. Okay."

"When you're ready, start talking."

Leo wished he'd had more time to wake up. Get his brain firing. He needed to somehow give a clue. But what did he know? That there were three men. Two were probably brothers. They were in an underground house. What were those called? Bunkers?

"Any time, Leo."

"Sorry. I'm cotton mouthed and having trouble waking up. My brain is fuzzy."

"Just do it."

Leo licked his lips. He spoke slowly. It wasn't hard to make himself sound confused. "I'm feeling under the weather, not able to raise Cain, got a killer headache. Today is the third, I think three. But definitely Monday. I'm supposed to say my name but it's like my brain is surrounded by mountains it can't climb. This is Leo Palmer." Had he been too obvious? Leo braced himself for a blow.

"You sound like an idiot."

He relaxed. This one wasn't on to him. He was glad it wasn't Challenger. He seemed like the brains of the group. "What's it for?"

"To prove you're alive."

"To who?"

"Now, who do you think? Your girlfriend, of course. She's doing us a little favor, then coming to pick you up."

The conversation he'd overheard the night before. Drugs were whack. He'd completely forgotten. They were setting a trap for Delaney.

He heard a chime from Whiner's phone. He prayed it was the sound of a text sending. Delaney was smart. She'd know he was sending her clues. She'd work on them. She'd get help. Drew. The police. Everyone.

Whiner cocked his head and grinned at Leo. "I met her, you know. She's hot, for a cop. I've decided to give her a try, even though she doesn't deserve it. Poetic justice and all. I've never had a lady cop before. What do you think? Is she worth it?"

Leo bit the inside of his lip to keep from screaming. If the hood had been off, he would have gone after Whiner with his teeth. He wouldn't need a reminder to make Whiner pay for what he'd just said about Delaney. Next time he got the chance, he had to remember to warn Delaney not to come.

No matter what, she could not come.

FORTY-SIX

Delaney set the brake on Gabrielle outside a boxy warehouse on the outskirts of Calgary. The vista reminded her of the book *Little House on the Prairie*, only she'd call this *Big City on the Prairie* with a killer mountain view. *And you sound drunk*, she told herself. It was the exhaustion. Her brain was alternating between zoned out and sheer loopiness now.

A message was in from Skeeter.

Sorry, I got nothing on the phone yet.

She hoped the big man was taking her request seriously. *Please expedite.* She deleted the second word and instead typed *hurry*. She hit send.

Then she fired off a message to Fabi.

Arrived. Proof of current life.

Seconds later, a video arrived without any text. The image was so horrifying that at first she didn't hear the words. Literally, did not even register anyone was speaking. It was a man. Ankles bound. Wrists tied in front of him. Hood over his head. He was lying on his side. The room he was in was dark, with the only light for the video coming from the camera. She replayed it, now purposefully ignoring the words and just watching the screen. A bucket. A water bottle. A bag of some kind. No furniture. No windows? He might be underground.

Then she turned her volume to max and focused on the words.

"I'm feeling under the weather, not able to raise Cain, got a killer headache. Today is the third, I think three. But definitely Monday. I'm supposed to say my name but it's like my brain is surrounded by mountains it can't climb. This is Leo Palmer."

It was definitely Leo's voice, even muffled by the hood. And the body looked like his, albeit contorted into an unnatural position. Her forehead fell onto her steering wheel. *He's alive. He's still alive.* He sounded awful. Groggy. Drugged. His voice was hoarse. But he was alive. Tears sprang to her eyes. She wished she could put her arms around him and whisper that it was going to be okay. That she was coming for him as fast as she could.

She wiped her eyes then played it again, now focusing on *what* he was saying, not just whether it was him. Honestly, he came off like a patient in a psych ward. What in the world was he talking about? She took it one sentence at a time, pressing stop when he transitioned. None of it sounded like him. "Under the weather" was something her grandmother would have said. No doubt he didn't feel top notch. But he would have said he felt like crap. And "not able to raise Cain"? Never. Not in a million years. A "killer headache" sounded more like something Freddy would say. So, his choice of phrasing—was that the drugs talking or was it deliberate? Was he sending her a clue?

Think, Delaney. Think.

A knock on her window startled her. Her phone clattered to the floorboard. She pasted on a smile and turned to the window, then lowered it. As she did, a white Nissan Rogue drove past. Was this the most popular car in the great white north? She tried to see the license plate, but the angle of her view made it impossible. She had a bad, bad feeling she was being followed.

"Yes?" she said.

A man in a red wool cap with side tassels and wavy blond hair that curled up from under the bottom of it said, "You can't park here, lady."

"I'm actually here to pick up a load. My contact is Jordan Iles." She held up her paperwork.

"Oh, beauty. He's in the washroom. You want to follow me in? There's a place you can wait while he gets you squared away."

No, she did not want to. She wanted to turn around and drive home where she would find Leo waiting for her. Today, she was not getting what she wanted. "Sure," she said, then gathered her handbag, backpack, and the phone.

They entered a door on the far corner of the building, away from the loading docks and roll-up doors, but not away from the strong diesel odor.

"These are our offices, and this is the waiting area." He pointed at a couch and some uncomfortable-looking chairs. Two of the walls were navy blue. The third was white. Photographs of Alberta's Rockies were the only decoration. A standing water dispenser stood in the corner, but it had no little paper cups. "Take a seat. I'll tell him you're here, eh?"

She hefted her bags onto the couch. "Thanks."

A second man walked in, rail thin and standing approximately Kat's height. "Tell him who is here?"

"A driver, bud. Hey, I'm running to Timmie's. Want a double-double?"

"Make it two. One for me and one for our driver."

Delaney didn't argue, and she even understood their conversation after all the miles she'd logged and hours she'd booked in Canada in her old life. The double-double—a coffee with double cream, double sugar—sounded wonderful.

Her host disappeared.

The other man stuck out his hand, shaking his head. "That one's a keener. I'm Jordan Iles. Welcome to Cowtown."

They shook.

"Delaney Pace. Thank you." She offered her paperwork.

He read it quickly. "All right. We'll give'r and get you loaded up."

"How long?" She remembered Fabi telling her to pick up Gabrielle at one, but she still had to ask.

"About an hour. But don't worry. Your coffee will be back in half that time."

He whistled as he walked out.

Delaney sat on the couch which was as uncomfortable as the chairs looked and pulled the video back up. After watching it again, she pulled a piece of paper out of the trashcan and scribbled notes on it, listing the things she thought were weird.

- Under the weather
- Not able to raise Cain
- Killer headache
- The third, I think it's three
- Surrounded by mountains I can't climb

She stared at them until the letters swam in front of her eyes. She needed help. She texted it to Clint.

Today's proof of life. What do you make of it? I think he's trying to send us clues.

She had to rest her brain, but she couldn't sleep yet. She passed the time by booking a hotel for her afternoon nap. Then she checked the weather, and what she saw literally sent her into a cold sweat.

FORTY-SEVEN

Drew typed rapidly on his phone as he finished a midday report to Delaney updating her on the progress the team had made in the morning, from Leo's office. He'd moved there because it had more room to put up a second whiteboard. The small conference table would be perfect for Clara's spreadsheets tracking the different properties, when she finished them. He didn't mind the sheriff's view of the snow-covered mountains out the picture window either. And the chair. It was so much more ergonomically sound than the one at his cubicle. Hell, this office even smelled better than their bullpen. Lavender and vanilla. He saw one of those plug-in air freshener thingies. It was unnaturally civilized for a police station.

Skeeter walked in. "Does Delaney know you're using Leo's office?"

Drew frowned. "No, why?"

"She's pretty protective of him."

So what if he used the office? It was efficiency. That helped them find Leo. "What's up, Skeeter? Are you on to something?"

"I got a name. Ex-boyfriend of Jackie, from a few years back. Robby Sanders."

"What about him?"

"He followed her to Bozeman. I found a restraining order she had out against him there. Going on two years ago now. But after she got that, it doesn't look like she ever reported anything on him again."

"What were the grounds? Did he beat her up?"

"No. He was stalking her. Harassing her. Causing problems at work. Seems like he was obsessed and having trouble letting her go. A lot of trouble."

"Have you talked to him?"

"I've left messages where he supposedly works—an auction barn—but there's no home number for him. I just wanted you to have his name in case it comes up."

Drew nodded, feeling a warm rush. They were making progress. "Nice work. Thanks for the update."

Almost on his heels, Clara knocked. "Big desk to fill, there."

Why did everyone keep mentioning him using Leo's office? "Room to spread out. Like a task force room, you know."

She nodded, lips pressed together. "I'm coming up with property all over the country. I don't feel like I'm getting anywhere. And we're in a hurry."

Drew tapped his chin, thinking.

Clara said, "How far away do we think he is? I could focus within the number of miles they could have traveled."

"Well, that depends on whether they flew or drove."

"True."

"Still, my gut says keep it tight. Let's start with Idaho, Montana, and Wyoming. If nothing pans out, go wider."

"I like that. I'll be back when I finish those states."

"Thanks." He glanced at the time. Noon. His stomach growled.

Normally, Clara would bring lunch back, but there was no way he was asking her today. What she was doing was far more important. He'd raid the fridge later. He kept a stash of low-fat frozen dinners in there. Just thinking about his training-friendly meals brought on a little stress. He could feel his muscles atrophying. When Leo was safely home, he'd get his coach to help him redesign his training plan leading up to the competition, to make up for the time out of the gym.

He went back to his laptop. Checked for return messages from Delaney and his trustees. None. No voicemail either. He wondered what the secret leads were that Delaney was pursuing in the field and why she couldn't tell him about them. She'd asked for his trust, and he'd given it to her. She'd earned it. But something was up. Something big. He could feel it.

He sent a follow-up to his update text to her.

What's going on out there? If you let me know, maybe we can help you more.

He interlaced his fingers and inverted them, stretching them and his shoulders. Time for a deep dive on contestant number two. He'd finished the workup on Elan Mitchell that morning. It had been fruitless. The man had served on boards for major companies and charitable organizations—including as chair of the board at the gun company his family had founded—but other than a list of their members, his name never came up in connection with them again. He had no criminal history that Drew could find. No bad debts or tax liens. No property owned in his own name. Funny how the poor strived to own something in their name, but the rich had the money to keep everything out of it.

So, on to Greg Sones. *Google, show me what you've got.* He flexed his fingers, then started tapping away.

Time passed quickly as he browsed site after site. There was more information out in the ether on Greg, but not much. The most interesting thing he found was the clients of his political consulting company. One was the gun manufacturer Elan

Mitchell was tied to. The list was sprinkled with well-known companies. But there were more than a few recognizable extremist groups. He started running names through Google, and after only a few a picture began to form. Groups that were believed to be anti-establishment and militant. Ultra conservative, ultra-right, ultra left, ultra anything outside the mainstream.

Basically, ANTIFA, although they weren't mentioned. ANTIFA wannabes.

He shuddered. Who would want to make a career working with groups like those? So, Far West had one trustee who made guns, and another who lobbied on behalf of militant groups. He wasn't liking their vibe much so far.

"What the hell are you doing in here?" a man barked.

Drew looked up to see Deputy Joe Tarver, and he jumped to his feet. Only a couple of months ago, Joe had campaigned to fill this very office, and he was several decades Drew's senior in law enforcement. But wait—hadn't he been due in that morning? Joe's hours weren't his to monitor, but it was after noon.

He stumbled over his words. "Leo's been kidnapped. Delaney's out in the field on leads. I'm working with—"

"I know all that. I watch the news. I talked to Clara on the way in. I meant what in the hell are you doing playing sheriff while Leo's gone?"

FORTY-EIGHT

Leo woke to the sound of raised voices. He'd passed out again immediately after Whiner had videotaped him. Or had that been a dream? He rolled his neck back and forth. He felt better. More alert. Hungry, thirsty, but sharper. One thing was for sure. He wasn't eating anything else those jerks gave him for as long as he could hold out. Not after last time. He didn't need water yet either. It had been—what?—twenty-four hours or less since he'd last had anything to drink. He'd be fine.

The voices grew louder. Leo rose to his hands and knees and did a hopping, shuffling crawl to the door, where he sat with his ear against the slight crack in the jamb.

Boss was the yeller. "When were you going to show me the video you had Fabi send her?"

Fabi. The name rang a bell, but he hadn't heard them use it before. It was unusual. He'd definitely heard Boss talking to a woman the day before on the drive, although he'd been in and out of it at the time. For that matter, he'd been pretty dazed when he made the video. He remembered trying to send clues, but not exactly what he'd said.

"Why would I show you, Br—" Whiner asked.

"No names!" Boss thundered.

"Sorry. Jeez."

"I would hope because you realized it was a dumbass thing to do and came to me to beg for forgiveness."

"Agree to disagree."

"Did you actually listen to what the sheriff said?"

"He was drugged as shit. He babbled a bunch of nonsense. You should have heard him try to figure out what day it was. The lights were on, but no one was home."

"Jesus!"

"All right. Let's settle down." Challenger was there, too. He sounded calm. Maybe too calm. Something about him scared Leo more than the other two. Whiner was frightening because he seemed most likely to do something stupid. *Can't disagree with you, there, Boss.* Boss because he hadn't been happy the other two had dumped Leo in his lap and wanted him dead sooner rather than later.

"Settle down? Settle down? Look at this!"

Faintly, Leo heard his own voice. *"I'm feeling under the weather, not able to raise Cain, got a killer headache. Today is the third, I think three. But definitely Monday. I'm supposed to say my name but it's like my brain is surrounded by mountains it can't climb. This is Leo Palmer."*

He nodded, lips pursed. *Not bad.*

Challenger said, "It's not what we would have wanted sent to her."

"Damn straight. We know she's smart."

Whiner did his thing, his voice wheedling. "She won't figure it out."

"Maybe. But maybe someone else will. By now, every law enforcement officer in the country might have it, you idiot!"

"We told her not to tell anyone, or we'd kill Leo."

"I've demoted you. I've taken responsibility from you. Yet you keep fucking things up, little brother. Well, I'm in charge.

I'm the one who will answer for your mistakes, who *is* answering for them to DC. I'm sorry. I have to show I hold people accountable."

"No!" Whiner screamed. "You can't. We're family."

Boom! A gunshot rang out.

Thwump. Something hit the floor.

Leo grabbed the door handle, rattling it. It wouldn't budge. His breath came in ragged gasps. What the hell had just happened out there?

FORTY-NINE

The cheerful Jordan Iles hummed as he sauntered back into the waiting room. He stopped in front of Delaney and held out a sheaf of papers. "All's ready for ya with your crates."

Delaney blinked and took the paperwork as she stood. She'd been dozing on and off. Mostly on. So much for the double-double from Timmie's. It wasn't strong enough to combat her level of sleep deprivation. "Thank you."

He dapped his fist at her without touching her. "Our mutual client has been asking me about you. What gives with that?"

She had the sensation of bugs crawling over her skin. "I'm a first-time driver for them. I guess they're trying to get to know me. What did they ask?"

"Whether you're alone. Who you've talked to. What you've said to us."

"What did you tell them?"

"That you're a looker." He winked. "But they did ask me to pass you a message."

Delaney's hands automatically went to rub themselves on

her pants, but she stopped herself. She didn't want to betray her nerves. "Yes?"

"It was something like 'tell her not to worry, because we'll be able to keep an eye on things the whole way.' I hope you know what that means, since I didn't."

Boy, do I ever. It meant the monitoring. The question was how. Drones? Surveillance from planes? A tail, like the white Nissan Rogue? Did they have a tracker on Gabrielle or the trailer? Or in the crates she was picking up? Maybe a bug in her cab, sound or even video? Suddenly, she was jarringly wide awake. "Um, yeah. Sounds good."

"Any message back to them?"

"Nah. I'll take it from here. Thanks again."

"Be careful out there. And come back any time. You brighten up the place."

They shook hands, then Jordan pointed toward where Delaney had originally parked, and she went to claim her rig.

Delaney drove her load of God-knows-what to a hotel she'd booked because of its big rig parking out back. It wasn't how she rolled in her days on the road. The sleeping cabin was comfortable. Checking in and out of hotels was a chore. She'd be sleeping in her own bed that night. She had an ulterior motive, though. She wanted a place to park away from the Nissan Rogue that may or may not be following her and reporting back on her actions, because her feeble brain had been formulating a plan. Before she could put it in play, she needed to determine exactly what kind of illegal cargo she was about to transport into the United States. Plus, she was on a search-and-destroy mission for any tracking devices that could ruin that plan.

She coasted through the parking lot around the building, slow and careful. When she had made it around back, she found a space between two rigs pulling high-profile trailers. It was a tight squeeze but excellent cover. The only way to see her was from the front or back of Gabrielle. Or if someone became curious and walked right up on her.

Her phone rang with a Facetime call. It was Kat.

"Hello!" Delaney said.

Kat was scowling, arms crossed, sitting on the bed in her mostly black bedroom. Delaney couldn't wait for the day Kat wanted to give it a makeover. "Have you found Leo yet?"

"Not yet. But I will."

"He's not going to die, is he?"

"No. I won't let that happen."

"I gave you a hard time about dating him at first."

"Yes, you did." Delaney gave her a rueful smile. Kat had thought it would interfere with her fledgling relationship with Freddy.

"But he's all right. You're, um, good together."

Delaney could barely answer over the lump in her throat. "Thanks, Kitty Kat."

"Yeah, but also Carrie's treating me like a baby."

Sometimes Kat's shifts were like whiplash. Delaney wasn't going to engage in complaints about her sister. She thought about Carrie telling her Kat was acting weird. "This will be over soon. But how about you? Are you okay?"

Kat shrugged. "Fine."

Which meant not fine. Through the phone line, Delaney heard a horn honk before she could answer.

"That's Carrie. I've got to go, or she'll leave me."

"Okay. I love you."

"Love you, too. Bye."

The screen went blank. Delaney put her hand to her chest like it would keep her heart from spilling out on the floorboard. Then she took a few deep breaths and crawled into the sleeper cab. She had to keep moving forward. She had no choice.

After retrieving and donning her holstered Staccato, she got out and climbed up the side of the flatbed. She shimmied over to some strap and grabbed a loose tail. Her hand was able to easily wrap around it. She nodded, pleased with her idea and feeling a sense of déjà vu, sucked right back into her old life on the road. She hopped down and first unfastened the straps that held the lids down on a row of crates. Next, she threw a pry bar and a hammer on top of the boxes and filled her pockets with nails. Then she loosened the strap nearest to it and climbed up. She grabbed the strap in both hands, lowered her center of gravity, leaned back, and climbed. It wasn't easy, but in two minutes, she was at the top and able to reach over, wedge her hands oh-so-painfully under the strap, and scramble over the top edge of the boxes.

Leo would have been impressed. Leo. She closed her eyes for a second. Watching videos of him wasn't enough. She needed to see him, touch him. Free him.

She breathed heavily and massaged her hands for a minute. Tiredness weighted her eyelids and lapped at the edges of her consciousness. Every few seconds, things seemed to move in slow motion. She shook her head and pried a box open and began unloading it on top of the others. When it was empty, she was staring at nothing but a heap of boxes, all purporting to be car parts. She opened each, inspecting the contents.

There was no contraband, or, to her eyes, any trackers. She didn't know whether to be elated or disappointed. Was she nothing more than a free delivery service? That made no sense. This *had* to be about leverage against her or about jamming her up at the border. She couldn't give up after one box. If she didn't find illegal goods in this one, she'd have to keep checking boxes until she found some or finished with all of them.

But there were fifty of them. Twenty-five of which were underneath the heavy top boxes.

It would take her more time than she had left before she needed to leave, if it were even possible for her to do the bottom row manually. Meanwhile, there was Leo. He was being held prisoner. Waiting for her. With captors that might lose their patience and execute a different solution.

She couldn't push this off a day claiming mechanical issues. She had to get there.

So be it. She'd have to move fast.

She carefully repacked everything and was about to reload the crate, when she eyeballed the dimensions against the empty space in the box. Then she smiled. Sleep had made her less sharp. It was something she should have noticed before—there was more space in this crate. A false bottom. She got her crowbar out again and crowed softly with triumph when she found she was right.

The false bottom was wedged in tight. She couldn't risk damaging the outside of the crate, but she didn't care if she destroyed the false bottom. She'd deliberately started with a box in the top center. If she was checked at the border, they'd likely go with the first one they could reach.

She switched tools and started hacking with the claws of her hammer. By the second strike the claws broke through. The bottom was flimsy. She whooped.

"Someone up there?" It was a male voice.

She closed her eyes. *Oh, shit. Please don't let it be them.*

"Yes. It's my trailer. I had a problem. I'm fixing it."

"If you don't want me calling the cops, we need to have this conversation face to face."

Delaney felt for her waist holster. She checked the chamber and the magazine. The chamber was empty, the magazine full. She snapped the magazine back into place. "Give me a moment. I'm climbing out of a crate."

When she was standing near enough to see over the edge, she waved with her left hand at a gray-haired man the size of a gnome. Her right hand was on the hand grip of her gun.

"What's a beautiful woman like you doing driving trucks?" he said.

"I wouldn't have to if I had a dollar for every time someone asked me that."

He laughed. "You promise you're not a thief?" He jerked a thumb at the rig on her driver's side. "This one's mine. I don't want you coming back later for my load."

"I promise. My name is Delaney Pace."

"I'm Walt Feener. Wait—were you the one who was driving the ice roads a few years back? I heard about you."

Delaney had been the only women on the route at the time. "My reputation precedes me."

"Well, men never forget a pretty face. Plus, I heard you did your job better than most of the guys. They may not have liked it, but their buddies sure enjoyed telling stories about you showing them up."

"I don't hate hearing that. Well, I'd better get back to it. This won't fix itself." She smiled. "Thanks for keeping an eye out."

"Sure enough."

She was dizzy with relief, and the adrenaline rush of the encounter had brought her fully awake. She attacked the bottom with renewed vigor and busted through, then tore at the wood until she'd cleared most of it away. Curly packing paper an inch thick obscured the contents. She pawed it away, then jumped back like she'd been snake bit.

The familiar odor of gun oil met her nostrils. Five machine guns nestled in slots in the bottom of the crate.

"Dammit," she whispered.

This is what she'd been afraid of. Machine guns were illegal in the United States, for good reason. They were lethal on humans and had no real purpose outside killing people. Leo was being held by a group smuggling weapons like these into the country. They were armed. Secretive. Living outside the law.

Were they really going to let her go with Leo after she handed them two hundred and fifty machine guns? Highly unlikely. If this was an indicator of how well armed they were, she wasn't going to be able to fight Leo away from them either. They were a literal militia.

But she knew exactly who to call. She just didn't want to.

Clark Applewood answered on the first ring. "Have you reconsidered my offer to work with us?"

"Not in the way you think. I despise that you have been holding Leo's safety over my head. I know you don't care what happens to him any more than you care about the young girls Igor Salazar might hurt. You just care what happens to your sacred mission."

"You aren't saying anything you haven't said to me before. I won't respond by explaining to you the larger threat this group poses to more people. Is this all you called for?"

"No. I'm calling to offer you a chance to fulfill your mission by catching a militia group receiving a shipment of smuggled machine guns from Canada, if you'll cooperate with me to retrieve Leo from them. Alive."

"Deputy Pace, you have my full attention."

FIFTY

As the trained police officer in Leo pulled at his locked door—for what reason? What could he do?—shrill screams rattled the main section of the underground house. He could smell gun powder coming from the other room.

"Oh, my God! Oh, my God! What did you do?" The voice was unrecognizable in its sheer panic.

"Saved your life, brother. It's going to be okay." That one was definitely Challenger.

Leo stilled, trying to figure out what was going on fifteen feet away from him and how it would impact him.

"But you shot him. He's, he's... his head. His face. I think, oh God—I think he's dead." It was Whiner.

Leo's mouth dropped open. When he'd heard the shot, he thought Boss shot Whiner. But it had been Challenger who shot Boss. *Holy smokes!* There was a power vacuum about to be filled. Challenger was the stronger man. Would he fill it, or was this a family-run group? Leo squeezed his eyes shut. But wait—Challenger had just called Whiner brother. Were all three of them brothers?

"Of course he's dead. I made sure of that."

"But why?"

"Because he was about to kill you."

"He was bluffing."

"No. He wasn't. And I saved you."

"But he is—was—my brother. *Family*."

"I'm a better brother to you than he ever was. He disrespected you. He belittled you in front of the guys. He didn't see your value."

After a pause, Whiner said. "Yeah. Maybe."

"Not maybe. Definitely. The guys are on your side."

"Really?"

"Yes. They're behind you one hundred percent. You're the man now. The man in charge."

"What will we tell them?"

"We had a skirmish with the cops. He was shot. You saved us. Heroically."

"But will she buy it?"

Who—Delaney?

"She wants you to succeed. Needs you to. She's not going to question anything but results. She has people to answer to as well. We present a united front. You, me, her. Everything will be fine."

Not Delaney. But who?

"Even after Jackie?"

"Blame Jackie on me."

"Really?"

"Sure. All of it. All on me. I'll back you up. Tell them your brother was a lying piece of scum."

Whiner's sigh was like a sack of flour falling to the floor and splitting open. "I won't forget this. Any of it."

"I know you won't. We're going to do great things together." *A thump, thump, thump. Challenger is patting Whiner on the back.*

Leo slid down the door. Who was *she*? Fabi? And who did

all of them answer to? He shook his head, trying to slow down his thoughts. It had been a damn coup out there. He'd only been around these guys for one full day. Challenger had just eliminated the leader—Boss—and was propping up baby brother Whiner in his place. But not for Whiner to be the man like he was telling him. No. For Challenger to jerk his strings and run the show. It was clear as day to Leo.

Apparently not to Whiner.

Suddenly, Leo was more scared than he'd been since this ordeal had begun. Because Challenger was utterly terrifying. And any minute, that door could open, and Leo would have to answer to him for what he'd said on the video.

FIFTY-ONE

Delaney had been out as soon as her head hit the pillow in the privacy of Gabrielle's sleeper until her alarm woke her Monday evening, four hours after she'd talked to Clark Applewood. She had a micro-bathroom and tiny kitchenette in the cabin. She got to use her own pillow. She never worried about bed bugs. It saved time. All things she was extremely thankful for right then.

She moaned. "Not enough sleep. Not enough. Not enough."

But if she was going to stick to the plan Clark had signed off on, she had to get on the road. She crawled out of bed, splashed water on her face, then sat back down on the bed's edge and booted up her laptop, tethered to her phone's signal. She ignored the incoming emails, texts, and missed calls. There would be time for them later.

Through bleary eyes, she looked at possible routes toward Helena. The most direct was to return via Coutts–Sweetgrass on the Interstate. The port was open twenty-four hours a day, which she needed. The roads would be clear. But she'd face an army of agents and the probability of active law enforcement patrolling the interstate on the drive through Montana.

Not with the load of machine guns I'll be hauling. Not with the plan I have with the ATF. A plan she hadn't shared with Clark in full, of course. For starters, she'd told Clark only that she was getting texts from a supposed contact of Leo's captors with a burner number, which she'd refused to give up, citing it as insurance and a bargaining chip. Nothing about her mother or her suspicions about Liam. Also, Clark thought he and his team would take down the militia and she'd cart Leo away. Which she agreed with, except for one thing. She wanted the man who'd murdered Jackie Spurrier and was responsible for those unmarked graves, and she intended to get him by any means necessary. *Assuming I can figure out who he is by then.*

So, should she cross at Chief Mountain Pass or Carway? She leaned toward the cover the terrain would provide south of the Chief Mountain port. Then she slapped the bed. It closed for the season in the fall. She double checked. It had shut down in September. *Damn, damn, damn.*

She pulled the Carway information up. It stayed open year-round through eleven p.m. She checked the time. Six thirty. The drive would take three hours or more, depending on conditions. Leo couldn't afford for her to miss that crossing and lose twelve hours.

It would have to be Carway. And she would have to leave *right now.*

Delaney turned off her music. For some reason it was driving up her agitation. Her mind was consumed with endless worry about the Carway route. Taking it meant she'd have to drive through the Blackfeet Reservation. She knew from her driving days that they were an inhospitable bunch. Their communities were riddled with drugs, alcohol, and violence. It had never been the place for a middle-of-the-night breakdown. But recently she'd also read about a Mexican cartel infiltrating the reservation, so the cartel could operate in the US in a zone where not all the laws would apply to them—a semi-lawless zone with a much lower concentration of law enforcement. The Blackfeet Nation wasn't alone in this problem. It was happening on reservations across the US, and it was scary.

She was equally concerned about the terrain and weather. She would be battling the eastern slope of Glacier National Park's Lewis Range of mountains. The risk of a blow over from the downslope winds was high. Vigilance and strength would be required, at a time when she was sleepy and crossing bad roads in the pitch dark. Add to that the extremely low temperatures and the winter storm about to unleash its fury on northern Montana, and it would be tough going. If she'd been hauling a normal load, she would have bunked in Calgary. Hell, if she'd been hauling a normal load, she'd have retread the same Interstate route she'd used driving northward.

For contraband, though, the Blackfeet Reservation was just about perfect. For her plan with the ATF, too.

A reply to Delaney's earlier message that she was leaving Calgary had come in from Fabi.

You give us the crates, we verify the contents, then we give you Leo.

Delaney dictated and sent a reply with Siri.

Nope. I hand off to the #1 guy. Approx 250 machine guns—I won't be blamed for handing to wrong person.

The reply came fast.

Who told you to look in those crates?

Me. The one risking years in jail.

Fine.

And I want Liam there.

I don't know why you think I can make the impossible happen.

Delaney shook her head, "Oh, no. You didn't just say that." She dictated and sent another.

And I don't know why you think I believe they'll keep Leo alive. Maybe I hand this load over to the authorities. Or find a buyer for myself.

I can't raise a dead man.

That was not a no.

Leo will be in my control before anyone goes near the trailer.

No.

I will not show up with their guns without that.

If you don't show, they will hunt you down and make you pay for them any way they can.

Which won't happen if they promise.

There was a pause of several minutes.
Finally, Fabi sent another text.

Fine. You have the promise.

Delaney almost laughed. Like hell she did. But they wouldn't have expected anything less than for her to ask for it.

Delaney downshifted on the final approach to the Carway port of entry. She worked her jaw, trying to relax. She'd been practicing looks of boredom and nonchalance in the last few miles. Killing the motor with her shifter in neutral and coasting up to the window, she rolled into the oversized bay.

The smile that met her there was only half the size of the one she gave in return. It was Kammie, a border patrol agent who used to race at the same dirt tracks as Delaney's father back in the day. When Gabrielle first pulled up for inspection with her years ago, Kammie had remembered Delaney as the tagalong little girl who'd idolized her. Delaney and Kammie had never been close, but over the years, they'd had each other's backs on a few occasions. Delaney had literally punched a driver in the throat when he'd pinned Kammie against a wall outside a bathroom in a little bar in Montana. Kammie had started extending extra professional courtesy to Delaney after that incident. And it had come in handy. Maybe it would tonight, too.

Kammie threw a glance over her shoulder then spoke softly. "I heard you moved back to Wyoming and hung up your boots and spurs, Cowgirl."

The old nickname warmed Delaney. She'd never been an actual cowgirl, but Kammie had called her the Cowgirl of the Ice Roads. "I adopted my niece. She lost her parents."

Kammie nodded, suddenly looking very serious. "My supervisor is watching. Let's keep this moving. Empty or loaded?"

Delaney gestured with her thumb. "Loaded."

"ID and manifest, please."

Delaney handed both through the window.

Kammie scanned them but kept talking. "Any guns, alcohol, or cigarettes?"

Delaney maintained a steady gaze and just barely kept from licking her nervous lips. "No."

"Are you reloading and coming back through?"

"No."

"All right. I'd be remiss not to ask if you were aware of the weather and road reports?"

"I am." *And frankly, terrified.*

"Fuel tanks full?"

"Yes."

"Okay, then. Keep it between the lines." Kammie nodded at her.

"Thank you, agent."

Delaney turned Gabrielle's big motor over and pushed in the brakes to leave.

"Wait," a new voice called. A man's voice.

Delaney's heart sunk. She stopped her rig. "Yes?"

The second agent looked too young to be the supervisor except for a hairline that had receded halfway back his skull. "You came in for this load earlier today?" His voice was officious. *Little Napoleon.*

"Yes."

"Can you confirm where you picked it up?"

Delaney recited the address of the warehouse by memory.

"Have you driven for Far West before?"

"No."

"Would you be willing to let us inspect your cargo?"

"Of course. It wouldn't do wonders for my timeline, which wouldn't help me working with this new company. But you have a job to do, and I respect that."

"Did you witness the loading of your trailer?"

What is this about? "I did." *Not.* She'd have to get square with God later about the choices she was making to get Leo back. Hopefully He believed in the greater good and even more was rooting for their love story.

The agent frowned. Kammie kept her eyes cast down. He looked at his watch, then shook his head. "Drive on."

Delaney nodded at him. Her dash clock read ten fifty-five. Five minutes until closing time. *And that's the only reason I just got away with this.* "Thanks."

As she accelerated out of the station, she felt like she was going to throw up. That had been close. Too close, with Leo the one who would have paid if she'd been searched. She drove with her lips caught in her teeth, eyes darting back and forth to her sideview mirrors, watching for the wig-wag lights that would signal she was heading for the wrong side of the law with Border Patrol.

Skeeter's phone rang. He was about to answer it when he heard a commotion at Leo's office. He stood up and peered down the hall. It was Joe Tarver. Skeeter had never liked the deputy. Back in the day, Joe seemed to take too much pleasure bringing Skeeter in for a night in the drunk tank. He'd heard the jokes the older man had cracked about him. He would shoot the bird at Joe when his back was turned—it made Skeeter feel better.

It sounded like he and Drew were arguing now. Then the argument moved into the hall. Joe was red-faced from yelling. Drew was trying to get a word in edgewise.

Skeeter watched for a second, ready to rush in if Drew needed it. They'd become buddies of sorts since they both hung out at the Loading Shed. Skeeter because he watched Juan Julio for Mary and watched Mary while watching her son. She was the prettiest woman he'd ever seen and the nicest, too, so it was the perfect gig. Drew because he was dating Adriana. Poor guy. That woman was like a rat terrier. Cute and feisty, but sometimes they bite.

Joe let up on Drew. He started down the hall toward Skeeter.

Skeeter dropped back into his seat.

"What the hell are you doing here?" Joe lifted his chest and squared his shoulders. Skeeter stood a head taller, and it had always seemed to bother the other man.

"At Delaney's desk? I needed a place to work. I didn't touch any of her stuff."

"A place to *work*? On what?"

"We're trying to find Leo. I'm helping."

"You? On whose authority?"

Drew was barreling down the hall. "Back off, Joe. Delaney authorized it. We were short- staffed."

Joe was shaking his head. "No. No way. I'm in charge with Leo out."

"What?"

"I have seniority."

Drew crossed his arms. "I'll have to hear that from her."

Joe pointed at Skeeter. "We don't need your services. You can go now."

Skeeter looked from Drew to Joe. "Uh..."

Drew threw his hands in the air. "That's not right, Joe. We need Skeeter."

Joe strutted to his cubicle where he sat and leaned back in his chair, a smirk on his face. "There's nothing he's doing that I can't do."

"Of course not. But we can spread out the load. Now that you're finally here we need to update you and integrate you. There's a lot to do in a very short timeframe, if we're going to get Leo back alive."

"What do you mean, *finally* here?"

Drew tapped the top of his wrist. "The schedule said you'd be in at the beginning of the shift. It's midday. I thought you must have missed your flight home."

"What business is it of yours?"

"Whatever, man. I'm calling Delaney." Drew had his phone out, pressed a button, and put it to his ear.

"Do that." Joe stood back up. "Do I need to escort you out, Rawlins?"

Drew made a disgusted sound. "Skeeter, I'm sorry. I'll fix this."

Skeeter said, "Don't worry. You, Delaney, and Leo are my friends. I don't care where I work. And I don't need no escort, Tarver. I know the way."

Joe raised his eyebrows. "Stand down on our case. This is a police matter."

Skeeter saluted him with a bent wrist, a move that would have earned him extra physical training in the Army if his commanding officer had seen him do it. Joe could flap his gums all he wanted, but it didn't matter to Skeeter. He was working this case before Drew and Delaney brought him in, and he'd be working on it until Leo was back, whether in an official capacity or not. But that didn't mean he was happy about how Joe was treating him. A leopard didn't change its stripes. Or whatever the saying was.

He let his face go slack. "Uh huh."

"Dammit! She's not answering," Drew said. "Hang tight, Skeeter. I'll get you back in as soon as I can."

Back at his usual high-top table at the Loafing Shed, Skeeter waved to Mary. "Got a few calls to make."

She handed a beer to a customer. "What are you working on today?"

"Bringing Leo back."

She smiled at him. "You're good people, Skeeter. He's important to Adriana and Delaney. To all of us."

He nodded at her, suddenly unable to speak. He busied himself setting up his workspace.

Mary brought him a Diet Coke with a lime sidecar. "On the house." She reached out, touching his shoulder.

The warmth of her hand sent a buzz through him. He thought he detected mangoes or something tropical every time she was near. "Thanks."

"Of course."

He couldn't help sneaking a peek as she walked back to the bar. He loved the way her hair went sky high on top of her head. Her makeup, which made her eyes look sexy, pointy at the sides. He especially liked her jeans and the way she wore them with all the "look here" bling on the back pockets. She was an angel on earth.

He tore his eyes away. He had to get to work. Following up on the steroid head ex-boyfriend was the next order of business. He consulted his notes for the latest number he'd found for Robby Sanders. It was for a halfway house in Billings. According to a guy who used to work with him, Robby had gotten out of jail recently. Skeeter put on his headphones and dialed. The call rang through.

He cleared his throat, ready. Eager to be the one to break the case, not just for the group to find Leo. He wanted to shove it in Joe Tarver's face and all the way up his nose.

The phone rang and was quickly answered by a woman with a prim voice. When Skeeter asked for Robby, she said, "Robby is not available at the moment. May I have him call you?"

"Yes, please."

He ended the call after giving her his information.

Then he saw he had a voicemail from a number in his Recents. His outgoing Recents. He pressed play and listened.

"This is Alisha, we talked a few days ago. You said to call. I just had a visit from a man named Cole Atwell. I'm very sure he's the one who was following Janet, um, Jackie. He said that the police were looking for her, but that he didn't hurt her. He asked

for my help. I guess in his mind Jackie would have wanted me to help him, at least that's what he was trying to say. There was something not right about him. I got him out by promising him I'd do what I could. I'm really nervous and wondering if I should call the Sheridan police?"

Skeeter nearly dropped his phone in his excitement. *Take that, Joe Tarver.*

FIFTY-THREE

Delaney maneuvered Gabrielle away from the border station. She had a thought. The fact that she hadn't been detained meant that Leo's kidnappers wanted the load, not her incarceration. Otherwise, Liam would have tipped off the agents. She wasn't sure if that was good or bad for Leo, but she was glad not to face even a minute in a federal prison.

Her lowered stress was short-lived, though. She hadn't just entered the United States with a load of illegal machine guns. She wasn't just in Montana. She was in the Blackfeet Reservation.

She had very little cell signal already, and she knew she'd likely have none soon. Using Siri, she sent two texts. The first was to Clark Applewood.

Crossed.

The second was to her mother.

Crossed. Roads v bad. Progress v slow. No signal 4 hrs.

Then she sent another to the source of her maternal genetics.

Border agent said probs on 484.

It was a lie. But she needed a plausible excuse for her location if she was tracked where she was about to go.

Then she had Siri read her messages to her. Updates on the evidence the team was gathering—nothing yet to identify who had murdered Jackie Spurrier. One from Drew.

What's going on out there? If you let me know, maybe we can help you more.

She'd have to bring him in soon. But late at night driving in a snowstorm was not the time. Then another from him.

Tarver is back. He's causing problems. He kicked Skeeter out, but Skeeter told me he's still on the case.

She let out a string of words that would have earned her soap in the mouth from her grandmother. There was a voicemail from Joe, which she ignored. She had no bandwidth for his antics at the moment.

Siri played a voicemail from Carrie. *"Melaney, whatever Kat is saying about me is bull... corn. Don't let her stress you out when you're worried about Leo."* Delaney heard a snuffling sound and realized Carrie was crying. *"You're not going to lose him. When I lost my mom and my brother and my boyfriend, I had a bad feeling. Like I knew it was going to happen without knowing what it was. But I don't feel like that about Leo. I just wanted you to know that."* There was a long pause. *"Okay. That's all. Be safe."* Another pause. *"I, um, love you."* The voicemail ended.

Delaney tightened her jaw to keep from crying, too. Carrie was maturing into a truly kind human being. How lucky Delaney was that adopting her had turned out so well. It had been hard at times but could have been much worse, given the trauma the girl had endured. She would give her the biggest hug when she got home.

She flexed her fingers and rotated her neck, as her thoughts switched over to Leo. Worrying about Leo, no matter what Carrie had said. *Please let him still be alive.* Then she gave herself a mental slap. She required all her mental energy for this drive if she wanted to make it to Helena, or wherever the militia —as she now thought of them—would be sending her. Her skills were rusty.

She swigged down cold coffee. "Pay attention, Delaney. Inattentiveness kills. Falling asleep kills. Leo needs you alive. You can't bring in Jackie's murderer if you're dead either."

The snow was falling steadily now, creating a tunnel of white. White sky, white road, white shoulders, white all beyond the road. The reflectors were long since covered. Green metal fence posts on either side of the road were her best indicators she was still on it. She had about twenty-five miles of this until her date with the devil she knew, in her plan to outwit the devil she didn't. In these conditions, that was going to take an hour or more.

She checked her sideview mirrors for sign of a tail. Headlights. Or the movement of a vehicle running without them. The white Nissan Rogue that she hadn't seen since she left the hotel. She looked out and up at the sky as best she could. The limited visibility from the clouds made that less than helpful, even if her sightline hadn't been blocked by Gabrielle's bulk. At least she couldn't be tracked from the sky now.

She tapped her brakes, testing the road. The semi slipped. She cursed. Better to chain up than to end up stuck or—worse— flipped. It was conservative, given that she didn't expect ice, but she was completely alone in a remote area, and snow would pack under the weight of a heavily laden eighteen-wheeler. That could be plenty slick.

But chaining up wasn't going to be fun. Turning on her hazards, she slowed and stopped in what she hoped was the shoulder and not the middle of the road. She decided to chain up just her back drive axle. Just enough for a little extra grip. Not enough time that she'd be discovered and jumped or freeze to death.

Delaney pushed herself out the door and into the wind. *And this is why we stay dressed for the outside weather inside the cab.* Wrecks, flats, breakdowns, chain-ups, load shifts. The possibilities of problems were endless.

She opened a side hatch and pulled out one set of chains. The buggers weighed more than she did, which is why she kept them in their plastic container until the last second, to slide across the ground. She grabbed the chain's end, dragged on it, and grunted as she tossed it over the tire. Talk about a dead lift. Leo always marveled at how strong she was. It didn't come from a gym, although she kept her strength up there now that she was no longer on the road. When she had the chain on, she realized she was wet from her own sweat and already tired, but she repeated the process on the other set of chains.

The last thing she did was drive a mile down the road, park again, and tighten the chains one more time. Loose chains did no good and she'd be more likely to lose them. Of course, they were only rated to twenty-five miles per hour, so if she went over that, they would break apart and fly off anyway.

When she got back in the cab, she took off her gloves and wiped her neck and face with a cloth she kept in the glove compartment. Her arms and legs were quivering. *Real-world strength beats gym strength every time.* She switched off her differential lockers, essentially making her back two axles into one. Big rig four-wheel drive.

Now the hum of her tires was accompanied by the percussive noises of the chains.

"Hey, Siri," she said.

"Mm-hm."

"Play Dad's List."

After a polite, confirming discussion, Siri initiated the classic rock play list. It boomed through the speakers. The grinding guitars and frenetic drum solos were like Xanax to Delaney. The soundtrack of her best memories with her father and of her years of meditative time on the road as a truck driver. Delaney touched her fingertips to her sternum. Her heavy coat was unzipped just enough that she could feel a medallion through the layers of clothing. A talisman. *Eastern Wyoming Dirt Track Champion*, it read, commemorating a big win by her father. She wore it nearly every day, near her heart.

Feeling him with her, she sang along with Van Halen, then Heart, and was screeching the lyrics to "There's No One Like You" when she saw the lights of Babb, Montana, in the distance. The western-most towns of the Blackfeet Reservation, like Babb, were overrun by visitors to Glacier National Park in the summertime. In the winter, they shrank to almost nothing. And the people who stayed were often the ones she didn't want to meet up with on a dark night when she was carrying cargo that probably looked pretty valuable—and that was not counting the machine guns. Cargo she needed to barter for Leo's life.

She cut her headlights and slowed further. She'd navigate by the image on her phone screen. As she did, she had a bad thought. Someone following her at this speed could be doing exactly the same thing, and she wouldn't know they were back there. Well, she couldn't do anything about it.

She switched off her Jake Brakes. No way was she going to take a chance on the loud engine brake announcing her presence in the middle of town. Then she killed her running lights and marker lights. She'd used this trick many times at weigh stations—granted, she'd navigated by moonlight reflecting off the tiny glass beads embedded in the paint in the roadbed. With Gabrielle's dark colors and the sleek flatbed profile, they were now cloaked against the night sky and curtained by the snow. With any luck, she'd skate past any hoodlums up drinking and raising Hell in the middle of the night. Even if they heard the sound of her truck over the scream of the wind and the noise inside the bar, it would be confusing without a visual to match it to. Her biggest risk would be if someone was outside as she passed by.

But Siri and the map had her back.

She muted her radio and let off the gas as she entered town. Then she held her breath as she glided past a bunker-like bar with a crooked half-lit neon sign. She smelled hamburgers and French fries, but it was the last place in the world she would have stopped to eat. Ramshackle trucks were crowded up to the building like bugs to a blue light. She didn't see anyone in the parking lot. She chanced a breath.

Her turn was on the edge of town, and, using her manual downshift, she didn't even have to hit her brakes and show the telltale red of her brake lights for it, nor did she signal. She made the right and immediately began skirting the eastern side of Lower St. Mary Lake. She was very near the edge of the reservation and the entrance to the national park now.

She was also close to her ATF rendezvous point, although they were driving in from the south. She checked her mapping. Only three miles to go.

Her eyes lit on her sideview mirror as she reached to begin switching lights back on. What she saw chilled her to the bone.

Headlights, closing fast.

FIFTY-FOUR

At the end of her shift Monday night, Tabby stopped by the manager's office. He was a decent enough guy. A kid really. The son of the owner. Sometimes he blushed when he talked to her, so she always made sure to dress in street clothes—sweatpants and a bulky sweatshirt—before stopping by. Tonight was payday. Most of her money came from tips, but she wasn't passing up even the meager base wage.

She rapped on his closed door. "It's Tabby. Picking up my check."

"Just a minute."

She heard thumps and rustling. Whatever he was doing in there, she did not want to know. She heard him unlock the door. Then she heard his footsteps walking back to his desk.

"All right. Come on in."

She entered to the stink of too much Axe body spray. He was sitting in a cushy chair behind a desk piled with invoices, schedules, and inventories. The set-up consumed nearly the whole space but left enough room for one wall to be covered with pictures of rodeo celebrities posing with his father in the club. *Paid appearances, I'll bet.* "Sorry to bother. My check?"

"Yes." He thumbed through a stack of envelopes and held one out to her.

She reached for it, put her hand on it, even pulled at it, but he held firm.

"Some guy was in here looking for you. I'd never seen him before."

The blood left her face and her head and she had to put her other hand on his desk to keep from falling right over on it.

"You okay?"

"Yeah, sure. I didn't eat on break. Low blood sugar. What was his name?"

"He didn't say."

"Give me a hint. A description?"

"Tall. Dark hair. Spooky green eyes."

She almost smiled. *That's not him. It's not anyone I can remember.* She sighed. "Huh. Well, get a name next time."

He released her check. "Want someone to walk you to your car? In case he's waiting for you out there?"

"No. I'm fine. Thanks, though."

But she held her bear mace in her hand when she exited the building five minutes later.

FIFTY-FIVE

The vehicle behind Delaney started honking and flashing its lights.

"Great." All she had to do was drive three more miles. There'd be an unpleasant surprise waiting there for whoever was signaling her. She couldn't outrun them, though. She was limited to twenty-five miles per hour in the chains, and the vehicle behind her was closing fast.

Limited? That was fatalistic thinking. She mashed her accelerator. To hell with the chains. Let them break apart. These weren't Leo's captors—the kidnappers wanted delivery of the guns. These guys intended to pull the truck over and steal her cargo. When they discovered she was a woman, what would they do—rape her before they tortured and killed her? She patted her belly. There was no reassuring presence of a Staccato in its holster. She hadn't retrieved it from its hiding place after she crossed the border.

"*Joshua 1:9. Have I not commanded you? Be strong and courageous. Do not be afraid; do not be discouraged, for the Lord your God will be with you wherever you go.*" The words, the verse had come to her automatically, a vestige of her childhood learning Bible verses, or, more often, kneeling in rocks when she or Liam failed to do so. No matter how she'd come to know them, no matter how she resented the knowledge, they came to her in moments like this one.

Her eyes flashed around the interior. She was without a firearm at the ready, and she'd be stronger and more courageous with a weapon. She spotted her multitool in the console. She also had a six-inch pocketknife on her hip. Those would help in close quarters fighting. She unzipped her coat and hiked up her layers of clothing for easier access to the pocketknife, then activated her electric locks.

Maybe I'll have time to go for my gun.

A truck whipped around her, horn blaring again. When it drew even with the cab, a man leaned out the passenger window with a gun. She ducked and swerved, but his shots pinged off Gabrielle in front of Delaney. *He's trying not to endanger the load by killing me when I'm still driving.*

"You son of a bitch!" Her beautiful tractor, marred by the bullets of thugs trying to disable her.

The pickup accelerated. She tried to count heads from the back. Two. Three at the most. She watched for smoke, sniffed for it, but didn't smell any.

She swung the nose of the semi at their truck, clipping its bed.

The truck spun, and she plowed into it. Gabrielle shoved it down the road. She whooped and pumped her arm. Her joy was short-lived, though. She'd caught the back end of the truck. It jerked forward from Gabrielle's front bumper and pulled away.

Two more trucks drove alongside her. She hadn't been watching her sideview. Hadn't seen them coming. There were no more shots at the semi, but the trucks darted in front of her. All three led her now.

"Oh, no." Delaney could see what was coming.

The three trucks threw up brake lights and stopped hard. She was tempted to accelerate and bust through their line, but she knew it was pointless. Gabrielle would sustain damage. She might crash or slide off the road. And the way they'd staggered their vehicles, she wouldn't be able to take them all out at once. Going around them was no use either. She'd end up stuck in the snow.

Her mapping showed a road toward the lake on her right. She strained to find it in the dark. There it was, she realized, in twenty feet. Did she dare take it? She could get trapped back in there. But if she didn't take it she was trapped out here. *Live to fight another day.*

She swung the steering wheel to the right, holding on tight to the wheel. She would keep fighting.

The unmaintained road was snowy, but not so deep that Gabrielle couldn't handle it. Maybe six inches, and she had a good eighteen of clearance. Delaney kept her speed up. She was hoping for a way out on the other end of the road. She chanced letting go with one hand for a quick swipe on her map. In only a few hundred yards, the road ended. She frowned. Did it end at the lake?

If there was one thing Delaney knew, it was ice driving. She did a quick analysis of the situation. She needed eleven to sixteen inches of thickness to safely drive Gabrielle across ice. The only way to know for sure whether she had it was to measure it. *And that's not going to happen.* Her eyes flicked to her sideview. Headlights. More than one set. She lacked the certainty of precise measurement, but she was familiar with the average monthly temperatures of the area. She'd driven Montana in the winter for years. Most Rocky Mountain West citizens such as herself watched weather like sports scores or market stocks. This had already been a colder-than-normal season in the Rockies for three solid months.

The ice should be all right. Maybe. She had about one hundred yards left to decide.

Gunfire erupted behind her. Serious gunfire. She chanced another look in the mirror just as one of the trucks following her careened off the road and smashed into a tree. The other trucks seemed to be slowing down. Then they stopped.

She couldn't believe it. She saw another vehicle behind them. Maybe reservation police or the feds? That would be a miracle akin to a second virgin birth. They were as scarce as... as... women driving trucks on the ice roads. Which she knew was very scarce.

In front of her, she could now see where land met lake. It was a very gentle slope. If she had to try to make the transition from land to ice, she couldn't ask for a better natural ramp. But she didn't want to do it if she didn't have to.

She skipped downshifting and stomped on her brakes. "Come on, come on." Gabrielle behaved and did not fishtail. When the rig was at a nearly complete stop despite the incline, she reached down and pulled the parking brake. The rig lurched to a complete stop. Diving into the cabin, she jerked out the compartment under her bunk and pawed through it for her gun case. She'd never opened the combination lock faster, never jammed a magazine in and loaded a cartridge with more speed. She kept the gun in her right hand and grabbed a shotgun with her left.

The sound of gunfire in the night outside hadn't let up.

Whoever was out there holding off her pursuers would need help. Delaney was pretty darn invested in their success and only too happy to come to their aid.

FIFTY-SIX

Snow crunched under Tabby's boots as she walked from her car across the backyard Monday night. Not really her car. The car that had belonged to her landlady's husband before he died. Not only was she living rent-free, but the woman had insisted she borrow the car, too, when she saw Tabby taking taxis.

"That's too much money. I won't hear of it when Ron's car is just collecting cobwebs in the garage," Mrs. Owens said.

Tabby hadn't known there were people on earth as nice as Mrs. Owens. It was a shame she was going to have to move on. In another world, she would have lived here forever. But not in this one, so close to where *he* was. She'd decided on the way home that she couldn't take a chance any longer either. No one should have known who she was. Not in this town. It didn't matter if it was a stranger.

She shouldn't have used her name at the club. Only they'd refused to hire her without documentation. She had tried. At least she hadn't had to rent this place under her name.

No one had followed her home—she'd been watching for that. She hurried across the postage stamp backyard to the red door and unlocked it with shaking hands. She would just get all her cash and a toothbrush and stuff some underwear in her purse. If she didn't eat the whole way to West Virginia, she had enough money.

She ran inside without even turning on the lights. The moonlight through the kitchen window was bright enough for her to see her hiding places in the pantry and under the stove. She stuffed cash into her bag. In her bedroom, she scooped panties from her drawer. On her way back out, she grabbed her toothbrush. She paused, then sprayed on some of the fancy perfume she'd splurged on two weeks ago. She hated leaving it.

It had taken her only two minutes to get her things, she guessed. She'd done good. Her only regret was not saying goodbye to Mrs. Owens. She'd just write her a letter when she made it to West Virginia.

"Goodbye," she whispered.

"But I just got here," a male voice said. A voice she didn't know.

A light came on. Terror froze her in place.

He lifted his phone and spoke into it. "I found that other leak that needed plugging. Do you want the pleasure, or shall I take care of it myself?" He listened, smiling, then said, "Got it." He put the phone back in his pocket.

She knew who sent him. This one would kill her, or he would. She had nothing left to lose by fighting with everything she had, but she didn't want him to hurt Mrs. Owens, so she didn't scream as the man with the spooky green eyes walked toward her.

FIFTY-SEVEN

Delaney rolled down her window to check out her situation. The scene was unexpected, to say the least. She'd seen the first vehicle crash head-on into a tree. The cab of the old truck was crumpled. She couldn't be sure, but it looked like there were still two people inside. Dead? Injured? The second vehicle had flipped and was sliding upside down. As she watched, it slipped past Gabrielle and ended up twenty feet out onto the ice. Back toward the road, the third vehicle had stopped. The two occupants were on the ground with their hands on their heads, rifles in front of them.

But now there was that fourth vehicle behind them. It was a white Nissan Rogue. She was too far away to be sure, but she would put a twenty on it bearing North Dakota plates. It appeared her minders had come to her aid to protect their cargo. Now she wasn't sure which set of bad guys to be more afraid of.

She pulled her latch and kicked the door open. The aroma of pine trees filled her senses. The area was beautiful and pristine—like something out of a fairy tale turned into a James Bond movie. Leaving her shotgun behind, she was shouting before her feet hit the ground. "Wyoming Deputy Delaney Pace, stay down with your hands where I can see them. And you there—identify yourself!"

Walking toward the men on the ground was a tall silhouette holding a shotgun pointed at the men. She felt a frisson of recognition. The figure said, "It's me, Delaney. Clint Rock-Below. I've got them."

Clint?!? There was no time to ask what he was doing. He was here. The minders weren't. This was great news.

"We need to hurry. I've got a place I'm supposed to be," she said.

"You're welcome, I think." Clint kicked the guns further from the two men on the ground.

"Sorry. I'm very grateful."

"Help me get everyone secured. Five minutes and you'll be back on the road. Flexicuffs on my belt." Clint was in plain-clothes but wearing his duty belt over heavy-duty winter gear.

"Got it."

Clint said, "These men don't look Blackfeet."

Closing the distance between herself and Clint, she took a supply of the cuffs. She secured the first two suspects' hands behind their backs but opted to leave their feet free. They might need to walk back to Babb. She noticed they weren't wearing gloves, but that was on them. She owed them nothing.

One man turned to the other and whispered. They looked nothing alike—one was all forehead, the other had a completely round face offset by a pointed chin— yet they shared traits. Neither seemed particularly tall. Both had dark hair and light-brown skin.

Delaney could hear them clearly. "They're speaking Spanish."

To the man closest to him, Clint said, "*Sí, te entiendo.*" He lowered his voice and moved closer to Delaney. "I think they're cartel."

It was her guess, too. She picked up the first semi-auto and fired it into all four tires of the intact truck. It sunk a few inches. Then she gathered the rest of the rifles. She'd stow them with her guns in the sleeper berth. "I'm worried about the guys in the other trucks. They could still fire on us."

"Yeah, but not if we get out of here. Their vehicles are disabled, so they can't follow us."

"I like the sound of that. I want as far away from cartel as I can get."

"We can call 911 from the road."

"Maybe. Let's talk after my meetup."

He nodded. "I can live with that."

She smiled. "You've been following me."

"I told you I was going to protect you." He was staring at her, as if he wanted to hug her. She liked the idea of additional help in this phase of the operation. She was relieved and a little bit emotional that he'd ridden up on his white Rogue at just the right moment. But—no hugs.

She took a half-step back. "I made you, I just didn't know who you were. Are you good in that rental for the conditions?"

"I paid the upcharge for the snow tires. I've got chains if I need them."

"Stick close behind me. I'll explain more when we get where I'm going."

"Okay."

She jogged through the snow with her armload of semi-autos, staying low, trying not to look like a target. The chains on the driver's side were intact, she realized. *Good. That will help me get out of here.* Breathing a sigh of relief when no more shots were fired, she hauled herself back into Gabrielle. She set the long guns in the passenger floorboard to deal with later and took a seat and tucked her Staccato under her thigh.

She put the rig in reverse and pressed the gas pedal. As she was slowly making her way up the incline, cold steel pressed against her neck. She immediately recognized her error. She hadn't locked the doors. The men in the other vehicles—this had to be one of them.

"Got you now, bitch." He spoke with a Mexican accent.

Think again, buddy. She stomped the brakes to the floor, which caused the muzzle of her stowaway's gun to leave her neck as he tumbled forward toward the dash. She pulled her gun from under her thigh and chopped him across the back of the neck. When he didn't move, she pulled one of Clint's flexi-cuffs from her pocket and trussed him up like his cohorts.

Then she resumed backing up but stopped beside Clint. She rolled down the passenger window and unlocked the doors. "Do you mind grabbing someone out of my passenger seat?"

He opened the door and lifted one eyebrow. "This one failed the IQ test. He must have come from the truck on the lake."

"More like I did. I left Gabrielle open."

"The two that hit the tree didn't make it. No airbags, no seatbelts. I guess this means we're still missing one of them."

"I'm not missing him."

"Me neither." He pulled the man out by his shoulders and propped him in the snow on his behind beside the others. "*Adiós, cabrones.*"

Delaney finished backing onto the main road and pulled forward. When Clint was visible in her sideview mirror, she drove the final two miles to the tiny town of St. Mary, Montana, winter population fifty-four, hopefully with no public drinking establishments open. She turned right near the edge of the lake and then into a closed seasonal campground a few hundred feet down the winding road. The place was deserted with picnic tables and hookups covered by tarps and snow.

She parked and blinked her headlights. Clint pulled in beside her.

Two white vans emerged from the cover of the trees.

Delaney had been expecting the vans, but they had been

expecting only her. She exited Gabrielle, shoulders hunched against the wind. She turned and held up one finger to ask Clint to stay put before she walked to the van closest to her. The passenger window began to lower, so she steered toward it. Peering in, she found Clark Applewood at the wheel. The rest of the vehicle was crowded with unfamiliar faces. The only other time she'd met Clark, he'd been in a very federalistic black suit and *Men in Black* shades. Tonight, his muscular body was squeezed into a winter white snowsuit that matched those worn by the others and looked a lot like those of the suspects in Jackie's murder. His face was uncovered, revealing a nose crooked from unnatural reasons and his characteristic scowl. She was surprised by eyes almost as green as her own in his dark face.

"Who's that with you?" Clark said.

"Hello to you, too, Clark. Yes, I'm well after a very harrowing drive, thank you."

"Cut the shit, Delaney."

"That is Police Chief Clint Rock-Below from Kearny, Wyoming. Apparently, he's been following me for my entire journey. When I was run off the road by a gang of cartel thugs outside Babb, he rode in guns blazing, thank God, or I would not be standing here now."

Clark's scowl deepened. "Do you think it was a hit or an opportunistic attack?"

"Opportunistic."

"Where are they now?"

"Five out of six were dealt with. One got away. As did we."

"I don't like hearing one got away."

"Likewise. But we weren't prepared to launch a cross-country search for him at night during a storm on the Blackfeet Reservation. After you load your guys in my truck, though, you can be my guest to try it yourself." Delaney turned and waved to Clint, beckoning him to join her. "Tactically, this means we have an additional vehicle now. One that's more nondescript than your vans."

"Does he know the plan?"

"Not yet."

Clint approached, a big frown the centerpiece of a suspicious face. "What the devil is going on, Delaney?"

She made introductions. Clark did not introduce his stony-faced agents to either of them. *Such great manners.*

Clint crossed his arms. "Bureau of Alcohol, Tobacco, Firearms, and Explosives? When did you partner up?"

Delaney explained to Clint exactly what she'd found in the crates loaded on her flatbed. "I called Clark as soon as I saw my cargo. As you've probably already gathered, Clark hasn't had a reason to take down the group that has Leo or he would have already. I have a trailer full of reasons. He agreed that catching them red-handed would be ideal for their operation, in tandem with my rescue of Leo."

Clint interrupted. "No one in their right mind believes they're planning to let you and Leo leave alive."

She tapped her temple. "Exactly."

Back on the road, Delaney tried to ignore the fact that her sleeper was filled with federal agents, including one she hated so much it made her teeth ache. But it was hard to do when Clark kept leaning out of the sleeper to go over tactical details with her. At least she didn't have to worry about getting rear-ended by friendlies. They'd decided to space out fifteen minutes apart with Gabrielle in the lead going twenty to twenty-five miles per hour, because of the still inclement roads and her chains.

Clark had introduced the other five other agents she was transporting as they'd filed in. They were each carrying a small armory. In their winter camo, they looked fairly similar—serious, muscular, and gaunt—except for varying skin tones and the fact that one was a woman. Past that, she didn't bother to imprint them. They were a means to an end. She hated Clark, she hated the ATF and most feds, and she didn't plan to trade friendship bracelets with any of them. They'd do jobs adjacent to each other, and that would be all.

The snow was slowing, but exhaustion was creeping over Delaney now that the adrenaline of the cartel attack had ebbed. She needed to consume more caffeine, but she'd been trying to minimize stopping for bathroom breaks, especially now that she had six agents outside its door. She popped open a Monster and chugged it down. In the sleeper, the agents were breaking out their snacks. She smelled Cheetos and beef jerky. No one offered her any.

After ten minutes of Clark's yammering, irritation got the better of her. "In case you haven't noticed, I'm trying to deliver us in a tinder box on an ice-skating rink. I have to focus on the road and my driving."

"I'd think you'd care about this going well, seeing as it's your boyfriend we're trying to rescue."

"Don't pretend you care about Leo."

"I won't. But I need to know you won't mess us up or get in our way, and that means drilling on all the possibilities."

Delaney had no illusion that the feds would help her. *Clint will.* She just hoped they didn't actively sacrifice Delaney and Leo to accomplish the ATF mission. "I'm fine with that when..." Her voice faded as she caught sight of headlights in her side-view mirror.

It couldn't be one of her colleagues. She hadn't seen any open establishments in St. Mary. No vehicles on the road, even. Who else would be driving in the middle of the night, in a storm? Overdriving, given how fast they were closing on Gabrielle. She listed the possibilities in her head. People with an emergency. People traveling cross country. People up to no good.

"Earth to Delaney," Clark said.

She held up her hand. "Incoming." And then she frowned. The truck. It looked familiar.

She heard pings from the back of the trailer. "They're firing on us. It's one of the trucks that ran me off the road earlier, back for more."

"I told you I didn't like the one that got away."

She needed him to shut up so she could think. "Not now, Clark."

Should she stop? The agents could pulverize the truck. But their firepower might draw unwanted attention. Maybe she could outrun it. The truck was a beater, and—she now saw—was smashed on top from its slip-and-slide across the frozen lake. *The guy must have freed his buddies. They could have flipped it together.* What were conditions like ahead? Now would have been a great time for other truckers to be on the road offering information and advice over CB radios, but there were none. When she'd checked the radar earlier, it hadn't looked like the storm had extended much further south than where they were, and they were still heading that way.

So, the roads wouldn't be as bad. Could she outrun the truck? It wasn't like she was driving a race car, but she was a professional ice driver with a triple-digit truck. Surely she could outdrive a transplant from Mexico on these roads in a truck on its last legs.

She punched her accelerator to the floor and started shifting through gears as the big rig gathered speed. She'd driven this route several times in the past, albeit in daylight and decent weather, and a memory hit her. If she was remembering right, it might be just what she needed. Enlarging her map, she evaluated the road ahead of her, honing in on the spot she had in mind. Her idea could work, with a head start, her Jake Brakes, and some fancy driving. The cover of darkness would help, too, especially if her pursuers weren't using a map, which was likely — they were following her.

The peppering of gunfire against the trailer had stopped. The pickup was visible but growing smaller in the sideview. A loud *thwump, thwump, thwump* sound startled her. It only took a spit second to identify it—her chains. They'd broken and were beating the daylights out of one of Gabrielle's beautiful fenders.

"What in God's name is going on?" Clark said.

Delaney's voice was clipped. "I'm going to outrun our cartel tail."

"In an eighteen-wheeler on snow in the mountains?"

"There's a lot you don't know about me."

"Your truck is breaking apart!"

"Not my rig. Just my snow chains."

Clark climbed into the passenger seat. "But you need those."

"I've got great snow tires. If you're going to sit up here, buckle in."

The second set of chains busted and started their assault on the other fender. Delaney sent up a quick prayer to the god of trucking that she didn't get a piece of chain in an axle. She side-checked—she was still pulling away from the smaller truck. According to her map, she had about half a mile to go. She decided to mess with the driver's depth perception and switched off her running lights and marking lights, leaving on her headlights for the time being. Then she shifted into neutral and started coasting.

Clark's face looked like a bulldog's. "I don't like this."

"Where are you from, Clark?"

"Georgia."

"Not surprising. You know the most important thing you can do to stay safe in a situation like this?"

"What?"

"Shut up and let me do my job."

A quarter mile to go. If Clark said anything else to her, she didn't hear it, because she went deep inside herself, listening to Gabrielle, the road, and her instincts. As she'd recalled, the road flattened out before it entered the switchback turn she was aiming for, which suited her purposes. She didn't want to use her Jake Brake on an incline. The Jake was the best tool ever invented for slowing heavy trucks as far as she was concerned. It allowed compressed air from the engine cylinders to be released rather than combusted. That created pressure against the rotation of the engine. Then, voila, the truck slowed. The problem was that it could make traction on a slippery road a little dicey, especially in the high setting, even more so going downhill.

She engaged the Jake on low and began downshifting, sharing the work of slowing Gabrielle with the gears. The semi kept a grip on the road, so Delaney moved the Jake to medium. She waited a few seconds, trying to sense even the slightest change in traction.

Still good.

With the dangerous curve approaching fast, she wanted her speed at five miles per hour. This curve was nearly one hundred and eighty degrees. She hadn't cut off enough speed. Did she dare try the Jakes on high?

She bit her lip. If she tapped her brakes, the red lights on the back of the trailer would telegraph the slowdown to the truck behind her. She didn't want that.

She was going to lose traction one way or another—by taking the turn too fast or with the Jake on high. The end result was the same. Well, maybe not exactly the same. Taking the turn too fast could cause Gabrielle to slide off the road, which was bad. The Jake problem risked a jackknife, with the trailer swinging up to greet them in the cab. This was because the Jake only affected the drive wheels under the semi—not the trailer wheels, which spun freely.

But that wasn't really much worse than sliding off the road, if she remained in control. And bottom line—she had to get her speed down.

She flipped the Jake setting to high.

Gabrielle jerked and slowed. The impact wasn't as dramatic as going from no Jake to high, but it still created a floating sensation in the trailer, one obvious enough that Clark screamed, as high-pitched as Kateena when she'd found a mouse in her shoe before school one day. Delaney swore under her breath. She moved the Jake back to medium. It was time to start the turn, their trailer wasn't gripping right, and they were going faster than she wanted. Still, they hadn't jackknifed.

She looked as far ahead as she could see. There were no headlights coming from the opposite direction. The middle of the road was clear of snow, comprising roughly half the oncoming lane and her own lane. Clear didn't mean ice-free, but it was likely good since the temperature hadn't risen enough to melt the snow and risk a re-freeze. She aimed Gabrielle for the visible pavement and steered into the sharp turn, cutting her headlights as she did so.

"Have you lost your mind?!" Clark shouted.

His voice was joined by others from the sleeper now. They sounded scared and angry. A mob.

There was no time to explain that she didn't want their tail to see her headlights when they reversed direction on the other side of the turn. That she needed the guy to miss the hairpin in his crazed effort to overtake the big truck. If he crashed in the middle of the night, Delaney and crew would remain safely on mission. Maybe it would even rid the world of a few more dangerous creeps.

But for that to happen she needed the tires on that load of car parts and machine guns to start spinning in contact with the road again.

Gabrielle seemed to coast the curve in slow motion. It felt

like an eternity. Long enough that a myriad of images played through her mind. Mostly of Leo. Leo eating summer sausage and cheddar cheese cubes with her and the girls at their favorite picnic spot. Leo making faces behind the trainer's back at the gym. Leo with his stupid tablet and investigation templates and databases and apps that he patiently kept teaching her how to use. Leo's blue eyes, his lips, his shoulders, his skin, his touch.

But as the trailer continued to glide through the turn, the images changed to mayhem. Trailers snapped off semis, semis rolled by trailers, and even the one time she'd had a trailer jackknife on her on an ice road. She slid at a terrifying snail's pace nearly one hundred yards until through divine intervention or dumb luck she bumped into the high side of a frozen wave. It was just enough to stop her tractor, which caused the trailer to slingshot slowly, slowly into the same wave, where it crested, slid jerkily over, and lost momentum.

"We're not going to make it," Clark said, his voice tight. He wasn't screaming anymore.

She heard one of the agents in the sleeper praying.

She breathed steadily and stayed loose but ready. She just needed the team to hold it together and not rush her or touch her until she got them through this. Honestly, they were going ten miles per hour on flat ground. How bad a crash did they think this would be? They weren't going to die. The risk was to Leo. Their timeline. His rescue. They were grown-ups acting like babies and needed to snap out of it. She wished she could have partnered with Army Rangers instead.

Behind them, she heard the sound of metal making impact. Seconds later, an explosion so loud it punched her ears painfully. If she hadn't had to hold the wheel steady, she would have clapped her hands over them.

"Holy shit," Clark said. "That was the pickup truck!"

Delaney felt the trailer's wheels catch. She exhaled loudly. "We're good." She flipped on her headlights, running lights, and marking lights, but she didn't accelerate. They had another sharp turn to make before she could do that.

The sleeper erupted into whoops, clapping, cheering, and laughing.

Clark abstained from the revelry. "Did you expect that to happen?"

"I hoped it would."

"Are we going back there?"

"I'm going to get Leo."

Clark stared at her for a moment, then he grinned. "You've got ice running through your veins. I knew you were cut out for federal work."

Delaney's instinct was to argue with him, especially on the federal point. The cartel members had come after her. She'd only fought back. Her primary objectives as a law enforcement officer were to prevent and detect criminal activities, respond to emergencies, and assist those in need. That had been drilled into her throughout her training. She tried to embody those values every day. But sometimes, it was kill or be killed. Those guys could have kept her from getting to Leo. They still could if she went back and waited on someone to haul away bodies and start an investigation.

No way. She wasn't going to let anything stop her. If that was ice in her veins, she could live with it and worry about personal penance later.

FIFTY-EIGHT

Leo woke and sat up. It was disconcerting to have no idea what time it was or whether it was day or night. He rolled his neck. Everything hurt, but he was alive. Challenger had visited him privately after Whiner had gone outside to smoke. When he'd shown up, Leo thought he'd be following Boss into the hereafter.

But Challenger hadn't said a word when he'd come in. He'd just stood Leo up then started punching him. In the gut, on his sides, in the head. Leo tried to block the blows, but between the sedatives in his system and his bound hands and feet, his reactions and balance were off. He was on the floor within a few hits. He curled into a protective ball as Challenger kicked him.

As fast as it had started, it ended. Afterwards, Leo had fallen into a restive sleep.

But something had woken him. Sounds, he realized. They were different from the ones he'd heard since they'd arrived at the bunker. He heard them again. Was it a coyote howling? Someone crying? Or maybe it was something coming from a phone or a television?

He strained to hear more, but whatever it was had stopped.

The last thing he was aware of as his heavy eyelids closed was someone saying, "She's in Montana. She'll be here in the morning."

FIFTY-NINE

Skeeter shuffled into the Loafing Shed with Juan Julio after Mary unlocked the door Tuesday morning. She and the skeletal staff were there to prepare for the breakfast shift. He liked the bar best at this time of day, smelling of stale beer and the sawdust Mary left on the floor overnight to absolve the sins of the evening before. Not that he often came before it opened. Usually just after. Adriana's daily breakfast specials could bring a man to religion. He needed to get back to work on finding Leo, but he'd agreed to watch Juan Julio for the first half hour. The boy was easy, though, and Kat would take over child-minding duties when she and Carrie arrived.

His phone was ringing before Mary had shut the door behind them. A Montana number. "Sorry, Mary. Can you give me five minutes to take this?"

She took her son by the hand. "Come to the office with Mommy, Juan Julio. I have a new toy for you." She kept a small stash of inexpensive new toys hidden for moments like these. Skeeter couldn't imagine a better mother than her.

"Yay!" the boy screamed. He did his funny hop alongside

her, which he called skipping. It was in fact not quite skipping and it usually made Skeeter smile. Now he was preoccupied with the call that would go to voicemail any second.

"No problem. Let me know when you're off," Mary said over her shoulder.

Skeeter said, "Thanks," as he accepted the call and identified himself.

"You called me yesterday? This is Robby Sanders."

Yes! "Thanks for returning my call." Skeeter explained the reason for it. Jackie's murder. Robby's past association with her. He didn't mention the restraining order, yet.

Robby reacted emotionally. Sad, not angry. "It's the worst. Just the worst. I can't believe she's gone. I got clean in jail. I was going to show her. I was hoping now would finally be our time."

Skeeter had been told he wasn't that good at taking hints from women when they weren't interested, but even he could see Robby should have taken one from Jackie. "When did you get out of jail?"

"Yesterday, man. I was at Walmart with a social worker when you called, getting clothes and supplies. The news about Jackie was on TV when they dropped me off at the house. It's a setback, I'm not going to lie. I've got to keep working the steps. Working the steps."

Skeeter hated losing a great suspect. No matter the restraining order or how good Robby looked on paper, he couldn't have killed Jackie. Someone else could have done it for him, maybe. There was nothing about him to suggest he had the money to hire a killer. It would have to have been a favor. Adriana slid a plate onto the table. Huevos rancheros and hash browns. It smelled delicious. She mouthed, *Thank you.* He mouthed, *You're welcome. Thanks for the food.*

He turned the plate to put the hash browns on his right. He'd attack them first. "What were you in for?"

"I got in a fight at a bar in Billings. The guy ended up in the hospital. He started it, but I shouldn't have fought him, I know that now. The funny thing was I was on my way back to Georgia from Bozeman. I needed money, and they were looking for help at the auction house. I was just gonna do it for a few weeks before I went home. Maybe that fight was fate. It changed my life."

"Was it over Jackie?"

"Nah. It was over who was next at the pool table."

"Jackie had a restraining order out against you."

He sighed. "She did. That was the old me. I needed so bad to apologize to her for the stuff in Bozeman. It's part of my twelve steps, but it was more. I really wanted to, you know? It was the right thing to do. Now I'll never get the chance."

Either this guy had become a saint in prison, or he was covering up any ongoing animosity toward Jackie. "Do you know of anyone who might have wanted to hurt her?"

"No. She was the sweetest person. The most beautiful, sweetest person."

"Okay, then. If you—"

"Wait."

"What is it?"

"I thought of someone."

"Okay—who is it?"

"When I came to Bozeman she was pretending to like this guy to, you know, just let me down easy. She took a trip with him. But I know her. She's gonna leave him. She's a heart-breaker. Guys never get over her either. Hell, I'm living proof of that! You should look at that last boyfriend."

"Do you know who that was?"

"If it's the same one, yeah. I'll never forget his name. He was trying to steal the love of my life from me. He thought he was some kind of bad boy, but he was a ninety-pound weakling compared to me. I could have squashed him like a cockroach if I'd wanted to."

Skeeter waited, pen over paper. This guy was drama with a capital D. But was he killer with a capital K? "The name. Please."

"Randall Miller."

SIXTY

By the time Delaney neared Augusta, Montana—well clear of the southern border of the Blackfeet Reservation, to her immeasurable relief—on Tuesday morning, her resentment over the chorus of snoring from the sleeper had reached epic proportions. First, they chowed down on snacks, then they criticized her driving, then they rubbed their slumber in her tired face. She'd literally slept only eight hours of the last forty-eight. Fitfully, those. Not that she would have let them drive, but not one of the lazy asses had offered to spell her or help her in any other way.

It was with great pleasure that she put the Jake Brake on high to wake them up on the outskirts of town.

"Good God," Clark said amidst the groans of the others.

Delaney adopted a sickeningly sweet tone. "This is your first-class flight attendant slash captain. We're coming in for a landing. Please fasten your seatbelts and return your tray tables to their upright and locked positions. No one will be coming around to pick up your trash, so don't be pigs."

"Seriously?"

"I'm stopping to check in with my contact, refuel personally, and use the facilities. You guys, on the other hand, cannot leave this vehicle for any reason." The militia would have eyes on them, but the robocops would survive. Planning ahead, she'd refueled Gabrielle at the only truck stop they'd passed during the night.

"Are we in Helena?"

"No. My latest instruction was to stop here for GPS coordinates. I expect someone will be watching for me to report on my status."

"Finally. GPS coordinates. Let's rock and roll!" one of the agents said. Delaney couldn't see which it was. One of the men.

"Easy for you to say, Sleeping Beauty. But I'm sure we will be told to make haste. They want to keep me as sleep deprived as they can for this interaction. I'll be pushing for as much time at this pit stop as possible." She put on her blinker for the bar and grill she'd been advised was the only place open at this hour in early January. As she turned in very slowly, she said, "I'm closing the sleeper. Don't open it. Don't make a sound. Don't screw this up for Leo."

"Or for our takedown. We know how to handle ourselves, deputy," Clark said.

"Then see that you do."

She parked and disembarked carefully with her purse under her arm. Parking lots were often icy, but the gravel in this one made for decent footing. The cafe was dismal, with a sign on the side of the building hand-painted in cursive and weathered to the point of illegibility. Red and white curtains faded to pink and cream-framed dingy windows.

As she approached the door, she saw a worse sight in the glass—herself. Her braid had come apart under her wool cap. Her eyes were puffy, red-rimmed, and surrounded by black hollows. Her skin was sallow. She looked like she'd just fought off a tropical fever or six months of pneumonia.

She pushed open the door. A bell hanging from red yarn

overhead rang. A blast of electric heat hit her in the face. Sleepiness pulled at her like an undertow as the eyes of all five patrons turned to her. She wondered which people were there to watch her. Would the report include that she looked like a feral raccoon?

A woman stepped in front of her. Her hair was coiled Princess Leia-style like her own personal earmuffs. She smiled, and Delaney saw Invisalign braces. "Good morning. Will you be wanting something to eat?"

Delaney smiled back. "Good morning to you. Yes, please. And lots of hot coffee."

The woman pointed to an open table near a door that said RESTROOMS above it. "You can sit over there. I'll bring you coffee. Cream and sugar?"

"Thank you. Yes on the cream and sugar. And water please."

Delaney went to splash cold water on her face. She used wet hands to smooth her hair. Rebraiding it was too daunting. When she returned to her table, the drinks were already there, as was a teenage girl. A young teen. Around Kat's age, maybe a little older, sitting on one of the bench seats.

"Hello," Delaney said, taking the other side.

"I'm Fawn. What is your name?" the girl said with a lisp. Her top lip was twice the size of her bottom and her nose very flat. Her eyes were wide set and small. Was this her watcher?

"Hi, Fawn. What can I do for you?"

"Fawn! Leave the poor lady alone!" The woman hurried over, pulling the girl up by her elbow. "Your pa wants help in the kitchen."

"Ah, no. I'm tired of helping. I want to sit here."

The woman pointed. "Now, Fawn."

Pouting, which did not work well with her small lower lip, Fawn stalked off behind the counter and into the open kitchen, where a man with a dirty apron tied under a protruding gut handed her a tray of silverware. She lugged it to a sink.

"I'm sorry about that. We don't get a lot of women alone in here. She was excited."

"It's quite all right. I have a daughter about her age."

"You ready to order?"

Delaney hadn't even looked at the menu. She was starving. "Three eggs over medium, hash browns, sausage, and do you have tomato?"

The woman screwed up her lips. "It's not very good."

"Fruit?"

She waffled her hand. "It's better than the tomato."

"Fruit, then. Whatever you have."

The woman scribbled on a notepad. It took her a minute, but then she looked up and said, "And then you'll be checking in and on your way?"

"What?"

"I was told to pass you a message to be sure to hurry."

A chill raced down Delaney's spine, even though she'd anticipated this interaction. "Who asked you to tell me that?"

The woman shrugged and looked off into the parking lot. "They didn't say. It was a phone call."

"Man or woman?"

"Some guy."

"And what are you supposed to tell them?"

"What do you mean?"

"About me—what do they want to know? What time I was here? Was I alone? What I said? What time I left?"

"Um, he didn't ask me any of that."

But he would when he called back, that Delaney was sure of. "How did you know it was me?"

The woman averted her eyes, turned, and took Delaney's order to a pass-through window into the kitchen, then returned to the front counter, where she picked up her phone and studied it.

Delaney's skin crawled. There might be more of them in here. She laid her coat on the bench beside her and put her phone on the table. She unscrewed the top to a white coffee carafe releasing a smell like salvation. She added sugar and packets of cream to a cup of it, stirred it, and drank it down, then chugged a water. She made another coffee and filled another glass of water. She was dehydrated from the road.

Biting the inside of her lip, she texted her mother. Her mother. A woman she'd hated and missed in equal measures for so many years. Now that she was back in touch with her, all that missing had shifted to a full measure of hate. She'd had lots of time to think about her on the long drives in the last two days. About her relationship with her compared with the ones with her own daughters. With her brother. Delaney could acknowledge the possibility of extenuating circumstances for her mother's involvement in Jackie's murder and Leo's kidnapping. When it was over, she might have explanations for Delaney. Delaney just didn't know if she could stomach hearing them.

Exhausted. Roads terrible. In Augusta waiting on food. Send proof of life. Needs to answer this question on video. What is the name of Kat's dog?

Three dots appeared. It was early on the west coast. Fabi must have been sitting up waiting on Delaney. The dots disappeared. Reappeared.

It was like watching paint dry. Time to bring the team in on all the information. She sent a text to Drew.

In Augusta MT w/ATF. Clint followed and saved me from cartel on Blackfeet Res. We're raiding the militia who have Leo v v soon. Clint in on Op. HIGHLY confidential. Waiting on GPS for meetup and current proof of life. Need identity of Jackie's killer ASAP. Haven't read your updates bc driving. Will soon. Lots to tell when safely home. Thanks for all the help.

Still dots from Fabi.

The cook slung two plates in front of Delaney. Hot food. Cold fruit in the form of slices of browning apple and half a banana, unpeeled.

She flipped her phone face down.

When the cook left, she turned her phone back over. No dots. She took the time to text her daughters before eating, though. In case... in case the worst happened, she wanted them to have heard from her this morning. She used the group text.

Love you both. More than you know. Hope to send good news soon.

A new thought occurred to her. What if Leo survived today and she didn't? She sent a text to his phone.

Thank you for loving me almost as much as I love you.

She dug into the hot plate. Greasy, salty, and wonderful. She'd eaten more meals like this than she could count in her decade on the road. She hadn't been ready to give up that life. There had been so many things she'd loved about it. But she wouldn't trade what she had now for anything.

She checked her phone again. The dots stared back at her, like the screen was frozen. She powered it down. Tears pricked her eyes, and she dabbed them with her rough paper napkin. Anger ignited like a prairie flash fire. Where was her proof that Leo was okay? How hard was it to shoot ten seconds of video of him?

She shoveled down the rest of her meal so fast it was a wonder she didn't choke. She turned her phone back on. While it booted up, she ate the fruit. Tasteless winter produce. She didn't care. She needed the energy. Chasing it with coffee, she read through her texts. The updates from Drew were inconclusive, just leads with no certainty about Jackie's killer. She was running out of time. A few messages from the girls that made her smile. They could both be very sweet when they wanted to.

She returned to the thread with Fabi. No dots. No new text.

She messaged Clint, who had driven ahead to Helena with the ATF vans to avoid detection by the wrong people.

The ATF can have everyone else. I want Leo and Jackie's killer. And, if he's there, my brother. You and me. Okay?

His reply was fast.

Agreed.

She looked to the Fabi text string. A video had finally come in.

Hands shaking, she prepped another coffee and drank it like a shot, using water to cool the scald it left in her throat. She took her phone and purse to the bathroom. No way was she watching the video in front of anyone else.

In the tiny room, she locked the door, put in the AirPods Leo had bought her for Christmas, and pressed play. Onscreen, the bright light of a camera pierced the darkness. The view closed in on a man huddled on the floor, fetal position. A booted foot entered the bottom of the frame, toed the man, shoved him around, then kicked him.

Delaney clenched her fist, wanting to swing it at something, anything. Wanting to cry. Wanting to throw her body over Leo's.

A man's voice—not Leo's—gravelly and threatening in a querulous way said, "Hey! Leo! Wake up! Your girlfriend wants to see your pretty face."

A low groan, then Leo's head lifted and turned toward the camera. His eyes squinted, zip-tied hands coming up to shield them from the intrusive glare. "Delaney?"

"What's the name of the cat?"

"What?"

"No, the cat's dog?"

"Uh, Jack. Jackie."

"As you can see, deputy, he's just fine." The voice gave the time and date.

Leo screamed, "Don't come, Delaney, that's an order. It's a—"

The video ended. Delaney verified the time and date against her phone. The video had been shot five minutes ago. Her hands trembled. Leo had just told her in a way only she could understand that he was in the presence of Jackie's killer. If she didn't figure out who he was herself, Leo would be able to identify him. As for his order, she appreciated the warning and caring behind it but disregarded it without a second thought. A thought hit her. Leo hadn't said anything about Liam, not in any of his videos. Surely, he would have mentioned it if he'd seen her brother? She didn't know what to make of that.

A text came in.

Satisfied?

Far from it. But he's alive.

The next text contained **GPS** coordinates.

Should take you less than an hour from where you are. Get on the road now.

Delaney closed her eyes. It was time for her to dig deep for her inner warrior. There would be no room for doubts or hesitation or fear. In her head, she said, *You will let nothing stop you from getting Leo.* Again, *You will let nothing stop you from getting Leo.* She kept repeating it until a warm confidence took root in her core and started spreading outward in her body. Then she added, *And after you get him, you'll bring in a killer.*

When she opened her eyes, she felt ready to fight a pack of wolves. Anything for Leo. Which was good, because she was afraid that was exactly what she was about to have to do to get him back.

SIXTY-ONE

Drew had come to the office at six that morning, after a night of no sleep, but he didn't beat Clara there. They'd greeted each other solemnly as he marched back to his cubicle. He'd spent the night obsessively checking his phone for updates. He'd gotten one from the Sheridan police in the wee hours. They'd found Cole Atwell and pulled him in for questioning, which Drew had prepared them for earlier. Joe was copied on the message and had immediately replied that he was on his way to handle the interrogation personally. It was the lack of other updates during the night that kept him awake. Where was Delaney? What was she doing? Devon Peele said Clint Rock-Below had gone AWOL, too. It was hard to argue against Joe that she was in charge when no one had heard from her.

He just had to keep doing his job the best he could.

Yesterday, he'd finished digging into Greg Sones and today he'd research the final trustee—Tanya Sones. He had finally found one useful tidbit on Monday afternoon. He'd found a marriage license for Greg and Tanya. At first glance, Tanya seemed the least likely of the three trustees to yield anything of significance. Drew had halfway assumed she'd been given the third trustee spot by default. He imagined a conversation between the other two along the lines of "better three than two of us and an attorney would look good, hey, how about my wife?" Was that sexist of him? Probably. He wouldn't admit it aloud, certainly not in front of Adriana.

Tanya was a partner in a law firm with offices in DC and a few other large US cities. She and Greg owned a luxury brownstone in Georgetown. He'd already pulled up pictures. He wouldn't have wanted to live there, but it looked expensive.

Drew became aware of a presence. Joe, lurking.

"Morning, Tarver," he said.

The older deputy smirked. "I broke Cole Atwell. He's confessed to stalking and harassing Jackie Spurrier. He's being charged later today."

Drew frowned, momentarily at a loss. *Ah, Cole Atwell.* "He said he killed her?"

"Not yet. But he will. I've been up all night, so I'm going to finish some paperwork over coffee then go home to sleep." Joe disappeared toward the breakroom.

It didn't sound like Joe had broken anything.

There was nothing more Drew could do on Atwell at the moment, so he went back to browsing Tanya's firm's website. With a Monster in one hand, he read her page. The picture was of a woman with dark curly hair and an intense gaze from eyes of two colors—one brown and one green. It gave her an unsettling look. She had a litigation practice, representing all kinds of clients but specializing in non-profits. At first, he was thinking *big city millennial do-gooder*. But he skipped down to read the list of clients and changed his mind. One domestic troublemaker after another scrolled down his screen. The anarchists, militias, fascists, and anti-fascists. The eco-terrorists, the animal rights crusaders who tended toward violence and property destruction. Religious cults. Basically, it was like reading a list of subjects to plug into the day's clickbait headlines.

A text came in. It was from Delaney, finally!

In Augusta MT w/ATF. Clint followed and saved me from cartel on Blackfeet Res. We're raiding the militia who have Leo v v soon. Clint in on Op. HIGHLY confidential. Waiting on GPS for meetup and current proof of life. Need identity of Jackie's killer ASAP. Haven't read your updates bc driving. Will soon. Lots to tell when safely home. Thanks for all the help.

Drew's eyes felt like they were about to pop out of his face. He reread the message three times. Holy shit. Delaney. The ATF. Clint. Leo. OMG.

He texted.

Do you need me to do anything there? Coordinate with local law enforcement?

Her reply was quick.

ATF has it handled.

What did Drew have that would help her take out Jackie's killer? Really, they had nothing to identify him. Maybe if he just did a little more research. He'd send more in a few minutes.

He scrolled back to Tanya's degrees. And that's when his pulse began to race. Undergraduate and law degrees from the University of Wyoming.

Finally! A trustee with a tie to Wyoming.

He read her sparse bio. It added nothing about her outside the information already on the page. So, he plugged her name into Google and began perusing search results. Case after case after case came up. Of course it did—she was a litigation attorney. He felt like he was getting nowhere. He didn't have time for this level of detail now.

He added *Wyoming* to the search. Skipping over all the regurgitations of her educational credentials, a result at the bottom of the second page stopped him cold. The word "Kearny." He clicked on the headline: KEARNY DEPUTY RECEIVES TWENTY-FIVE YEARS IN MURDER CONSPIRACY.

His mouth dropped open. He leaned forward. His lips moved as he read. And then he sat back in his chair and said, "Son of a bitch."

Tanya Sones was the sister of former Kearny deputy Tommy Miller, who had been convicted along with their sister Riley Miller Tucker in the murder of Riley's husband Brock and his lover, politician and activist Annabeth Dillon.

Not only did Tanya have a Wyoming connection she had a Kearny connection. A criminal Kearny connection. If Tommy was a Miller, that had to be Tanya's maiden name. He checked her law firm page. She didn't use anything but Sones.

He ran another search, this time for Tanya Miller. Too many irrelevant results. He tried Tanya Miller Sones and didn't get squat. He shrugged and typed in *Tanya Miller Sones Tommy Miller Riley Miller*.

His eyes popped. The first result made him scared for Delaney.

FOUNDER ANDREW MILLER SENTENCED TO FIVE YEARS IN MONTANA.

He scanned for the part related to Tanya.

Andrew's siblings, Riley Miller, Tanya Sones, Brandon Miller, and Randy Miller, were not charged, although all have been tied to the anti-fascist militant Western Pride group in the past. The Miller siblings lost their parents in a shootout with the ATF and were split up and raised separately in foster families. Andrew has refused to answer questions about his siblings' involvement or his unconventional childhood in an off-the-grid mountain compound.

What in the hell was Delaney walking into? These were the people that had Leo? His heart was thumping wildly. These people were dangerous. Professionally dangerous. At least Clint and those ATF agents were with her.

His phone rang. The department line. "Hello?"

Clara said, "I have Sheriff Wilcox for you."

"Okay. Thanks." Drew sucked in a deep breath. His coordination phone calls with the Big Horn sheriff had not been pleasant. He should have handed the call over to Joe, but, well, he didn't want to. Joe shouldn't have been such a weasel if he wanted people to respect him. "Sheriff Wilcox?"

"What the hell is this shit that's landed on our desk, deputy?" Wilcox's voice sounded like a roll of thunder.

"I'm sorry, sir. What are you talking about?" Drew held the phone from his ear for the reply.

"This rucksack. Is this some kind of sick joke? We found an ID for Paul Lester in it."

Drew had no idea who Lester was. "I don't see what the problem is."

"Oh, you don't? Well, google Paul Lester. I'll wait."

Drew typed it in. His jaw dropped as he scanned the results. Paul Lester was Delaney's brother, Liam. He kept reading. Liam was presumed dead after falling from a cliff when Delaney shot him. His body had never been found. "Liam Pace."

"Yeah. Deputy Pace's long-lost brother. So, I was thinking it was some kind of joke, until we took fingerprints. We ran 'em. Guess who they match?"

Drew was struggling to connect the dots, but this could have only one answer. "Liam Pace."

SIXTY-TWO

Drew pressed his palm against his temple, having trouble processing what he was hearing. The rucksack from the snow-mobile trail belonged to Delaney's brother?

Sheriff Wilcox's voice was cold and angry. "Yes. And he is supposedly dead. Now, this bag coulda been his from a year ago and it just got coincidentally dropped on that trail. But I don't believe in coincidences. And I also don't believe your Deputy Pace doesn't know more about this than she's telling people. You tell that woman if her brother is alive and we need to be watching out for him, she damn sure better tell us. He's one of the most dangerous fugitives in the history of Wyoming."

"I'll, uh, pass along that message, sir. This is the first I'm hearing of it."

"It won't be the last. This whole thing is nothing more than spillover from Kearny County not taking care of its own business. There are four unmarked graves on Snow Hare Ranch. Four! I won't let that be a black mark on me, you can be sure of that."

Drew didn't follow his logic, but he scribbled down the final grave count. "Noted. What will be happening with the bodies?"

"A team from Cheyenne is coming to exhume them. They'll try to identify them and the causes of death. You'd better pray for natural causes. And one more thing. Tell whoever is in charge over there that it's near time to cut Mark Scarpetta loose."

"Who?"

"You don't even know who he is? He's the caretaker from Snow Hare Lodge!"

"I knew. Our connection was bad." Which wasn't true. Drew was tired, and Wilcox was being a bully. He'd blanked out the name for a second.

Shannon snorted. "He hasn't given us jack shit, he's a complainer, and he eats too much."

The connection ended. Apparently, Shannon was done talking.

Drew was shook. Well and truly shook. From not enough happening, things had gone quickly to too much. Delaney, Clint, and the ATF were about to raid a militia and rescue Leo. Tanya Sones—a trustee connected to Snow Hare Ranch where Leo was being held—was the sister of Western Pride militia members and a former member herself. The crime scene investigators were processing information from four unmarked graves at the ranch. And now Sheriff Wilcox wanted to scalp Drew because Delaney's brother Liam might be alive and involved?!

Joe poked his head in. "Done. Going home. If you talk to Delaney, tell her she owes me a report on what she's doing."

Drew barely glanced up. "Uh, yeah."

He had to finish the research he was doing. He knew it was important. Then he'd send Delaney everything he had. Hands quaking, he typed in *Tanya Sones* and *Western Pride*. The same article popped up, as did another where Tanya disavowed ongoing connection to Western Pride, claiming she disassociated with the group years ago. A picture accompanied the story, in which Tanya wore a winter camo suit next to identically clad people identified as Western Pride members, including her siblings. He frowned and rechecked her law firm page. Western Pride was not listed as a client.

A text notification distracted him. It was from Delaney. GPS coordinates.

Tell me about this place. It's where we meet up to get Leo.

He stood and shouted, "Clara, Delaney has coordinates for where Leo is!"

He heard running footsteps. Clara appeared wide-eyed at his cubicle.

He stood. "You'll be better at finding this than me."

She took his chair. He stood behind her as she plugged in the coordinates.

"Can we figure out who owns this place?" he said.

"Yes," she said. "And hopefully a lot more."

Drew's phone flashed a notification. Another text, this one from Skeeter. He'd talked to the steroid head ex-boyfriend, but he'd been incarcerated at the time of Jackie's murder. Skeeter would explore whether the guy could have called in favors for someone else to kill her. The ex said we should look at Jackie's last known boyfriend in Bozeman, the one she'd left town with —Randall Miller.

Drew felt like sirens were going off in his head. Miller. He looked back at the article and then at the pictures. Randall Miller. Randy Miller. Tanya's brother.

Typing fast he said, *Thanks. This is great, this is it!*

Clara was zooming in on the location with Google Earth. She pulled an address from the screen and opened another tab. This time she used Google Maps to pull up the parcel by its street address. The same place appeared. Opening a third tab, she ran a search on the address.

Drew scanned the results over her shoulder.

"Nothing here that I can see. But this address looks familiar. Hold on. Let's see if it's in the properties I've already identified." Clara switched to a spreadsheet. In a few keystrokes she'd honed in on a line in the results. "I thought so. It belongs to Far West Ventures."

"Which we already know is owned in turn by Far West Ventures Trust. Our trustees again. One of whom is Wyomingite Tanya Sones, sister of Tommy Miller, formerly of Western Pride."

"Our former deputy Tommy?"

"Yes. And there's more. Skeeter just texted that Jackie was dating *Randall Miller.*" He showed Clara the article listing him and his siblings as Western Pride members.

"Oh, my God."

Clara read over his shoulder as he typed as fast as he could. It was past time to send Delaney all the updates, including the picture of Jackie's former boyfriend Randall Miller with Western Pride in their white camo suits, and the flood of information from Sheriff Wilcox. At the last second he included the details about Cole Atwell, too, with a picture he pulled from Facebook.

He finished with, *We think Randy Miller is the one who killed Jackie.* He wished he had more for her. He hoped this was enough.

SIXTY-THREE

Delaney turned out of the parking lot and worked her way up through the gears as she accelerated out of Augusta. She was chewing the inside of her cheek, having just read a text from Drew that had been full of bombshells. As soon as she wasn't needing all her attention to be sure not to mow down residents or motorists with her big rig, she ripped open the divider between her and the ATF agents.

"Clark, why the hell didn't you tell me we were dealing with Western Pride? I could have been preparing for them," she said, her voice lethally tight and low.

There was a rustling as Clark moved to the front of the sleeper, still invisible to people outside the truck, but closer to Delaney's ear. "You didn't need to know."

Her voice began to rise. "Didn't need to know? I'm driving into a meeting with them in an hour. They're holding my b... our sheriff hostage. And I don't need to know?"

"Well, you know now. And what good does it do?"

"My co-deputy tells me that the property we're meeting them on is owned by an LLC owned by a trust. One of the trustees is Tanya Sones. She's a former member, and the sister of a former co-deputy of mine. He and another sister are murderers the sheriff and I arrested and helped put away. The Millers are not Leo's biggest fans. And I'm fairly sure that another criminal we arrested is the confidential informant you have placed with them. Igor Salazar. Last but not least, we've learned Jackie Spurrier left Bozeman a year ago with her new boyfriend—Randall Miller. Ring any bells?"

He sighed, like she had worn him down. "On the ground, Western Pride is run by two of the Miller brothers. Brandon and his younger brother Randy." *A murderer. Maybe a serial killer.* "The eldest, Andrew, is still in prison as are Riley and Tommy, as you said. Their parents died years ago. Hopefully, by the end of today we'll have the rest of the criminal family pending trials and life sentences."

"I thought Tanya got out."

"We think she's lying. We think she's in charge."

Delaney thought back to Leo's proof of life video. Not the one today. The one she'd seen in Canada. Something about it was ringing alarm bells now. She needed to watch it again and send it to Drew, now that he was in the need-to-know loop. For the tiny bit of information Clark had just given her, Delaney decided to share in turn.

"I want to show you something," she said.

"What?"

"Hey Siri, play Leo Proof of Life Video Two," she said to her phone, which was in the holster.

Leo's voice filled the cab and Delaney had to bite her lip to hold back tears. *"I'm feeling under the weather, not able to raise Cain, got a killer headache. Today is the third, I think three. But definitely Monday. I'm supposed to say my name but it's like my brain is surrounded by mountains it can't climb. This is Leo Palmer."*

Clark said, "When did you get that?"

"Yesterday. It's very oddly phrased. He was clearly trying to pass us clues. I also think he was drugged. I'm interested now in that line 'not able to raise Cain.' Cain and Abel. I think he's saying he's with two brothers."

Clark started nodding. "Play it again."

She did.

"Yes. I can see that. He's being held in a mountainous area. He's feeling sick?"

"I'm not sure."

"Well, not that we needed further confirmation, since our source is a good one, but there's information there that may yet help. Can you send it to me?"

Delaney asked Siri to send the message to Clark. For the briefest of moments, she considered telling Clark she believed her brother was with the Millers—a third person, hence Leo saying, "I think three." She'd just attacked him for withholding on her after all. She decided against it. She'd given him the video. She didn't want to admit the possible connection to any of her family members yet, although word was bound to get out soon with Sheriff Wilcox on the warpath about Liam.

She said, "We only have forty-five minutes until touchdown." They needed to discuss the mission. And she needed to forward Drew's text about Randall Miller and Tanya Sones to Clint, without Clark seeing her do it, since it contained info about Liam.

"I still don't love going in on the ground. We could get trapped if there's no secondary exit. Air assets would solve that. They're on standby. We still have time."

"We talked about this from the jump. That's a no-go. You'd leave me on the ground without backup."

Clark harrumphed. "That's the only reason I'm going along with this plan."

"Good. Then we don't need to discuss it again."

Clark initiated a group call with the other three vehicles. "We'll keep this call active until the operation is over. Wear the earbuds I gave you." Delaney would be in close contact with the Western Pride members. The earbud was flesh colored, but she was still nervous it would be detected. "First and foremost, Delaney is going in alone initially. If you need a rescue, the code word is 'Sheridan,' Delaney. We'll all know to respond to it."

"What happens to your mission if I use the code word?"

"We'll abort." He held her gaze. She didn't believe him. He turned and spoke into the sleeper. "You lightweights have a plan yet?"

Delaney grabbed her phone and quickly forwarded Drew's text to Clint.

The miles flew beneath Gabrielle's tires. With Clark perched in the opening between the cab and the sleeper, they spent the rest of the drive talking topography, roads, drones, weaponry, and strategy with Clint and the agents in the vans on speakerphone. The ATF had deployed a high-altitude drone that paced them, flying ahead and then back to keep an eye on what they were driving into. The roads became increasingly bad—snowy and curvy with elevation changes that tested Gabrielle. Delaney wished she hadn't sacrificed her chains back on the Blackfeet reservation, and that Clint and the vans hadn't stayed behind on paved roads awaiting their signal to join them.

Clark said, "Your rig isn't made for this."

She shook her head. "If it doesn't get much worse, we're okay."

"Unless we need to get out of here quickly."

Or unless we need our backup.

The forest here was vastly different from the Bighorn National Forest near Kearny. The trees were spinier, shorter, and spaced further apart. Even with the snow cover, the rocks had a redder tint, and the land appeared more arid. She imagined it was brutal in the summer months. It wasn't very hospitable in the dead of winter.

She rounded a bend into a large open area.

"According to my GPS, this is it," the unit's female member called out from the back.

Delaney shook her head. There was no one there. "There are vehicle tracks, but I don't see anyone. Is it possible it's a little further along?"

"No. This is definitely it."

"Maybe they gave us the wrong coordinates. Or they messed up when they got out here and drove too far."

Delaney's Spidey-senses began to tingle. As she eased Gabrielle to the far side of the clearing, those senses escalated to a full-blown neuropathic storm. She stopped, checked her mirrors, and said, "This doesn't feel right."

Clark barked into a radio the group had brought with them. "Drone, what do you see?"

A woman's voice answered. *"Trees. Rocks. Snow."*

"That's it?"

"Wait... I see movement in the trees off to your left. I'm getting a glint that may be metal."

Delaney had already picked her escape route and took Gabrielle off road and into a big loop to turn her around. "We're getting out of here."

Clark grabbed her shoulder. "Not yet."

She couldn't release the steering wheel as the big rig bounced over ruts, rocks, snow, and fallen branches. "Do not touch me while I'm driving. Or ever."

"We don't know—"

The drone operator's voice rose. *"Movement in multiple locations now, all around you, converging on the meadow."*

"Oh, shit," Clark said. "I see them. They're everywhere."

The crack of automatic weapon fire came at them from three sides, although still too far away for the bullets to reach Gabrielle. That would change fast. Delaney didn't see any vehicles on the road back toward civilization, but she expected them any moment. Unless they had an armored tank, though, she and

Gabrielle had the advantage of size and momentum, as long as she stayed on the road and built up her speed.

"I'm activating our backup," Clark said. "We need to abort the mission."

Gabrielle gave a slight wobble as it regained the road. Delaney felt the trailer tilt and recover as well. "No," she said.

"It's not your call."

Accelerator to the floor, Delaney waited as long as possible to shift. "No effing way."

"If we have to protect you in a shootout, our cover is blown. We need help! Help will blow cover, too. We're out of options."

The turbo whined. Delaney waited, maximizing acceleration before shifting. "Do not ask for help. I will get us out of here. Cover will not be blown."

"Good God, you're going to kill us!"

"No, I'm planning on saving you." She had to outrun the militia members back to pavement. But how? Block their progress by weaving Gabrielle from side to side down the narrow road? That wouldn't keep them at bay forever. They had a couple of miles to go. The speedometer read thirty miles per hour. It wasn't fast enough. Their pursuers—who she could now see coming at them at ground-covering angles from both sides—had faster vehicles. They had weapons. They would be trying to take out the tires. Cripple the tractor.

Maybe I can't do this... But she banished the thought. She refused to accept defeat because to do so meant giving up on Leo.

Be smarter if you can't be stronger.

And in an instant it came to her. She knew exactly what to do.

"Clark, text my contact right now. Tell them I've rigged the trailer with explosives and I'm going to blow it sky high if they don't back off. You'll see the string. It's a Washington area code."

To his credit, the ATF agent moved fast as a rattlesnake strike, unlocking Delaney's phone by holding it in front of her face, then voice texting her words.

Now the bullets were pinging wildly off the truck. Delaney had eighteen wheels. She was sure they'd gotten some of her tires. So far, they hadn't hit the front two, and those were the most critical.

"Come on, come on," she breathed. *Read the text. Act on it. Stop them.*

"You've got a reply," Clark said.

The whine of the off-road vehicles suddenly stopped. The crack of weapons, the ping of bullets grew silent. *Yes!!*

"You bet I do. And I didn't have to read my texts to receive it. Let's get out of here."

SIXTY-FOUR

Drew's head felt like it was about to explode from the tension. Delaney had just messaged him. The meetup had been an ambush. She'd escaped without her cover blown, but now she had no idea where Leo was.

Are there properties near me where he might be?

She sent a Pin. Then she'd sent a video.

Watch this. Clues to Leo's whereabouts?

He shouted for Clara. He heard pounding footsteps. He twirled his chair to face her as she approached.

"What is it?" she said.

He showed her Delaney's messages.

"Oh, no! Have you watched the video yet?"

"No. Let's do it together." He pushed play.

Leo's voice said, *"I'm feeling under the weather, not able to raise Cain, got a killer headache. Today is the third, I think three.*

But definitely Monday. I'm supposed to say my name but it's like my brain is surrounded by mountains it can't climb. This is Leo Palmer. Does any of that sound like a clue to his whereabouts?"

"Not that I can tell."

"Me either. We can keep thinking while we work. Can you see if Tanya or the trust or the LLC or anyone we've come up with so far has property near this Pin that Delaney sent?"

"Give me five minutes."

"Make it three and I'll come with you."

The two of them ran to Clara's desk.

She typed like she was a video set to double playback speed. "I'm mining zip codes around Helena. Okay, now I'll just search my spreadsheet—copy and paste the relevant data into a new one—and sort it by owner. Got it." She lifted her hands from the keys, a virtuoso pianist at the end of a performance. "Three possibilities."

Drew read the list over her shoulder. "One looks like the place of the original meetup."

Clara pointed at the second entry. "This one is nearest to where she is. Let's see if I can find some visuals." She opened the Google Earth app and typed in the address.

Drew eyed the screen hungrily, looking for any kind of structure where someone could be held. "I don't see any buildings."

"What if they have him in something portable, like an RV or a mobile home? Or a tent?"

He hit his forehead with his palm, one time, two times. "Things that won't show on Google Earth."

"Or anywhere."

Clara pulled up the third property. It looked similarly uninhabited. She moved to Google Maps and typed in the nearer of the two addresses. The words "T Bar M ranch" were superimposed over the outline area on the screen. She typed the same address into the Google search engine in a new tab. A listing on Zillow appeared.

"This is out of date. Far West bought this place since the time this was posted. These listings usually have pictures.

"It says in the specs that there are three homes, but I don't see anything," Drew said.

"Me either. I see some doorways, but I don't know where to. They're not to houses. Maybe they're so rundown they didn't want to scare people off by including them." She hesitated on a photograph of a sign over the entrance. "Looks like they used to call it the Parker-Shelton ranch. Let me search on that."

In a new tab, she ran the search. She clicked in the results on an article titled, UNDERGROUND BUNKERS ABOUND IN REMOTE MONTANA PROPERTIES, then did a find on her search term.

Drew read aloud. *"The Parker-Shelton ranch near Helena is a prime example with three underground bunkers, each the size of modest traditional homes."* The article went on to describe the history of the property. A previous owner had created the bunkers in case of nuclear war. *"Owners since then have lauded the privacy and low power bills of underground living."*

"The pictures of the doors from Zillow. They were doors to bunkers. Underground!"

Something about her words made Drew play Leo's video again.

"I'm feeling under the weather, not able to raise Cain, got a killer headache. Today is the third, I think three. But definitely Monday. I'm supposed to say my name but it's like my brain is surrounded by mountains it can't climb. This is Leo Palmer."

Drew snapped his fingers. "He feels under the weather. Like underground."

"Surrounded by mountains. This ranch is definitely surrounded by mountains."

Drew could barely breathe. Had they found Leo? Could this be where he was being held captive? He wished he could type as fast as Clara as he sent the information about the T Bar M ranch on to Delaney.

SIXTY-FIVE

Miles flew by—more mountainous winter beauty Delaney didn't have the bandwidth to appreciate—as the agents in Gabrielle's sleeper pored over online maps, photographs, and literature. Delaney was driving at a pace just under the speed limit toward the site Drew and Clara had identified. Of course, Clark had one of his guys verify every bit of the information, but they agreed it was solid. *Found by our newest deputy and our department admin, not the ATF.* Of course, there was no guarantee Leo was there. But it was possible, and it was all they had.

Clark was facing his agents in the sleeper, talking fast. His words were also going out to the other vehicles on the operational group call. "If they're in bunkers, let's talk about how we draw them out, so they don't just hole up in there pretending no one's home or sniping us off one by one."

This was one time Delaney wished she wasn't behind the wheel. She wanted to be in the thick of this discussion. "We have to draw them out. Nothing happens unless Leo is out and safe."

"More to the point, we have no arrest to make unless they take delivery of the machine guns," Clark said.

His point, maybe. Not mine.

"I've told them I've got my finger on the trigger to blow their machine guns up. That should get them to send Leo out at least."

"I hate to rely only on that."

"What else do you have?"

"Plenty. These prepper types think they're clever, but we've seen it all. I assume if they send Leo out you won't go to war with us over more aggressive means to flush the others from underground?"

Delaney was too near to the ranch to push Clark for a more complete answer than "plenty." She'd grown up in a household of preppers. Her grandfather could teach the ATF a thing or two about the mentality. If it wasn't that she had extreme personal dislike for the man, she'd invite Clark to the basement of her house for a master class. Once, she and her grandfather had visited one of his friends who lived in an underground bunker. While she'd mostly played with his dog, she'd followed the grown-ups around while the man showed her grandfather everything he'd done to prevent being flushed out. The methods were fascinating and stuck in her young mind. The ways vent pipes could be hidden, and people could escape through tunnels and camouflaged alternate exits.

"Once I have Leo, you can do whatever you want to them." *Although Clint and I will be looking for Randall Miller and my brother.* Randy had to answer for his murders in Wyoming—four unmarked graves plus Jackie Spurrier. She added, "Two miles out."

Clark pointed to a spot on the mapping application, talking softly to Delaney. "Somewhere short of this ninety-degree turn looks good for parking your rig. It's only a hundred feet from the gate into the property, which we need to stay clear of. But God only knows where the doors to those bunkers are. They aren't usually visible from major roads as that defeats the security and privacy reasons for installing them in the first place."

His voice became clipped and forceful. "Van one, drive ahead and report any sightings of bunkers, persons, weapons, vehicles. You know the drill. Van two and Kearny, stay apart and at least a half mile from the entrance of the property and no more than three miles away. Don't drive by. Be ready to deploy on my mark." Kearny was how Clark had taken to identifying Clint Rock-Below and his SUV. Delaney wondered what was wrong with just using Clint.

She pulled over and left Gabrielle in neutral with the parking brake on. A hill obstructed any view they might have had of the gate. There were no visible signs of the bunkers, either.

A reply from van one came over Clark's speaker phone. *"Snow, tire tracks, and hills. Nothing else."*

"It's less than ideal," Clark said, "but we're all professionals. Stick to the plan and follow orders."

"I'm texting my contact," Delaney said.

"What do you plan to say?"

"That I'm here for Leo."

Clark nodded. "I'll see if the drone has some good pictures for us."

She took his nod as understanding rather than permission, because the latter would have been too infuriating. She typed, *Tell them I'm here for Leo.* She hit send.

The reply came quickly.

Where is here?

T Bar M ranch. Same deal. I'll wait near the gate. If any vehicle comes in sight, I'll blow the trailer.

She sent a quick text to Clint.

Priorities 1. *Leo* 2. *Randy* 3. *Liam.* 4. *Igor Salazar, who kidnapped the Crow girls last yr.*

Clint had been very helpful in solving the case that ended in Igor's arrest and would know him by sight. The memory of Clark taking Igor from Kearny to continue as a confidential informant still burned. In her world, justice required that murderers like Randy and people who hurt children like Igor pay for their crimes.

She followed up with, *We take them all alive. We put them away for life.* If Clark tried to take Randy, Liam, or Igor from her today, she would not make it easy. She'd play as dirty as she had to.

Clint responded with a thumbs-up emoji, then, *What about Brandon?*

Let the ATF have him.

Does Wilcox know Randy killed Jackie?

I don't think so. I don't know.

"You're doing a lot of texting," Clark said.

"I'm reminding them of my terms."

"You're dictating terms to them?"

Delaney scowled at him. "I have their guns. I'll use that until the last possible second."

Then the reply she was waiting for came in.

They have to send three vehicles. One is the semi to haul the trailer. The other two will bring the men to unload the crates.

No. Not until I see Leo, Liam, and whoever is in charge here. Not until Leo is in my custody.

They are discussing it.

"What are they saying?"

"Still arguing. They're trying to set me up for another ambush. I'm trying to keep that from happening."

She replied to her mother.

Tell them they have one minute, then I'm leaving.

Clark said, "The drone operator sent us an aerial marked with three doors. He said one of them just opened. Two men have come out."

Two men—that is not what I asked for, she thought.

There was no answer. No three dots.

"Text me the aerial of the doors."

Clark nodded. "Done. It's go-time for you, Delaney. Don't forget, if you need us, just say 'Sheridan.' Your earbud will pick it up as long as you keep the line open. It wouldn't hurt if you'd tell us when they've got guns loaded into their vehicles, but we'll be listening from inside, too. Can't count on you in case you lose that earbud. Now, get yourself to that gate."

Don't accidentally say "Sheridan." "Can your drone operator confirm that one of the men is Leo?"

Clark asked via radio. The reply was that Leo's identity was inconclusive.

"Swell." She patted the holster under her bulky jacket, which was itself over a heavy bulletproof vest. She was bringing the Staccato for herself and a Smith & Wesson Shield that she hoped to get to Leo. She'd already checked the magazines. "See you soon." She opened the door, got out, and started jogging. She felt preternaturally calm, the opposite of how she'd felt since the moment she'd figured out Leo was missing. She rounded the corner and came upon the gate. Looking up the dirt lane into the property, she saw two men approaching.

Her heart soared. She'd recognize the shape of Leo anywhere. He was alive! "Leo!" She waved her arms.

He didn't wave back. It wasn't surprising. His hands would be bound. The other guy wasn't Liam, though. She recognized him from the pictures sent by Drew. It was Randy Miller.

She texted Fabi.

Where is Liam? That is not Liam. I'm leaving.

Aren't you going to take Leo with you?

Delaney hesitated, her eyes on the beautiful sight of her man. His feet were shuffling. His arms were behind his back. He looked hollowed out and thinner in sweatpants and a short-sleeved T-shirt despite the cold winter weather. He seemed to be in tennis shoes. She hadn't seen any of the clothing items before. She wanted to weep for what he'd been through. To run to him and kiss him senseless. But she could do none of those things. There would be a time for all that later. For now, there was work to do, and she needed a laser focus on the operation.

But his head was up, and he clearly saw her. There was no smile on his face. Instead, he looked frantic. Panicked. He was shaking his head back and forth.

Randy Miller spoke, his high-pitched voice malevolent. "If it isn't Liam's baby sister. Delaney, you're a vision. Even prettier than when I met you on the mountain. This ol' sheriff has been missing you, haven't you, Leo?" He elbowed Leo in the side.

Leo didn't react.

"So, I get to meet another Miller. Murder runs in the family, I guess." *Multiple murders apiece.*

"We're just misunderstood."

Leo muttered, "Well, now things make more sense."

Delaney said, "Leo can walk the rest of the way to me himself."

"Not until I have a word with you both about Riley and Tommy."

"And I said I wanted to meet with Liam and whoever is in charge. We can't always get what we want."

"Unless you're in charge, which I am. You'll see them when the time for it comes. After we finish our business." He and Leo were less than ten feet away now.

"When will your trucks be here?"

"Any minute, sweetness." Randy pulled Leo to a stop just beyond her reach. "I just want you to know, Delaney, that everything I'm going to do to you is for Riley and Tommy." He leered. "Well, that's not true. Some of it I'm going to do just for me."

She could see a wildness in his eyes. A shiftiness. Her skin crawled. *Don't let him see he's getting to you.* "Give Leo to me."

Leo's eyes were locked on Delaney's. He was mouthing something to her. She watched his lips, not understanding him. Then he shouted, "Watch out."

A gun barrel jammed into her ribs as another arm caught her in a loose sleeper hold. "You should have been watching your back instead of Leo. Hand me that detonator, Laney."

She'd know the voice anywhere. It was her brother.

SIXTY-SIX

"Hello, big brother," Delaney said, praying the group call was still connected with Clint and the ATF. *So much for drone support.* She hadn't heard a word through her earbud about another person above ground and approaching her. "Not a very hospitable greeting."

Randy grabbed Leo's shoulder and put a gun to his neck, the threat clear. Leo's eyes were bugged out. Liam, she realized. Leo hadn't known he was *that* Liam, not even when she'd said his name a few moments before. He hadn't been aware of Randy Miller's identity either. She couldn't imagine the hell of his last few days, underground, captive to strangers, drugged and beaten.

"Just be glad I haven't pulled the trigger. You deserve it."

She couldn't escape Liam without Randy shooting Leo. She had to keep Liam from finding her earbud or confiscating her weapons and phone. He would see the phone was connected to a multiparty call. If he searched Gabrielle he'd discover the Trojan horse waiting inside before she could get Leo to safety. Before Western Pride had accepted delivery of the illegal machine guns.

The team had anticipated situations like this one. All she had to do was utter "Sheridan" and help would come. But she would not. Not while there was still hope that the rescue and the operation could be salvaged.

She said, "Kateena is fine by the way, not that you'd care."

"I keep tabs on her."

Delaney hated the thought of that. They were changing the girl's phone number as soon as she got out of this mess.

"Clever using Fabi in your scheme." She hoped Clark wouldn't realize she was talking about their mother. To her dismay, she felt a wave of emotion behind her own words. After every way in which her mother had failed her, in the end she had chosen Liam, too.

"It didn't take much convincing."

"What about—"

"Detonator, now."

"I don't have it on me."

Liam cursed. "I don't believe you."

Randy cackled. "I'm going to enjoy this."

Leo's shoulders jerked, his face contorted. "Delaney, Randy shot Jackie Spurrier. Liam is the one who took me from the lake, and he killed Brandon."

Brandon is dead?! It was one less Miller to worry about in the next few minutes.

"I only killed her because Brandon made me." Randy wheeled on Leo, grabbing him by the elbow at the same time as he swept a foot under Leo's legs. Leo toppled to the ground. Randy put one foot in the center of his back. "Every word you speak is another day I keep Delaney alive after you're dead. Please keep talking, Sheriff."

"Enough." Liam's mouth was inches from Delaney's ear, luckily the one that did not hold the earbud. "Give me the detonator or we'll do this the hard way."

"I told you. I don't have it on me. I threw it in the grass

halfway between here and my truck, just so this couldn't happen."

Liam's cursing intensified. "Randy, cuff her."

"You can't do that if you want me to be able to find it."

"You'll do it in cuffs so you can't use it if it's still on you."

Randy kicked Leo in the ribs before strutting to Delaney. Leo's body jerked. Delaney flinched, too. Randy strutted over to her. The stench of cigarette smoke was nauseating. She held her hands in front of her and he began zip-tying them together. He pulled tight, and she grunted.

"You like that?" Randy said. "You and me, we're just getting started." He crouched at her feet and used two zip ties around her ankles.

Leo looked up at her, gravel pressed into his face. She winked at him and mouthed, *It's going to be all right.* His blinked slowly three times. Then he rolled onto his back, began rocking from head to toe against the ground, and kipped up.

Liam nodded at Leo. "Grab him before he does something stupid. I've got her."

"For now. But I get her later."

"Yes, for now." Liam whirled Delaney by the shoulders, then grabbed her by the wrist binding and jerked her toward him. "Now, show me this detonator."

Another reason to hate her brother. He'd promised her as a sex toy to Randy Miller.

Three noisy trucks rumbled past them toward Gabrielle. One a semi and trailer, the others two long-bed pickups. She jerked her head toward them. "Your crew?"

"Yes." He dropped Delaney's wrists, got out his phone, and pressed a button on it before putting it to his ear. "Were the roads all clear?" Liam nodded, apparently getting the answer he wanted. "Okay. Get to work."

Delaney said, "They better not scratch my tractor or trailer."

"Walk."

Liam jabbed his gun barrel in between her shoulder blades. Delaney took short, quick steps, shuffling to keep her balance. She looked over at Leo.

He widened his eyes at her in question.

She smiled at him, conscious of Randy watching her. "Are you okay, Leo?"

He smiled for the first time, although he still looked grim. "I am now that you're here."

Randy rolled his eyes. He'd placed a cigarette between his lips and stopped to flick a lighter at its tip. When it caught, he took a few quick steps to catch up with Leo.

"Hurry up," Liam said.

When they turned the corner and Gabrielle came into view, the two pickups were parked in the road alongside the trailer. Men were piling out. They had a military look, other than the beards some of them wore. Short haircuts. Winter white camo gear. The way they moved briskly in response to the orders one of them was shouting out. A few were swinging crowbars. Others were carrying hooks and straps. They began scampering up the sides of the stacked crates on her flatbed like monkeys. When they reached Gabrielle, Delaney saw their semi had backed in, so their trailer was bumper to bumper with her flatbed.

"Be careful of explosives," the crew lead shouted.

She heard the sound of heaving wood.

Liam's fingers wrapped around her upper arm. "Who has the most explosives experience?"

The smallest of the men raised a hand. He'd been about to scale the crates.

"Check the trailer." Liam pointed underneath it.

"Yes, sir."

A deep voice shouted from atop the cargo. "Three crates intact. No sign of explosives yet. Want us to check more of 'em?" A face peeked over. Wide set, hard eyes. Hooked nose. Thick neck.

Randy said, "Start moving them. Offload the guns to the pickups as you go. We've got a buyer for those auto parts, so be careful."

"Yes, sir."

Within sixty seconds, Delaney heard the first of the gun cases clattering into the pickup beds. She turned to Leo. "It's going to be okay," she said to him.

"I know," he said.

"No matter what."

"I know. I love you."

Liam sneered at Delaney. "That's so cute."

Then a man's voice said, "All clear under the trailer."

"There was no detonator, was there, Delaney? No explosives." He laughed. "Well played, but pointless now."

While you've lost your edge. She wondered why he hadn't checked her truck or searched her, beyond his inherent belief in his mental superiority. Was it because she was incapacitated, and he thought her incapable of getting free? Or because he believed he would have learned of help through their monitors if she'd arranged for it?

"You got what you wanted from me. You have your guns. It's time to let Leo and me go, like you promised." Her words were intended for the team. It was time for the ATF to raid.

"I didn't promise shit—did you, Liam?" Randy said.

"I didn't either. "

Delaney seethed. Liam had to have been the source of much of what Fabi had said to her. She was ashamed they were related. She couldn't believe she used to idolize him as a young girl.

"Liar," she said to Liam. "He's lying to you," she said to Randy.

Liam grabbed her chin, twisting it. Delaney glared into the eyes that matched her own.

He said, "Last time I saw you, you shot me. Today it's my turn. But I have a much better aim." He summoned one of the men away from unloading. "Take her to Randy."

The man dragged Delaney across the road and into the snow beyond the shoulder, beside Randy and Leo. Liam waved the helper away.

Then he said, "I want them side by side on their knees, heads down." Smiling, he added, "I'll shoot Leo first, Delaney, so you can watch. Right between the eyes, just like Brandon."

"I should have killed you in Sheridan," Delaney said. She made sure to speak clearly and loudly.

Randy's voice was shrill. "You said I could have her."

"I changed my mind." Liam raised his gun. "Put them on the ground. Now."

Randy knocked Delaney to her knees then shoved her face into the ground. Her mouth filled with snow. "Don't move."

She shot a last glance at Gabrielle. The ATF agents were still inside the cab.

What the hell is Clark waiting for?

SIXTY-SEVEN

Randy forced Leo to the ground beside Delaney. His dirty face and unkempt beard were inches away from hers. How she wished she could hold his hand. At least hers were bound in front of her. She moved them over and placed her fingers on his cheek. The smile he gave her was like a caress. Time slowed down. She wished she could make it stop altogether.

"Move out of the way, Randy," Liam said.

Delaney was conscious of Randy standing in front of them. "Come on, Liam. You promised her to me. You can still make her watch Leo then kill her later, like we planned."

As softly as she could, she whispered to Leo, "Gabrielle is filled with ATF agents. I gave them the signal to come out. Stay low. Be ready to move to cover."

His eyes widened.

Liam said, "I killed Brandon and handed you Western Pride on a silver platter. Isn't that enough for you?"

And then pandemonium broke loose from Gabrielle. Helmeted agents spilled out of both doors, their weapons locked and loaded, their torsos bulky with bulletproof vests. They ran toward the pickup crews, their guns pointed at them.

The two vans and Clint's SUV pulled up before all of the agents were even out of Gabrielle. More agents poured into the road.

Clark led the charge. "Police! ATF! Drop your weapons and get on the ground! Hands where we can see them!"

Gunfire erupted from atop the crates on the flatbed. In front of her, Randy and Liam crouched and began shooting. The agents returned fire toward the trailer. The horrible sound of bullets hitting flesh was unmistakable, the screams chilling.

"We're exposed out here," Delaney said. "We've got to move and keep it low."

Leo nodded. "I can't get anywhere fast without my hands."

She looked around for something to break his zip ties. Randy and Liam had disappeared but were replaced by a welcome sight. Clint bent horizontal at the waist and running in a crouch toward them, his gun pointed at the ground but ready.

Clint slid the last few feet like a runner into home, set his gun down, grabbed his pocketknife, and slit the ties between Delaney's hands and feet, then did the same for Leo. "Good to see you alive, Sheriff."

"Great to be above ground, in more ways than one. Thanks for coming for me." His voice was rough, but he was sounding stronger with every word.

"Delaney wouldn't have had it any other way."

Delaney unzipped her coat and pulled both guns from her holster. She handed the Shield and an extra magazine to Leo, who stopped rotating and massaging his wrists to take the gun. "For you."

Leo hefted the Shield, getting a feel for it. "And it's not even my birthday."

Clint rose on his elbows. "Liam and Randy just snuck behind a hill. What do you know about that, Leo?"

"There's a lot I don't know. I was drugged most of the time. I don't think that's the way back to the bunker where they kept me, at least not the front door. They did come and go without using it sometimes, though."

"There are three bunkers," Delaney said. "Maybe more. Could be tunnels and an entrance to another over there."

"Sounds logical."

"That or they have a vehicle out there and they're making a run for it."

"Who else is in there?" Clint asked.

Leo said, "I think it was just those two and me. Randy and Liam. At least in the bunker I was in."

"What about Brandon?"

"He's dead," Delaney and Leo said at the same time.

The gunfire exchange between the ATF and Western Pride had slowed, but there was no sign the ATF was claiming victory. Both sides seemed to be hunkered down in a standoff with the occasional spit-spit of a weapon.

Delaney said, "Clint and I are going after them. Leo, are you up for it?"

"As I'll ever be."

"Clint, you go first. Leo and I will take turns covering. Although hopefully no one is looking in our direction. I'll bring up the rear."

Clint looked about to argue, but instead he turned and began running after the two Western Pride leaders. Leo went next, slow but steady. Then Delaney ran, ducking her head around several times to see if they'd been spotted. Clint and Leo climbed a rise in between two taller hills, then she lost sight of them. Panic burbled up, making her throat feel closed off. She pumped her legs harder. When she was over the lower hill, too, Leo was there, waiting, pointing at a doorway in the side of a hill.

A bunker. And the door was ajar.

SIXTY-EIGHT

Delaney, Leo, and Clint were flat on their stomachs in the snow. She propped herself up on her elbows, careful she was out of the line of fire from the front door of the bunker.

Using an aerial still of the T Bar M ranch captured by the drone, Delaney pointed out the locations of and probable distances between the bunkers. "Let's assume each is connected by a tunnel. The question is whether they're still in this one or made a run for one of the others."

Leo tapped the screen to enlarge a section. "This is the entrance to a garage, I think. I didn't see it, but I know they used it on the first day I was here. It's also underground. That's where they'd hide their vehicles."

"It's not far. I vote the first thing we do is disable the vehicles."

Clint was nodding, but said, "How about I'll go for the vehicles, someone else check inside this bunker? I can enter the other bunker near the garage. Maybe that way we can herd them into the third."

"I like that. Here's that aerial photo." She airdropped it to Clint.

Leo was biting his bottom lip. "Someone needs to guard the door on the third bunker, then."

"Seems like that should be you, Leo. You've spent enough time underground for one week." Clint dug in the deep pockets of his coat and came out with two cannisters. He held one out to Delaney. "One of the guys in van two gave me smoke bombs. They really were ready for anything."

She took the bomb. "You should get moving. Leo and I will work the rest out."

Clint nodded at them, then spun around and jogged across the rough, snowy hill with the gunfire echoing in the valley behind him.

Delaney laced her fingers through Leo's. "We won't be able to communicate with you. I'm sorry."

He leaned in and kissed her, hard and fast. "My job is simple. Don't let Liam and Randy come out that door. I have two full magazines. I'm good."

"Listen, you know these guys are dangerous. But we found unmarked graves where they were holding you. Randy Miller is a possible serial killer. And you know all about Liam. Or at least a lot of the deaths he's responsible for. Kat's mother. My father. Sheriff Coltrane. As much as I want to send my brother to his grave, I want justice more."

Leo growled. "I feel the same way about Randy."

"Keep them alive if you can. But not at the expense of yourself." Now she kissed him, softer than he'd kissed her. *Don't let this be our last one.* "I love you."

"I love you, too. See you soon."

She felt choked up, but she steeled herself. With a deep breath, she took off toward the bunker. She couldn't bear the thought of watching Leo go, so she didn't look back. When she reached the side of the door, a thought stopped her. Their operations group call was muted on her phone. If Clint needed her, she wouldn't hear him. For a moment, she considered jumping off the call and initiating one with him directly. Then she decided to keep it as a failsafe, in case things went really bad in the bunkers. She unmuted the call. The crack of rifle fire seemed louder through the phone, then the air.

"We need to flank them," Clark was saying. He issued a series of commands to his team about who went where and what to do when they got there.

What they were doing didn't affect her, so she turned the volume lower. It just had to be loud enough for her to hear Clint. She entered around the door quickly, making a hard right to get out of the backlit firing line, gun high but ready. The bunker was inky dark in front of her. She felt the light switch digging into her back and flipped it on. She had a quick impression of a dimly lit, low-ceilinged room with very little furniture and a kitchen to one side, before she crouched and dove behind an armchair.

There was no sound except the accelerated bass drum of her heartbeat.

She peered over the chair back. No movement. No human forms. She looked for closets or bulky pieces of furniture that might provide hiding places. Nothing.

She advanced to the hallway and moved through it sideways, holding her Staccato pointing slightly down and away from her chest with both hands. The sound of the ATF's fight with Western Pride started breaking up over the phone line. Silence then bursts of chaotic sound then silence again.

She counted three doors and went to the first, throwing it open from the side. It bumped into the wall in the room and bounced back at her slowly. *No door stop.* When no one fired on her, she buttonholed around the jamb then found the light switch and turned it on. No furniture. No closet. No people.

One down.

She repeated her cautious entry on the second room. What she found there was quite different, however. A room filled wall to wall with furniture, like a storage room. Two beds, or rather, two box spring and mattress sets on the ground. Two armoires. Two chests of drawers. She checked behind the tall furniture.

Another empty room.

Once she was back out in the hall, her phone made a beeping sound. It had lost signal. She gave a quick glance back into the living room and kitchen. It was still clear.

Last room.

This was the tricky one, as it was directly at the end of the hall. There wasn't much wall to shield herself behind for entry. She tried to minimize her side profile and opened the door. Inside, was nothing but a bathroom with no shower curtain.

Anticlimactic.

She needed to communicate with Clint. Back in the living room, her phone reacquired signal, but she was no longer connected to the group. There would be no crying "Sheridan" again. An eerie sense of aloneness crept over her. *Leo must feel it even more.* She couldn't think about him. If she did, she'd worry. If she worried, she'd lose her edge and get herself killed. Then she'd be no help to Leo or anyone.

A text came in from Clint. It was of voice-to-speech errors, but understandable.

I tried the call but you'd dripped. Two vehicles in a two-car hay. I slashed tires and shot into engines. I'm gong under-ground now.

The text was from two minutes before. It would probably take him five to search the bunker. She'd use the time to locate the tunnel entrance. There had to be one, if Liam and Randy had entered this bunker. The door had been open, which suggested they had. Or that they wanted her to waste her time looking for them somewhere they weren't. She guessed they could have thrown the door open then kept running above ground, but she had to follow through with the plan.

She went back to the bathroom, checking under the sink and floor mats for floor hatches, then ran her hands along all the walls. Since it was the room furthest under the ground, it had seemed her best bet, but it yielded nothing. She repeated the exercise in the empty bedroom. It was even easier in there because there were no rugs, although the walls took her longer. In the other bedroom, she paused, thinking. Would they have moved furniture to get into the tunnel? If so, they'd have to have moved it back to disguise the entrance. The pieces in here were too bulky to move far once someone was in the mouth of a tunnel and trying to shut a door behind them. She decided she didn't need to move the furniture, but she examined the floor around the edges of it carefully. Then she smoothed the walls with her palms and fingertips, reading it like Braille for any change in the surface. Nothing.

Back in the living room, she rolled up rugs and looked under the couch and chairs. The walls were a bust. It was all a bust.

She texted Clint.

10-4. Bunker 1 clear. Leo guarding door to 3. Can't find tunnel entrance.

At least she hoped Leo was in position at bunker three. What if Randy and Liam were above ground and had found him? Again, she fought back her panicky thoughts.

Then she heard a noise from the bathroom, coming from above. She sprinted toward it, gun pointed at the ceiling where a trap door was hanging down. *The ceiling! I never thought!* She shut the door to the bathroom partway and put her body behind it, gun aimed at the hatch.

She heard whispering.

"...if that damn idiot hadn't shown up. I think I hit him. He wouldn't have been alone, though. Now how are we going to get to the truck?" It was Randy's voice.

Clint shot? If he'd been underground, the ATF wouldn't have heard it over the call, because he would have lost connection like she had. She felt split in two. One of her team members was possibly down, but she had no choice. She couldn't give her two suspects a clear shot at her by fleeing down the hall to go to Clint's aid.

Liam said, "If you hadn't taken so long, we would've been gone. Now, check before you jump out of here."

Half a face peeked out of the trap door. The eye blinked then it widened. "It's Delaney!"

Take them alive. She held fire. The face vanished. Then the tip of a rifle appeared through the hole and began spraying bullets down the hall.

SIXTY-NINE

Delaney crouched low and retreated down the side of the hall into the empty bedroom. She took cover behind the jamb, then turned to face the bathroom. She could see one side hatch. She fired two careful shots at the opening.

Their shooting stopped.

She closed her eyes and waited through fifteen more seconds of silence. Were they gone? She had to chance it, to get to signal and text Clint. She ran down the hall and into the living room, off to the side where a bullet from the bathroom wouldn't reach her.

Suspects shot at me thru tunnel door in ceiling. R U OK?

Three dots appeared.

Come on, Clint. Hurry.

She had to catch Randy and Liam before they reached Leo. Through the tunnel or above ground, though? If she was going after them in the tunnels, she needed a flashlight. In the kitchen, she opened drawers and cabinets. She found one, but when she turned it on, the batteries were dead.

Her phone rang. It was Clint.

She hit accept. "Are you okay?"

"I've been better." His voice was strained. "I shut the door on the bunker. Now I'm above it trying to bomb it so they can't come back, but I can't find the vent."

Delaney thought back to the prepper tricks she'd learned as a girl. "Sometimes they vent through hollow fence posts. Do you see any?"

After a few seconds of silence, Clint said, "Son of a gun, you're right. It was beside me this whole time. Bombs away."

If that bunker is totally unavailable to them, I should go to Leo above ground. "Leo's alone. I've got to go."

"My ankle is shattered. I barely made it up here. I don't think I can get to you guys."

"I understand. Call for help."

"Drop your bomb on the way."

"Roger that."

Delaney ended the call. She slammed the door shut on her way out and ran up, up, and around to the earthen berm that was the bunker's roof. Where was the vent? She looked for fence posts and stove pipes, but there were none. There were, however, two posts for a clothesline. One end of the line blew in the breeze between them.

She approached the first one. It was taller than her reach. She jumped and caught the top edge with both hands. She wiggled her fingers. It felt hollow. But since she couldn't see into it for confirmation, she repeated the move with the second one. It felt hollow, too.

So, which was the vent?

She only had one cannister. She eyed the ground, envisioning the footprint of the bunker below her. Returning to the first post, she stared at it. She hadn't gotten high enough before.

An idea came to her. She tested the clothesline against her weight. It was wire in a plastic covering, and it held. She measured a length with her eyes and wrapped it around her hand. Then she leapt and grabbed the edge of the pole again. Holding tight, she lifted her foot and felt around for the line. Her body swung as she searched. The soldered top edge of the pole was cutting in to her hands. Her abs were burning from the mid-air leg lift. Just as she was about to drop to the ground, her toe found the line. She stepped into it and propelled herself upwards. The line tightened around her hand and dug into it. The pain was sharp. Very sharp. She had to move fast.

She let go with the other hand, dug the cannister from her pocket, and used her chin and shoulder to hold it while she pulled the tab. Smoke poured from the top, and if it weren't for the wind, it would have enveloped her immediately. It stung her eyes and irritated her lungs. *And that's why a mask and eye protection should be worn at all times when using these things.*

Coughing, she felt for the opening at the top of the pole and dropped the cannister inside. More smoke billowed out of the top into her face.

Blind from the smoke, she grasped the pole's edge again, worked her foot out of the clothesline, and dropped to the ground. She landed with an audible, "Oof." She rubbed her face in the snow, trying to speed up her recovery. After a minute, she stood, still coughing. Her eyes smarted like mad but she could see. The smoke was clearing. Whether or not her bomb was smoking the interior of the bunker, she had no way of knowing, but she'd done her best.

She pulled the drone photo up on her phone, squinted to eyeball it against the terrain in front of her, and ran a straight line toward the third bunker as fast and hard as she could across the slippery, uneven ground.

. . .

When Delaney crested the last rise, her smarting eyes found Leo below her. He was on his belly, carefully firing at the open doorway of the third bunker. He must have just started, because they were the first shots she'd heard. A burst of semi-automatic rifle fire answered from inside. Leo flattened his head and shoulders into the snow.

Silence.

Delaney evaluated her options quickly. The two men inside didn't know she was out here. They now knew Leo was. She'd probably have a minute or so while they regrouped. If she joined Leo, they had only one angle on the door. She eyed the grassy area above the opening. It put her in the line of Leo's fire, but it also gave her the element of surprise if and when Randy and Liam came out. There was almost no way she could miss an incapacitating shot from that range.

But first she had to let Leo know what she was doing.

She bent at the waist and sprinted the last fifteen yards to reach him. He turned when he heard her, gun drawn, then lowered it. She slid to the ground beside him.

"I'm glad I didn't shoot," he said.

"Me, too." Breathlessly, she said, "Clint's hurt. He won't be coming. We lost our connection with the ATF, so they won't either. But the vehicles are disabled. The other two bunkers have been smoked, after confrontations in both of them. Hopefully, that means they're cornered in this one. But I don't have another cannister of smoke."

"Okay. I've only taken three shots. Lots of ammo left."

"Did you hit them?"

"I don't think so. I guess now we just wait. The ATF will show up eventually."

"Which is why I think they're going to shoot their way out. If the ATF gets here they know they're caught. They have a chance against one guy. But I have an idea." She told him about it quickly. "Just please don't shoot high."

"I don't like it."

"After I incapacitate them, I'll jump down between them and the door."

His voice grew harder. "This is a bullshit plan."

"Advance on them as soon as I have them down."

"Seriously, Delaney."

"Order me not to."

"I order you not to."

"Sorry, you're out of jurisdiction. My brother is not getting away from me this time. And I'm not letting them mow us down with AK-47s after we run out of bullets. We don't know how long it will be until the feds show up. If they do. But I have to leave now while they don't know I'm here."

Leo sighed. "I don't know why I bother arguing with you. Okay, I'll try not to shoot you."

"Cover me." She jumped up and ran a wide approach to the snowy hill.

Leo fired two more shots at the doorway, letting several seconds elapse between them.

Delaney slowed on the ground above the bunker. Would they hear the thud of her boots below? Or her gasping breaths? She moved soft-footed to the edge of the earthen berm that surrounded the door and centered herself above it.

From inside, she heard Liam's voice. "I'm not going to prison. We've got to make a break before the ATF gets here. It's just Leo with a handgun. He's too far away for much accuracy. We've got superior fire power. We unleash on him then take off cross country to the shed. The two-seater is waiting for us there."

"I'm low on ammo," Randy said.

"I'll cover you, then I'll follow."

Delaney knew she couldn't fire on Randy. It would drive Liam back inside the bunker. She'd have to wait for Liam to emerge. *If Randy gets away, I'll send the ATF after him.*

"Fine."

A rifle appeared out of the doorway and began shooting at Leo, who was lying face first in the snow. Delaney couldn't do anything to help him now. All she could do was her job. She huffed a breath out.

"Go, go, go!" Liam shouted.

Randy darted out the door, cutting immediately to his left. More bullets sprayed toward Leo's position. Delaney stayed crouched and ready with her gun trained a few feet from the door, along the path Randy had used.

Liam burst from the doorway.

She stood, aimed, and fired.

Liam tumbled to the ground. Delaney leapt through the air after him.

SEVENTY

Delaney saw blood on the back of Liam's thigh before she landed with her chest on his feet. *Got you.* He kicked ferociously, catching her in the solar plexus. It drew an "oof" from her but she half rose and threw her weight on the back of his legs. Somehow, she got her arms around them. Liam kept kicking, shaking her like the rattle on a snake. Then he twisted his upper body around so his shoulders and head were facing her, which was far worse. She looked up and into his maniacal eyes. His rifle was in his right hand, and he was bringing it around. The very definition of point-blank range.

"Looks like I get to show off my aim after all," he said.

A single shot shattered the silence. Delaney felt it as much as she heard it, the whooshing displacement of air near her ear as a lethal projectile passed close by, like someone walking across her grave. She ducked and braced herself automatically, even though she knew it was already too late. If the shot was going to hit her, it already would have been embedded in her flesh.

Liam screamed. His gun fell to the snow. He lifted a bloody hand, or what was left of it. Were some of his fingers missing?

Delaney wasn't going to waste any time figuring it out. She jumped to her feet and snatched up the rifle.

She pointed it at his chest. "Looks like you don't."

Leo slid to his knees beside Liam. "Zip ties."

She pulled them from a pocket and tossed them to him.

Liam was holding the wrist of his one arm with the other hand. Blood was soaking into the snow. As Leo reached for him, he tried to writhe away, making it impossible for a single person to cuff him.

Delaney threw the rifle in the snow, far, far away from her brother. "Sit on him. I'll cuff him."

Leo grunted and spread his weight out over the front of Liam's body. From an inside pocket, Delaney fished out her metal cuffs. Liam released his injured hand and started swinging at her with the good one as she came at him. She stepped on the wrist of his injured side. He screamed as she snapped one side closed around the wrist under her feet. Leo reacted quickly, rolling Liam to his stomach while Delaney pulled the cuffed wrist behind him. Leo brought the other arm around and Delaney cuffed it, too. Then Leo slid back to Liam's calves, rotated to face his feet, and helped control them while Delaney used the flexicuffs to secure his ankles.

"Randy's getting away," she said. "I have to go after him."

Leo shook his head. "Call it in. We've got a team."

She texted the entire operations group.

Randy has made a run for a shed at the back of the property. There is a two-seater ORV back there. Send agents. Leo and I have Liam.

A reply came quickly from Clark.

Western Pride subdued. Sending team after Randy.

She sent another.

Clint shot, injured at far west bunker. Liam injured, too, at far north bunker. Need a ride.

She said, "The ATF is going after Randy. They may need my help."

Leo stood, one foot on Liam's back. "Randy hasn't committed any crimes in Kearny County. Liam has. Let's bring him in together."

Delaney knew Leo was right. One cop wasn't enough to contain Liam, whether he was cuffed or not. She helped Leo jerk her brother to his feet.

Liam was still making a pitiful noise. "I need medical attention. I'm going to bleed out."

"Then I'd never have to worry about you bothering Kat again." Delaney looked at his hand. He'd definitely lost two fingers. "Sorry to say, but hands don't bleed much. You'll be fine."

"My fingers. Where are they? They can be reattached."

Delaney was going to look half-heartedly until she heard a sound from inside the bunker that sent chills through her.

"Help." The voice was faint. "Help me."

"Do you hear that, Leo? It sounds like a girl." She ran to the doorway.

Leo pulled Liam along behind her.

"Somebody. Please help me," the voice said.

"It seems like it's coming from a room down the hall." Delaney turned and shook Liam. "Who's in there?"

He spat in her face.

She wiped the thick glob away. "Let's secure him. Then I'm going in to help that girl."

Leo used his head to indicate direction, into the living room. "There's a D-ring in the trapdoor."

Delaney saw a rug rolled back. The entrance to the tunnel was in the floor in this bunker. Leo dragged him over to it. Delaney used more flexicuffs to attach him to it.

She said, "Ready?"

He nodded. "Gun pointed at his head."

Delaney took off down the hall. She paused at the first door, listening. A person was whimpering. She tried the knob. Locked. But it was a simple spring latch, not a deadbolt. If she'd had a credit card, she'd have made quick work of it, but her wallet was in Gabrielle.

"Hello in there. My name is Deputy Delaney Pace. I came to get you out," she said.

A young woman's voice said, "Thank God. Yes! Yes!"

"I need to kick the door down."

"Okay!"

"Can you move away from it?"

Delaney heard scuffling inside.

"I moved."

"Are you ready?"

"Yes. Very."

Delaney tapped her fingertips on the door. Old and cheap hollow-core. The trick to kicking in a door, Delaney had learned, was not to kick the door itself or throw weight against it. It was to visualize kicking *through* it, past the other side. Unless, of course, as had been the case in the barn on Snow Hare Ranch, it was a steel door or had a deadbolt lock. But this door couldn't keep her out. If it didn't give, the spring latch would.

She reared back and kicked just below the handle. It only took two kicks for the door to fly open.

The girl screamed, "Oh, my God."

Light spilled into the dark room from the hallway. A beautiful young woman was bound and lying on the floor, hands behind her back. Long blonde hair hung in her face. Her blue eyes were huge, frightened, and teary. One of them was heading toward a shiner, and her lip was bloody and swollen. "You're really a deputy?"

"I am. All the way from Wyoming. I'm going to cut you loose, okay?"

"Th-th-thank you."

"What's your name?" Delaney crouched beside her.

"Tabby. Tabby Teller." She gave a nervous laugh. "It's a horrible name. I should have changed it."

"I like it." Delaney moved quickly, flipping open her pocketknife and cutting through the restraints.

The girl groaned. "My shoulders. They really hurt."

"How long have you been here?"

"Not long. A day. But I was with them before. Then I got away."

"Them is Western Pride?"

"Yes. They brought me back for *him*." Her eyes flew wide. She clutched Delaney's hands. "He's going to kill me. Is he out there? We have to go!"

"Randy? No, he's gone."

The girl looked confused. "Not Randy."

"Liam?"

"Is he the one who brought me here? The one with the creepy green eyes?"

"Yes." A strange understanding was falling into place. "Who is *he*, Tabby? The one you're scared of?"

"The one who hurt me. The one who killed the others. Brandon."

For a few beats, Delaney held perfectly still, letting the revelation sink in. Brandon was the serial killer.

Frustration and fury surged through her. Liam had denied this girl and others like her justice when he shot Brandon between the eyes in the takeover of Western Pride. A dangerous man was dead, but he wouldn't have to answer for his crimes.

Did this mean Delaney owed Liam some debt of gratitude for it, like he'd done the world a favor?

No. I will never feel gratitude for anything he's done.

She pulled the shivering younger woman into her arms. "You don't have to worry about him, I promise. You'll never have to worry about him again."

SEVENTY-ONE
ONE WEEK LATER

Leo walked into the station, out of the bright winter sun. In the week since he'd returned home, he'd showered three times a day. After he'd been cleared at the hospital, he'd slept twenty-four hours the first day. Then he'd eaten his body weight in steak and potatoes over the next few. All of it with Delaney by his side as much as she could be. Physically, he was fine. But he was shocked how volatile his emotions had been at first. Angry one minute. Guilty the next, because of the ATF agent who'd died from a shot fired by a member of Western Pride. Happy. Grateful. Inexplicably sad about humanity. Inexplicably hopeful. And worried about Delaney. He was glad to be returning to work where he could keep an eye on her.

She hadn't been the same since they'd come back from Montana. He was improving. She was going in the other direction.

Clara stood when he entered. She threw open her arms and he walked into her hug. "I'm more than glad to see you."

"Thank you. For that and for everything you did to help find me and Jackie's killer."

"It was a team effort." She winked. "Drew hit a few speed bumps, but he's coming along."

Leo laughed. "That's good to hear."

"He's going to tell you Joe was awful."

"Okay."

"I don't like to talk out of school, but he'll be telling the truth. We found you despite Joe."

Leo wasn't surprised but hated hearing it. "Thank you for letting me know."

"Of course. Now, they're waiting for you."

Leo whistled as he walked the hallway. He wasn't going to let this closeout meeting with Clark Applewood ruin this day. He opened the door to the conference room.

Balloons floated into the hall as people shouted, "Welcome home, Sheriff!"

He accepted hugs amid tears and laughter. A sheet cake that read WE LOVE YOU grew smaller by the piece. He saw Delaney over a sea of heads. Deputies, city officers, state cops, the crime scene techs. Clara, who'd snuck in behind Leo. A few civilians. Adriana, Freddy, Kat, Carrie, and Skeeter. Clint Rock-Below, who was on crutches. The police chief had followed Delaney to Canada and back. *There's something going on with him when he's around Delaney. I can feel it.* He would talk to Delaney about it, but not until she was back to her old self.

Delaney looked up and saw him watching her. She mouthed, *They want to hear from you.*

He groaned but held up a hand. "Can I speak for a second, everyone?"

Voices died down, stragglers were shushed.

"Thank you for this." He paused. "So, you may have heard I had a rather unpleasant visit to Montana."

At this, Drew chuckled.

"But our team never quit. Thank you to all who helped but especially to Drew, Skeeter, Clara, Clint, and Delaney. The scope of what you did and how you managed it so quickly makes me very proud. That you did it for my benefit means the world to me." He met each of their eyes and smiled directly at them. He'd make time to talk to them individually soon.

There was loud, extended applause and whoops, except for Joe, who was leaning against the wall furthest from Leo, a sullen expression pulling his whole face downward. *I'm going to have to do something about him.* Now that he had a new deputy starting, he'd begin recruiting for the next one. As soon as that one was onboard, he'd deal with Joe.

"Not only did they rescue me—Clint and Delaney under gunfire and in hand-to-hand combat—but they partnered with the ATF to confiscate two hundred and fifty illegal machine guns and take down key members of the Western Pride militia."

More cheering, but this time it was Clint whose clapping slowed. Randy had shot Clint, and Clint was now recovering from ankle surgery earlier in the week to repair the damage. Leo knew personally how hard it was to get over the ones who got away. Clark Applewood felt the same as Clint, he imagined. When the ATF team had gone after Randy at the shed Delaney had told them about, the off-road vehicle and Randy were gone. It was the same with Tanya Sones. The agents who showed up at her office and her home found she'd already cleared out.

Two Millers were in the wind.

The only Miller in Western Pride leadership gone was Brandon, who was found in a shallow grave on the T Bar M ranch, and only because Liam executed him. *Saves the state and county the money and uncertainty of prosecution.*

The excavation of the Snow Hare Ranch graves was ongoing, but one of the Western Pride witnesses had given up information on Brandon in hopes of leniency from the feds. It hadn't worked, of course. But, thanks to that witness, they had a good idea of the names of the four young women they'd found in the graves and who put them there. He'd also said Randy Miller didn't kill his women, that they were paid off for secrecy when they left the group, which was the problem with Jackie, who had run off without a nondisclosure agreement. Brandon, on the other hand, was like a cat with his. Torture, then kill. The witness had told them one last horrifying detail—there were other graves at properties elsewhere in Wyoming and Montana. The investigation was expanding.

Meanwhile, Sheriff Wilcox was taking credit for multiple solved murders while casting shade on Leo and Kearny County. Leo decided he wasn't going to be voting for him for governor.

As for Tabby, her landlady in Helena had paid for a plane ticket back to West Virginia. Delaney had spoken to Tabby and said the young woman was doing as well as could be hoped.

"Last but not least, our team apprehended one of the most dangerous outlaws in Wyoming history. The lion's share of that credit goes to Delaney Pace. And this one was personal for her. It is our intention to see Liam Pace stand trial for all of his many crimes in the state of Wyoming. I have it from the most reliable of sources that Montana wants a piece of him, too."

The clapping was loudest for this announcement, but the mood turned solemn. It wasn't hard for people to understand that having a criminal in the family was painful. Having to be the one to apprehend him was worse. One by one, people shook Delaney's hand.

The party ended quite naturally after that, leaving only Drew, Clara, and Skeeter with Delaney and Leo. Delaney was humoring their thirst for action stories, but she looked antsy. Finally, it was just Leo, Delaney, and Skeeter, who they hadn't been able to shake. Leo suspected he wouldn't leave until the last of the cake was in his belly.

Skeeter tucked a bite in his mouth then talked through it. "I finally got the information on that number you asked me to trace, Delaney."

Delaney said, "Now that all this is over, I want you to know that it was my mother who was in possession of that phone. Liam was sending messages to me through her. I'm sorry I couldn't tell you earlier."

Skeeter held his next bite aloft. "Sorry about that, boss-lady."

"I'll be okay."

"Anyway, the address was in Puyallup, Washington, and the registered owner was Far West Ventures, LLC. The address is a no-go, it's just one of those places where people have mailboxes and send packages. But maybe she's in the area."

"Maybe so. Thank you."

"Course, the SIM has disappeared."

"I'd imagine she was told to destroy it if something went wrong. We don't need to look for her anymore. I've talked to her. I'm at peace."

Leo saw the pain in her eyes. There was no peace there.

Skeeter nodded solemnly. Then he added another scoop of ice cream for the remainder of his extra-large piece of cake.

Delaney said, "But how come we couldn't find her on that number if it wasn't a burner?"

Leo said, "It's pretty easy to mask a location with virtual private networking. You can make a phone or computer look like it's almost anywhere in the world."

"Could it have been Liam talking to me all along?" Then she shook her head. "Sometimes, I know it was her. There were things she said that only she knew."

"If it was an iPhone, Liam could have been logged into iMessages on an Apple laptop or tablet under the same number. Then he could have participated in the chats you had with her directly, and it would have shown as coming from the same phone number."

"How did I not know about this?"

Leo smiled. "It's a good thing for a parent to keep in mind."

Skeeter said, "On another topic, when I talked to Jackie Spurrier's parents they said something that got me to thinking."

"Yes?" Leo said.

"She called them a week before Randy killed her. I'm thinking that's how they found her—when she reached out to her parents."

"The timing fits. They could have been bugged." Leo rubbed his eyes. "That's really sad."

Delaney abruptly headed for the door.

"Where are you going?"

"I need some air." Her voice sounded hoarse. She slipped out without looking back, shutting the door behind her.

Leo thought about going after her. He'd learned that sometimes she needed to be alone, preferably on the road driving too fast. Was this one of the times to let it happen? He shared a look with Skeeter, whose face was sympathetic. It seemed the other man understood the pain of loving a woman who had trouble loving herself.

SEVENTY-TWO

Delaney washed her face in the women's bathroom. She hated crying. Hated it even worse when she did it in front of other people, and she nearly had in that conference room. Over what? Jackie's parents' joy in hearing from their daughter leading to her murder? She hadn't cried all week, and that was what finally set her off? She allowed herself five minutes of messy, unrestrained sobbing.

When she had slowed to hiccups and sniffles, she checked her phone. Leo had texted, checking on her. Several times. And called, which she hadn't heard because her ringer was off.

She texted him back.

Hope Clara told you real mtg time/place.

She did. You OK? You coming?

There was no use pretending that she *had* been okay. It would be clear when she came out.

I will be. See you there.

She washed her face then looked at herself in the mirror. "Buck up, buttercup." She was dreading the next meeting. Clark Applewood was due any minute.

When she emerged from the bathroom, Clara was escorting Clark into Leo's office just ahead of her. Delaney couldn't believe he'd agreed to the location. Coming to Leo's office was the opposite of a power move. Was that because he was saving up his real ones for the battle over Liam? Or in deference to what Leo had gone through at the hands of the Western Pride? Because Clark bore some responsibility there in Delaney's opinion for withholding evidence and protecting his federal turf.

She entered the office after Clark and Leo had shaken hands.

She nodded at the ATF agent. "Hello, Clark."

Clark was always good at reading the room. He sat without giving her a chance to reject him. "Delaney. Hello."

Leo opened his blinds, displaying his killer view of white mountains. "Thanks for coming here on my first day back, Clark."

"You okay? No medical surprises?"

"No problems."

"That's good news." Clark side-eyed Delaney and said, "I can't tell you how impressive your deputy was in this operation."

"She's pretty amazing," Leo agreed.

"Her driving is terrifying, though."

Leo laughed aloud. If that was funny, Delaney couldn't detect it in her current mood.

Clark then launched into the story of Delaney losing their tail at the switchback. He segued into their harrowing escape from Western Pride at the ambush. Delaney hadn't gone into detail with Leo about the challenges she had faced on the road. She wasn't sure why she was feeling clammed up, but it just hadn't come out of her mouth.

Now, Leo's eyebrows were in his hairline. He shot her a look that held hurt.

Delaney said, "You're not here because we're all besties, Clark. Get to the point."

Clark said, "You won't be surprised, Leo, that I didn't find her any less prickly than in the past on this operation."

Leo half-smiled at Delaney and withheld comment.

Delaney rolled her hand.

Clark leaned forward with his palms on his thighs. "Well, then. Let's start with the good. We seized two hundred and fifty machine guns. We apprehended fifteen Western Pride members and another seven are dead. Brandon Miller is dead. Liam Pace is off the street. The bad. We did lose a team member, which never gets any easier."

Leo looked down at his feet. "I'm sorry about that. Very sorry," he said.

Clark nodded. "We didn't arrest Tanya Sones. You have a misguided notion we're going to let you prosecute Liam Pace in state court. And you chased off Randy Miller before we could arrest him."

Delaney turned in her chair. "We did *not* chase him off. And he shot Clint. We weren't your assistants."

"I made it clear we were there to bring in the leadership."

"Reference my earlier statement. 'We' should have kept him in your sights and taken him down."

Clark continued speaking as if she hadn't. "Yet we brought in none. Brandon is dead. Tanya and Randy are probably in a country with no extradition. Now we can't find our confidential informant, Igor Salazar. And Liam is here in Kearny County."

Delaney was vibrating. She felt out of control, wanted to be gone. Her vintage Chevelle SS was in the parking lot. Shotgun Shelly. Her father's old car. Restored to its former beauty and as fast across prairie roads as a pronghorn antelope. She could excuse herself and be flying toward the foothills in two minutes.

After this is over. Just get through this.

"Which is where he should be, as many of the outstanding warrants against him for earlier crimes are here," Leo said. "As should Igor. And if we find him, we'll bring him here."

"None of Liam's federal crimes committed with Western Pride occurred in Kearny County. I'm here to take him off your hands. As for Igor, we'll see how all this shakes out down the road."

Delaney jumped up, finger pointing at Clark, but Leo stood and held out a hand to stop her.

He said, "Last time you took one of our prisoners, it *was* Igor. You sent a kidnapper and rapist back on the street."

"As a confidential informant. To our mutual benefit this time. And that's not what I'm doing today. I'm taking Liam to a federal detention center where he'll stand trial for federal crimes."

Leo put both hands flat on his desk and leaned toward Clark. "We can put him away on multiple life sentences for murder. We can get the death penalty."

"But the ATF needs a win. A big, visible win. It's why I cooperated with Delaney and risked the lives of my agents. Besides, this will save Kearny and Wyoming from a protracted trial. You can get on with your lives and focus on your community. And your relationships."

Delaney was almost holding her breath, standing poised for what she didn't know, as she waited to see what Leo would do.

"If you're asking for my blessing, you will not get it," Leo said. "And if you're telling me to release him to your custody, I absolutely refuse without a court order." Leo straightened and crossed his arms.

Delaney sank back into her seat. Leo had stood up for her

and what she needed. Tears threatened her again. *So inappropriate.*

"Then you shall get one. I'd hoped we could do this collegially."

"No chance," Delaney said.

"One more thing. Delaney, you'll be hearing from me to collect what you owe us."

"What I *owe* you? We're square. I got Leo, you got a mega bust."

"Both you and Leo would be dead without us. We'd have still brought down Western Pride without you."

Delaney flipped him the bird.

"But as a thank you, I wanted to give you something I think you'll want." He handed her a slip of paper.

She glanced down. It was a street address in Puyallup, Washington. Not the address for the mailbox store.

Clark interlaced his fingers and inverted his hands, then released them and returned them to his lap. "Fabiola Pace is residing at this address. I know you thought you kept your communications with her a secret, but we have that house wire-tapped. We knew from the beginning. I decided not to press the issue since you were giving us the content if not the source of the messages. Also, because Clint Rock-Below said you had told him, I won't call it what it feels like, which is obstruction of justice. I can forgive withholding from partners you're not sure you can trust. Because, as you can see, I did that with you as well."

Delaney's anger was so all consuming that she couldn't speak. Couldn't move or think. Suddenly, Leo was at her side. She didn't know how or when he got there. He took the paper from her hand.

Clark's phone rang. "One moment."

He went into the hallway to answer it.

Leo put his hands on Delaney's shoulders. "This isn't over."

"I hate him."

"I do, too."

"They knew about my mom and never told me."

"I know."

"They tried to order me not to go after you. They withheld information about where you were. Who you were with. Then, this."

Clark came back in. "It appears we have nothing to discuss anymore about Igor Salazar."

"Why?" Leo asked.

"He was found dead with the word PAYBACK branded into his chest."

SEVENTY-THREE

The second Clark was gone, Delaney leapt to her feet and hurried to her cubicle for her purse and keys. She expected to hear Leo's footsteps behind her. She didn't. She thought he'd call after her. He hadn't. *Fine. It's better that I'm alone anyway.*

She was out to Shotgun Shelly as fast as she could speed walk out of the station, saying goodbye to no one, just throwing a wave at Clara as she stormed out. She was so blinded by her short-circuiting emotions that she was all the way to the Chevelle before she saw Leo leaning against it.

"I thought you might let me come with you," he said.

"You're not going to tell me to calm down or to let you drive or to come back inside and talk or... or..."

"Nope. I'm going to put my life in your hands. You're my ride or die. If you're going out, I'm going with you."

She stared at him, aware that her lips were moving. *No. No. No.* She couldn't let him go. If he saw her like this, it would change how he thought of her forever.

"You want to say that out loud?"

She shook her head.

"Okay. Let's do this."

She opened the car and slid into the seat. Even though it was cold outside, the leather was warm from the sun. Leo buckled in beside her.

"I don't want to talk." She turned on the engine. Backed up. Laid rubber in the parking lot.

"You don't have to."

She kept Shelly reined in until they were out of town. Then she coaxed the car up to one hundred. One ten. One twenty. Leo stayed silent beside her. He didn't hold onto the arm rest or grip the edges of the seat. He kept his head turned, watching the scenery streak by outside the window. For ten minutes, Delaney drove like she was running from the devil herself, slowing just enough for the curves, enjoying the centrifugal force pulling at her.

But far before she usually turned around when she pulled a scamper like this, she slammed on the brakes and spun the car around so that it faced the opposite direction where it stopped in the middle of the road. She was panting like she'd been pushing the car instead of driving it.

Leo didn't move a muscle. After several long, quiet seconds, he said, "Clint told me what happened with the cartel on the Blackfeet Reservation. You've been keeping a lot to yourself this week. That's fine if you need to but understand that your feelings aren't a burden to me."

Her lips felt like ice. "It's not that."

"I'm still here if you want to tell me now."

She swallowed down a lump in her throat. "You took the permanent sheriff's job. I hadn't thought about what that meant until this week."

"And what does it mean?"

"The last few sheriffs died in office."

"And many before them didn't."

"I lost you on the mountain. Liam was going to *kill* you. The cartel guys on the reservation were probably going to kill me. Randy sure would have after he finished with me."

"Yes." His eyes were bright. His voice held heat. She wanted to warm herself with him like he was a damn flame. She wanted to run from him like he'd burn her to ashes.

Her voice rose, pushing outward against the confines of the Chevelle. "Don't you get it? There are so many ways to lose you. People die. We're around death all the time. So much of it."

"Yes."

"My father died. Fentworth died. My mother is dead to me. Liam is dead to me."

"You've known a lot of loss with nothing to fill up the holes it left behind in you. Until Kat and Carrie. And me, I hope."

She buried her face in her hands. "I can't function under the weight of this fear." She lifted her head, not looking at him. "If this is what love is, it's too hard. It's just too hard."

Leo reached over and put his hand on her knee. "This is what love is. And you're plenty strong for it."

She looked up at his beautiful face. His beloved face. She whispered, "But what if I'm not? Look at me. I'm falling apart."

He took her face in both of his hands. "I don't think so. I think you're putting up the fight of your life."

"This isn't about fighting you."

"Not against me." He smiled. "You're fighting vulnerability."

"I don't want to be weak."

He stroked her cheek with his thumb. Played with the end of her braid with his other hand. "Not weak. Vulnerable to the possibility of loss. If you can do what you did in the last week to bring me home, you're plenty strong to face your fears. You're strong enough to be vulnerable."

"Last week was different. I didn't have time to be scared. I couldn't let anything happen to you. Now... now..."

"You're not doing it alone. I'm right here going through it, too."

She snorted and wiped her damp eyes on her arm. "You're not a basket case like me."

"That doesn't mean I'm not terrified of losing you, Delaney."

She put her head on his shoulder as he pulled her into his arms, his chest. "So, what can we do about it?"

"I think this is a pretty good start."

SEVENTY-FOUR

Back at the Pace homestead, Leo and Delaney walked in through the back door of the house.

"Want to stay for dinner?" she said. "It's the least I can do after going mental on you."

"I guess I have to. I don't have my truck."

Delaney laughed. She hadn't thought she'd ever laugh again an hour ago. How could her emotions be so all over the place? She'd take this one, though. Joy was creeping up on her. Love.

The smell of something yummy greeted them. Her daughters were scurrying around the kitchen, which looked like a nuclear waste site.

"What are you two up to?" She was tall enough to kiss both of them on their heads, which she did with a hand to their hair. They were so different. So wonderfully different.

"Hey, Melaney. Hey, Leo." Kat held up oven mitt-covered hands. "We made homemade pizza."

Carrie shut the refrigerator with her hip. "School starts Monday. We decided we won't have time after this. Not for a while."

"And Skeeter said you were having a bad day."

"We bought the pre-made crusts, though."

Delaney was delighted. It was rare that they did something for her, because, well, they were teenage girls. "What a fantastic surprise. Thank you."

"Also," Carrie said, "we both have announcements. Sit down. We'll bring the pizza."

Carrie opened the oven and Kat retrieved one pizza, then popped another in. Carrie set the timer on her phone. She sliced the pizzas with the rolling pizza cutter they'd gotten Delaney for Christmas.

Delaney and Leo sat, holding hands.

Kat brought a bottle of red wine and poured them each a glass, bowing with one hand behind her back. "I may have had one little taste. It was gross."

"Forgiven. Such great service," Delaney said.

Kat sat down and Carrie brought the pizza over and placed the pan on trivets.

"*Bon appetit!*" Carrie said.

They all repeated her salutation, then dug in. The pepperoni pizza was cheesy and delicious. Everyone consumed a first piece with the only noise their groans of ecstasy.

Delaney pulled a second piece from the pie. "Announcements time."

Carrie said, "You go first, Kat."

Kat cleared her throat. "I have found a horse I would like to buy with your help. I am going to pay you back in chores and I'll work at the Loafing Shed and anything I need to do if I can have her."

Kat's surprise wasn't very surprising. "What does Clara think of your choice?"

"She thinks Leopard is perfect."

"You can show her to me this weekend, and I'll see what I can do."

"Is that a yes?!" Kat shrieked.

Delaney put her hands over her ears and laughed. "It's a yes, you can have a horse. It's a maybe whether this is the right one for you."

Kat started dancing around the table, humming the music to a silly cartoon ditty. When she got to Delaney she sat in her lap and threw her arms around her. "Thank you, thank you, thank you, thank you!"

"You're welcome."

Then, speaking so fast that Delaney almost couldn't understand her, Kat added, "And the other thing is I broke up with Freddy because having a boyfriend is a little more grown up than I realized and it's okay we're still going to be friends, but I think I hurt his feelings, and I don't want to talk about it."

"Oh, my." Delaney found this news shocking but also kind of wonderful. Maybe Kat could remain a child a little while longer.

Kat tilted her head at Leo. "Sorry, Leo."

He smiled. "No need for that. He wasn't my boyfriend."

Kat laughed. She had more pizza in her mouth before her behind hit the seat. She toasted Carrie with her slice. "Your turn."

Carrie took a deep breath, then pushed back from the table. She wiped her hands on her blue jeans. "I've made a decision about next year."

Delaney crossed her fingers under the table. She had traded teaching Carrie to drive Gabrielle to get her to fill out college applications. Carrie had sent out two for schools in Montana, one in Wyoming. "And what is your decision?"

The pizza timer sounded, and Carrie turned it off on her phone. Then she slipped on the oven mitts. "I'm going to commercial driving school. I want to be a trucker. Like you were."

Leo grabbed Delaney's hand and squeezed. She looked over at him. He was grinning at her. She was at a loss for words.

She licked her lips. "But Carrie, you'll be missing out on so much. The college experience. Freedom without financial obligations." She'd been saving money for it and knew that she had enough, even if it made things a little tight.

Carrie turned away to get the pizza out of the oven. She set it on the counter. "I know. But I'd just be wasting your money because I want to be a truck driver."

"Education is not a waste of money."

Carrie was shaking her head. She crossed her arms over her chest, oven mitts still on her hands. "It would be for me right now. Maybe later."

Delaney sighed. At least you're not telling me you're taking a gap year to backpack around Europe and find yourself."

"You'll let me?"

"I will continue to try to talk you out of it with the knowledge that I might be fighting a losing battle."

Carrie lunged toward her. Delaney stood and met her hug. They rocked back and forth.

Carrie said, "If I do really good, can I buy Gabrielle from you? After you fix the bullet holes."

Delaney sighed. "One step at a time, kiddo."

They both sat back down. Delaney took a sip of her wine. *What a day this has been.*

Kat said, "Want to know something weird that I forgot to tell you?"

"I'm not sure I do."

"Your mom texted me one more time, but when I tried to answer her, it just bounced back a message failure."

Delaney took a bigger sip of her wine. "What did she say?"

"I'm sorry."

"You should be. I told you not to text her anymore."

"No, that's what she said. 'I'm sorry.'"

The treacherous emotions that had been plaguing Delaney all week threatened her again. "What was she apologizing for?"

Leo squeezed her knee.

Kat's voice was light. "Dunno."

"To you?"

"I guess."

"Did she say anything else?"

"Yeah." Kat took another big bite and started chewing. She pointed at her mouth.

Delaney wanted to strangle her.

Kat swallowed the pizza and washed it down with water. Her glass clunked on the wooden tabletop. *Put it on the placemat*, Delaney thought. Then, *Something mothers think. Mothers.*

Kat turned her long-lashed eyes toward Delaney. "This is the weird part. She said, 'You have the heart of a dragon in you.'"

Delaney felt her dragon heart shattering into millions of tiny crystals that fell like snow to the floor. Her head slumped. She put her face in her hands. The message was to her. It was the first *real* thing Fabi had said to her.

Leo jumped up so fast that he knocked his chair over. He was kneeling beside Delaney, holding her hand, murmuring comforting sounds.

"Did I say something wrong?" Kat sounded worried.

Delaney looked up at her daughter with more tears in her eyes. Today, she had an unlimited supply. She lifted her shoulders and dropped them with a watery smile. "I guess I have an announcement, too."

"What is it?" Carrie asked. "Are we going to hate it?"

Delaney cocked her head. "I don't think so. Leo has been asking me to take a trip with him. Haven't you, Leo?"

He was righting his chair, but he hadn't taken his eyes from her face. "That I have. But someone has been too busy."

"If I were going to go on a trip with Leo, I would need something from you, girls." She smiled at them. "I'd need you to let me go for a week. Do you think you could do that?"

Carrie said, "When? You were just gone."

"Maybe in about a month."

She wiped her mouth. "Yeah. That would be fine by me."

Kat eyed them suspiciously. "You're not going to get married without us, are you?"

"What?! No. We aren't engaged. No wedding."

"Okay. Then I don't mind. I've just always wanted to be a bridesmaid."

Delaney said, "I'm sorry, Leo."

He made a zipping motion over his lips, but his eyes were alight with laughter.

Delaney tilted her head and met his eyes, the eyes she'd been worried she'd never see again, the ones she might lose someday. "All right then, Sheriff Palmer. I hereby accept your invitation to go on a vacation with you."

Leo looked around the room like she was speaking to someone else. "Who, me?" Then he walked over and put the back of his hand on her forehead. "She's not ill," he said to the giggling girls. He turned to Delaney, fists on his hips. "If you're serious, I accept your acceptance. Where would you like to go?"

Delaney said, "Puyallup, Washington. I have some unfinished business there."

"What's Puyallup?" Kat said.

"Why Washington?" Carrie said.

Leo took both Delaney's hands and pulled her to her feet. "I'd be honored. There's nowhere I'd rather go than on that journey with you."

A LETTER FROM PAMELA FAGAN HUTCHINS

Dear Reader,

Welcome to the end of *Her Cold Heart*! Whether this is your first or sixth Delaney Pace crime thriller or somewhere in between, thank you with all my heart for joining me in this story. With all the choices for and demands on use of your time, I am honored that you spent hours of yours reading it.

If you would like to receive email alerts of all my latest releases, just sign up at the following link. Your email address will never be shared, and you can unsubscribe at any time.

www.bookouture.com/pamela-fagan-hutchins

I've been excited to write this particular story since this series began. The winter books are especially fun, and I felt like all the circumstances in Delaney's life inevitably led to this adventure. The irony of me writing it from the southern coast of France instead of snowed in at our Snowheresville, Wyoming, cabin in the depths of winter is not lost on me, but I think my husband enjoyed the break from plowing our mile-long driveway!

It has been such a thrill to read your reviews of the first few books in the series and share my love for Delaney and her world with you. I can't believe I get the privilege of continuing her stories. In a crazy twist of fate, I've been writing this series in Denmark, the UK, France, and California, far from my home base in Wyoming, or even our family cabin in Maine. This particular book was written in Martigues, France, one thousand meters from the Mediterranean Sea on Le Côte Bleue. Writing Delaney here has made me both more and less homesick.

I hope you enjoyed *Her Cold Heart* and if you did, I would be very grateful if you could write a short review online. I'd love to hear what you thought about it, and reviews make such a difference helping new readers discover one of my books for the first time.

Writing is a solitary experience, and I am somewhat of a hermit anyway. I split my time between two rustic homes—when I'm not traveling the world. The one in Wyoming, on the face of the Bighorn Mountains, and the other on a remote lake in Maine. No matter where we are, my companions are my husband and our sled dogs, with visits from our adult children and grandchildren.

So, I *love* hearing from my readers out there in the real world. You can get in touch with me via my Facebook page where I am fairly active, through Instagram, Goodreads, or my website. I also so very greatly appreciate follows on Amazon and BookBub.

Thanks,

Pamela Fagan Hutchins

www.pamelafaganhutchins.com

instagram.com/pamela_fagan_hutchins
facebook.com/pamela.fagan.hutchins.author
goodreads.com/pamelafaganhutchins

ACKNOWLEDGEMENTS

Her Cold Heart may be the book I've been most excited to write, definitely for the Delaney Pace series anyway. I've been dreaming of a book to show off Delaney's superpowers—the skills that make her different from other law enforcement officers and most people—and to aggravate some of the lingering wounds from her past. Hopefully I succeeded in these pages.

A few years ago, my husband posted that we were giving away rusty, fire-damaged barbed wire. One of the takers was Daisy, who showed up with her family to claim some to use for a project. We soon learned that she'd given up oil field trucking in North Dakota—and a side gig as a reality star—for taking over the family homestead, raising her second daughter twenty years after her first, and being a service to others through philanthropy and her physical labor. She was a key player in organizing one of the largest agricultural relief efforts in the history of the United States through a huge convoy of truckers, donors, and volunteers after historic fires devastated America's Midwest. She and her family raise (and butcher) a large flock of turkeys every year to feed three hundred-plus people at a free community Thanksgiving dinner. Daisy's the one you want as your second in a knife fight, who could have been a model or actress instead of a rodeo star and extreme trucker, and she's the friend you can knock back a cold one with or take to meet your pastor (after you've done your best to prepare them for the encounter). If by some small miracle you find her in a church, you won't see her sitting in the pews... she's the one standing in the back. She was forged in the kind of volcanic upheaval that can result in smoking rubble or beautiful rocky mountain ranges. Daisy, through character and force of will, is the latter. If you enjoy Delaney as much as I do, it is because of my friend Daisy. Daisy, thank you for agreeing to let me reshape you in fiction.

When it comes to creating a fictional law enforcement world, you have to start with the real thing. I am so lucky to have Police Chief Travis Koltiska of Sheridan, Wyoming, in my corner for this. A fourth generation native of Wyoming (with his kids the fifth generation like Delaney), Travis is a bit larger than life. I know him as the generous guy with the heart for his family and animals, a big laugh, and endless stories, but trust me that you would *not* want to be the perp who faces him! Which is ironic since we met him through his wife after my husband accidentally broke into a house she was listing for sale. (It's a long story that ends in years of friendship, and I swear, it was an accident!) I've included anecdotes, quotes, history, and ideas from Travis in many books. I even have a Deputy Travis who shows up from time to time in several interconnected Wyoming series. This time, he took it a step further and acted as my beta reader and coach. Any mistakes are mine alone. He improved the book immeasurably and put up with dumb questions in texts all hours of the day and night. Please email Travis some love through me as I am praying he wants to continue in this role! Thanks, Travis, for your friendship and your help.

Huge thanks to my creative, firm, encouraging, brilliant editor Helen Jenner for her patience and collaboration. Thank you for your confidence in me. Helen, you've pushed me through walls I didn't know I'd built to shelter deeply buried writing fears. I'm very lucky to collaborate with you on Delaney and her world. I hope there are many more to come.

Thanks also to the wonderful team at Bookouture. As a rugged individualist/indie since 2012, I didn't think there was a publisher I would ever be willing to work with. Nimble, lean, flexible, strategic, mission driven, and reader centric, Bookouture is everything I was looking for, and I appreciate them taking a chance on me. The support has been incredible, in every step of the process.

Thanks to my husband Eric for brainstorming with me, dreaming up ways to exhibit Delaney's superpowers and mechanical prowess, encouraging me endlessly, beta reading, and much more despite his busy work, travel, and workout schedule. Special thanks for taking me on our grand French adventure for the last year. Your brilliance and sacrifice keeps bringing wonderful things into our life. I am blessed to be your wife and spoiled by you beyond belief... and I love it.

Thanks to our five offspring. I love you guys more than anything, and each time I write a parent/child relationship like the ones Delaney has with Kateena and Carrie, I channel you.

Finally, to each and every blessed reader: I appreciate you more than I can say. It is the readers who move mountains for authors, and you have done so for me, many times over.

PUBLISHING TEAM

Turning a manuscript into a book requires the efforts of many people. The publishing team at Bookouture would like to acknowledge everyone who contributed to this publication.

Audio
Alba Proko
Sinead O'Connor
Melissa Tran

Commercial
Lauren Morrissette
Hannah Richmond
Imogen Allport

Data and analysis
Mark Alder
Mohamed Bussuri

Editorial
Helen Jenner
Ria Clare

Copyeditor
Jon Appleton

Proofreader
Liz Hurst

Marketing
Alex Crow
Melanie Price
Occy Carr
Cíara Rosney
Martyna Młynarska

Operations and distribution
Marina Valles
Stephanie Straub
Joe Morris

Production
Hannah Snetsinger
Mandy Kullar
Ria Clare
Nadia Michael

Publicity
Kim Nash
Noelle Holten
Jess Readett
Sarah Hardy

Rights and contracts
Peta Nightingale
Richard King
Saidah Graham

Dear Reader,

We'd love your attention for one more page to tell you about the crisis in children's reading, and what we can all do.

Studies have shown that reading for fun is the **single biggest predictor of a child's future life chances** – more than family circumstance, parents' educational background or income. It improves academic results, mental health, wealth, communication skills, ambition and happiness.

The number of children reading for fun is in rapid decline. Young people have a lot of competition for their time, and a worryingly high number do not have a single book at home.

Hachette works extensively with schools, libraries and literacy charities, but here are some ways we can all raise more readers:

- Reading to children for just 10 minutes a day makes a difference
- Don't give up if children aren't regular readers – there will be books for them!

- Visit bookshops and libraries to get recommendations
- Encourage them to listen to audiobooks
- Support school libraries
- Give books as gifts

There's a lot more information about how to encourage children to read on our websites: **www.RaisingReaders.co.uk** and **www.JoinRaisingReaders.com**.

Thank you for reading.